Afterlight

Alex Scarrow

An Orion paperback

First published in Great Britain in 2010
by Orion
This paperback edition published in 2011
by Orion Books Ltd,
Orion House, 5 Upper St Martin's Lane,
London WC2H 9EA

An Hachette UK company

3 5 7 9 10 8 6 4 2

A CIP catalogue record for this book
is available from the British Library.

ISBN 978-1-4091-0306-6

Typeset at The Spartan Press Ltd,
Lymington, Hants

Printed and bound in the UK by
CPI Mackays, Chatham, Kent

The Orion Publishing Group's policy is to use papers
that are natural, renewable and recyclable products and
made from wood grown in sustainable forests. The logging
and manufacturing processes are expected to conform to
the environmental regulations of the country of origin.

www.orionbooks.co.uk

Alex Scarrow is the author of three previous novels, *A Thousand Suns*, *Last Light* and *October Skies*. He lives with his wife and son in Norwich. He spent the first ten years out of college in the music industry and the next twelve years in the computer games industry before turning to fiction. To find out more about Alex's books visit www.scarrow.co.uk

By Alex Scarrow

A Thousand Suns
Last Light
October Skies
Afterlight

'Me, Nathan and Helen, we're going down to London.'

'Oh.'

'The lights have come on in London.'

She frowned. 'What?'

'Mr Latoc said he saw them . . . from a long way off. A big glow over the Thames.'

Leona stirred in the chair. 'He said that?'

'Yeah.'

'Across London?'

She missed the hesitation in his reply. 'All along it, all over, that's what he said.'

Some sense of *possibility* tingled inside her. An alternative to sitting here in the middle of the road until she could muster enough willpower to push that stupid blunt tip all the way into her wrist.

An alternative.

'They've been rebuilding quietly,' continued Jacob. 'Nathan reckons they wouldn't be radioing out and telling everyone that they're rebuilding things 'cause it might draw too many people at once. Swamp them, you know?'

Hannah loved the stories you told her of the past, didn't she? She loved the idea of shopping malls, ten-pin bowling, IMAX cinemas, fun fairs . . .

'That's why we haven't heard about it on the radios,' Jacob continued. 'It's a secret. They've been doing it bit by bit. Otherwise there'd be people coming across from other countries too, probably.'

'It's one of those safe zones, I reckon, Lee. One of them that's come to life after all this time, and now it's rebuilding the city. It's remaking our home.'

To Jacob, Leona and Nathan. I started out using you guys as inspiration for the characters and about halfway through this book realised I wished I hadn't. You'll see why. This book is dedicated to the three of you.

Acknowledgements

This book required a lot more research than I expected it to. The person to whom I'm most indebted is Chris Gilmour, a man with a lot of experience in the North Sea and knowledge of the oil and gas rigs out there. Without his help this would have had to be a very different book.

I also owe a big thanks to my hardcore team of beta readers; John Prigent, Robin and Jane Carter, and Mike Poole, who waded through my first draft and returned copious notes of feedback.

Finally, as always, Frances, for the many thorough read-throughs and attendant margin notes that help me turn my unintelligible ramblings into 'books'.

Prologue

There are many names for what happened in 2010: The Big Die Off, The Crash, The Long Darkness, The End of the Oil Age. It was the week that crude oil was stopped from flowing and the world catastrophically failed.

My head still spins when I recall how quickly it all happened. A complete systemic collapse of the modern, oil-dependent world within the space of a fortnight. Events chased each other around the globe like a row of dominoes falling. It started with a series of bombs in the Middle East. Bombs deployed in the holiest of places that set the whole of the Middle East on fire with a religious civil war; Shi'as fighting Sunnis fighting Wahhabis. Then, later on that first day, I remember there were other explosions; an oil tanker scuttled in the busiest shipping channel in the world, a gigantic South American refinery, an oil processing hub in Kazakhstan . . . and a dozen more. By that evening, something like ninety per cent of the world's oil production capacity had been disabled.

What we were spoon-fed by the news on the first day was that oil prices were going to skyrocket, and that . . . yes, we'd be in for a sharp and protracted recession.

It was on the second day, or maybe the third, that everyone began to wake up and realise that billions of people were very quickly going to starve . . . and that was in the western world, not the Third World.

The moment people collectively understood what 'no oil'

actually meant, that was the tipping point; the point of no return. Panic and rioting swept like wildfire through every city and town in every country. No nation was immune. At the end of the first week of anarchy, as cities smouldered and streets lay quiet, littered with shattered glass and looted goods, broken and spoiled things, most of the tinned, preservable food was gone. Around the world, ready-to-harvest crops that might have been speedily gathered, processed, tinned and shipped to provide emergency supplies to feed us as the dust settled and we picked ourselves up . . . well, all of those crops rotted in the fields because tractors were sitting with empty fuel tanks . . . the Big Die Off began.

For a long time after the crash, the world really was dark. With no generated power, there were no lights at night except for the flickering of campfires, candles and oil lamps; the pinprick signs of life of small communities dotted here and there that had found a way to keep going. The UK resembled some collapsed east African state; a twilight world. Empty towns, burned-out farms with gone-to-seed fields, empty roads, abandoned cars.

And I must admit, I'd completely lost hope. I was ready to face the fact that where I was, I was going to slowly starve until my weakened immune system finally succumbed to a minor cut or a cold or tainted water.

Then I met her. Ten years after the crash, I met her.

She lived in a community of the weak and the vulnerable, living in isolation aboard a cluster of rusting gas platforms in the North Sea. There were four hundred and fifty of them living there and, I realise this only now, back then that was quite probably the largest self-sustaining community left in Great Britain.

She was to become the driving force for recovery. It was this remarkable woman who kept things together as we rebuilt our country from the abandoned ruins of the Oil Age.

2

I'm an old man now, too bloody old. If we still used the pre-crash calendar it would be the year 2061 as I write this.

Today, the world has lights again, computers, even trams and trains, technology that was once taken for granted before the crash. It's a very different world. There are far fewer people, owning far fewer things. The skyline no longer bristles with telecoms pylons sprouting satellite dishes and mobile phone antennae. There are no longer garish advertising billboards or phallic mine's-bigger-than-yours high-rise office towers. Instead, our horizons are broken by a sea of wind turbines, big and small.

I think of it as her *world.*

She helped make it. She helped define it. I see her stubbornness, her determination, her common sense, her sense of fair play and her maternal wisdom in everything around me.

But sadly she's a footnote in history. The e-books being written on the Oil Crash by academics today tend to focus on the things that went wrong in the first weeks and months of the crisis. Not on the rebuilding that began ten years later.

So her name is a small footnote. Just a surname in fact.
Sutherland.
But I met her. I actually knew her.

Adam Brooks
21 December, 51 AC [After the Crash]

Chapter 1

2010 – Eight days after the Oil Crash

North London

'I'm really, really thirsty, Mummy.' A quiet voice – her son.

'Yeah,' whispered her daughter, 'me too.'

Jenny Sutherland realised they'd not stopped since the first light of dawn had made it possible to pick their way through the rubbish strewn streets without the help of a torch.

Her mouth was dry and tacky too. She looked up and down the deserted high street; every shop window a jagged frame of threatening glass shards, every metal-shutter-protected shopfront was crumpled and stove in. Several cars, skewed across both sides of the road, smouldered in the pale morning light, sending up acrid wisps of burning-rubber smoke into the grey sky. She glanced at the stores either side of them, all dark caves within, but all promising goods inside that had yet to be looted.

Jenny would much rather have stayed where they were, out in the middle of the road, well clear of the dark shadows, the interiors. But water, *safe* bottled water, was something not to be without. Her children were right, this was probably as good a place as any to see what they could find.

'All right,' she said.

She turned to her daughter, Leona, and handed her one of their two kitchen knives. 'You stay here and mind Jacob.'

Leona's pale oval face, framed by dark hair, looked drawn and prematurely old; she had eyes that had seen too much in the last few days, eyes that looked more like those of a haunted veteran from some horrible and bloody war than

5

those of a nineteen-year-old girl. A week ago at this time of the morning Jenny could imagine her daughter lying under a quilt and wearily considering whether to bother dragging herself across the university campus to attend the first study period of the day. Now, here she was being asked to make ready to defend her little brother's life at a moment's notice with nothing better than a vegetable knife whilst the matter of a drink of water was seen to.

'Mum,' she said, 'we should stay together.'

Jenny shook her head firmly. 'You both stay here. If you hear me shout out to run, you run, understand?'

Leona nodded and swallowed nervously. 'Okay.'

'Mummy, be careful,' whispered Jacob, his wide eyes hidden behind cracked glasses and bent frames.

She ruffled his blond hair. 'I'll be fine.' She even managed a reassuring smile before turning towards the nearest shop: a WH Smith newsagent.

She could see it had been repeatedly visited and picked over in the last week from the litter strewn out of the doorway and into the street. It was surprising, even now, after so many days of chaos, how worthwhile finds could still be had amidst the debris – a can of soda pop here, a packet of crisps there. Looters, it seemed, weren't the systematic type; the shadowed corners of a floor, the spaces behind counters, the backs of shelves, still yielded goodies for someone patient enough to squat down and look.

She stepped towards the shop, her feet crunching across granules of glass. Outside the door – wrenched open and dangling from twisted hinges – sat a news-board bearing a scrawled headline from last Wednesday.

OIL CRASH – CHAOS ACROSS LONDON

Wednesday seemed so long ago now; it was the day this country flipped into panic mode, completely spiralled out of control. The day the government suddenly decided it needed to be honest and tell the public that things had become extremely serious; that there would be severe rationing of food and water and there'd be martial law.

Actually, Wednesday was the day the *world* panicked.

She'd witnessed snarling fights, torn hair, bloodied knives, things set on fire, bodies in the street casually stepped over by wild-eyed looters pushing overladen shopping trolleys, and woefully few police, who watched, powerless to stop any of it. A madness had descended upon everyone, particularly here in London, as people desperately scrambled to grab what could be taken, and were prepared to kill in order to keep hold of it. Jenny remembered the news stories of the Katrina survivors in New Orleans; those stories paled against what she and her children had seen.

She stepped inside, holding her breath as she did so.

Standing still, she let her eyes adjust to the dim interior. Like every other shop it looked like a whirlwind had torn through. The floor was a mash of spoiled goods, newspapers, magazines and paperback novels; shelves dangled precariously off the walls and a row of fridge doors stood open, the contents long since emptied.

A plastic CD case cracked noisily beneath her shoe as she slowly moved deeper into the store, her eyes working hard across the carpet of trampled and soiled stock, searching for an overlooked bottle of water, a can of Coke. Something.

'You okay, Mum?' called Leona.

'I'm all right!' she replied, hating the feathery sound of growing fear in her voice.

The sooner they cleared London the better. After that . . . Jenny didn't have a clue. All she knew was that this city was death now. There were too many people tucked away in the dim corners of every street, cowering in dark homes, ready to use a knife or a smashed glass bottle or a gun to take what they wanted, or keep what they had. She really had no idea what they'd do once their feet hit a B-road flanked by open

7

fields. She entertained a fanciful notion of living off the land, Jacob trapping rabbits and cooking them over a campfire; all thick jumpers and outdoors rude health. Almost idyllic, just like that old BBC show, *The Survivors*. If only Andy was with them . . .

Not now, Jenny, not now.

Her husband – their father – was gone. Dead in the city.

Crying comes later when we're clear of this place. All right?

She thought she saw the glint of a soda can on the floor – dented, but quite possibly still full of something sickly sweet and bubbly. She was bending down to pick it up when she heard a noise. A plastic *clack* followed by a *slosh* of liquid. An instantly recognisable sound; that of a plastic two-litre bottle of some drink being casually up-ended and swigged from.

'All right?' A boy's voice, a teenager perhaps; the cadence wavering uncertainly between choirboy and manhood.

Her eyes darted to where the voice had come from. Adjusted to the dark now, she picked out a row of four . . . maybe five of them, sitting on crates, buckets, boxes. She could see the pale outline of sporty stripes and swooshes, trainers and caps, and the soft amber glow of several cigarette tips.

'Uh . . . fine . . . thanks,' she replied.

'You after somethin'?' Another voice, a little slurred this one.

'I . . . I was looking for something to drink,' she replied, taking one small step backwards. 'But forget it, you can have this shop. I'll try another.'

Keep your voice calm.

'Don' matter,' said the first voice, 'we got loads. Wanna share?'

She heard a snigger. Several cigarette tips pulsed and bobbed in the dark. She recognised the smell – a familiar

8

odour from long ago, from college days, the same smell she picked up occasionally off the dirty laundry Leona brought back from university. Dope.

They're just kids, she told herself. *Just boys*. Boys who could be scolded and cowed if one picked just the right tone of voice.

'So where are your parents?' she asked.

Another snigger.

'Who cares?' replied one of them.

'Fuckin' dead for all I know,' said another.

Jenny took another step backwards, hoping it was too dim for them to see her attempt to put further distance between them.

'You should get out of the city, you know,' she said, trying hard to sound like a voice of authority. 'Seriously. You'll starve when there's nothing left to pick up in the shops.'

'Thanks, but we're all right, love.'

She saw the pale outline of a baseball cap move, the scraping of a foot and the tinkle of broken glass. One of them getting up.

'Hey, why don't you give me a blow job? An' I'll give you a fag.'

A snort of laughter from the others.

Oh, God, no.

'How dare you!' she snapped, hoping to sound like an enraged headteacher. Instead it came out shrill and little-girly. She stepped back again, her foot finding a plastic bottle that cracked noisily beneath her shoe.

'Hey? Where you goin'?'

She saw more movement, they were all getting up now.

'I'm going,' she announced. 'You boys stay here and get pissed if that's what you want, but I'm leaving.'

'Look,' said one of them, 'why don't you stay?' Phrased as a question, as if she was being given a choice in the matter.

9

The nearest boy took another step forward, wobbling uncertainly on his feet and swigging again from his plastic bottle.

Her hand closed around a wooden handle poking out from the waistline of her skirt. She pulled the knife out, feeling emboldened by the weight in her hand.

'You stay where you are!' she barked, holding the bread knife out in front of her.

'I just wan' you to give me a little *luurrve*.'

'Yeah, me too,' said one of the boys behind him.

'I've got a knife!' shouted Jenny, 'and I will fucking well use it. Do you boys understand?'

That drunken giggling again.

'We're going to a *part-eee*,' one of the others cheerfully announced from the back with a sing-song voice.

'She's doing *me* first,' insisted the lad nearest her. He lurched clumsily forward, reaching out for her with big pale hands. Instinctively Jenny slashed at one of them.

'Ahhh, fuck!!' he screamed, tucking his hands back. 'Shit! Bitch!! Bitch fuckin' well cut me!'

A torch snapped on and, for a moment, she caught sight of the boy's face. Beneath the peak of his hoodie-covered baseball cap she saw the porcelain skin of a child, pulled into a rictus sneer of hate and anger. Surely no more than fifteen, sixteen at a stretch, his big hands, one gashed, reached for the knife. It happened too quickly to remember anything more than a blur of movement. But a moment later she could see the handle protruding from the side of his waist, a dark bloom of crimson spreading out across his Adidas stripes.

The boy cried out, all trace of his puberty-cracked voice gone, now screaming like a startled toddler stung by a wasp. He collapsed heavily onto the floor of the shop, his desperate whimpering accompanied by the clatter of displaced bottles and cans, the scrape of feet as his mates drunkenly clambered forward either to help him or, far more likely, to overpower her now she no longer held her knife.

Jenny turned and ran, stumbling across an overturned newspaper rack, her foot slipping on the glossy covers of a spread of gossip magazines scattered across the shop floor. She headed towards the front of the store and grey daylight, leaving the drunk boys behind her.

This is how it's going to be from now on, she realised with a growing sense of dread; the world Jacob and Leona will inherit is a world of feral youths, a lifetime of scavenging for the last tins of baked beans amidst smouldering ruins.

The Beginning

Chapter 2

10 years AC

'LeMan 49/25a' – ClarenCo Gas Rig Complex, North Sea

Jenny sat up in her cot, a scream caught silently in her throat.

That nightmare again.

There were others, of course. Plenty her subconscious mind could choose from, but that one in particular kept returning to haunt her sleep. It was worse than the other memories perhaps because the boys had been so young, just babies really – drunk, dangerous babies. Maybe because that particular encounter had happened the day after Andy died. She'd still been in shock then, confused. Running on auto-pilot for her children's sake, her foggy mind making foolish decisions.

She rubbed the sleep from her face and tucked the nightmare back in its box along with the others, hoping for a few nights of untroubled sleep before another managed to creep out and torment her.

Through the porthole beside her bunk a grey morning filled the small cabin with a pallid light. The North Sea, endlessly restless, seemed calmer than usual today. She could hear the persistent rumble of it passing beneath the rig, feel the subtle vibration in the floor as gentle swells playfully slapped the support-legs a hundred and forty feet below.

Newcomers to their community always seemed terribly unsettled by that – the slightest sensation of movement beneath their feet. Once upon a time, this archipelago of man-made islands had been called 'LeMan 49/25a'; a cluster of five linked gas platforms, in the shape of an 'L', a couple

15

of dozen miles off the north-east coast of Norfolk. Now it was called 'home'. Five years of living here and even when the North Sea was throwing a tantrum and sixty-foot swells were hurling themselves angrily against those tall, hollow support-legs, she still felt infinitely safer here than she did ashore.

She heard the *clack* of hurried footsteps on the stairs outside her cabin. The door creaked open. 'Breakfast time, Nanna.'

Jenny smiled wearily. 'Morning, Hannah.' She slipped her legs over the side of the cot, her feet flinching on the cold linoleum floor, and glanced at the empty bunk opposite, the blankets tossed scruffily aside. Leona was gone.

Hannah grinned cheerfully, eyes too big for such a small face tucked beneath a fuzz of curly strawberry-blonde hair.

'Mummy's up already?' Jenny asked, surprised. Usually she had to kick Leona out of her bed in the mornings.

Hannah rolled her eyes. 'Lee's eating breakfast already.'

Jenny sighed. She tried to encourage Hannah to call her mother 'Mummy', but since Leona actually encouraged the first name thing — sometimes it seemed like she almost wanted to be more of a big sister than a mother — it was a futile effort on her part.

'Okay . . . tell her I'll be down in a minute, all right?'

Hannah nodded and skittered out of the cabin, her wooden sandals rapping noisily along the floor of the passageway.

Jenny unlatched the porthole and opened it a crack, feeling the chill morning air chase away the cosy fug in the cabin. She shivered — awake for sure now — and pulled a thick, chunky-knit cardigan around her shoulders and stood up.

'Another day,' she uttered to the woman in the mirror on the wall opposite. A woman approaching fifty, long untamed frizzy hair that had once been a light brown, but was now streaked with grey, and a slim jogger's figure with sinews of muscle where soft humps of lazy cellulite had rested a decade ago.

16

A poor man's Madonna.

Or so she liked to think.

She smiled. The Jenny of before, the Jenny of ten years ago, would probably have been thrilled to be told she'd have a gym figure like this at the age of forty-nine. But then that very different, long lost, Jenny would probably have been horrified by the scruffy New-Age-traveller state of her hair, the lined and drawn face, tight purse-string lips and the complete absence of any make-up.

She was a very different person now. 'Very different,' she whispered to no one but the reflection.

The smile in the mirror dipped and faded.

She pulled on a pair of well-worn khaki trousers and a pair of hardy Doc Martens that promised to out-live her, and clanked downstairs to join the others in the mess room.

Four long scuffed Formica-topped tables all but filled the mess; utilitarian, unchanged from the days when gas workers wearing orange overalls and smudged faces took a meal between shifts.

Busy right now. It always was with the first breakfast sitting of the day. There were nearly a hundred of them sitting shoulder to shoulder; those on the rota for early morning duties. Potato and fish chowder steamed from plastic bowls and the room was thick with chattering conversation and the chorus of too-hot stew being impatiently slurped.

Jenny spotted her daughter. She grabbed a plastic bowl, ladled it full of chowder and squeezed in beside her.

Leona looked up. 'Mum? You okay?'

'Fine.'

'You were whimpering last night. Bad dreams again?'

Jenny shrugged. 'Just dreams, Lee, we all have them.'

Leona managed a supportive half-smile. 'Yeah.' She had her nights too.

Jenny cautiously tested a mouthful with her lip. 'I noticed it's a good sea and fair wind out there today. We're overdue a shore run. Could you get together a shopping list and I'll grab it off you later?'

'Yeah, okay,' Leona replied, picking an escaped chunk of potato off the table and dropping it back into Hannah's bowl. Nothing wasted here. Certainly not food.

'Anything you want to put on the list?'

Jenny's mouth pursed. 'A couple of decent writing pens. Some socks, the thermal ones . . . oh, and how about booking me in at a posh health spa for a weekend of pampering.'

Leona grinned. 'I'll join you.'

Jenny hungrily finished her breakfast before it had a chance to cool; too much to do, too little time. She clapped her hands like a schoolteacher and the hubbub of conversation slowly, reluctantly, faded to silence.

'It looks like a good day for a shore run. The sea's calm and we've got a westerly wind. So Leona's going to be coming round this morning to get your "wants and needs".' She picked out a dark-skinned and broad-framed woman halfway down the table. 'And, Martha Williams, let's try and keep George Clooney off the list this time.'

There was a ripple of tired, dutiful laughter across the canteen and a loud cheerful cackle from Martha. Her grin and the musical lilt in her accent still hung on to a fading echo of Jamaican beaches.

'Aye, Jenny, love. How 'bout me 'ave some Brad Pitt, then?'

Martha got a better response; popular with everyone.

Jenny grinned; to do less would be disingenuous. She gave the room her morning smile; even those who she knew sniped at her behind her back, those who muttered and complained in dark corners about *Jenny's Laws*. A smile that assured them all she'd weathered far worse than sticks and stones and whatever bitchiness some of them got up to out of her earshot.

'Busy day today. We've got seedling propagators to

transfer from Drilling to Accommodation, slurry from the digesters to bring out and spread; we had some rain last night so all the water butts and catch-troughs to check.'

There were some groans.

'First teatime sitting will be at four-thirty; a little later since we're getting more evening light now.' She nodded. 'Okay?'

Chairs and benches barked on the scuffed floor as everyone rose to go about their morning duties. The mess door opened, letting in a lively breeze. Outside on the deck, those waiting to come in for the second breakfast sitting rubbed their hands and shuffled impatiently.

Jenny felt her sleeve being tugged and looked down to see Hannah cocking a curious barrister's eyebrow. 'Who's *Brad Pitt*?'

Chapter 3

10 years AC

'LeMan 49/25a' – ClarenCo Gas Rig Complex, North Sea

The catch bell jangled. Jacob looked up from his pack of weathered and faded Yu-Gi-Oh cards to the net cables tied off along the platform railing. They were both as taut as guitar strings and twitched energetically – a sure sign there was enough squirming marine life in the net to make it worth his while pulling it in.

He crawled on hands and knees out of the sheltered warmth of the rustling vinyl one-man tent and onto the grating of the spider deck – an apron of metal trellis running around the bottom of the accommodation platform's thick support-legs, no more than thirty feet above the endlessly surging swells. The tent snapped and rustled in the fresh breeze as he stood up and leaned over the safety rail.

The sea gently rolled and slapped against the side of the nearest leg, sending a languid spray of suds up towards him, but not quite energetic enough to reach him. He grabbed the winch handle and began to wind the net up, a laborious process that seemed to take ages, each creaking turn on the winch hoisting the laden net just a few inches.

He gazed out at the sea as his arm worked the handle. It was well behaved today, mottled with the shadows of clouds scudding across the sky. He pushed a long tangled tress of sun-bleached hair out of his eyes and squinted up at the platform towering above him. From down here all he could see was a large messy underbelly of welded ribs, giant rivets and locking bolts sporting salt and rust collars, and criss-crossing support struts linking all four enormous support-legs together.

This early in the day, the sunlight was still obscured by the body of the tall, top-heavy accommodation module perched on this platform, like an elephant balancing on a barstool. It towered a hundred and thirty feet above him, a multi-storey car-park on stilts. On top of the module he could see the large circular perimeter of the helipad. Faint rays of sunlight diffused through the safety netting and promised to angle down here to the spider deck come midday, but for now he had to shiver in the accommodation platform's tall shadow.

The fishing net was out of the water now and he could see amidst the struggling tangle of slippery bodies a healthy haul of mackerel, whiting, sand eel and other assorted specimens of marine life drawn to graze for food in and around the man-made ecosystem below; a thick forest of seaweed that propagated around the support-legs below the sea like a fur stole.

He smiled, satisfied with the haul.

Enough there.

He could finish early, pack up his tent and join the second sitting in the mess. Occasional wafts of chowder and stewed tomatoes had been drifting down from the galley's open window, accompanied by the faint clink and rattle of cutlery and ladles.

His tummy rumbled for breakfast.

Above him feet clanked across the suspended walkway from the neighbouring gas compression platform – people on their way over for second sitting. Most of the machinery, cooler tanks, scrubbers and pumps that had once been installed over there had been stripped out before the crash when these rigs were being mothballed. Now, about a hundred and fifty members of the community were sheltered on the compression platform amidst a cosy, often noisy, cavernous interior; a rabbit warren of towelling 'cubicles', bunks and hammocks, and laden washing lines strung across the open interior space from one gantry to another; a many-layered bazaar of multicoloured throw rugs, bedsheets and laundry.

The second, smaller, compression platform, also stripped from the inside out, played host to another technicoloured shantytown; just over a hundred of them living cheek by jowl in a warm, stuffy, smelly fug. Both compression platforms linked to the accommodation platform overshadowing him. That was home to the most; about two hundred and forty people lived there. The cabins, once designed to keep a crew of fifty in home-from-home comfort, were now cosily filled four to a cabin, and, like the compression platforms, a noisy maze of chattering voices and clothes lines strung across hallways.

Beyond the smaller compression platform was the production platform. It hosted the generator room and the stinking methane room with its digesters full of slurry – a mixture of human and chicken shit – with the chicken deck directly above. No one lived there. It would be a resilient person who could endure both the rancid stench of fermenting faeces and the endless clucking of several hundred brainless poultry.

At the furthest point of the cluster of platforms, flung out at the end of the longest linking walkway, beyond production, was the drilling platform. Just under fifty people lived out there. It was quieter than the other places, and a much longer walk for breakfast, the evening meal and any community meetings that needed to be attended. But it was where those less sociable preferred to bunk.

All five platforms, unique in shape and purpose, were united in one thing, though: they were green. Every walkway, every terrace, every gantry, every external stairwell, every cabin and every Portakabin rooftop was overgrown with potted vegetables, grow-troughs, bamboo frames holding up rustling mini forests of pea and bean climbers. Approaching the platforms from a shore run, Jacob always thought that, from afar, they looked like a sea-borne version of the Hanging Gardens of Babylon, a towering wedding cake of rustling green.

He heard his name being called out and looked up, a hand shading his eyes from the pale glow of the morning sky. His mum was leaning over the railing of the cellar deck.

'Jake!' she called, her voice competing against the thud and spray of languid swells and the clanking of feet across the walkway above. 'Good haul?' she smiled.

'Yeah, Mum.'

She disappeared back out of sight and then a moment later he saw her making her way down the ladder to the spider deck. She stopped midway – close enough to talk.

'We're doing a shore run today. You okay to go with Walter?'

'Yup.'

'Go get some breakfast first, love, all right? Walter's going to lower the boat in about an hour.'

'Okay,' he called back.

She gave him a hurried wave then clambered back up the ladder and out of sight.

On her rounds. She was busy paying each platform a visit, checking every deck and walkway of plants, conferring with those tending them, ensuring every chore that needed to be done was being done, settling minor disputes, soothing ruffled feathers and petty egos . . . tirelessly keeping this little world of theirs ticking over.

He shivered as a teasing gust played with his anorak. He zipped it up and resumed winding in his catch, a smile spreading across his face. The shore run was a welcome departure from his daily routine. The foraging trips to the coastal town of Bracton came with much less frequency these days, not like in the early days when they'd first settled on the rigs and needed so many things that they were constantly ferrying supplies from the mainland.

He cherished the trips ashore. An opportunity to explore, to see something other than these windswept islands of paint-flaked metal. He savoured the fading reminders of the past, often wandering a little away from the others as they busily foraged for the things that were needed. He enjoyed standing in the silent high street. The shop signs were all still there: WH Smiths, Boots, Nationwide, Waterstones . . . but the storefront windows were long since gone. If he half-closed his eyes, let them soft-focus, and used a little imagination, he could almost *see* the high street busy once more; the soft creak of swinging signs replaced with the hum of traffic, the boom of music from the back of a passing car, the pedestrian thoroughfare filled with mums pushing buggies, the jingle of a newsagent's door opening.

His smile turned into a cheerful grin. 'Shore run,' he announced happily, as he hauled the net over the rail, 'cool.'

Chapter 4

10 years AC

Bracton Harbour,
Norfolk

Walter Eddings dropped the sails twenty yards out from the concrete quayside and let the thirty-foot yacht glide forward under its own momentum. The boat drew parallel as he steered her to a gentle rest. He watched as, on the foredeck, Jacob and his friend Nathan flipped tethered buoys over the side to cushion the boat's fibreglass hull. As they bobbed gently, drifting the last few yards to a standstill, both young men equipped themselves with boat hooks and reached out to snag the moorings.

Jacob hopped across onto the quayside, Nathan tossing him a couple of lines which he secured fore and aft.

'Good enough,' shouted Walter, a ruddy face half hidden by the thatch of a grey-white beard and framed by thick salt-and-pepper hair pulled back into a ponytail that fluttered in the breeze like a battle standard. He looked like an ageing biker, like an old roadie who'd happily tell you how many groupies he'd once banged in the back of Status Quo's tour bus. However, in the Sealed Knot uniform that he kept safely tucked away and took out and wore on very special occasions, he looked every bit a musketeer from the King's Royal army, snatched from the seventeenth century and dumped into the twenty-first.

Jacob loved listening to him describe the battles of Nazeby, Edgehill, Marston Moor, as if he'd actually been there. He could almost smell the acrid smoke of gunpowder, feel the thud of cannons firing and the grunting of massed pikemen going toe-to-toe . . . and he could certainly imagine Walter, thickset and ruddy-faced, in the middle of it, pouring powder from a horn down the long barrel of his musket.

It was gone two in the afternoon. They'd made good time from the rigs to Bracton Harbour with the wind behind them. Walter had got them across without needing to turn on the engine once. Something he preferred to do whenever the wind was in their favour. Even though they'd discovered a diesel tank still half full in the marina from which they topped-up each time they visited, and promised to last them a good many years yet, he was determined to use as little of it as possible.

Walter looked at his watch. 'We've got about five hours of daylight left,' he announced.

Enough time for them to forage for most of the items on the very long shopping list, whilst Walter did a water-run. Across the marina was a tugboat moored on a side canal. It was tethered up to the delivery jetty of an old ale brewery. The brewery had its own well, tapping the very best of 'natural Norfolk drinking water', or at least that's how it was described on the labels of their traditional brown glass bottles. It was in fact clean enough to drink and showed no sign of running out any time soon. Every time they did a shore run Walter filled the several dozen brewery drums in the back of the tug with well water, piloted the tug out to the rigs and exchanged the full drums for empty ones. It supplemented the rainwater they managed to catch in their water butts.

He'd usually returned, refilled the tugboat's fuel tank and moored it back down the canal by the time the others had returned from their foraging. They'd then overnight at the quayside aboard the yacht, spending a few hours the next morning looking for whatever was left on the list, before heading home.

'All right then, gents, it's gun time,' said Walter.

Four guns in the cockpit, the community's entire arsenal. Jenny had appointed Walter – her right-hand man – as sole custodian of them a long time ago, fed up with being pestered by the boys, Jacob included, to get them out so they could hold them.

Walter picked up a shotgun. 'As normal, we're pairing off. One gun per pair.'

He handed the shotgun to a tall, narrow-shouldered guy called Bill Laithwaite who pushed scuffed glasses up the bridge of his nose and grimaced uncomfortably as he took possession of the gun.

'Bill, you can take young Kevin with you.'

Kevin pulled a face. 'Can't I go with one of *them*?' he whined, pointing towards Jacob and Nathan. Kevin was just thirteen, yet considered himself to be one of the 'big boys'. The last thing he wanted was to be paired up with Bill who fretted and worried like an old woman.

Walter scowled. 'Excuse me, you'll do as you're told. You're with Bill.'

'Great,' Kevin pouted.

Walter picked up the second gun. 'Jacob and Nathan, you can have the SA80.' He passed it over to Nathan, who took a moment to pose with the army assault rifle like some urban gangster.

Jacob snorted.

'For Christ's sake, Nathan! It's not a frigging toy!' snapped Walter irritably.

Chastened, but still flashing a conspiratorial grin at Jacob, Nathan passed it carefully over before hopping across to join him on the quayside.

'Howard and Dennis . . .' Both men were old, older even than Walter. The three of them regularly played cribbage together in the mess during the evening lights-on hours. 'You chaps can have the HK carbine.'

Walter picked up the remaining weapon and looked at David Cudmore. 'And we'll have the MP5.'

'Righto,' replied David, running a hand through the thin wisps of hair on his head.

'Okay then,' said Walter impatiently, 'you've all got your lists?'

They nodded.

'Back here no later than eight this evening, please. We should have supper on the go by then.'

Jacob pushed the shopping trolley down the aisle. The wheels squeaked with an irritating metronome regularity. However, unlike most of the other trolleys discarded outside in the high street, exposed to ten wet English summers and ten even wetter winters, at least the wheels hadn't seized up with rust.

It was piled almost to overflowing with medicines requested; antibiotics, antiseptics and a variety of painkillers. This particular chemist had weathered the looting better than most stores. Of course, the windows had gone in and all the energy drinks, fruit juices and bottled water had vanished a decade ago within the first few days. But most of the rest of the shop's stock was still patiently sitting on shelves or scattered across the floor collecting dust. For those who needed to dye their hair, wax their legs, or colour their nails this was going to be the place to visit for many more years to come.

Jacob looked down at the list. They'd ticked off most of the items, mostly the different branded painkillers. Of the four hundred and fifty-three members of their community, a large proportion were women between the ages of sixteen and fifty. On any given day there were at least half a dozen of them reporting to Dr Gupta — once upon a time a GP — for something to ease stomach cramps.

Jacob wheeled the trolley through the checkout, Nathan walking behind him with the SA80 held casually in both hands, the muzzle pointing safely at the ground, just as Walter warned them, ad nauseam, to do.

'Nah, it was definitely a game on me PlayStation,' said Nathan, continuing a conversation Jacob had almost forgotten they'd been having. 'I know it was. I think it was the last game me dad got me.'

Jacob shook his head. 'But I'm sure I played it on my Nintendo, though.'

'Nope, you didn't . . . couldn't have, Jay. Was a PlayStation-*only*, man.'

They emerged outside onto the high street. The sun was just dipping behind the flat roof of the multi-storey car-park opposite; the dark shadow it cast slowly creeping across the thoroughfare of weed-strewn paving.

Jacob stepped through tufts of waist-high nettles, the trolley squeaking and rattling before him, the small wheels juddering over a broken paving slab.

He let go of the trolley and rested for a moment.

''Sup, Jake?'

He shrugged. 'You ever stop and pretend?'

'Pretend what?'

'That the street's still alive.'

Nathan looked around at the overgrown pedestrian way, the dark shop entrances, the jagged window frames, cars resting on flat tyres, many of them displaying tell-tale bubbles of rust beneath the paintwork.

'Used to. Sort of gets harder to imagine each time we come ashore, though. You know what I'm saying?'

Jacob looked at the signs above the shop doorways. Most of them — the homogenous chain stores — were plastic façades, perfectly well preserved, some still bright and colourful. Here and there, fractures in the moulded lettering had allowed thin veins of moss to take hold and spread bacilli-like fingers of growth. The sign above a phone store in front of him had slipped down from its mount above the shop's front window at some point in the past and lay on the ground, cracked on impact with the street, weeds and grass growing around it.

'We used to live in London.'

'I know, Jay.'

Jacob turned to him. 'Can you remember how streets used to sound?'

Nathan's dark features clouded for a moment; he tucked a wiry dreadlock behind one ear and scratched at the meagre tuft of bristles on his chin. 'Shit . . . not sure,' he replied, the soft echo of Martha's accent in his. 'Where me mum 'n' me was livin', it was sort of always *rumbly*.'

'The cars?'

Nathan nodded. 'And car music. Sort of a boom . . . boom . . . boom . . . kinda thing?'

'Yeah, I remember that.'

'And police cars and fire engines sometimes. Me mum said it was a rough place.'

Memories from a younger mind flickered momentarily in front of Jacob. He remembered so little from before the crash. It was that chaotic week that formed most of his recall of the old world; the wailing of sirens, trucks full of soldiers on a gridlocked high street. People hurrying, not yet running . . . but hurrying; not quite ready to be seen panicking, but eager to get home and lock the door. Harried-looking newsreaders on the TV talking about oil, and food rationing and martial law. Images of Oxford Street full of people smashing windows and running away with arms full of stolen things.

'Yeah,' he said, 'I remember those siren noises.'

They stood in silence for a moment, listening to the fresh North Sea breeze hiss through the leaves of a young silver birch tree, growing out of a decorative island in the middle of the shopping centre's thoroughfare. It had probably been little more than an anaemic sapling when the crash happened.

'What do you miss the most, Nate?'

Nathan pursed his lips in thought. 'Gonna have to be me game consoles. There was great games and graphics that was, like, real enough you could be in there.' Nathan's hands absent-mindedly cupped around buttons and joysticks in the air. 'I guess I miss all that. And the telly,' he said wistfully. 'What about you?'

Jacob rubbed his eyes irritably. Since his glasses had finally fallen to pieces several years ago he'd had to make do without. It left him too often nursing a headache and tired eyes. His face creased with concentration. 'I miss the orange.'

'Orange?'

'At night time,' added Jacob, 'the orange. Night wasn't black like it is now. It was always sort of orange.'

Nathan's face clouded with confusion for a moment, then cleared. 'Oh yeah, man. It was, wasn't it? You talkin' about the street lights.'

Jacob nodded and smiled. 'I remember even the sky was a dull sort of orange. And those lights always had a glowy fuzzy sort of halo round them. I remember there was one outside my bedroom window. It used to buzz every night.'

Nathan shrugged. 'We lived up high. I was always lookin' down on 'em.'

Jacob watched the evening shadow complete its slow crawl across the high street as the sun set, and begin to climb the deserted shopfronts. The setting sun, warm and blood-red in a vanilla sky, glinted off the few shards of glass that remained in the store windows.

'I suppose I miss that the most – the night time lights.' His face cleared, brushing away hazy childhood memories. He turned to look at Nathan. 'And TV, too. I miss *The Simpsons*.'

Nathan's face cracked with a broad grin. '*D'oh . . . stoo-pid oil-crash apocalypse.*'

Jacob doubled over. Nathan could do Homer's voice perfectly. He could do all of them brilliantly. Many's the

31

time he had the mess filled with laughter, impersonating some old TV personality from the past. Just like his mum, Martha — very popular, because he could make smiles happen. And, *fuck*, you needed a reason to smile every now and then.

Jacob slapped his forehead Homer-style. 'Duh!'

'No, man, it's *d'oh*!'

Nathan did it so much better.

'Doh.'

'Nearly, Jay.'

Chapter 5

10 years AC

Leona sat on the accommodation platform's helipad savouring the warmth of the evening sun on her back. Hannah, her best friend, Natasha, and several other children were chasing each other across one side of the open deck. On the other side, tomato plants grew in endless tall rows, sheltered beneath a large plastic greenhouse roof. The tangy odour of the plants drifted in pleasant waves across to her, alternating with the faint stench of fermenting faeces coming all the way across from the production platform.

Nice.

Apart from that particular fetid odour, which fluctuated in strength from one day to the next, this was her favourite place on the platform. Up here on the highest open space amongst the five linked platforms, she had a three-hundred and sixty degree panorama to enjoy. The sea varied little, of course, always dark, brooding and restless, but the sky on the other hand was an ever changing canvas, sometimes steel-grey and solemn, sometimes like this evening, splashed with mischievous pinks and livid crimson.

Strings of light-bulbs began to wink on as the sun dipped closer to the waves and the evening light waned. She could just about hear the distant chug of the generator. The lights would stay on until an hour after the last dinner sitting in the canteen. Time enough for everyone to eat and make their way safely back home, perhaps read a chapter of a book, darn a sock, tell a bedtime story or two, play a card game . . . then lights out. Thanks to Walter's technical know-how and hard work, they generated a modest but steady supply of methane gas. Enough to give them a few hours of powered light every evening and no more.

Leona heard soft footsteps and the rustle of threadbare khaki trousers behind her as her mum approached and squatted down beside her.

'Hey.'

'Hey back.'

They watched Hannah get tagged by another little girl and resentfully have to stand still like a statue until 'freed' by someone else. She lasted all of ten seconds before getting bored and pretending that she'd been released. She rejoined her friend, the same age, same size . . . they even looked similar; frizzy hazel-coloured hair, tamed, more or less, by bright sky-blue hair ties. That was *their* colour. Sky blue . . . for some reason. Leona squinted her eyes as she watched them play – they could almost be twins.

Tweedledum and Tweedledee.

'She's so like you were,' said Jenny. 'Always cheating at games.'

Leona smiled.

'And stubborn.'

Above the soft rumple of the wind and the chatter of the children, she could hear people emerging from the mess and clanking back across the walkways to their platforms for the night. Another routine, uneventful evening.

'I know you still pine for the past, Lee. But it's gone. It's not coming back.'

Leona shrugged. 'I know.'

'I listened in on your school class this morning. You were talking to the kids about how music used to be.'

Leona nodded. She ran classes, along with another woman, Rebecca, for the younger children. It wasn't much of an education, truth be told; basic reading and writing and a little maths, that's all. This morning one of the children had asked about what music she used to listen to before the crash and, before she could stop herself, she was telling her class about the gigs that she'd gone to as a student. About how electricity used to go into guitars and make them sound fantastic and big. About how the shows were flooded with powerful flashing lights and dazzling effects and lasers. They'd sat and listened, spellbound, all of them born after the crash, all of them used to nothing more than campfires, candles, oil lamps and, only recently, the miracle of flickering strings of light-bulbs. The only music they heard were nursery rhymes and Bob Dylan songs strummed rather badly by an old Buddhist earth-mother called Hamarra.

'It's not good for them, Leona. You can't fill their heads with things as they *were*. They're never going to see any of those things. *This* is all they'll have.'

Leona sighed. 'It's hard not to want to tell them, Mum.'

'But it's kinder not to. You have to let go. That world's really not coming back any time soon.'

Leona said nothing. This was an old conversation, one they'd had too many times before.

'We've witnessed enough to know that,' added Jenny, 'haven't we?'

Witnessed enough. She was right about that. They'd seen that world collapse up close, living in London – the worst possible place to have been during that first week. After the dust settled on the riots, there was a hope that order would somehow be restored. But it was soon clear things had gone too far. Too much damage done, too many people killed. The food that had been in the stores on the Monday was cleaned out by the Wednesday; stolen, spoiled, eaten, hidden. And with no power there was no clean water. People were very quickly dying of cholera, or killing each other for bottled water.

There'd been many small communities outside the cities

that were better prepared; foresightful people with beards and chunky-knit jumpers who'd been rattling on about Peak Oil for years and preparing for the inevitable end. The sort of scruffy new-age weirdy-beardies that Leona had once turned her nose up at; that reminded her a bit of her dad. They had their freshwater wells, their vegetable plots, their chickens and pigs.

The one thing they didn't have, though, was guns. So many of them were overrun and picked clean by the starving thousands flooding out of London, Birmingham, Manchester. Picked clean . . . and in many cases, since there was no sign of the police or the army or any sense that law and order was going to return, the women raped and the men killed. Years of foreknowledge and preparation accounted for nothing. It had simply made them a target.

Survival through those first few weeks and months turned everyone into a brutal caricature of themselves. Everyone had done something they weren't proud of to stay alive. For a while it was nothing more than a twisted form of Darwinism at work; it was the most selfish who managed to survive: the *takers*.

Hordes of people emerging from the cities – running from the rioting and the gangs making the most of the anarchy, they choked the roads, endless rivers of people on foot, all of them hungry. At first it was begging, when they came across the well-tended vegetable gardens and allotments and chicken runs out beyond the urban sprawl. Soon it became a matter of stealing after dark. Finally the migrating hordes just picked clean anything they found, and if a person was stupid enough to try and explain they'd been preparing for this for years and tried to stop them stripping his garden clean, then it turned even nastier.

Leona remembered the day their small settlement had been raided by a gang of about thirty men, several *years* after the crash. By then, they'd assumed roving bands of scroungers were a thing of the past, died out, killed by others or starved long ago. Then one cold winter morning they turned up, armed with guns, some of them wearing ragged police and army uniforms, emerging from the trees, drawn by the smell of woodsmoke.

She shuddered at the memory of what followed and forced her attention back on the playing children. But her mind wasn't done yet.

They were always men, though, weren't they? The 'takers'. Groups of men with guns.

Her mind played flashes of that winter morning; the raping in the barn. The ensuing struggle. Spatters of blood on the snow. Screams. Gunshots.

Stop it.

Leona turned to look at her mother watching the children play; always on guard, always on duty.

That's why she doesn't trust men any more. That winter morning . . .

It was why they now struggled on out here on these windswept rigs. In the aftermath of that morning, after the men had gone, Mum had gathered her and Jacob and a few others who'd decided to leave, and she'd left. Soon after, they'd found the rigs, and she'd decided that's where home was going to be.

What happened that morning to her, in the barn, mum never spoke of. But she'd never trusted men since. Well, that wasn't entirely true. She trusted Walter, but only because she knew she had a hold over him. He was like a puppy, always eager to please her, always around their quarters, like a live-in uncle, always there.

Mum trusted him and herself. That was it. When they first moved onto the rigs there'd been about eighty of them; mostly those from the raided settlement. Now there were over four hundred and fifty; people they'd encountered in and around Bracton, looking for safety from men with guns.

Quite possibly the same ones. And mum had allowed them to join – safety in numbers and all that. Mostly women and children, a few old men.

Leona watched as her mother goaded Hannah to chase down one of the other kids.

But now there's too many people, aren't there?

Too many for Jenny to indefinitely remain an undisputed leader. There were grumblings amongst some of them that Jenny Sutherland was unelected and yet making all the rules. A self-appointed dictator and Walter, with the only pair of keys to the gun locker, her lackey.

Leona suspected that one day Mum was going to have to face down an open challenge to her authority. It could be over any number of contentious issues; her refusal to allow any prayer groups to be organised, the relentless work-schedule for everyone, her insistence they remain hidden away on these gas platforms with no clear indication for how long. Surely not for ever? And, of course, they were welcome to leave if they didn't see things her way.

One day, Leona suspected, a group of them were going to down their tools and defy Jenny. If for no other reason than to see what she would do in the face of such a challenge – to see what sort of a person she really was. And then, in that moment of truth, what would she do? Evict them at gunpoint? Mum was tough, she had to be to make this place work, but Leona hated the idea that she was paying for that with what was left of her old self.

'I'm sorry to moan,' said Jenny, breaking into her thoughts. 'But you can't dwell on what's gone. Our children need to be happy with what we've got, Lee. Not pining for what you once had.'

'Our children can't live their *whole* lives here either, Mum. I won't do that to Hannah.'

Jenny's face tightened. 'Look, one day we'll settle back on the mainland,' she said after a while. 'When we can be *sure* it's safe again. When we can be sure that the bastards who take what they want at gunpoint have run out of things to scavenge and have starved to death.'

Leona shrugged.

Jenny turned to her, softening her voice, realising how harsh she must sound. 'Hannah *will* inherit a better world. One day it'll be better than this. Better even than it used to be before the crash.'

Leona offered a wan smile. *The old spiel, again.*

She had heard that speech about a million times, 'All That Was Wrong With The Oil Age World'; greed and consumerism, borrowing and spending, debt and negative equity, haves and have-nots; *me* generation people living lonely lives in their own plastic bubbles of consumer comfort. Maybe she was right? Maybe it was a miserable world full of discontented people, but in a heartbeat, *in a heartbeat*, she'd have that shitty old world back and thoroughly embrace it. So would Jacob.

'Mum . . .'

Jenny looked at her.

'You know, one of these days, Jacob will go out on one of our shore runs and he won't be coming back.'

Jenny's face pinched and she sat silent for a moment. 'I do worry that will happen every time I send him.'

'So why do you send him?'

'Because I hope he'll see enough to realise there's nothing ashore, nothing to run away *to*, only overgrown streets and buildings falling in on themselves.'

Leona knew he felt differently. 'Several of the older boys, Jacob included, are convinced that things are rebuilding themselves on the mainland. That somewhere in the big cities they've already got power going again, that street lights are coming on and the like.'

Jenny sighed. 'We'd know, Lee, wouldn't we? We'd have

heard something on the radio about it. Something from a passer-by.'

'I know that. I'm just saying Jacob's becoming, I don't know, sort of *taken* with the idea that out there, some sort of . . . glittering metropolis is waiting for him.'

Jenny watched as Hannah flopped to the ground, exhausted from her running around. Natasha flopped to the ground beside her, and the pair of them, for some reason, suddenly decided to waggle their feet and hands in the air like struggling house flies.

'You can talk to him, Lee. He listens more to you than he does me now. Tell him that's a bloody stupid idea.'

Leona shook her head. 'I *do* talk to him. But, you know, I guess sometimes I feel a bit like that too.'

Jenny turned towards her. 'Leona, it's a dead and dark world. You've seen it for yourself. If there are any people left, they're dangerous and hungry and looking for people like us to strip bare.'

Leona noted mum had kept that comment gender neutral. But by 'them' she meant men, and 'us' she meant women.

'Here, on these platforms, we're safe. We've had time to consolidate, to build things up. We can feed ourselves now, we aren't relying on a dwindling supply of canned goods in some grubby warehouse. We're not scavengers, Lee.'

Jenny reached out for one of Leona's hands and squeezed it. 'I know it's tough, it's cold, it's wet and boring out here. But one day, Lee, one day the last of those bastards will have starved to death and it'll be safe. Then we can move ashore.'

Leona watched as Hannah and Natasha got bored with playing dead flies and scrambled to their feet, ignoring the other children and playing their own game of tag, chasing each other towards the swaying field of tomato plants, along the faint, peeling lines of the helipad's giant 'H'.

'But look . . . will you talk to Jacob? Assure him we're not staying here for ever? One day, right? One day we can go back.'

'I'll try,' said Leona.

Chapter 6

10 years AC

Bracton Harbour,
Norfolk

Sitting on the foredeck of the boat, secured alongside the harbour's quayside, Jacob listened to the noises of the night. The rhythmic slapping of water on the hull, the sporadic whisper of a fresh breeze and the clatter and tinkle of loose things teased by the wind amongst the quayside warehouses.

On occasions such as this, on guard duty, there had been times that he'd heard other noises; the haunting echo of a faraway cry; once, the solitary crack of a distant gunshot; often the sound of someone, or wild dogs, rifling through crates and cargo containers in the warehouses.

Less so with each visit, though.

Tonight it was the tide, the breeze and shuffling debris skittering in wind-borne circles and nothing else.

He reached out for the SA80 and stroked the smooth cold metal of its barrel. He'd only ever had one go at firing the thing; a dozen test rounds out into the North Sea. The punch on his shoulder, the bucking in his hands, the crack of each shot – it had been exhilarating. One burst of fire and then Walter had snatched the gun off him saying that was enough. Ammunition couldn't be replaced, and now he knew *how* to fire the thing, he was trained enough.

Walter had been part of the community from almost the very beginning; after the crash, back when they lived for several years amidst a cluster of barns. Jacob had been only twelve when the 'bad men' arrived. Hungry men, lean men in tatty clothes, some even in army uniforms. He wasn't certain whether they were really soldiers or not; he remembered some wearing trainers, some had the sort of tattoos he'd never imagined that a policeman or a soldier would have, and no one seemed to be in charge.

They saw the chickens, the pigs. They'd followed the smell of frying bacon and woodsmoke through the thick forest that thus far had hidden them from the world outside.

He shuddered at the memory of that particular day. An initial polite request for a meal and a little hospitality had quickly escalated to something very different. After they'd eaten the bacon, a girl only a couple of years older than him was taken by several of the men to a nearby barn. That was the first. They took other girls and women, one by one. Mum included.

The fighting started soon after. It was probably all over in ten minutes, but to Jacob it seemed like that whole winter morning had been filled with the crack of gunfire, screaming, crying. Seven of the bad men were killed, the others melting away into the woods.

But so many more of their own people had died – mostly they'd been women, girls. It was as if the soldiers had decided that if they couldn't *have* them, they might as well *kill* them.

Leona lost the young man she was with; a tall guy with long hair called Hal. Jacob remembered Hal's father – he couldn't remember the man's name – had used a kitchen knife to make short work of one of the bad men left wounded in the snow. He'd dragged him into the barn and finished him there.

He returned with Mum, helping her back across the paddock, she was covered in scratches and cuts and blood, her clothes ripped, her face a hardened stare. Their little community never really recovered from that morning, and a few weeks later the survivors were split down the middle; those that were going, those that were staying.

Over the years Jacob had often found himself wondering whether those they'd left behind – people who had almost been like extended family through the early years after the crash – had managed to carry on there. Or whether those men had come back as promised and this time finished them all off.

It was certainly a morning no one *ever* discussed. When newcomers arrived and asked how the rig community started out, Mum always fluffed the question, and Walter usually said nothing.

That day was just over five years ago and Jacob was certain that all the bad men must be long gone by now – run out of things to steal and people to kill, and just faded away. What was left of the UK had to be safe now.

He looked out at the dark skyline. Bracton was just empty buildings, wild dogs and weeds. But London? That's where the government, the Prime Minister and all the important men lived. He remembered listening to the BBC emergency broadcasts just after the crash mentioning the safe zones in and around the big cities. There were about twenty or so of them; big buildings guarded by soldiers and full of emergency supplies of food and water and taking in civilians who sought their protection.

Yes, some of the zones had gone wrong in the aftermath, he'd heard about that, too many people, too few troops. But surely not all of them? Right?

At least one or two of them must have muddled through, especially in London where there were several of the biggest zones. Surely, by now, they'd managed to get things up and running again; had powered up lights like they had on the rig, perhaps even had enough power to make hot water, to run some street lamps, perhaps even a few shops selling their wares once more. It was possible, wasn't it?

He smiled in the dark.

It's inevitable. You can't keep a great country like Great Britain down. Called 'great' for a reason, right?

He knew he was right. He knew something else too. One day he was going to find out for himself.

Soon. One day soon.

Chapter 7

The Day of the Crash
10 a.m.

RAF Regiment, 2 Squadron mess hall,
RAF Honington, Suffolk

Flight Lieutenant Adam Brooks sat in the corner of the mess hall, his eyes glued to the small television set, as were those of several dozen of the lads from 2 Squadron. The rest of the gunners were out on rotation manning the front gates and beating the airfield perimeter with the dogs. Security readiness at Honington had already been upped this morning, as a matter of precaution, from amber to red. Adam suspected it was almost a certainty that all leave and weekend passes were being revoked right now as they sat here watching the telly.

On the small screen BBC24 was covering the story — already somebody had managed to throw together some computer graphics to sex up the visuals. As if shaky mobile phone footage of columns of flames was not enough.

'. . . *and then there's the Paraguana refinery in Venezuela which is the main processing facility in the country — in fact for all of South America — for their light crude. We have no details on how much damage has been done there and whether that's going to have an effect on oil output from the region but . . .*'

'They're all *oil* targets,' grunted one of the men sitting next to Adam. It was Lance Corporal Sean 'Bushey' Davies. 'Someone's just hitting the oil!'

'Jesus. Well spotted, Bushey, you stupid twat,' someone a row back quipped.

'Fuck off,' he grunted over his shoulder.

Adam watched as the talking heads in the studio were replaced by a Google Earth map that panned silky-smooth across the screen. Slick explosion graphics were peppered across the Arab states, several more around the Caspian Sea. He counted two dozen. More were being added to the map as they spoke.

'. . . Nigeria, the Kaduna refinery. That's just come in. Again no idea of the size or damage or how many fatalities. So, the question being asked is just what is going on out there? Who's doing this?'

'It's . . . uh . . . really too early to be putting the blame on any group in particular,' replied a freshly scrubbed and suited industry expert. To Adam, the poor young man appeared to be an unprepared and none-too-willing participant, pulled without notice from some back office and thrown before the glare of studio lights. He cleared his shaking voice with a self-conscious cough and took a quick sip of water. 'But this does appear to be an attempt to disrupt as much global oil production as possible.'

'What about the earlier bombs in Saudi Arabia at Medina and near the Kaaba in Mecca? Neither one, apparently, to do with oil.'

The expert looked awkwardly at the camera – a complete no-no. His skin turned a blotchy corned-beef red, uncomfortable, nervous, before turning back to the well-groomed news anchor.

'Well . . . uh . . . that's obviously an attempt to incite widespread Sunni–Shi'a retaliatory violence . . . religious civil war. With just two bombs in those very sacred places, you've got a peninsula-wide tinderbox going up. It'll completely destabilise Saudi Arabia, Kuwait, Iraq . . . and other producers in the region, the core OPEC producers.'

The young man's helpless face was replaced with shaking camera footage of an enormous oil slick, entirely aflame, spreading across a slim shipping channel. The towering pyramid of fire tapered into a thick black column of smoke that, in terms of scale, reminded Adam of photos of the pyroclastic cloud above Mount St Helens. The morning sun was lost beneath it. The sea that should have been a bright blue was a dull twilight grey. Beneath the shaking pixellated footage, red tickertape indicated further explosions in the Strait of Malacca.

'And that, of course, is a very dangerous scenario. Just by taking Saudi Arabia and two or three of these other key producers out of the loop we're looking at a shortfall of fifty-five to sixty-five per cent of the world's oil production capacity right there.'

'Now that sounds quite serious,' said the anchor with a thoughtful frown spreading across his tanned face. *'Presumably we can expect some sort of impact on us here in the UK. Are we going to be looking at queues at the pumps?'*

The expert stared back at him, not studio-savvy enough to dial-back the look of utter dismay on his face. *'Uh . . . no, you . . . you're missing the point. It's a lot more serious than that. In the oil markets, we call this type of . . . of scenario, well there are a number of what are called Perfect Storm Scenarios—'*

A cocked eyebrow from the anchor. *'Perfect Storm?'*

The expert nodded silently.

Dead-air time. The anchor prodded him gently. *'Which means what exactly?'*

'Enough wild-card events occurring synchronously to completely shut down oil processing and distribution—'

'Affecting, of course, the price per barrel; presumably a major blip on the price of other commodities. So, this kind of an interruption of oil availability . . . how long before we can expect to feel the impact of this on our wallets? How long before we—'

'You really don't get it, do you?'

The anchor stared at his studio guest, his mouth hanging open.

'It's a Perfect Storm . . . there's no contingency for it. We're screwed.'

Adam glanced at the men in his unit, silent now, boots shuffling uncomfortably beneath the tables.

'We . . . we're a net importer,' the expert continued, 'a net importer of oil and gas. More importantly, we're a big importer of everything else . . .'

The anchor nodded, an expression of practised gravitas easing onto his face, as if he'd known exactly how serious things were all along.

'. . . Food, for example,' continued the expert. 'Food,' he said with added emphasis. 'There's very little storage and warehousing in the UK because it's a drain on profit. What we have instead are "just-in-time" distribution systems; warehouses that need only store and refrigerate twenty-four hours' worth of food instead of two weeks' worth. As long as haulage trucks and freight ships keep moving, it works just fine. But, no oil,' the expert shook his head, 'no food.'

The anchor's eyes widened. 'No food?'

'We could well be looking at a severe rationing programme, perhaps even some form of martial law to enforce that.'

'Martial law? Oh, surely that's—'

'A Perfect Storm . . . we're into uncharted territory this morning.' The expert's voice was beginning to waver nervously. 'There's no way of knowing how serious this could get . . . or . . . or how quickly. Believe me, there are industry doom-sayers who've long been pointing to this kind of event as a . . . as a global paradigm shift.'

'A global . . . a what?'

'Paradigm shift. A . . . well, a complete global shutdown.'

Adam turned to look at his men. Silent and still. The last time he'd seen the lads like this was when an unexpected *third* six-month extension on their rotation to Afghanistan was announced to them last year.

A moment later the first mobile phone began to trill.

Chapter 8

10 years AC

Bracton Harbour,
Norfolk

They all heard it and froze. It was unmistakable and instantly recognisable, an after-echo peeling off the myriad warehouse walls, across the open quayside and slowly petering out.

'That was a gun,' said Walter.

Like it needed saying.

Jacob lowered a sack full of boxes and plastic bottles of pills through the storage hatch into the boat's fore cabin and stood up straight, squinting as he scanned the buildings overlooking the quayside. 'It sounded pretty close to me.'

'Maybe we should leave,' said Bill. He pushed his glasses up the bridge of his nose and glanced anxiously out of the cockpit. 'Just leave the rest of the stuff and go.'

Walter was giving that consideration. They could always come back another day. But then if it was a rival group of survivors staking a claim, attempting to frighten them off, they'd be buggered. Bracton was their only source of essentials.

Another shot.

'Dammit,' the old man muttered unhappily.

'Shit, man, that was definitely closer,' said Nathan, his face in an involuntary nervous grin.

'Are we going or what?' asked Bill.

Walter's eyes narrowed. He remained where he was on the quay, scanning the buildings for signs of movement. Undecided.

'Walter?'

Dammit . . . we can't just go. He knew that. They needed to find out who was out there, what they wanted. Bracton was all they had.

'My gun,' he said, 'pass me my gun.'

Kevin reached down into the cockpit for the shotgun and passed it over the narrow sliver of choppy water to Walter.

'What the hell are you doing, Walt?' asked Howard. 'There's just you, me, Dennis and Bill . . . and the boys. We can't get into a fight!'

Walter was tempted to jump in the yacht, run up the sail, turn the motor on and flee. But that would be it. They needed to clear the marina, the warehouses, the brewery's freshwater well was already being tapped by themselves, and wasn't fair game for anyone passing through.

'We can't leave,' he snapped irritably. 'We have to find out who that is.'

'S'right,' Nathan nodded, 'this place is *ours*, man. They need to know that.'

Jacob picked up the assault rifle from the foredeck and hopped across onto the quay to join the others ashore.

'Hey, gimme the gun,' said Nathan.

'It's okay, I've got it.'

'But I got better eyesight, Jay.'

Jacob made a face, tight-lipped.

Walter nodded. 'He's got a point. Best give the SA80 to Nathan.'

Jacob passed the gun over to him resentfully.

Another couple of shots rang out across the open space of the quayside.

'Jesus!' hissed Dennis ducking down in the boat's cockpit.

'Look!' shouted Nathan, jabbing a finger towards the loading bay of the nearest warehouse. From the dark interior, out through large, open sliding doors, a man emerged, staggering frantically towards them. He'd seen them, was making his way towards them. He cried out something – it sounded garbled or perhaps foreign.

Following him, two more men appeared from the doorway, both armed. They walked unhurriedly after the first. He wasn't going to run anywhere. He looked weak and spent. No danger of him escaping. One of them shouldered his gun and fired off a shot. It pinged off the ground a yard away from the staggering man, sending a puff of concrete dust into the air, and ricocheted in the general direction of Walter and the others.

'Fuck!' the old man hissed, raising his shotgun. 'Ready your weapons,' he uttered to the others.

Nathan raised the assault rifle to his shoulder.

'Safety,' muttered Walter, 'lad, you need to take the safety off.'

'Oh, yeah.'

The man being pursued continued to stagger towards them. They could see now he'd already been hit in the thigh, the left trouser leg was dark and wet with blood.

'*Aidez-moi . . . aidez-moi*!!' he gasped, his eyes wide with terror beneath a mop of dark curls of hair.

Another shot whistled past the man, almost clipping his shoulder, and thudding into the fibreglass side of the boat.

Fuck this.

'STOP RIGHT THERE!!' bellowed Walter.

The two men slowed, but didn't halt.

The wounded man collapsed several yards in front of them. He groaned with pain as he clutched his thigh in both hands, sweat slicked his olive skin, sticking dark ringlets of hair to his face.

'*Ils essaient de me tuer*!!' he gasped. 'They going to kill me!' he said again with a thick accent.

'I SAID STOP!' shouted Walter again, shouldering his shotgun and aiming down the barrel at them, now standing only a dozen yards away. One of them was wearing a police

53

anti-stab vest, the other a grubby pair of red tracksuit bottoms and a faded khaki sweatshirt. Both of them, like Walter, with lank hair tied back into a ponytail and a face of unshaven bristles.

'Out of our fuckin' way,' snapped one of them. 'He's going to die.'

Walter realised he was trembling; the end of the shotgun's barrel was jittering around for everyone to see.

'You just . . . just bloody well stay back!' shouted Walter, breathing deeply, shakily, the air whistling in and out of his bulbous nose.

One of the men looked up at him and shook his head dismissively. 'Shut the fuck up, you old fart.'

The man in the stab vest took a quick step forward and lowered his gun at the foreign man on the floor. 'This is how we deal with dirty fucking Paki wankers.'

The wounded man screwed his eyes shut and uttered the beginnings of a prayer in French.

'You . . . y-you can't just . . . *shoot* him,' cut in Jacob. 'It's not right.'

'Yeah?' said stab vest. 'Is that right, son? Am I infringing his fucking human rights?'

Jacob swallowed nervously. He nodded. 'It's just not . . . you can't!'

'Yeah? You get in my way I'll do you next, you little prick.' The man levelled his gun at the Frenchman's head. 'Fuckin' scum like this . . . only way to deal with—'

Walter's shotgun suddenly boomed, snapping stab-vest's head back and throwing a long tendril of hair, blood, brains and skull up into the air. The other man looked up, startled, and swung his weapon towards the old man.

Instinctively Nathan squeezed several rounds off from his assault rifle. Only one of his shots landed home, punching the man at the base of his throat. His knees buckled and he dropped to the ground like a sack full of coconuts.

'Oh, fuck!!' whispered Walter. 'Oh, fuck,' he wheezed, 'I didn't bloody mean to. Damn thing just went off in my hand!'

Red tracksuit's legs scissored on the ground as he gurgled noisily, his hands clasped around his throat as if throttling himself, blood quickly pooling on the gritty concrete beneath him.

'Walter . . .' said Kevin from the back of the boat. He stood up, eager to clamber ashore and get a closer look at the mess. 'You blew his head off!'

'Dammit! Kevin, sit down and be quiet!' snapped David.

'Oh, shit, man!' said Nathan, his features ashen. 'He's dying! What – what the fuck are we gonna do?'

They watched the man squirm on the ground for a moment.

'We have to do something!' shouted Jacob. 'He's bleeding everywhere!'

Walter stared, dumbfounded, smoke still curling from the barrel of his shotgun.

'He's dying,' said Bill. 'We *can't* help him.'

Walter nodded.

'We could take him back to Dr Gupta,' said Jacob bending down to peer at the man convulsing on the ground.

'Don't be stupid!' snapped David. 'He's bleedin' out! He'll be dead before we get him back.'

The sound of the man's gurgling, bubbling breath filled the space between them.

'Then, shit, we ought to . . .' Nathan started, looking at the others. 'You know? We can't leave him like this!'

Walter nodded, finally roused from a state of shock. 'Yes . . . Christ. Yes, I-I suppose you're right,' he said quietly. He placed the shotgun carefully down on the ground and tugged the assault rifle out of Nathan's rigid hands.

'Best close your eyes, mate,' he said to the man on the ground.

The man struggled to say something. Bubbles and

strangled air whistled out through the jagged hole in his throat, whilst his mouth flapped uselessly.

'Look away, boys,' he said to the others.

Walter aimed, closed his own eyes and fired.

Chapter 9

10 years AC

'LeMan 49/25a' – ClarenCo Gas Rig Complex, North Sea

Jenny looked down and watched Dr Tamira Gupta take charge of lifting the wounded man out of the boat. Tamira – 'Tami' as she was more commonly known – small and delicate, her dark hair pulled back out of the way into a businesslike bun, bossed the men and boys as they eased the man out of the cockpit.

'Be very careful,' she heard the woman bark at Jacob and Nathan as they lifted him into the net swinging just above the rising and falling foredeck. The man groaned weakly as he flopped across the coarse netting. Tami threw a blanket over him to keep him warm then signalled those above manning the davit to start winching him up.

The net rose from the bobbing deck, swinging its catch in the fresh breeze. The sea was beginning to get a little lively, swells slapping against the nearby legs sending up small showers of salty spray.

'So what the hell happened?' Jenny asked Walter.

He leant forward on the railing, watching the net slowly rise, and Dr Gupta clambering up the rope ladder onto the spider deck. He breathed deep and swallowed, looking like someone ready to vomit.

'Walter?'

'He was being chased like it was some kind of . . . of a bloody fox hunt. The poor sod was already wounded, saw us moored up on the quayside and getting ready to go and made straight towards us. The blokes chasing after him . . .' Walter took another breath and watched the swinging net slowly rise for a moment.

'The two blokes chasing him fired shots at him that nearly hit us. In fact, they didn't seem to give a shit that they nearly hit us. They came over, standing right over him and were about to execute him when . . . when . . . the bloody gun just went off in my hands.'

'You killed them?'

Walter wavered for a moment, wondering whether he ought to tell Jenny that one of the men had been killed outright, but the other, they'd had to shoot like a wounded animal. 'Yes, we killed them.'

To his surprise she nodded approvingly. 'Well, then you did the right thing.'

'We checked around nearby. Didn't find anyone else. But that doesn't mean there aren't more of them out there.'

Jenny nodded.

'Seems like they were after this Frenchman for a bit of fun.'

'French?'

'He spoke something before he passed out.' Walter shrugged. 'Been a long time since I've been in school – it sounded like French to me.'

They watched as Tami climbed the last steps of the stairwell onto the cellar deck.

She pushed her way through the crowd gathered around the davit cranes, pulled the netting aside and knelt down beside the man, quickly checking the wound, the man's pulse.

'I wonder how far he's come?' asked Jenny. 'From mainland Europe?'

Walter shook his head. 'Or perhaps further? He's quite dark. Could be from somewhere Mediterranean, possibly Middle Eastern?'

'You think that made him a target? You know, being an outsider, a foreigner?'

Walter tugged on the grey-white bristles of his beard, the slightest tremble still in his fingers. 'By the look of those two men chasing him . . . who knows? Thugs with guns. You know the kind.'

Jenny nodded, biting her lip. 'I was starting to hope the mainland was a safe place again. I was hoping vicious bastards like that had died out long ago.'

Dr Gupta finished making an initial examination and had him transferred to a stretcher to be taken up to her infirmary. Jenny quickly excused herself to let Walter oversee the unloading of the boat whilst she pushed her way past the onlookers gathered along the railing.

'Jenny,' called out one of the women. 'You going to tell us what happened?'

'Not now,' she called over her shoulder. She quickly climbed the steps to the cellar deck and joined Dr Gupta as she packed up her medical bag.

'Tami, how is he?'

'He has lost a lot of blood from the wound. I cannot see if there are any broken bones in there, or fragments. I will need to clean him out and take a look. He is also very malnourished by the look of him. In a very sorry way, I am afraid.'

'Will he live?'

She shrugged. 'I really don't know, Jenny. We have got plenty antibiotics to combat any infection and I'll sedate him right now and take a look inside the wound, make sure there is no internal bleeding. I will see how we go from there.'

'All right, I'll let you get on with it.'

Dr Gupta flicked a stiff smile at her then headed after the stretcher, being manoeuvred awkwardly up the next stairwell to the main deck by half a dozen pairs of hands.

'Careful, Helen!' she barked out at one of the youngsters she'd drafted to help heft the stretcher. 'Both hands, please!'

'I'm doing my best!' the girl replied haughtily. 'He's heavy, though!'

Jenny watched them go, pitying the poor sod being rattled around on the stretcher, moaning with every jar and bump.

I hope he pulls through. There's about a million questions I'd like to ask him.

Walter puffed up the last of the steps and stood beside her, his red blotchy face dotted with sweat. 'It all happened so quickly.'

'I'd like to know where that man came from, and what he's seen abroad,' she replied. 'I wonder if the rest of the world is faring any better.' She looked down at the sea. Sixty feet below, the net, lowered once more to the boat's foredeck, rising and dropping on the swells sliding beneath her, was being filled with the goodies they'd found on the shore run.

Walter nodded silently. She could see he was still shaken by what had happened. She decided to direct his mind elsewhere. 'So, more importantly, how did your shopping run go?'

'Oh . . . yes, we got most of what was on the list,' he smiled, 'and a few little extras for the party.'

Jenny smiled wearily. *Good.*

Life was usually made a little easier after a shore run. Most people got something they'd requested and were less likely to bitch and grumble for the next few days at least. And the celebration party . . . well, that couldn't come soon enough.

They were soon to mark the very first anniversary of getting the generator up and running; Leona's suggestion – a good one too. The two or three hours of light every evening, afforded by the noisy chugging thing, made all the difference to their lives. More than a small luxury, it was a significant step up from merely managing to survive. It was a comfort; a reminder of better times; a statement of progress; steady light across the decks and walkways after dark.

Absolutely worth celebrating that.

Apart from anything else, the party would be a boost for their morale — hopefully shut the whingers and malcontents up for a while.

'Come on, Walter, what *extras* did you manage to rustle up?'

Walter tapped his ruddy nose and managed a thin smile. 'Just a few nice things.'

The net was full enough for the first load and Nathan flashed a thumbs-up to the people manning the davit. They worked the manual winch and the laden net swung up off the deck with the creaking of polyvinyl cables and the clinking of chains. As it slowly rose away from the rising and falling boat, Jacob, Nathan and the others worked in practised unison, bringing boxes of supplies from below deck and stacking them in the cockpit ready to fill the empty net again. Mostly medicines. But also items of clothing, woollen jumpers, waterproofs, thick socks and thermal underwear. She spotted a basket full of paperback novels and glossy magazines, cellophane-wrapped packs of cook-in-sauce tins, catering-size bags of salt and sugar and flour . . . amazing how, even now, if one knew where to look, what things could be foraged from the dark corners of warehouses.

Hannah clattered on noisy clogs through the crowd and found them, dragging Leona by the hand after her.

'Uncle Walter, did you find me anything?'

He hunkered down to her level and winked at her. 'Oh, let's just see.' He reached into the old leather bag slung over his shoulder, made a show of rummaging around inside. 'I'm sure I must have something in here for you.' Finally, with a little theatrical flourish, he pulled out a transparent plastic case containing what looked like a row of water-colour tabs and a paintbrush.

'Little Miss Britney make-up set,' he said handing it to her.

Her little caterpillar eyebrows shot up to form a double arch of surprise. 'Wow!' She threw an arm around his shoulders and planted a wet kiss on his rough cheek. Walter's face flushed crimson.

'Bit young for grooming, isn't she?' said a woman stepping past — Alice Harton, a miserable-faced bitch who seemed to make a life's work out of mean-spirited put-downs and caustic remarks.

Walter looked up and shrugged awkwardly. 'Well . . . I saw it . . . just thought she'd like it.'

'It's lovely!' cooed Hannah brightly.

'There, see?' said Leona, handing the woman a dry *now-why-don't-you-piss-off* smile. Alice Harton brushed on past them, shaking her head disapprovingly as she spoke in hushed tones and backward glances to the women with her.

Jenny squeezed his round shoulder affectionately as he slowly stood up. 'Don't listen to that silly cow, Walter. I don't know what I'd do . . . what *any of us* would do without you.'

He smiled at her and down at Hannah. 'I'm here for you, Jenny,' he uttered.

'And *I* got this for you, Hannah,' said Jacob.

He produced a Playmobil Princess and Pony set from his sack. It was still in its cardboard and plastic packaging; pristine and not sun-faded. He'd found it at the back of a children's shop on the high street. Her eyes instantly lit up, as much at the sight of the beautiful pink cardboard presentation box and the unscuffed plastic window than at the two small plastic play figures she could see imprisoned inside.

'Thank you, Jake,' she gushed, twining her short arms around his neck and plastering his grimacing face with wet kisses.

The large mess and the hallway outside were crowded with a couple of hundred of the community's members; those that had put a *must-have* on the list and turned up in the hope that there was something for them to collect. It was a deafening convergence of overlapping voices raised with pleasure and surprise or groans of disappointment.

Jacob extracted himself from Hannah's clinging embrace. Leona thanked him with a squeeze. 'Thanks, bruv. Two treats today, she's being spoiled.'

He shrugged. 'I used to love Playmobil stuff. It was proper cool. Those things don't ever break.'

She smiled. 'I remember. You had the Viking ship and all the Vikings in your bedroom, didn't you?'

'Yeah,' he nodded. 'So, I umm . . . I treated myself to a present as well . . .' He reached into his bag and pulled out a small pristine cardboard carton. 'Viking captain,' he smiled, opening the box and pulling out the plastic figure. He turned it over in his hands, his fingers stroking the smooth contours of plastic, his eyes drinking in the bright unblemished colours. For a fleeting moment – like a dormant memory stirred by a smell – he was back home in his bedroom, seven once again, sitting cross-legged on the blue furry rug that looked like an ocean, and steering his ship through a stormy furry sea. Beams of afternoon sun warming his face through the window; the reassuring sounds of mum in the kitchen, dad in his study watching the news on his laptop, Leona playing music in her room. A very ordinary Saturday afternoon . . . from another time, another life.

'The arms and legs can move,' he added thoughtfully, adjusting them in his hands.

'I know, little brother, I know,' she smiled.

He looked up and saw amongst the animated faces others like him, staring wistfully at mementos from the past, lost in a fog of nostalgic delight.

'So, there were some men, I heard,' said Leona.

He nodded. 'A couple of them.'

'Chasing the guy you saved?'

Jacob was reluctant to talk it out right now. It was still way too easy to conjure up an image of the Y-shaped splatter of blood and brain tissue across the concrete.

'We had to shoot them. Otherwise they would have killed the other man,' was all he wanted to offer just then. Leona was going to press him for more details, but Hannah was yanking impatiently on her hand, keen to show her the princess and pony. Leona relented and squatted down to her level and Jacob watched and smiled as his sister and niece cooed at the marvellously preserved plastic figurines.

Two men with guns.

Is it really safe ashore?

The question annoyed him, made him feel angry and his stomach lurch unpleasantly.

See . . . if you really want to go ashore, Jay, if you really insist on going ashore and exploring, then that's what you might be up against. Nasty men. Big guns. You ready for that? You a big enough boy to look after yourself now?

'Yes,' he muttered under his breath. A gun was going to be just as deadly in his hands as some wild-eyed thug playing fox and hounds.

'What's up, bruv?' asked Leona looking up.

He shook the Y-shaped splatter from his mind and smiled. 'Oh, nothing.'

Chapter 10

Crash Day + 1
11 a.m.

Suffolk

Adam looked out of the open canopy of their truck as it rumbled south along the A11's slow lane, towards London. The rest of the squadron's gunners, inside, were trying to listen to a small radio attempting to compete with the deafening snarl of the RAF transport truck's diesel engine.

Today, the second day of the crisis. The situation seemed not to show any sign of abating. On the contrary, the news seemed to be getting worse by the hour. The last soundbite Adam had managed to catch from the radio was that the American military forces in the region had begun redeploying en masse in Saudi Arabia. Although no one from the US Defense Department had made a public statement on this large scale rapid movement of muscle, it was obvious that the troops were being sent to defend critical installations in the Ghawar oil fields, an area that had yet to be wholly incapacitated by the widespread rioting.

The Middle East was sounding like one big battlefield, the fighting now not just between Sunnis and Shi'as, but between rival tribes, between neighbouring streets, seemingly in every city and town in many of the Arab nations; a chance in the spreading entropy to settle age-old dishonours and more recent disputes.

Then, of course, there was the bottomless plummet on the markets.

Adam, with ten thousand pounds of savings in a Nationwide Sharetracker account, had listened with increasing desperation as the FTSE had plummeted this morning to somewhere close to two thousand, losing just over fifty per cent of its value, the government apparently doing or saying nothing to halt the slide until half an hour ago when it announced, out of the blue, that the London stock exchange was being suspended for the day. Shrewdly, before Wall Street was about due to come online.

A voice on the radio reminded listeners that the Prime Minister was scheduled to make an important announcement at midday. Adam checked his watch.

An hour or so to go.

All ears in the truck would be cocked for that one.

He stared back out of the truck at the road filled with unhurried vehicles going about a normal day's business and wondered why he wasn't seeing any signs of panic yet. Why there were so many cars out there making routine journeys.

But then, of course, none of them had been there at the briefing yesterday. It had been little more than a hasty exchange over Squadron Leader Cameron's desk; enough to leave Adam with a cold, churning sensation in the pit of his stomach.

'Unofficially, Brooks, we're getting orders to redeploy the regiment. There's a lot of rear-echelon chatter buzzing around this morning. The word is we'll probably be pulling the rest of the regiment back from Afghanistan, Iraq, East Timor and Belize immediately. They want as many boots back on the ground in Britain, as soon as is possible.'

'In response to this oil thing?'

Cameron nodded. 'Yes. I'd say someone upstairs is anticipating laying down some degree of martial law in this country; guarding critical fuel depots.'

'It's going to get that bad, sir?'

'What do *you* think? We nearly had bloody riots over the duty being paid on petrol a few years back. I can only imagine what sort of fun and games we're going to have on our hands when petrol pumps start running dry.' Cameron, agitated, tapped his pen on a desk pad thick with scribbled notes. 'Our poor bastards, 15 Squadron, guarding Kandahar will no doubt be the last fellas out of the country. That is if we still have enough fuel to keep our planes flying.'

Jesus.

Being the last company-strength unit left on the ground in that hell-hole, even on a good day, was going to be hairy. He wondered, when the dust settled in the aftermath of this crisis, what sort of news stories would get top billing in the tabloids: A-list celebrities stranded on holiday islands, *X Factor* auditions postponed by the oil shock, or the massacre of an entire company of left-behind British soldiers.

Stranded celebrities, obviously.

Cameron looked at him. 'You know this has caught everyone on the hop. *Everyone.* I can't believe there wasn't a prepared contingency plan for something like this. You'd think the Russians buggering about turning off gas supplies in recent winters would have alerted someone to the possibility of an oil switch off.' He shook his head. 'I get the impression that everyone up the chain of command is simply winging it. It's a fucking shambles.'

Adam nodded at the pad on his desk. 'So, where are we redeploying?'

'I've got a list of places just come in, places the government want troops stationed round. Since we're perimeter defence specialists we've been handed a lot off the top of the list. Oil distribution nodes, government command and control centres.' He looked down at the list. 'I'm splitting 2 squadron between you, Dempsey and Carver. You're taking Rifle Flight one and two down to London. The O2 Dome, of all places.'

'The Millennium Dome?'

Cameron shrugged. 'Most probably be a regional

emergency co-ordination centre. It's not listed as such, but that's probably why they want guards on the gates there.'

'Right.'

'Get your boys ready to go. As soon as I've got a confirmation order on these deployments I'll let you know.'

'Yes, sir.' Adam turned to go.

'Oh . . . Brooks?'

'Sir?'

'Good luck.' The two words came out in a way he'd probably not intended. They sounded unsettling.

'You think it's really going to get *that* bad, sir?'

Cameron tried a reassuring smile, but produced little more than a queasy grimace. 'Just, good luck, Brooks. All right?'

He dismissed Adam with a busy flicker of his hand. As Adam pulled open the door Cameron called out for him to send in Flight Lieutenant Dempsey.

Adam watched the vehicle a dozen yards behind; a couple of scruffy teenage kids in a beaten-up white van, yapping merrily like they hadn't a care in the world. Beyond them, a Carpet World truck was rolling placidly along, the driver on his mobile. Overtaking in the fast lane a young lad with gel-spiked hair driving a bakery van like it was a performance racing car.

And life goes merrily on for some.

He shook his head at the surreal ordinariness of the scene beyond the back of their truck. People going about their business as if today was just another day.

'Surely they realise?' he muttered.

'What's that, sir?' asked Corporal Davies, sitting on the bench opposite.

Adam looked up at Bushey. He wasn't the brightest lad in the unit, but even in his bullish features Adam could recognise a growing unease that world events were beginning to out-pace the increasingly frantic news headlines.

'Nothing, Bush. Just singing.'

The big fool grinned; a stupid oafish Shrek-like grin that was probably never going to end up on a calendar. He turned to look back out of the truck at the white van behind them and leered at the teenage girl in the passenger seat in a manner he most likely considered rakish and charming.

She returned his unattractive leer with a cocked eyebrow and a middle finger.

Chapter II

10 years AC

'Mum, you really don't need to be shovelling this shit,' said Leona. 'Seriously, you're in charge round here, no one would expect you to.'

Jenny looked up from the foul stinking slurry before her. The odour rising from the warm, steaming bed of human and chicken faeces was so overpowering that she'd been fighting a constant gag reflex until she'd managed to adjust to the unfamiliar habit of breathing solely through her open mouth.

'I'm taking my turn just like everyone else,' she said, tucking a stray lock of hair behind her ear. 'If I ducked this job, the likes of Alice would have a field day with it.'

Alice was a miserable shrew. There wasn't a day that passed without Jenny hearing some little barbed comment come from the woman's flapping lips. There wasn't a day Jenny didn't regret allowing the woman to join them. She'd been so quiet and meek the first few months, no trouble at all . . . that is until she'd found her feet; found other quiet voices like hers. Voices that wondered why this community should have an unelected leader; why one woman should be allowed to impose *her* values, *her* opinions on all of them, when it was *everyone* who contributed to their survival.

Jenny suspected it wasn't the idea of democracy being shunted aside because it was a temporary inconvenience that so irked Alice Harton, it was the fact that some other woman was in charge . . . and not her. After all, as she constantly let everyone know, she'd had extensive management experience back in the *old world;* ran a local government department of some kind. Logically, it should be someone like *her* team-leading, not some workaday middle class mum.

'Sod Alice,' said Leona. 'She moans about everything anyway. You're damned if you do, damned if you don't with a bitch like her.'

'Still, we all should take turns doing this, Lee. It's going to be your turn soon.'

Leona grimaced. 'Oh, gross.'

'We've all got to do our bit, love.'

Walter nodded. 'Each digester stops producing methane after three weeks and needs emptying and refilling.' He gestured at the other two sealed eight-foot-long fibreglass cylinders that he'd rescued from a brewery. 'Huey and Dewey are doing fine right now. Week after next, I think it's your name up on the rota to clean out Dewey.'

The rota . . . *The Rota* . . . was the community's closest equivalent to a Bible. It was written out in tiny handwriting on a whiteboard in what had once been some sort of meeting room. There were four hundred community members old enough and fit enough to work one chore or another. Every day Jenny found herself in front of that whiteboard, shuffling names around, shifting groups of people from one chore to the next.

No one escaped the rota, she insisted, not even herself.

This task, though, was generally considered to be by far the worst; shovelling the spent slurry from the digester into several dozen four-gallon plastic drums to be taken up to the plant decks and used as fertiliser. There was always someone who refused point-blank to do it; like Alice Harton did, like Nilaya Koundinya who claimed it was unacceptable for someone of her caste to work directly with human faeces. On both those occasions she'd found herself in the middle of a shouting match, ultimately having to threaten eviction if they didn't shut up and take their turn.

71

This isn't a popularity contest, she told herself daily. *Remember that.*

'Next week is it?' asked Leona.

'Yup,' replied Walter.

'Fantastic,' Leona replied drily. 'And do I get *your* help as well, Walter?'

The old man grinned but didn't reply. He'd volunteered to come down to the 'stink room' to help Jenny out when her turn came up on the rota. His infatuation for her was embarrassingly obvious.

'What do you say, Hannah?' asked Walter. 'Want to help your mum, too?'

She shrugged. 'Maybe. I'll think about it.'

Jenny laughed. *Such a little madam.*

'I know it smells bloody awful down here,' said Walter, 'but if you get into the habit of breathing through your mouth—'

'Can't we move it to somewhere better ventilated?' asked Jenny.

He stood up straight, stretching his stiff back. 'It's the warmest location on the production platform.' There were no windows down here, the room was perfectly insulated on all four sides by other storage rooms.

'It's the easiest place for us to maintain a consistent fermenting temperature,' he said, 'and let's be honest, the chickens on the deck above are unlikely to moan about it.'

Hannah giggled. 'Moaning chickens.'

'It worries me,' said Jenny regarding the other two digesters. Thick rubber hoses attached with G-clamps ran from both of them up to the ceiling and there, attached with wire ties to a metal spar, snaked across towards a doorway leading to a second windowless room where the generator rattled away noisily.

'What does?'

'That we can't ventilate this place properly. Isn't that a bit dangerous?'

He shrugged. 'We just keep the door open. That'll be all right.'

'I know. But that's another worry – the door always open, one of the smaller children could just wander in and—'

Walter stood up and arched his back. 'They all know not to come down here.'

'Could you not rig up an extractor fan or something? Then that door could be closed and locked.'

He sighed. 'Another thing to put on the To Do list, I suppose. I could consider relocating all of this to a cabin with a window, for safety's sake, but then we'd need to heat the room to keep it warm enough for the slurry to ferment. That'd be a lot of work, Jenny.'

She nodded. 'Yes, I suppose.'

'For now, as long as the children know they're not to play down here, we'll be just fine.'

Jenny hefted another shovel of spent slurry into the barrel at her feet. 'Perhaps something to think about in the future, Walter.'

Hannah was doing her best to help out with a trowel, scooping small dollops out of the digester with a determined frown on her face. Leona grimaced at the sight of shit smudged up her daughter's arm. 'But did you have to rope in Hannah?'

'I want to help my nanna and Uncle Walter,' she answered.

Walter smiled at her. 'You're our little helper. Aren't you, poppet?'

Hannah scooped up another heavy trowel, carelessly flicking a small dollop of pale brown mush onto her forehead. 'Yup.'

'Ugghh,' Leona made a face, 'be careful, Hannah, you're getting covered in crap.'

'It's not crap,' said Walter. 'Just think of it as rocket fuel for our potatoes, onions and tomatoes. That's all it is. Everything gets used; there's no room for waste or slack on these rigs. You know that.'

Leona continued to curl her lip at the sight of the slurry as they shovelled and scraped it out of the plastic tube.

'Walter,' said Jenny after a while, 'how's our newcomer? I've not had a chance to drop in on him yet.'

'Tami says he's still very weak.'

'What do we know about him?'

Walter shook his head. 'Not much. I'd say he's in his late thirties. He's French, or at least he speaks French. He looks Mediterranean, perhaps Middle Eastern at a pinch . . . hard to say.' He stood up straight, leaning tiredly on the shovel. 'But, to be honest,' he hesitated a moment, choosing the right words, 'he looks like the type you wouldn't normally take on, Jenny.'

'Hmm?' she mumbled.

'A loner. The loners are always trouble. You know that.'

They'd had trouble before; a young man they'd encountered in Bracton harbour, foraging for things nine months ago. They'd taken him in and assigned him a cot on the drilling platform. A fortnight later he'd sexually assaulted a woman there. They'd nearly tossed him over the side. Instead Jenny decided he should be taken back to Bracton and left to fend for himself. A year before that there'd been a couple of younger men with guns who'd buzzed the platforms in a motorboat, demanding to be let on and firing off a few wild shots in anger when she'd refused them. And before them, there was the wild and ragged twenty-something lad they'd found living on scraps in Great Yarmouth. He'd ended up nearly beating Dennis to death because the old boy had complained about the lad's language in front of the young ones. Men of a certain age, in their twenties or thirties, seemed to be either dangerous predators who viewed this quiet world as their personal playground, or were unbalanced and unpredictable.

'This French chap was being pursued by the others,' added Walter with a cautionary tone to his voice. 'There could be any number of reasons for that.'

Jenny nodded. 'True.' She pursed her lips and took a moment. 'When he's well enough, I want to interview him, though. If he really is from France or further afield, I want to know what he's seen.'

'Of course,' said Walter. 'And then?'

'And then, yes . . . when he's fit enough that he can look after himself, maybe we'll send him back. I'll just have to see for myself. I really can do without worrying whether we've picked up another nut or some sort of an axe murderer.'

She realised an interview was very little on which to make a judgement. But, to be honest, she couldn't be entirely certain of any one of the men *already* on the rigs. There was no way of knowing if at some time in their past they'd been violent, abusive; perhaps taken advantage of the chaos and anarchy and done unpardonable things. She couldn't know that. All she did know was that the few men living here had behaved themselves thus far. More importantly, that these few men were vastly outnumbered by women.

Best to play it safe, she decided, and assume this man was potentially a danger until he could prove himself otherwise. After all . . .

After all, it takes just one fox to get into the hen house . . .

Chapter 12

10 years AC

'LeMan 49/25a' – ClarenCo Gas Rig Complex, North Sea

Hannah watched the man; his chest rising and falling evenly beneath the sheet. She felt sorry for him. He looked so thin and frail, his olive-coloured skin almost grey by the light seeping in through the round porthole above the bed.

Dr Tami told her the man was not to be pestered. She could look at him, but she wasn't to be a nuisance. Dr Tami was gone now, left the sick bay to visit someone who'd had a fall on one of the other platforms and possibly broken something.

The man's dark hair tumbled down in lank ringlets onto the pillow. He looked like the picture of Jesus Martha had shown her once; a peaceful, kind face, not etched with angry lines around his eyes, but kind lines . . . a man used to smiling.

A coil of limp hair was curled into his beard and stuck in the corner of his mouth. She reached over the bed and pulled it away from his dry lips.

'You poor, poor thing,' she uttered softly as if this sleeping man was a baby griping and mewling with wind. His eyelids quivered ever so slightly, then a moment later flickered open.

'Oooh,' whispered Hannah.

Brown eyes, unfocused and dazed, darted around the cabin walls, the ceiling above him, the small porthole opposite, then finally onto Hannah.

She smiled. 'Hello, my name's Hannah.'

He stared at her silently.

'You're sick,' she added, 'you got shot by bad men and

you're poorly. Dr Tami said you have to stay in bed and I'm not to be a nuisance.'

His eyes narrowed, dark brows locked as he studied her. Finally the thick thatch of bristles around his mouth stirred and parted. 'P-please . . . you have water?'

For a moment she struggled to make sense of the man's strange accent.

'Water?' he rasped again, voice thick with phlegm.

Then she understood. She grinned and nodded, eager to be like Dr Tami, caring for a patient just like a real doctor. She clacked quickly across the floor and poured treated rainwater from a jug into a plastic tumbler. She came back to the bedside and held it out proudly in front of her.

'Please . . .' he whispered softly.

He was asking for help to sit up. Just like she'd seen the doctor do before, she reached up on tiptoes to slide a small hand behind his head, tilting it as best she could so that he could drink from the tumbler. She tipped the cup carefully, some of the water going where it was intended, the rest soaking into his thick beard and trickling down either side of his face and onto the pillow.

'There, there,' she cooed softly. She eased his head back. 'Is that much better?'

He closed his eyes for a moment, then opened them and returned her smile. 'Better, thank you,' he replied, his voice a little stronger now; more than a dry rattling whisper.

'My name's Hannah,' she said again. 'I'm nearly five years old.'

He smiled. 'I thought . . . I thought you were an angel,' he replied. 'Just now . . . when I opened my eyes.'

'An angel!' Hannah giggled at the thought of that, grinning like a Cheshire cat. 'My nanna calls me that sometimes.'

His eyes went from her, back to the walls, the ceiling, the other cot in the sickbay. 'Please, what is this?'

She knew what he was asking. 'You're in our *home*. We live above the water on big legs.'

He licked dry lips and winced with pain as he tried to sit up.

'You have to sit very still,' cautioned Hannah.

'More water? Please?' asked the man, glancing at the tumbler.

She helped lift his head again and held the tumbler to his mouth. 'Dr Tami is going to make you better again with all her medicine.' She let his head rest back again on the pillow when he'd finished the water.

He nodded gratefully. 'Thank you.'

'You are French,' she informed the man. 'Mum told me.'

He shrugged weakly. 'No. Not French. Belgian.'

Hannah's brow knotted. 'Bell-gee-an. I never heard of that. Is it in Africa?'

'Europe,' he managed a wan smile, 'what is left . . . at least.'

'U-rope?' she repeated the vaguely familiar name. She repeated it again under her breath, her face locked in concentration. 'That's another place, isn't it? Is it an island? Like America?'

He shook his head, closing his eyes, dizzy and nauseous. 'No, not really.'

Hannah felt a passing stab of guilt. Dr Tami had told her not to pester the man; that he was weak and needed as much rest as possible. And here she was pestering him.

'I better go now,' she said. 'I have school soon.'

She turned to go.

'Please!' the man called out.

She stopped.

'You . . . what you say your name is . . . ?'

'My name's Hannah Sutherland.'

He nodded. '*Merci beaucoup* – thank you very much – for the water, Hannah.'

'What's *your* name?'

'My name is . . .' he licked his lips, 'my name is Valérie.'

Her eyebrows knotted disapprovingly. '*Valerie*? Ewww. That's a girl's name!'

He laughed tiredly, his head collapsing softly back against the pillow. 'Girl, boy, is same *en français*.'

She thought about it for a moment. 'You're very funny.'

His eyes remained closed, the rustling sound of his breath growing long and even. He nodded sleepily. 'I try.'

'I should go now,' she said again.

She thought he was asleep, but he cracked an eye open and winked. 'Thank you, little angel.'

She was grinning as she fluttered down the corridor to the stairwell to deck B, carried aloft by the invisible little wings she'd suddenly decided to grow.

Chapter 13

Crash Day + 1
1.15 p.m.

O2 Arena – 'Safety Zone 4',
London

The Millennium Dome loomed before Flight Lieutenant Adam Brooks. He refused to call it the 'O2 Arena' just because some profit-fattened telecoms company had bought the abandoned site at a knock-down price and decided to rebrand it.

Enormous, squat, daunting, the last time Adam had stepped inside he'd been going to a Kaiser Chiefs' gig. The dome, lit up at night, had looked like something out of Disneyland – the canvas cover illuminated from within by a spinning kaleidoscope of neon colours. It had looked like some sort of giant undulating pearl in the darkness.

This afternoon the canvas appeared a drab vanilla, worn by the elements, washed dull by ten years of interminably wet British weather.

The pedestrian plaza in front of the dome's entrance was thick with civilian emergency workers, all wearing requisite bright orange waistcoats to identify them. The vast majority of them were crisis-situation draftees: paramedics, firemen, GPs, security guards, health and safety managers, Scout leaders . . . community-minded civilians who'd registered online as willing emergency helpers last time there had been an avian flu scare. Many of them were queuing to be processed; name and national insurance number taken down, given an orange waistcoat, an ID badge and a supervisor to report to.

Adam returned from his hurried jog around the dome's perimeter – a cursory inspection to scc how much work they'd need to carry out to successfully contain the area. He found most of the gunners gathered around the backs of their trucks, amidst off-loaded and stacked spools of razor wire and equipment yokes laid out in several orderly rows. They were crowded tightly together, heads cocked and leaning forward; a circular and improbably large rugby scrum of soldiers, watching a TV in the middle.

Why the hell are those lazy fuckwits standing around?

'Hey!' he bellowed. 'Sergeant? What's going on here?'

Sergeant Walfield straightened up guiltily. 'Sorry, sir. Prime Minister's just come on the telly. Thought I'd let the lads hear what 'e's got to say.'

Adam crossed the plaza towards them, grinding his teeth with frustration and debating whether to give Danny Walfield a mouthful for letting the lads down tools when they were supposed to be getting a wriggle on and erecting a secure barricade across the front of the plaza. As he stepped through the tight knot of men he saw Bushey holding a small portable TV aloft, intently listening, his RAF-blue beret clasped tightly in one hand.

'PM's just coming on,' he explained to his CO.

The men wanted to hear what was to be announced. For that matter, so did Adam.

'All right then, let's see what he's got to say.' He turned round and picked out the sergeant. 'Then, Danny, I want them straight back to work.'

'Aye, sir,' replied Walfield.

Adam squatted down beside Bushey and listened in. The small TV screen flickered with the flash of press cameras as Prime Minister Charles Harrison, flanked by his ever-present advisor, Malcolm Jones, stepped up onto the small podium. Adam thought the poor bastard looked haggard and pale, his tie loosened, his jacket off and shirt sleeves rolled up; like some unlucky sod who'd worked through the night and been roused from a nap ten minutes ago with a strong black coffee.

The Prime Minister uttered some grateful platitudes for the press assembling here at short notice, and after steadying himself with a deep breath, he began.

'Yesterday, during morning prayers in Riyadh, the first of many bombs exploded in the holy mosques of Mecca and Medina, and in several more mosques in Riyadh. A radical Shi'ite group sent a message shortly after to Al Jazeera claiming responsibility for the devices. Similar explosions occurred yesterday in several other cities in Saudi Arabia, Kuwait, Oman and Iraq. The situation has continued to worsen in the region. Because of the potential danger this poses to our remaining troops, and after consultation with Arab leaders, a decision was taken to pull all of our troops out of the region until this particular problem has corrected itself.'

Adam shook his head. So far it seemed as if the Prime Minister was doing his best not to mention the word 'oil'. A lot of news time yesterday had been filled with industry experts talking about the drastic impact the unrest was going to have on crude oil supplies; assessments on reserves in the supply chain, reserves in the holds of tankers still at sea – unaffected and able to deliver – and the possible per-barrel price these reserves might hit in the next twenty-four hours. Five hundred, seven hundred . . . even a thousand dollars a barrel for the next few weeks – that was the kind of punditry they'd been getting all yesterday afternoon.

Today, however, it seemed by consensus between the news channels, no one was discussing barrel prices, reserves or shortfalls. Today's news agenda was all about getting the boys back home from the troubled Middle East.

It smacked of misdirection. Adam wondered if someone was leaning on the media to steer the agenda elsewhere; to keep people's minds on matters abroad. There had been endless news footage of our poor lads holed up, besieged and waiting for their planes home, market places running with blood, baying crowds dancing around flaming cars, blackened corpses being dragged behind rusting trucks through rubbish-strewn streets. Horrific attention-grabbing stuff, in marked contrast to yesterday's footage of smoking oil refineries, towers of orange flame licking through ruptured storage tanks, and twisted piping belching black smoke. The refineries around Baku in Azerbaijan, Paraguana in Venezuela, rendered useless; the striking image of a tanker ripped open and spewing gigantic black lily pads of oil across the narrowest section of the Strait of Hormuz, rendering this crucial shipping lane impassable. Yesterday's talk was all about how an oil stoppage was going to affect the UK – *what exactly this all means to me and mine.*

Clumsy misdirection. Adam was sure that, no matter how much everyone cared passionately about our boys trapped abroad, what they really wanted to know was *exactly how screwed are we here in the UK?*

Charles Harrison rounded his prepared speech off with some assurances that order was going to be maintained and all possible measures were being put into place to minimise the economic damage done.

Adam was surprised to hear no mention of any 'safe zones' being set up, or of the implementation of any sort of martial law. Perhaps that was going to come later? Perhaps what was needed right now were some calming assurances, not the announcement of a raft of specific emergency measures.

He realised the PM was doing his best not to spook the press or the general public. *No one's ready for a stampede, for a mass panic. This is about buying another twenty-four . . . forty-eight hours of prep-time.*

Adam looked at his men.

It's about getting more army boots back on the ground first.

The PM rounded off and then opened the floor to questions.

They came in noisy volleys. The first few he answered calmly with more assurances that this was a blip that the UK was well-placed to ride out. Then Adam heard one of the assembled journalists cut in — a sharp female voice that sounded as if it had already been spoon-fed enough bullshit for one morning — with a question specifically about how much stockpiled oil and food was on UK soil right now.

The Prime Minister blanched.

'How long, Prime Minister?' the journalist asked again, the press room silent. 'How long can we feed ourselves whilst this oil crisis is playing out?'

Harrison froze for too long with a rabbit-in-the-headlights expression on his face.

Shit, that looks bad.

'Twat,' one of the gunners muttered. 'He doesn't fucking know.'

'Look . . . th-there really is no need for *anyone* to panic,' the Prime Minister replied, his voice wobbling uncertainly. 'There has been a lot of planning, a lot of forward thinking about a scenario like this.'

A shouted question from the back of the press room. 'Prime Minister, is the army being brought back to enforce martial law?'

A pause. Another too-long pause. They listened to dead air for nearly ten seconds.

'All right.' Despite the small tinny sound of the television's speaker, Adam could detect that the Prime Minister sounded tired, resigned. 'All right . . . look, that's probably enough crap for one day. So, I'm going to tell you how it is.'

Adam and Bushey looked at each other.

Did the PM really just say 'crap'?

'The truth is, everyone, the truth is . . . we *are* in a bit of trouble. Whilst this mess is sorting itself out we're going to have to make do with the resources we have. I'm afraid nothing is going to be coming into the UK for several weeks. So we're all going to have to work together. We are going to need to ration the food that is out there in the supermarkets, corner shops, warehouses, grocery stores. Food vendors are going to be asked to cease trading as of now. We're also locking down the sale of petrol and diesel from this point on. That has to be reserved for key personnel and emergency services.'

The Prime Minister paused for breath. It was silent except for the rustle of an uneasy press audience stirring. Adam noticed a subtle tic in the man's face. He looked like someone on the very edge of a nervous breakdown.

'Look, it's going to be a very difficult few weeks . . . perhaps months. But, if we *all* pull together, like we did once before, during the Second World War . . . we're going to be just fine. If we panic, if people start hoarding food and water . . . then . . .' His voice faded.

Prime Minister Charles Harrison suddenly stepped away from the podium, knocking a microphone clumsily with his arm. He walked quickly to the press room door flanked by his advisor and a bodyguard. The stunned silence was filled a second later with an uproar of questions shouted at the Prime Minister's back, as the Home Secretary replaced him at the podium and attempted to call the press conference to order.

Adam leant over and snapped the television off. He turned to look at his men, two squadrons of gunners, forty young lads; a good half of them still in their teens and sporting pubescent acne; but all of them silent and anxiously regarding their CO.

He looked across at Sergeant Walfield.

The sergeant shrugged casually. 'I believe, sir, the shit 'as just gone an' hit the fan.'

Adam nodded. 'I think we had better get on with securing this place.'

Chapter 14

10 years AC

'LeMan 49/25a' – ClarenCo Gas Rig Complex, North Sea

The foreign man looked up at Jenny from the steaming bowl of chowder, and around at all the others who had gathered in the mess to get a good look at the new arrival.

'Valérie Latoc? Is that right?'

He nodded, spooning soup into his mouth. 'Yes. I am from the south of Belgium, Ardennes region originally.' He pushed a tress of dark hair out of his eyes; brown eyes that her gaze lingered on longer than she wanted.

'We don't get many visitors out here,' she said.

Which was true. The community had grown over the last five years as a result of the people they'd come across whilst foraging ashore for essentials. People in small numbers; a family here, a couple there. It was an unspoken rule, though, that no one could join them on the rigs until Jenny had sat down and spoken with them. *The Jenny Sutherland Entrance Examination*, that's what she'd overheard Alice scathingly call it.

There'd been those she'd turned away, those she considered might cause trouble for them. Those she didn't trust. Some she simply didn't like the look of. Unfair, discriminatory, but Jenny didn't give a damn what was being muttered, the last thing she was going to allow aboard was some schizo who might go off like a firecracker amongst them.

It was men mostly. Men she didn't trust; males of a certain age. Young boys and old men she felt comfortable with. But men, particularly very masculine men, who oozed testosterone and smelled of hunger; who looked upon her female-heavy community with hungry eyes like a child in a candy store . . . they had no place here.

'I want you to tell us about yourself,' she said.

Valérie spooned another mouthful of chowder, wiped the hot liquid from the bristles of his beard. 'From the beginning?'

'From the beginning.'

He shrugged wearily. 'I was living in Bastogne in Belgium when it happened. The second day, the Tuesday, you remember your Prime Minister's television appearance?'

She nodded. Everyone behind her nodded.

Valérie shook his head. 'A big can of snakes he opened. No . . . *worms*, is it not? Can of worms?'

Jenny nodded for him to continue.

'It was on *TV5 Monde* only minutes after. Your leader was the first one to come out and tell the people how bad things were. Then our President Molyneux had to do the same, and then every other leader. It was the *significatif* word, you know? The *trigger* words that people heard; ration, curfew, martial law . . . words like this that made people panic and riot.'

He sat back in the chair. '*Le jour de desastre*. Like a modern day *Kristallnacht*, you see? Every shop window in Bastogne was broken that night.' He sighed. 'We had power in Belgium at the time, you know – nuclear power from France, not like you British needing the Russian gas and oil. But even so, we also lost our power on the Wednesday. There was the complete black-out. The French stopped the power to us . . . or their generators had problems. But we had better order in our country. No riots yet. Our government had made much emergency preparations for this kind of thing. Much more than yours, I think?'

He was right. Jenny recalled the appalling state of panic

the British authorities went into during the first few days. A complete lack of communication from the Cabinet Office during the first twenty-four hours, the Prime Minister's disastrous performance on the second day, then there was nothing else from them except one or two junior members of government wheeled out to broadcast calls for calm.

'But then things became much more worse for us in Belgium in the second and third week. There were millions of people who come up into northern Europe. They were coming from the east, from Poland, from Czech Republic, from Croatia, from Bosnia. We had much, much many more come north, up through Spain, from Morocco, from Algeria, Tunisia. Even from further south; Zimbabwe, Uganda, because of tribal problems in these places. You know?'

He hungrily spooned some more soup, then continued. 'In week three we became like you people in England. Fighting in the street; my city, Bastogne, on fire. No control by the leaders. Soldiers without clear orders.' He shook his head sadly. 'And many, many people dying when the water stopped pumping. You remember? It was very warm that summer?'

She remembered all right. The UK hadn't been particularly hot, but it had been very dry. When the oil stopped, the power stations, without adequate oil reserves, had soon ceased functioning, and with that so did the flow of water through pumping stations and purification plants. In London, bottles of unopened drinking water became like gold dust; vending machines were wrenched to pieces to reclaim cans of Coke buried inside them.

'I suppose, I guess a month after the oil stopped, most people not killed in the riots and fighting were sick with the water diseases in my country. You know, cholera, typhoid.'

'So, Mr Latoc, how did *you* manage to make it through the early days?'

It was a question Jenny always asked. The answer given to

this question was, more often than not, the answer that decided her. The type of person she didn't want on the rigs with her family was the type who *boasted* about their survival skills; their ability to fight off others for what they needed. They didn't need fighters. Not out here. What they needed were people prepared to muck in and work a long day, prepared to share, to compromise.

'I wandered,' he said. 'I stayed away from cities and towns and prayed like crazy I get through this nightmare. After many months I found some good people who took me in.' His eyes drifted off her, down to the steaming bowl of soup in front of him. 'Good people who let me – a stranger – join them during the time when *charognard* meant danger. You understand what I mean, yes? The people who take your food?'

'Scavengers,' said Jenny, nodding.

'Yes, *scavengers*. On the continent there were many, *many* . . . perhaps even still.'

She had hoped that those desperate people content to endlessly drift and live off what could still be foraged from mouldering shops would surely be scarce now. Isolated loners, unbalanced, dangerous and best avoided. What she'd been hoping to hear was that the only people alive now were communities likes theirs, people like themselves knuckling down to the business of making-do.

'I lived with these people for seven years. Then strangers came.' He shook his head sadly. 'Men and guns.' The expression on his face told her more than his fading words. 'They came. Smoke brought them . . . they came for food, but then they wanted much more,' he said.

Jenny felt her heart race, memories of a winter morning.

'Children, women,' Valérie shook his head, his voice failing for a moment. 'They,' he took a deep breath, 'they shoot the men first. The others, they *play* with.' He looked up at her. 'You understand?'

'Yes,' she nodded. 'But you . . . ?'

'How come they did not shoot me?'

That was her question.

He dropped his gaze, clearly ashamed. 'I hid and saw these things. Then I ran away.' He placed his spoon back in the bowl and pushed the bowl away; his appetite understandably seemed to have gone. He dropped his head and a moment later Jenny realised from the subtle heave of his shoulders that he was crying.

She reached across the table and rested a hand on his forearm. 'It's okay, Mr Latoc.'

He raised his face, cheeks glistening with tears. 'I did nothing . . . I was frightened. I ran.' He shook his head angrily. 'I did nothing.'

'There isn't much you can do,' said Jenny softly, 'not against armed men. It's just the way it is. That's why we stay out here.'

He accepted that with a hasty nod.

'So what happened after that?'

'I ran. I keep moving.' He composed himself, wiped the tears from his face and took a deep breath. 'I went south-east for some time, towards the Mediterranean.'

'Tell me, is it as bad over there?'

His eyes met hers. 'Yes. I will tell you . . . I saw tanks, some burned. Many abandoned tanks.'

'Did you say *tanks*?' cut in Walter.

'Yes. Russian ones.'

'My God! You remember, Jenny?' said Walter. 'Remember the rumours we kept hearing on the radio a few years after?'

She nodded. They'd heard garbled reports of short and frantic wars in Asia; resource grabs around the Caspian and several months of fighting in Kazakhstan. 'Let him continue, Walter.'

'I travel down to Croatia. And then I find a sailing boat in

Rijeka. I know a little sailing so I went across Adriatic, along the Italian coast. It is all much like the UK, some small communities making food. But small, you understand? Several dozen, no more. But one group tell me that they hear Britain survived much better. That they have built these big *safe zones*. So then I sail to Montpellier, and I cross France. Head north up to Calais.'

'Why not just sail around?'

He shrugged. 'I am not so confident with a boat – not to go out of the Mediterranean into rough sea.' He grimaced like a naughty child. 'I cannot swim. So, I go through France instead. And then I find another boat at Calais. I sailed across the Channel this last summer. To Dover. I walk towards London hoping to find one of these safe places. Order, you know?'

She nodded sympathetically.

He scratched at his thick dark beard. 'But I soon see that this country is no better; just like Belgium, like France. Empty towns, burned homes, abandoned car and trucks.'

She leant forward, almost tempted to reach out and comfort him. 'Tell me, did you see *any* signs of rebuilding going on? Did you see anything like that?'

He shook his head. 'I saw . . . very little. Smoke a few times. I saw horse . . .' he looked up at Walter standing just behind him.

'Shit?'

'Oui, horse shit, on some roads. You know? There are some people, like yours, surviving. But nowhere as big as this place.'

'And no lights?'

He shook his head. 'I saw no lights. There were no safe zones.'

There was a sombre stirring amongst the crowd gathered behind Jenny. A long silence punctuated by the soft rumple and languid thump of the sea below, and the steady patter of rain on the plexiglass windows of the mess.

'Those men that were after you at the harbour,' said Jenny after a while, 'why did they want you dead?'

He shrugged. 'I do not know.'

'There must have been a reason, Mr Latoc.'

'Really?' He glanced up at her, his tired voice pulled taut with irritation. 'I have come across too many men who kill you for a . . . for a fresh egg . . . or a rusty tin of food. Or just because you are a stranger to them, look different. Or because for fun.'

'I want you to tell me what that was about,' she insisted, feeling the slightest pang of guilt for pressing him.

'Okay, so, I found a settlement. They let me stay for a while. But then . . .' He looked up at the sea of faces standing behind Jenny. Eyes judging him silently, waiting for him to give them a reason to ask him to leave.

'Please go on,' urged Jenny.

'But then a woman was . . . was killed.' He lowered his voice slightly. 'You understand before she was killed she was . . .' He paused and Jenny knew he was omitting the word *raped*. She nodded silently. 'Go on.'

'They pull me out of my bed at night and did a . . . a *trial*. They decided I am guilty—'

'Why would they do that?'

He shook his head, genuinely exasperated. 'Why do you think?' He laughed. 'Maybe it is because I support the wrong football team, uh?'

Jenny acknowledged the naivety in her question. The dark ringlets of his hair and a black beard long enough to lose a fist in reminded her vaguely of the sort of firebrand mullahs who once preached outside the overcrowded mosques in Shepherd's Bush. She could easily imagine how that made him a target.

'They take me in a truck, away to be killed. To the town where your people found me . . . to Beckton?'

'Bracton.'

'Yes. The men said if I manage to get to the water and jump in and start swimming back to *Paki-land*, they will let me live.' Valérie sighed. 'I tell them I am actually Belgian. But do they listen to that? Of course not.'

'Mum,' called out Jacob. He was standing at the back of the small crowd. He squeezed his way forward until he was standing beside Walter. 'Mum, it *was* just like he said. Those men were hunting him, you know? Like it was a sort of *game*.'

Valérie nodded; he recognised Jacob from the quayside and offered him a hesitant smile. 'Hunting, yes . . . I suppose. Like your fox and hounds hunting.'

Jacob nodded. 'Yeah . . . that's what it looked like.'

'I would be dead now,' Valérie added, looking up at Jacob and Walter, 'if not for you. Thank you.'

Walter shrugged. 'That's okay.'

It was quiet for a moment, save for several whispered exchanges amongst the crowd.

'So,' Jenny sighed, 'that's how it still is, then.' She was tempted to turn around and say *I told you so*. To direct that at Alice and her small circle of nay-sayers. Even to direct that at her own son, who seemed so certain the world was putting itself back together without him. She could have scored some cheap and easy points saying those things right now. Instead she shrugged. Valérie Latoc's story argued her point – that the world beyond their little island was still a dangerous place.

'I . . . I would very much like to stay here,' said Valérie. His voice strained and stretched, the voice of a man not too proud to plead. 'I do not want to go back. I have seen enough of . . . of . . .' A pitiful tear rolled down his sallow cheek and lost itself in the dark thatch of bristles. 'Please . . .'

Jenny found herself reaching across the table again and gently patted his thin forearm. The gesture seemed to weaken his resolve and more tears rolled down into his thick beard.

'Okay,' muttered Jenny. 'Okay, that's enough for now.'

'Please may I stay?' he asked.

Jenny glanced back over her shoulder, keen to get a feel for what the others felt. She could see eyes that regarded him with pity, eyes red-rimmed with sympathetic tears. Heads that silently nodded their approval at her.

Let the poor sod stay.

She turned back to look at him. 'We'll see, Valérie. You can stay for a while, whilst I give it some thought.'

'For a while?'

'A probationary period. We'll see how things go, okay?'

His face crumpled. 'Oh, thank you!' he sobbed, grasping her hand. 'Thank you!'

She smiled awkwardly and pulled her hand back. 'All right.' She turned around in her seat. 'Right, the show's over, folks. We're done here.'

Walter clapped his hands together. 'Come on then, ladies and gents! Come on! You heard her, jobs to go to!'

'You like him,' said Leona softly, 'don't you?'

Jenny turned on her side to face Leona across the narrow floor space, the cot's springs squeaking noisily beneath her. She could hear Hannah's even breathing in the darkness, coming from the other end of Leona's cot.

'I suppose I feel sorry for him.'

Despite her initial knee-jerk reaction at the first sight of him, the poor man didn't seem to have either the masculine swagger of a predatory male nor the dangerous glassy-eyed stare of a nutcase. He seemed beaten, tired, dispirited . . . perhaps even broken. Years of travelling, he'd told them, years of bearing witness to what was left: the ruined shell of the old oil world had taken its toll on him.

Jenny could only imagine how much worse conditions must be on the continent. She'd been hoping he had a more heartening tale to tell but deep down she'd always suspected it was every bit as bad as he'd described.

Poor bastard.

She'd seen some awful things over the last ten years; once, the blackened and twisted carcass of someone tied to a stake in the middle of the ash-grey mound of a bonfire; someone she could only hope had been dead long before being burned. Once, a row of desiccated corpses lined up along the bottom of a wall riddled with bullet holes. Perhaps they'd been looters shot by soldiers or an armed police unit.

She could only imagine what other sights this poor man could add to that. Many more, no doubt.

She realised that there were also a few selfish reasons to let the man stay. Perhaps Valérie Latoc might be someone that Jacob would actually *listen* to. Perhaps in time the man would be ready to talk about what he'd witnessed in greater detail and maybe, just maybe, that would be enough to convince Jacob that there was nothing out there but empty towns disappearing beneath spreading weeds . . . and dangerous, armed people.

'You going to let him join us, Mum? We could do with a few more men here who, you know, *aren't* old age pensioners.'

'We'll see, Lee.'

Mr Latoc had been found a space out on the drilling platform. Howard and Dennis lived over there. David Cudmore and Alice Harton — who were a couple, she was almost certain of that — and Kevin whom they seemed to have adopted between them. The Barker sisters bunked there, all four of them very quiet and introspective. She suspected they held prayer meetings, but at least it was kept over there and in private. Mrs Panhwar, her mother and her two daughters, they spoke a little English — the daughters doing a better job at picking it up. The drilling platform was as good a place as any for the man to find peace and quiet and recover.

He could remain on probation until the anniversary celebration was out of the way, and then she'd have to make a decision. She smiled. The celebration party was just a week away and exactly what they needed after hearing Mr Latoc's depressing account. There'd been some silly rumours going around over the last year, that a UN force had landed on the south coast of England and was even now organising a major humanitarian effort. A silly rumour that had found traction because one of the women was picking up intermittent signals in Spanish on long wave on one of their wind-up radios. And, of course, there'd been that supposed sighting of a vapour trail in the sky last spring by one of the children. Things like that made everyone feel unsettled; made people want to put down their tools, forget their work assignments and go rushing ashore.

Valérie's words seemed to have completely scotched those hopeful rumours. Shot them down in the most brutal way. Jenny had felt her heart sinking just like everyone else as he'd told his story.

The party at least was something for them to look forward to; a celebration of Walter's wonderful methane-powered generator, a reminder that despite all the hard work, the cold winter nights, the monotonous diet, the discomfort, the damp, the wind, the rain . . . they were very lucky. That they were safe, and that slowly, little by little, things would get better again.

'He seemed really nice, in a sad kind of way,' uttered Leona.

Jenny sighed. 'I'll decide *after* the party. Anyway, get some sleep, Lee. Don't forget you're on morning-chickens tomorrow.'

'Oh, wonderful,' Leona huffed, and turned over noisily in her cot.

Chapter 15

10 years AC

'LeMan 49/25a' – ClarenCo Gas Rig Complex, North Sea

27 May
It'll be a lovely celebration this year. Walter brought back dozens and dozens of strings of Christmas lights on this week's shore run. We're having it on the production platform because of the open deck space and I've had Martha, Leona and Rebecca help me drape the lights all around there. Walter's run a cable feed off the walkway lights and while we know it all works, we've yet to see how pretty it's going to look when we switch it on.

Our new arrival seems to be mending well. Dr Gupta says the gunshot wound looked worse than it was. He's stitched up and bandaged. Mostly, she tells me, it's malnutrition that's weakened him. He does look a lot better now he's had a chance to clean himself up and trim that awful beard – at least he doesn't look like some mad Rasputin character.

Hannah's very taken with him. She's really quite sweet, helping him over the lips to doorways. I think she likes the idea of playing nurse and has made Valérie her pet project. She can be a bossy little madam, though; last night in the canteen she was really laying into him for not finishing up the fish in his broth.

Poor chap.

The rain is getting me down. So far this summer it's been almost constant drizzle and overcast skies. Good for all our crops, of course, and good that we've spent less diesel having to refill the freshwater tank so often, but the endless tapping on every porthole, the dripping of water from leaks seems to be everywhere. It depresses me. Reminds me that this is a prison just as much as a safe haven. When there's enough of a break in those bloody clouds the helipad is usually almost full to bursting with people grabbing a little sun. Not exactly bikini weather with that North Sea wind tugging away at you but it's so nice to feel the warmth on your face. Close your eyes and dream of a sun-kissed beach, sangria and topaz-coloured water – what I wouldn't give to walk away from this fucking place.

Anyway, I'm looking forward to tonight, those Christmas lights. They're going to look lovely.

'So, it's our first anniversary of having power,' announced Jenny proudly. Some of the audience around her cheered and whooped.

Jenny stood on the main deck of the drilling platform, lit by the faint amber glow of several plain bulbs in wire safety cages from the walkway leading across to the production platform. The deck was filled with expectant faces standing amidst the stacked Portakabins, sitting on them, hanging out of open windows, squatting in rows on those gantries not cluttered with growbags and foliage, and all of them waiting, full of excitement, for Jenny to get on with proceedings.

The middle of the deck was open to the sea sixty feet below. When the rig had been active the drill core had descended through that opening to the cellar deck and down to the sea. Thick support struts ran across the open space now and sheets of metal grille were welded on top of them to fill the gap and create sturdy additional floor space. They'd done that a couple of years after settling here, after they realised this platform was the most practical outdoor space on which the entire community could assemble together. It was their public forum, their civic space, a place for announcements, celebrations and, so far occasional, burials at sea. According to Walter the metal-grilled floor was secure and utterly safe, however, Jenny found it disconcerting standing on the mesh and seeing the water, a long way down, churning menacingly beneath her feet.

'A special day for us,' she added her voice croaking already as she did her best to be heard by everyone congregated around her. 'A celebration of our ability to make our own electricity. And, you know, it's also a reminder that things *will* get better; get easier for us. We'll get better at the business of survival . . . and maybe one day soon, whcn we know for certain it's safe enough, we'll *all* return to the mainland.'

She heard several voices amongst the crowd muttering. She'd like to think, just for once, that sour-faced cow Alice wasn't sticking her oar in.

'So, that's why we're having this anniversary bash, to remind ourselves that these rigs are just a *temporary* home . . . that things will improve. I promise you.'

Several voices called out in agreement. Another good-natured voice heckled her from the back to get on with throwing the switch.

Jenny laughed. 'All right.' She gestured towards Walter, standing beside her.

'As always, Walter's been working tirelessly for us. We have some homebrew booze that he's managed to distil.'

'Not from chicken shit I hope!' cried someone.

A peel of laughter rippled across the crowd. Jenny smiled. 'Potato peelings . . . so he tells me.'

Several people groaned at the thought.

'I'm sure it tastes better than it looks.'

Walter strode forward to stand beside her. 'That's right, ladies and gents! Several gallons of the highest quality *Spudka*. So you'd better bloody appreciate it!' he chipped in gruffly. The crowd rippled dutiful laughter.

'And, of course, we have our wonderful Christmas lights.

Shall we get them on now?' She smiled at the gathered rows of faces in front of her; pale ovals fading out into the dark night.

The chorus was deafening.

God help me if this trip switch doesn't flippin' work.

She turned to Walter. 'Walt, would you like to do the honours?'

He grinned as he reached down to his feet and picked up a length of yellow flex with a junction box attached to it.

'Ladies, gentlemen and children,' he pronounced grandly. 'Happy anniversary!'

Around the edge of the drilling deck hundreds of tiny coloured bulbs, strung across from one side to the other, suddenly winked on, lighting the platform like a Christmas tree.

The night was filled with a collective gasp.

Jenny found herself joining them. Even though she'd done her bit threading the power cables and strings of lights around the metal spars this afternoon, and took turns standing guard, banning anyone else from coming down on to the deck so that it would be a big surprise for them all; even though she had a rough idea where all the lights were strung and how many of those twenty-five watt bulbs were going to come to life, her breath was as much taken away as anyone else's.

Oh, God . . . it's beautiful.

Impulsively, she reached out and hugged Walter, looking over his rounded shoulder for her kids in the crowd.

Leona's gaze drifted along the strings of bulbs; red, blue, green, orange; beautiful carnival pinpoints of light that fogged and blurred with her tears. Hannah was chuckling with delight and swinging on her arm.

'Hey, Lee? Why you crying?'

Leona laughed, shook her head and wiped the dampness away. 'I'm not, Han. It's . . . it's just . . . so pretty!' She felt her throat tighten and knew that saying anything else right now would mean she'd probably end up blubbing like some old dear. She noticed amongst the other faces around her, turned upwards to gaze adoringly at the lights, the telltale glint of moist eyes.

Not just me then.

Hannah's attention returned to the lights and she whooped with joy, then tugged Leona's hand. 'Can I go give Nanna and Uncle Walter a "well done" hug?'

Leona nodded and let her hand go, watching Hannah scoot off through the crowd towards her grandmother, realising how old she felt just then. Only twenty-eight and yet she felt like one of those sad old soldiers who got misty eyed at the sight of an RAF flyover on Remembrance Sunday. Old before her time.

Oh . . . to hell with it.

She let the tears roll; the lights becoming a blurred kaleidoscope. Laughing and crying at the same time as she suddenly realised all those pretty lights winding their way up the comms tower reminded her vaguely of Trafalgar Square on New Year's Eve, Oxford Street at Christmas.

There was an orderly queue already forming beside the huge plastic ten-gallon drum containing Walter's potato brew and Hamarra had started bashing out an old folk tune on her acoustic guitar. Rowena Falkirk – a silver-haired surly stick of a woman, unsurprisingly a friend of Alice's – joined in on the fiddle; a playful tune that instantly lifted everyone's spirits and had toes compulsively tapping.

Leona found herself humming along in her own tone-deaf and tuneless way before she even realised she was doing it.

Jacob and Nathan had managed to sneak a second tumbler of Walter's brew before Jenny spotted them both queuing for a third and turfed them out of the line.

Sitting on the steps leading up to a Portakabin, Jacob found

Valérie, smiling at the revelry going on around him. Walter's concoction – limited to a mug per child and two per adult – had begun to weave its magic, taking the edge off the cool breeze and the damp and drizzle in the air.

'It is a good party,' said Valérie.

Nathan nodded. 'Walt and Jake's mum done well cool with them lights.'

Jacob found space on the step beside Valérie and sat down. 'How's your leg feeling?'

'It is very sore, but it is healing well, I think.'

He looked at the man. Valérie looked much more presentable now he'd tidied himself up a little. He'd borrowed some trousers and a thick woolly jumper from the clothes-library. If Mum decided to let him stay, he'd be able to pick a whole wardrobe of clothes from the communal pile, and those would be his to wash and repair as needs be.

He wanted to quiz Valérie further on what he'd seen ashore whilst on his travels. Mum had said she'd heard enough from him for the moment and when he was feeling better she'd want to hear more details. But Jacob was eager to know more now. Stone-cold sober it would have felt presumptuous to corner him like this; emboldened by the drink, this felt as good a time as any.

'You said there was *nothing* out there, Mr Latoc. Not a thing.' He looked up at Nathan, standing with a foot on the bottom step and distractedly watching the party going on. 'Me and Nate thought maybe, by now, there would be things getting themselves sorted out?'

Valérie shrugged sympathetically. 'In the Europe that I have seen . . . no. There was too much migration of people. Eastern Europeans, North Africans all assuming France and Germany would be better organised to cope. Too many people. It was a very bad mess.'

'And the United Kingdom?' asked Nathan. 'Is it really as bad as that?'

'I sailed across to Dover,' Valérie replied, shuffling on the hard metal grating of the step to find a more comfortable place. 'Then I walked through, uh, *Kent*? Yes. Then north towards London.'

'What did you eat?'

'There is still food to be found. Much easier to find food actually in your country than in Europe.'

Jacob cocked his head. 'Why's that?'

'You British died much faster at the time. The water was stopped when your power stopped, yes?'

Jacob nodded.

'People drinking bad water and getting diseases very quick. In Europe; France, Germany had much better emergency plans, reserves of food and water, and some power in areas. More people survived for much longer . . . a year, two years. All this time, they are finding food in damaged shops and warehouses, but not making new food. So, you know, eventually, we have too many people coming in, our emergency plans collapsed too. But by this time too many people had been picking for food and it is now all gone.'

Mum had said something along the same lines once, that in a way it had been a good thing that the die-off in Britain had been so incredibly rapid. It meant there'd been much more left behind to be foraged; it had given those who'd survived a better chance of keeping going whilst they prepared to feed themselves on what they could grow.

'What about those men who chased you?' asked Nathan. 'What was their place like?'

Valérie shook his head. 'Scavengers mostly. Just a few of them, maybe twenty. They were growing a few things, but not growing them very well.'

'Surely there were others you came across?'

'I just saw some signs of other people. The horse droppings . . . I saw a horse-drawn cart far away, I think. I saw a woman on a bicycle on a motorway bridge. She did not stop to talk to me.'

'But you never saw any lights on at night?'

Valérie nodded. 'Once or twice, you know, perhaps candlelight, a campfire maybe.'

'But no electric lights?'

Valérie hesitated. It was long enough that both Nathan and Jacob sensed he was holding something back from them.

'Hang on,' said Nathan, quickly ducking down to sit on the step. 'You saw something, right?'

'Did you see street lights?' asked Jacob.

Valérie's jaw set, reluctant to say any more. 'It is nothing. Your mother is right. This is the best place to—'

'Come on, what did you see?' urged Nathan.

'Please,' said Jacob. 'We need to know.'

Valérie studied their faces with a long considered silence. 'Very well. I think . . . I maybe saw electric lights . . . once. Perhaps.'

Both boys' eyes widened. 'Where?'

'It was very faint. Very far.'

'Where?'

Valérie bit his lip. 'Your mother would not be happy with me. It is still a very dangerous place on the land. I know she does not want—'

'Where?' asked Jacob. He leaned closer. 'Please!'

Valérie looked up at the party going on across the deck. Some of them were dancing in a circle, singing along and clapping to the accompaniment of the guitar and fiddle. The babble of merry voices, the incessant rumble of the sea below, more than enough going on that nobody but the two boys sitting beside him would hear their conversation.

'I was crossing the River Thames at a place near your Big Ben. I saw a glow of lights in the east.'

'Shit!' uttered Nathan, 'you mean the City of London, don't you? East? That's the *Bank* and *trading* bit.'

'Yes. That part.'

Jacob slapped his hands together. 'Shit! I knew it.'

'Government, like,' said Nathan. 'Westminster and stuff.'

Jacob nodded. 'Keeping it quiet. I fucking well knew it would start there!'

Valérie reached out and grabbed Jacob's arm. 'It was just lights. That is all. It could mean nothing.'

'But you saw it from far off?' asked Nathan.

'I only saw some light shining up on the clouds,' he said warily. 'That is all.'

'Shit!' Jacob's eyes widened. 'Really?'

The young men looked at each other. 'That could be like a floodlight?'

Nathan nodded. 'It would need to be powerful, right? To bounce off the clouds.'

Valérie looked uncomfortable at their growing excitement. 'I should *not* have told you this! Your mother will throw me off!'

Nathan patted his arm, his face widening with a grin. 'We won't tell, Mr Latoc.'

Valérie looked at them both, his mouth drawn with worry. 'It is still *very* dangerous ashore. You are better to stay here where it is safe. Look, I have made a mistake to tell—'

Jacob shook his head. 'No. We nccdcd to know. My mum shouldn't keep this kind of thing from us. It's only fair that—'

'Please,' begged Valérie. 'Forget that I told you this. The lights . . . perhaps I—'

Nathan rested a hand on the man's arm. 'You didn't tell us nothing, all right? Nothing we didn't already suspect. S'right innit, Jay?'

Jacob nodded. 'S'right.'

'It's been ten years,' said Nathan. 'Never believed we'd be the first to make some 'lectric again.'

'We won't tell Mum, Mr Latoc, okay?'

Valérie looked at them both. 'You are planning to leave here, aren't you?'

Nathan and Jacob shared a glance.

'I see it, you are. You should know it is very dangerous still,' he repeated.

'We'll be careful,' said Nathan. 'And we'll take a gun.'

Jacob looked out across the deck at a knot of people dancing. He saw Walter bopping around with Hannah bouncing on his shoulders; she was giggling. He could see Leona spinning, arm-locked hokey-cokey circles with Rebecca. He could see Mum laughing as she waltzed energetically with Martha.

Mum laughing . . . she rarely seemed to do that these days.

'We have to go and see,' said Jacob. He looked at Valérie. 'You understand? See for ourselves. I can't just stay here for ever not knowing. You know?'

Valérie nodded slowly. 'Of course, I understand.'

'Please don't tell my mum.'

'Seriously . . . don't,' added Nathan. 'She'll stop us going ashore again.'

'She would blame me when you leave.'

'Why? You haven't mentioned about the lights to anyone else have you?'

He shook his head.

'Then we won't mention it to anyone, will we, Nate?'

'Nope. Our secret.'

Chapter 16

Crash Day + 2
4.45 a.m.

O2 Arena – 'Safety Zone 4',
London

Adam Brooks looked out across the spools of razor wire stretched across the pedestrian approach and the acres of open coach-parking tarmac in front of the Millennium Dome. Beyond the glinting coils of wire he could see thousands of them. Tens of thousands of people filling up the open tarmac and spilling back past the football academy towards the front of a boarded-up and abandoned dockside factory – still patiently awaiting its time to be knocked down and turned into expensive dockside flats – and down the car-free Blackwall Tunnel Approach towards the low rows of terraced houses and south London beyond.

Their spools of razor wire were stretched thinly across a quarter of a mile of urban landscape from one part of the Thames to the other as it looped round, sealing the tip of the Greenwich peninsula from the rest of south London. A quarter of a mile of wire and just two sections of gunners and half a dozen police officers to hold in check thirty, perhaps forty, thousand people, all of them desperate, thirsty, hungry and frightened.

The wire was shaking and rattling here and there – the press of people from behind forcing those at the front into it. The people, frustrated and angry, were beginning to break up the tan-coloured tarmac and hurl chunks of it over the barricade. Adam could see absolute terror on the faces of many of them, and absolute rage on the rest. They all wanted in, many desperate for something clean and safe to drink, to escape the violent, feral chaos ripping through London.

Adam could see a mother directly in front of him waving her crying baby above the glinting coils of wire, screaming that she needed formula milk, or anything, for it.

Jesus.

He looked sideways at Sergeant Walfield. Normally the grizzly-faced bastard was a rock that Adam relied on. But right now, he was glancing at Adam with a face that said *what-the-shitting-hell-do-we-do?*

Several more bricks and clumps of dislodged tarmac arced over the top of the wire and clattered noisily on their side of the barrier. The wire loops bulged further along.

Bollocks . . . we're going to have to let them in.

There were standing orders from Safety Zone 4's supervisor, Alan Maxwell, that the growing crowd was to be processed in an orderly manner; no more than twenty at a time, details to be taken down, a medical check, sleeping cots assigned before another batch was allowed through. He'd been very specific about that; he wasn't going to allow a stampede to happen.

But this . . . batches of twenty, it was taking far too long.

The number of people outside had swollen drastically this morning after last night's riots. Adam had been walking the wire perimeter since yesterday evening. He'd witnessed the flickering glow of countless fires, heard the crash and tinkle of glass breaking, the distant whooping of delight from gangs of youths making the most of their new playground, sporadic screams here and there amongst the far-off terraced houses, and the occasional unmistakable crack of a gun.

Adam imagined that, to those poor bastards out there, it must have been like the night after Baghdad had fallen; British and American soldiers standing behind compound walls watching bedlam unfold before their eyes, under orders to do nothing. Just watching as the city tore itself to pieces through the hot and stifling night.

He glanced back at the dome, a drab whale's hump of canvas in the lifeless grey light of pre-dawn. The very tips of the support spars, arranged like a thorn crown at the top, glowed as they caught the very first vanilla rays of light from the early morning sun breaching the urban, smoke-smudged horizon.

Just outside the entrance he could see orange-jacketed emergency workers processing the recently admitted civilians. He could see several hundred more civilians inside the entrance atrium, many exhausted, stretched out on crash mats and cots, set out in orderly lines across the floor. He could see workers moving amongst them handing out bottled water, first aiders working on cuts and burns, wrapping grey blankets around those in shock.

But he couldn't see any bloody sign at all of Maxwell.

We've got to let them in. Now.

They needed to throw aside the barrier and worry about getting names and National Insurance numbers later. After all, that's what they were here for; food and water and safety for these people. Surely the damned paperwork could come later.

'Sir!' shouted Sergeant Walfield. 'Look!'

A hundred yards to his right Adam saw the wire coils beginning to bulge and flatten out.

'Bastards are trying to get over!'

A group of men, fed up with hurling tarmac over the top, had found a large panel of chipboard and hefted it across the wire. One of them stepped onto the board, his weight pushing down the wire coils, twenty yards either side, almost flat beneath it.

Shit.

Forty yards of breached perimeter; the coils of razor wire

were compressed enough that it was possible to cautiously pick a way through.

'Get that fucking board off!' bellowed Sergeant Walfield, his voice carrying above the rising roar of encouragement from the crowd.

The nearest of the men temporarily under Adam's command, half a dozen sequestered constables from the Metropolitan Police, jogged over towards the board, their guns aimed at the man standing astride it.

The man ignored their barked orders to get the fuck off; instead he was beckoning others to follow him up and over. He stood alone for a moment, deaf to the police and soldiers shouting at him to get off immediately. Then he was joined by two or three others clambering up on the board, their combined weight pushing the coils flatter across an even wider span.

Shit, shit, shit.

Adam racked his assault rifle and fired three shots in quick succession up into the air. It had the effect he wanted. The first half a dozen ranks of people beyond the wire ducked and froze and a hush descended for the briefest moment.

Adam finally found his voice.

'YOU!' It rang out across the tarmac in the moment's silence. 'Yes, YOU! Get the fuck off that board right now!'

For a moment Adam was convinced the man was going to comply. But the brief moment of hush his three shots had won them was already beginning to wane. The man stepped forward, the board tilted downwards as the wire twanged and rattled beneath his weight. He leapt down onto the tarmac, on *their* side.

You stupid fucking idiot.

A Berlin wall moment — the first man safely across inspiring all the others to surge forward in his wake.

A dozen others — men who on any other day would look unremarkable waiting outside a school playground to pick up their kids, or buying a sandwich and a coffee for lunch, grabbing a newspaper and some milk from a corner shop – encouraged enough by the first stupid bastard, barged and wrestled with each other to clamber onto the chipboard ramp.

It was one of the policemen who opened fire first. The shot punched a ragged hole in the first man's face and took off a section of the back of his head. His legs instantly crumpled beneath him and he flopped backwards over the end of the board and onto the compressed loops of wire, where his still body dangled untidily from the barbs.

For a fleeting moment Adam thought that would have been enough of a demonstration to the others that any further reckless stupidity like this was going to be met with more of the same.

He hadn't given an order to fire. The policeman didn't have the discipline of his gunners – wasn't waiting for the order; instead the copper had gone off-piste, popping like a poorly made firework. Still, it had bought them a second or two; a pause for thought from those nearest the splayed body. But that's all it bought. Now there were people tiptoeing through the flattened coils either side of the board, some of them flapping their hands in front of their faces, frantically waving at the young soldiers, screaming at them not to shoot.

Sergeant Walfield turned to look at him. 'Sir, what do we do now?'

Oh, Christ.

There were a dozen over the wire now, more snagged on the razor sharp blades and tugging their clothes clear, being pushed forward by a growing momentum from behind.

Adam swallowed anxiously. Walfield again looking back at him.

More of them were stepping over, and more behind them. The policeman who'd fired the shot was struggling with his weapon; the thing had jammed or he'd slipped the safety catch on in panic. Then suddenly he was down, clutching at

111

his head. Someone had thrown a brick at his face. And more projectiles were arcing over the top.

If this barrier folds these people will flood into SZ4. We will have lost control and they'll strip us clean – Maxwell's briefing from several hours ago as the crowd outside had started to swell in the darkness. *Do you understand? If you have to shoot, do it.*

'Open fire!' Adam heard himself utter to Sergeant Walfield.

Walfield bellowed the order again a dozen times louder.

The crackle of gunfire oddly reminded Adam of bubble wrap being twisted tightly. The gunners in his platoon fired single and double taps, the policemen emptied their magazines. A dozen people, probably more, flopped like pathetic rag dolls amidst the wire; England football strips, FCUK tops, sensible Primark shirts . . . exploding in unison, spraying curious Rorschach splatter patterns and question marks of dark crimson onto the tarmac, leaving dust motes of polyester and cotton fibres to float lazily to the ground like cherry blossom.

Behind the downed civilians the crowd ducked as one, an instinctive acres-wide herd response. Then they broke and ran, tangling with each other, falling over those behind who reacted with less urgency. The coach-parking area cleared rapidly from the front, rolling back like a receding Mexican wave, leaving behind a mess of items dropped in the panic; and those wounded and twisting in pain on the ground, or who'd stumbled in the rush and were now scrambling away on twisted ankles.

Most of his men ceased fire. One or two of the coppers – unforgivably in Adam's mind – fired further opportunistic shots at the backs of the parting crowd.

'For Christ's sake, STOP FIRING!' he shouted.

Walfield bellowed the order and the popping of gunfire halted.

The backs of a sea of bobbing heads receded into the distance, still running, swerving around the football academy, streaming down a sloping grass bank towards the Blackwall Tunnel Approach. Adam could hear the awful chorus of screams and slapping feet diminish leaving them now with an unsettling quiet punctuated by soft moans of agony coming from the prone bodies in front of them.

He realised his hands were trembling violently, the muzzle of his assault rifle wavering erratically. Not a good thing for his men to see. He clicked the safety on then lowered it until it was pointing harmlessly at the ground.

In front of him, just a dozen yards away, the mother he'd spotted earlier was rocking backwards and forwards on her knees, lacerated and encaged amidst the shaking coils of wire, expanding again now no one was weighing the board down. She seemed to be unaware that she had a gunshot wound to her arm, instead she stared dumbfounded at the ragged and inert remains of her baby.

Adam dropped down to a squat, feeling a wave of nausea roll up from his cramping stomach. He dry-heaved, not giving a thought to how it looked to his men.

He straightened up after a while and felt the first warm rays of the morning sun on his face.

Oh, Jesus, what the fuck have we done?

Chapter 17

10 years AC

'LeMan 49/25a' – ClarenCo Gas Rig Complex,
North Sea

'I don't know, Walter. I haven't made up my mind about him yet.'

Jenny hunkered down amongst the troughs of compost lining the walkway along the front of the second tier of the accommodation module. Clear plastic sheeting, attached to the safety rail and stretched up to the overhanging ceiling of the tier above, protected the newly sprouting plants from the occasional drops of salt spray. The sheets flapped and rustled noisily in the breeze like the slack sails of a yacht luffing close to windward.

Walter shot a glance over Jenny's shoulder at several ladies carefully watering the onion sprouts further along the walkway.

'You know,' he lowered his voice, 'he's been on his own for a long, long time.' He squatted down beside her. 'He's exactly the *type*, you know? The type you worry about. The type you don't normally allow to join us.'

'Walter,' she looked up at him, 'I said I haven't decided yet.'

He recoiled ever so slightly. He looked wounded.

She immediately felt guilty and reached out for his arm. 'Look, it's not entirely up to me. It's how everyone *else* feels about a newcomer as well. From what little I've seen of him, I . . .' She shook her head, searching for words. 'He doesn't seem the *troubled* kind. I've given him another month's probation, and we'll see how he gets on.'

Walter's jaw worked silently.

'And if anyone, including you, Walter, feels really twitchy about him after that, then we'll sit down and have it out with him. See what he's all about.'

He still looked unhappy.

'And believe me, if there's *anything* at all about him that worries me, then he'll have to go.'

Walter nodded. 'All right.' It looked like that wasn't what he wanted to hear, but it was going to have to do. She knew what was behind this. It was jealousy. And that irked her a little. She knew Walter considered himself to be the alpha male of their community. If she was some sort of mother figure then by default he viewed himself as the father, and that didn't sit well with her. By implication, it meant Walter saw himself as a potential suitor for her. A potential lover, one day, when she was finally ready for it.

The thought of that kind of a relationship with Walter didn't really do anything for her. He was ten years older. His florid face, salt and pepper bush of a beard and lank long hair reminded her of Billy Connolly.

A poor woman's Billy Connolly.

Ever since losing Andy she'd been without a partner. Too busy surviving, too busy fighting for her children, lately too busy peacemaking every petty squabble, managing the lives of four hundred and fifty-plus people to consider a partner.

If she ever did consider another man, well, it wasn't going to be Walter. He was the best of friends, a reliable second-in-command, an invaluable Jack of all trades. Without him she wondered whether they could have survived *at all*, let alone have electricity. But she could never imagine ending up lying in a cot with him, surrendering and sighing under the touch of his rough and callused hands.

'Where is he now?' he asked.

'Who?'

'Latoc.'

Jenny stood up, feeling her worn knees creak. 'Jacob, Nathan and Hannah are giving him the grand tour.'

'What if he's a spy?' said Walter, his face immediately colouring after he'd spoken. She knew he'd just realised how silly and desperate that had sounded.

She reached out and squeezed his hand. 'A spy for *who*, Walt?' she replied softly, offering him a tender smile. 'Who's out there now, organised enough to despatch a spy our way?'

'The chickens give us eggs,' said Hannah. 'Eggs and lots of poo.'

Valérie tilted his head thoughtfully. 'You have very many chickens.'

'I reckon we're up to about seven hundred of them now,' said Nathan. 'That right, Jay?'

Jacob nodded. 'At the last count. Some escaped Chicken-Land a few weeks ago.'

They called this deck that – the birds had the run of virtually the whole of the first floor of the production platform's main module. Wire mesh covered one or two opened portholes and an outside gantry had been wired in to give the birds an exterior run to scratch around on. Most of the floor was open plan. It had once been a series of work-shops; several large areas divided by wide, sliding doors on runners. Like the rest of the rig, the rooms had been stripped bare of machinery before the crash. On the linoleum-covered metal floor, faint stains of rust, divots and grooves showed where heavy equipment had once been secured. Now, though, the floor was mostly a carpet of chicken droppings, shed feathers and idling hens that stepped around the inert bulk of the remaining equipment – old lathes, milling tools. The nearest birds stared up at them stupidly.

Through windows along one wall, looking across the walkway leading to the drilling platform, they could see several supermarket shopping trolleys loaded with seed trays being wheeled along, clattering and rattling their way across. The mesh on the small round windows was garnished with tufts of fluffy feathers fluttering gently in a soft moaning draught that chased itself through the rooms of ChickenLand.

'It is a very good set-up,' Valérie smiled approvingly. 'You have done well.'

'You want to see the magic source of our power?' asked Nathan.

'Yeah!' said Hannah enthusiastically. 'Wanna see our lectrik power?'

Valérie smiled hesitantly. 'All right.'

'Not hard to find.' Jacob led the way out of the chicken rooms, shooing a few of them away as they opened the door. 'All we need to do is follow the stink,' he said, pulling a face.

They stepped out onto an external walkway, thick with the rustling leaves of runner bean plants climbing panels of green plastic trellis on either side of them. If the metal grating beneath their feet had been covered with a thick bed of spongy moss they could almost have been walking down a jungle trail.

'This way,' said Jacob leading.

They made their way carefully along it, passing several children and an elderly couple carefully picking pods from the stalks. Hannah announced to one of the children with solemn authority that she was doing her *official* job showing the newcomer around.

Jacob and Nathan grinned at each other.

Presently Jacob stepped to the left, and reached through a veil of leaves dangling down from the gantry above and doing their best to completely obscure a doorway. 'Guess you can smell it now?'

Valérie wrinkled his nose and nodded.

Jacob pulled the leaves to one side and opened the door. They stepped into an almost completely pitch black interior.

'Just a sec,' said Jacob. He fumbled in the dark for a

117

moment before finding the torch dangling from a hook just inside the door. He snapped it on. They were in a narrow passageway, ahead of them a steep flight of steps leading down to the module's bottom floor. The smell of fermenting faeces quickly grew unpleasantly strong as they made their way down the steps and along a passageway lined with tall lockers on which were fading name tags.

'Down here used to be the shift workers' changing room,' said Jacob. 'Walter said it's the best place for our digesters because it's insulated. It's the warmest place on all of the rigs.' He opened a door and led the way in, holding his nose as he did so. 'Here we are . . . the stinky rooms.'

Valérie and Nathan stepped inside, wincing at the over-powering odour.

'Sorry, Hannah,' said Jacob, gently holding her arm. 'You know the rules, no children inside.'

She frowned indignantly. 'But I want to show him the jenny-rater.'

Jacob smiled. Hannah frequently heard Walter referring to the generator as the 'genny'. Knowing how her faultlessly logical mind worked, Jacob suspected his niece assumed, quite reasonably, that the machine was named after her grandmother.

'No children inside without Mum or Walter around. You know that, Han.'

She scowled at him, but stood obediently out in the passage watching Valérie intently studying the machine by torchlight.

Jacob stepped across the floor towards the doorway to an adjoining room. 'In here is where the methane is brewed up,' he said.

Valérie followed him inside. The smell was almost over-powering in the generator room, but in this room the odour was even more pungent.

'Can you feel how warm it is?' said Nathan.

'The crap actually generates its own heat as it ferments,' said Jacob. He stepped across to the nearest plastic drum and rested his hand on it. 'Feel it.'

Valérie touched the plastic and nodded. 'Oh, yes . . . it is almost as warm as a radiator!'

The room was quiet, save for a gurgling coming from inside the large plastic containers. The only place on any of the rigs that seemed almost completely devoid of sound; the endless rumble of the sea, the whistle and moan of wind, insulated from them. Just that soft contented gurgling and bubbling from inside.

Nathan grinned. 'What do you think?'

Valérie studied the plastic drums, the feed-off pipes coming from them and leading to several gas storage containers. Another pipe winding its way across the low ceiling and out through the door they'd entered, into the generator room.

'That's the feed pipe,' said Jacob. 'Feeding methane to the generator.'

They stepped through the doorway back into the generator room. Hannah was tapping one foot impatiently out in the passageway.

'We make enough fuel for about three hours of power every night,' said Nathan. 'Walter said maybe one day he'll improve it so that we get even more power and we could have spare for things like music systems.'

'Maybe even a TV and we could watch movies and cartoons,' added Jacob.

'Or even, if we find a working PlayStation,' added Nathan, 'we could play video games again.'

Hannah, standing out in the passage, giggled. 'Viddy-oh games!' she chorused. She'd heard the term many times. Jacob had even described to her what they were. But in truth she had no idea – just that they were fun and happened on TV screens.

Valérie stared silently at the equipment.

'So? It's cool, isn't it?' said Jacob, certain Mr Latoc was impressed with the progress they had made here, bringing power and light again to a dark world.

The cushioned silence in the small room became awkwardly long.

'So . . . uh . . . didn't *anyone* else you come across have stuff like this?'

Valérie shook his head slowly. He glanced at them both. 'It is frightening.'

Nathan looked confused. '*Frightening*?'

Valérie shook his head sadly. 'Do you not see? It is taking us back to what we were *before*.'

'Yes! That's what we—'

'Before was a very bad time. You know this? Too many of us, all in our big cars, in our big homes. Eight billion people all wanting the new TVs, the new music systems, the new video games. The more things we had the less content we became. You would want that world again?'

Jacob and Nathan nodded.

'You want to live in a big city, full of noises and lights?'

'Yeah, 'course,' replied Nathan.

The man shook his head with incredulity. Both Nathan and Jacob stared at him, bemused.

'I believe the world was sick then,' he continued. 'And people were sick with a disease of the soul. You understand me?'

Neither boy did. Not really.

'Most people were not really happy. Most people were sick in their heart, unhappy with their lives. We all lived our isolated lives in our little homes and saw the world beyond through a tiny . . . *digital* window. People did not talk to each other. Instead they typed messages to complete strangers on the internet. The more things we had the unhappier we become because there was always people on the TV who had very much more.'

Valérie shook his head and smiled sadly. 'You do not see how much *better* your life is now, do you?'

Jacob, Nathan and Hannah continued to stare at him in bewildered silence.

'I think your mother understands this. It is not *things* – and all the electricity that makes those things work – that makes a good life. They are just *things*; distractions, you know? Shiny little amusements made to look so wonderful and fun and the answer to your unhappiness. But you get the shiny things home, you unwrap them, you hold them in your hand . . . and they are just shiny things, that is all. They mean nothing.'

Valérie looked at the generator. 'You know what it is that really destroyed the old world?'

They shrugged.

'It was greed.'

Nathan and Jacob glanced at each other.

'You know children killed each other for things like training shoes? Or mobile phones?' Valérie continued. 'The time just before the crash was mankind at his most evil. There were wars for oil, wars for gas. People killed for things, for power. Killed for oil. It was a world filled with jealousy for all the things we would see *others* have on the TV. A world of greed. Anger. Hate.'

He ran a hand through his dark hair, pushing it out of his eyes. 'All the bright shiny lights and the noises . . . video games, the TV, the internet, the music, the shopping, the arcades . . . these things were made by the governments to distract us; to keep our minds full and busy.'

Hannah leant into the room, her feet still obediently out in the passageway. 'Why . . . why did the guvvy-ments want us to have busy minds?'

Valérie turned to Hannah. 'So we did not realise how unhappy we all were.'

They stood still and silent.

Valérie clicked his tongue then rapped his knuckles on the generator's iron casing. 'Maybe machines like this are the first step back to bad, bad times, eh?'

The three of them stared at him, bemused by the comment.

'I wonder,' said Valérie, 'do you ever think that this planet would be better off without people on it? Do you ever wonder if the oil crash happened for a reason? Just like the asteroid that finished off the dinosaurs because their time was done. Maybe it was *our* time.'

The words hung in the air, echoing off the hard rusting metal walls.

'Uh . . . okay,' said Nathan quietly. He pointed towards the doorway. 'So . . . that was the generator room, anyway. Would you like to go see the tomato deck?'

He led the way out, stepping past Hannah. Valérie followed, and Jacob emerged in his wake.

'You coming, Han?'

She looked up at him, her face ashen. 'Is Mr Latoc right? Will the jenny-rater make everyone unhappy again?'

Jacob sighed. 'No . . . he's just, I dunno, exaggerating a bit. Ask Leona, she'll tell you we weren't all miserable.'

'Mum always says it was better then.'

'There you go.'

Jacob followed after Nathan and Valérie, whilst Hannah looked back once more at the dark generator room, listening to the sound of gurgling and bubbling, echoing along the feedpipes like the stomach of some large and hungry monster.

'You coming, Han?'

'Coming,' she replied.

Chapter 18

10 years AC

'LeMan 49/25a' - ClarenCo Gas Rig Complex, North Sea

Hannah watched him eat breakfast. He spooned the porridge into his mouth and smiled courteously at those who were speaking to him across the table. He said little himself. His eyes drank in the details around him, but his mind seemed elsewhere, far away.

As was Hannah's.

Mr Latoc troubled her. What Mr Latoc had *said* troubled her.

Leona urged her to eat up whilst the porridge was warm, and then continued in conversation with Rebecca, the other woman who taught classes at their school. They were heatedly discussing what sort of subjects they wanted to bring into the classroom. Leona wanted to add some complicated things like science and technology; stuff to do with machines. Rebecca, on the other hand, wanted to add more 'farmy' things.

She ate in silence and continued to watch Mr Latoc smiling politely at all the right times, even laughing occasionally, but just not there.

Elsewhere.

Finally, he finished his porridge and excused himself, standing up from the long table as he fiddled clumsily with his crutch and began to limp across the floor. Arnold Brown, old as the hills, offered him a steadying hand and offered to take his dirty bowl to the canteen counter for him. Mr Latoc smiled and thanked him, then shuffled towards the door of the canteen. It opened and the ladies coming in for the second breakfast sitting stepped aside and allowed him through on to the gantry outside.

Hannah hurried to finish her breakfast with three well-laden spoons, piling in one after the other until her cheeks bulged like a hamster. She almost gagged on it. She wasn't hungry. In fact, something was gnawing away at her tummy, making her feel sick. But Leona certainly wouldn't let her step away from the table with anything less than a scraped-clean bowl.

She stood up.

Leona stopped talking and glanced at the bowl. 'That was quick.'

Hannah nodded and smiled as she worked the porridge down.

'You all right there, honey?'

'Yes,' she managed finally. 'Want to go play for a bit before school.'

'Okay, but class starts in half an hour.'

Hannah nodded.

'And only inside or on the tomato deck. The wind's up today.'

'Okay,' she replied, scooping up her bowl from the table.

She walked over and placed it on the washing-up counter, then hurriedly stepped out through the canteen door onto the gantry. The wind tossed her blonde hair in all directions, stinging her cheeks with one or two spits of rain.

She saw him standing at the far corner, leaning on the safety rail and looking down on the decks below. Right now it was a hive of activity as people emerged from all corners to head up to the canteen for breakfast or in different directions for their morning chores.

She approached him warily, the wind teasing his long dark hair as well. The rumple of wind covered the soft clank of her sandals on the metal grating. She was standing right beside him before he seemed to notice and turn his gaze from the decks below towards her.

'Oh,' he said, 'hello, Hannah, I did not see you there.'

Hannah didn't do 'good mornings', 'how are you doing today', 'it's blowing lively this morning, isn't it.' Those were the kind of boring openers she let adults waste their time on. She had something far more pressing to deal with; something she'd been stewing on all night.

'Is Walter's jenny-rater really a very bad thing?'

He seemed taken aback by so direct a comment out of the blue. But after a moment, seemingly recalling his tour from yesterday, he nodded slowly. He lowered himself down, squatting so that his face was more on a level with hers, grimacing with pain as he did so.

'How much do you know about the times *before*?'

Her eyes rolled up to the sky as she attempted to retrieve some of the many potted descriptions she'd been fed over the years. 'Leona said those were fun times. But Nanna says things weren't so good. That most people pretended to be happy, but weren't.'

'Your grandmother is right. Even I did not see this back then. I pretended to be happy like everyone else. We had our cars, our gadgets, our internet, our shopping malls. And the nights glowed with neon signs, telling us to buy even more things, to wear more things, to eat more things. But I am sure now few of us were happy.'

'Why?'

'I think . . . because deep down, we knew it was wrong. I know now there was a . . . a voice, a quiet voice telling me that bad things were coming. That the food we were eating was poisoning us. That the electricity we were using, the materials we dug out of the ground, were not going to last for ever. That there were too many of us being much too greedy.'

Hannah thought she understood that quiet voice. There were times she'd been naughty, doing something she knew she shouldn't be doing, and not even enjoying it, because that annoying little voice was telling her there'd be hell to pay when Leona or Nanna found out.

'I think there were some who sensed that a . . .' Valérie looked around for the right word, 'that a *storm* was coming. And that storm would kill many people.'

'A storm,' she echoed quietly.

'But we did not stop or change our ways.' He looked sad. 'We were like caterpillars.'

'Caterpillars?'

Valérie nodded. 'A type of caterpillar that eats much too much. I remember reading about them – they are a species that live in some jungle. They eat and eat these green leaves, and then, when the leaves have all gone, they will just eat each other until only one of them is left on the plant.'

'Oh.' Her favourite picture-book in the classroom's small library was *The Very Hungry Caterpillar*. She wondered whether she might start seeing that story differently.

'God made such a beautiful world, Hannah. Then he put us on it and all we have done is destroy it. We have suck it dry of valuable resources and in turn fill it with useless things we do not need. We turn a beautiful thing into an ugly thing.'

Hannah looked down at the decks below; rusting, cluttered and messy. He was right.

'I feel this now, that the crash was like a judgement on us. Out there I have seen nothing but darkness and evil left behind, Hannah.' He smiled. 'But here, in *this* place, maybe I see goodness for the first time, in a long time. I see hope.' He looked out across the rigs, pushing dark hair from his eyes. 'This is a special place your grandmother has created; like an Eden. But . . . yes, the generator, it worries me.'

'Why?'

'Your friend, Nathan and your brother, Jacob?'

'He's my uncle.'

Valérie shrugged. 'They, and Walter and others will want

more electricity soon. And they will want other things, more and more things. And so I think we will head back to the way we once were. We will not learn.'

Hannah's eyebrows furrowed as she thought about that.

'Your grandmother, I think, sees that the past was very bad times,' he continued, 'and that is good. She is a clever woman. But, I wonder if she sees that the generator is *not* a good thing; the first step back towards the bad times.'

'The bad time before the crash?'

'Yes. Perhaps life is better here just as it is? You see that, yes?'

Hannah could hear the wisdom in his voice, even if she didn't entirely follow the logic. The jenny-rater rooms did in truth smell awful, and all that smell and hard work just to make a few light-bulbs glow? They had candles for that. She'd heard Leona and Jacob go on about the old world so much. Hannah often wondered what was really so *bad* about *this* world? The last time she'd actually felt genuinely sad was ages ago – when she'd accidentally lost a doll over the side and watched it tumbling in the wind all the way down into the sea, making hardly a splash.

And Nanna said the same things as Mr Latoc. It sounded like people spent so much time being unhappy in the old days. Sad, and angry too, because they didn't have the same shiny things as someone else had.

'I think it is a mistake.'

She sensed Mr Latoc was somehow disappointed in them, as if he'd hoped they were better people than they'd actually turned out to be. That thought burned her – like a telling-off.

It's the jenny-rater's fault. That's what was letting them down, that's what really disappointed Mr Latoc. She wondered if that meant he was thinking of leaving them as soon as his leg was all fixed up, go and find better people to live with; people who could live quite happily without silly 'lectric. She'd hate for him to go, especially after she'd worked so hard to make him better again. He seemed to be the only grown-up who really listened to her. When he talked to her, he actually looked at her. Other grown-ups always seemed to have their attention elsewhere, on things-that-needed-doing, they gave her an *uh-huh*, or a *really?-that's-nice.*

But Mr Latoc really listened; listened with his eyes as well as his ears.

He was looking at her now. He reached out and gently held Hannah's shoulder. 'You are crying. I am sorry. I think I have upset you?'

Hannah shook her head. 'Are you going to leave us?'

He shrugged. 'I . . . I see things I would want to change if—'

They heard the faint sound of a bell ringing out across the platforms.

'You have school now?'

Hannah nodded absent-mindedly, her face clouded and deep in thought.

'You should go. Before you are late and get me in trouble.'

'You won't go, will you? I can ask Uncle Walter not to put the jenny-rater on tonight, if you don't go.'

His smile was warm as he gently squeezed her shoulder. 'I do not think I am leaving today, Hannah.'

Jenny admired Martha's handiwork in the mirror.

'Oh, blimey! I can't believe what a difference it makes!'

Martha beamed cheerfully, scissors in one hand, comb in the other. 'I told you, Jenny. Didn't I say? It's the length that ages you. I been tellin' you that since I don't know.'

She studied her image in the mirror. Her hair, long and coarse and frizzy, had been tamed by Martha's hand into something she could be proud of. Instead of carelessly pulled back into a ponytail – out of sight, out of mind – it now framed and flattered her face.

'A little conditioner, and a trim . . . you look flippin' gorgeous now, sister!'

Martha's enthusiasm was infectious. Jenny found herself borrowing some of that smile for herself.

'It does make me look . . . yes, younger.'

She realised she looked a lot more like the old Jenny, the long-forgotten Jenny who once wore pencil skirts to work and looked good for thirty-nine with a little warpaint.

'Oooh, he'll love it, girl. He'll be all over you like a bloody rash.'

Her cheeks coloured ever so slightly. 'What?'

'Oh, come on, Jenny. You know who I mean.'

'No . . . I—'

'Our newcomer?' Martha grinned in the mirror. 'Monsieur Tasty?'

Jenny's jaw dropped. 'You think I got you to cut my hair *for him*?'

Martha's raucous laugh filled the cabin. 'Oh-my-days! Of course you did, love! It's obvious you like him. Lord knows, we *all* know you're goin' to let him stay.'

Jenny was appalled that they actually thought she'd put her own desires before the good of the community; that she'd let her loins do the thinking.

Desires? So, you're admitting it, then?

She shook the thought out of her head. 'Look, Martha, no.'

Martha cocked a sceptical eyebrow at Jenny.

'Seriously, no,' said Jenny. 'If he stays, it's because he can add something; knowledge, a skill set, a useful pair of hands, whatever. And that's the *only* reason.'

'Be nice though, to have a man 'round who ain't either some old goat or a young boy,' laughed Martha, her broad frame shaking. She sighed. 'A *real man* at last. Perhaps I'll get a bit of the real t'ing between my legs instead of me trusty ol' faithful.'

'Oh, Martha!'

'See, the batteries have been flat for years. I have to shake the thing like a salt cellar.' Martha cackled again.

Jenny found her own shoulders shaking. 'God, too much detail!' she snorted. 'Were you always this candid with your customers?'

'That's *why* they came to my salon, girl – for a little dirty talk an' a cup of tea.'

Jenny shared some of that infectious smile again. A raucous giggle with Martha every now and then was just about as good as any medicine Dr Gupta could hand out. She wondered whether she'd have gone mad years ago on these rigs if it weren't for Martha.

'Honestly, girl, if you're not going to wiggle for him,' Martha added, 'then I gonna be the first one in the queue!'

Their shared mischievous witch's cackle was brought up short by the sound of feet clanking up the steps towards Jenny's cabin. Jenny looked at Martha's face in the mirror.

Fast-approaching footsteps . . . something's up.

It was Rebecca who stuck her head in. She looked pale.

'It's Hannah.'

Chapter 19

10 years AC

'LeMan 49/25a' – ClarenCo Gas Rig Complex, North Sea

Jenny felt her insides turn instantly to stone. 'What's happened?'

Rebecca's mouth hung open, panting for a few seconds, gathering breath to speak, but also the words she should use. 'She's missing, Jenny. She's missing. She never turned up for the start of Leona's class.'

Jenny looked at the watch on her wrist; a clunky man's watch with a winder and no need for batteries. It was 10.37 a.m.; classes began at ten.

'Leona waited a while,' Rebecca continued, 'said Hannah woke up cranky this morning and was moaning about going to school today.'

Jenny nodded. She most definitely had awoken in a funny mood. Very quiet and sulky.

'Where is Leona?'

'I don't know. She's out looking for her. I don't know where exactly.'

Missing. The word had a deadlier meaning out here on the rigs.

'Get everyone looking,' she said, getting up and pushing past Rebecca into the hallway, 'everyone!'

Outside, on the top deck of the accommodation platform, she could already see the flitter of anxious movement, people leaning over rails and scanning the sea below.

Oh, God, no, please . . . not that.

Word was already spreading. She could hear distant voices

calling her granddaughter's name over and over. Martha, standing beside her, instinctively followed suit calling out for her.

Below, spreading out amongst the winding pipes, scaffolding and a mess of stacked Portakabins on the compression platform, she could see the children of both Leona's and Rebecca's classes crouching, ducking, calling, stretching, looking into every awkward recess for their missing classmate.

'She knows to be sensible,' whispered Jenny. 'She *knows* not to play near the edges.'

'Didn't Lee say she could play on the tomato deck?'

Jenny turned round to look up at the overhanging helipad. She could see movement up there. Could hear someone calling Hannah's name.

'Oh, God, Martha,' she whimpered, 'what if she's—'

Martha put an arm around her. 'She'll turn up, love. She just playin' silly buggers.'

Jenny heard the bang of a doorway below and then Walter emerged from the canteen onto the gantry beneath them. He turned round to look up at her.

'There you are! Someone said Hannah's gone missing!' he called out.

Jenny nodded, unable to speak for the moment.

'I saw her earlier,' he said quickly. 'Not long after breakfast.'

'Where?'

'I saw her with Latoc.'

Their eyes met and wordlessly exchanged between them was every conversation ever had over a kitchen table on the subject of a missing child, taken . . . the type of monsters that prey on children and the punishment *creatures* like that deserved.

She felt her blood flush cold, her scalp prickle at the

thought that she might have stupidly allowed a monster in amongst them; that Hannah . . . ?

'No,' she uttered. Her freshly cut hair suddenly felt like a badge of betrayal, a dunce-cap of stupidity. If she believed in such things, why not a punishment from God for allowing herself a foolish moment of vanity? Whilst she'd been preening, outside, somewhere, the man whose eye she'd been hoping to catch had been busy doing God-knows-what with her granddaughter.

'Where is Latoc?' she barked.

Walter shook his head. 'I've not seen him since.'

Then she saw it, half a mile away, the white blob of a sail. She leaned forward over the rail and looked down at the davit winches on the neighbouring compression platform. The chains dangled and clinked idly against the spider deck: one of their two boats was gone.

Oh, God . . . he's taken her.

She sheltered her eyes from the glare of sunlight and the glints on the sea, beautifully blue this morning and reflecting the azure sky. The boat was turning lazily, only the mainsail up, no jib. It seemed in no particular hurry to put distance between itself and the rigs.

A spark of hope ignited inside her. Perhaps Latoc had taken Hannah for a go on the boat? An innocent, but ill-judged kindness. That being the case, she decided she'd give him a very public bollocking for lowering the boat into the water without getting permission first. It wasn't there for joyrides.

They watched in silence for a few moments as the vessel slowly came about, the boom gently swinging across. Jenny squinted, trying to make sense of the distant flicker of movement in the cockpit.

'I think the boat's comin' back now,' said Martha.

They were waiting down on the spider deck, perhaps a hundred of them, assembled like a lynch mob, many more

133

lining the railing above, watching the boat peacefully carve a return passage across the docile tide, the mast tilted, the mainsail full.

Leona was shaking with rage beside Jenny. Rage, and anxiety.

'Come on . . . come on,' she hissed under her breath. 'Hurry the fuck up.'

Jenny rested a hand on her arm. 'I'll deal with him, Leona. I won't let this happen again.'

Her daughter stared at her silently. Jenny wondered if some of that anger was directed her way. 'If he's touched a hair on her—'

Jenny squeezed her arm. 'She'll be fine,' she smiled. 'I'll let you deal with Hannah, though.'

The boat's return was painfully slow. Although Jenny didn't say anything, she was nervously wondering if the boat might suddenly swing about and head away as soon as Latoc spotted the reception awaiting him. But it didn't.

As it entered the loom of shadow cast by the rigs, the mainsail dropped to the foredeck and the yacht slid slowly forward under its own momentum. William Laithwaite's narrow frame stepped up from the cabin and into view. Eyebrows arched in surprise from behind his glasses as he finally noticed the sea of faces lining the safety railings.

'What . . . uh . . . what's the matter?' he called out.

'Hannah's gone missing,' shouted Jenny. 'Is she with you?'

William shook his head. 'No.'

'Oh, God . . . Mum,' whispered Leona beside her.

'Why'd you take the boat out, Bill?' asked Walter.

The boat softly nudged against one of the support-legs and Kevin emerged from the foredeck hatch, grabbing at the collapsed mainsail and pulling it down through the hatch to store it in the fore cabin.

'I was changing over the sails, thought, uh . . . thought it

134

would be a good opportunity to give young Kevin some practice. Also, Mr Latoc fancied a ride with—'

'He's on there with you?'

'Yes! I am here!' Valérie stood up awkwardly in the cockpit, leaning around the boom and the fluttering folds of sail.

'What the fuck are you doing on there?' snapped Walter.

Valérie recoiled guiltily. 'I am sorry . . . I . . . thought it would be—'

Jenny waved impatiently for him to stop. 'Mr Latoc, you spoke to Hannah last. You were seen—'

'What has happened to the girl?'

'She's gone missing. Hannah's gone missing,' she replied. Next to her, she heard Leona's breath hitch, followed by a quiet keening whimper.

'You were seen talking with her last, Mr Latoc.'

'What have you done with her?' Leona suddenly screamed. 'You fucking bastard . . . what've you—!'

Martha reached for Leona, and held her tightly as her cries diminished to a whimpering.

He shook his head. 'Nothing. I spoke with her after break-fast, yes.'

'We can't find her anywhere,' said Jenny, struggling to keep her own voice even. 'She knows to be careful near the edges. There's no sign of her on any of the—'

'Did you try your generator room?'

Jenny looked around to her left and right. Heads were shaking. She certainly had not thought to look down there.

'The generator room,' continued Valérie, 'your children showed me this the other day. They are very proud of it.' He shrugged. 'That is all I can suggest.'

'She knows not to play down there on her own,' Walter said defensively. 'None of the little ones are allowed in there without me or Jenny with them.'

Leona shot an accusing glance at Walter then Jenny before

hurriedly turning and pushing her way through the gathered crowd and up the steps. Jenny followed in her wake, wondering what accusation was wrapped up in that look.

You should have had Walter put a lock on that room, Mum.

'Stay back!' said Walter to the others outside the generator room. 'Hannah!' Walter called as he pushed the door wider and stepped in. His voice bounced back at him off the hard metal walls. The room's pitch-black darkness was pierced by the fading beam from his hand-trigger flashlight. He pumped the trigger several times, setting the dynamo whirring, the beam brightening once more.

Behind him footsteps echoed noisily along the passageway outside and up the stairs at the end; a procession of the concerned.

Walter turned round and raised a hand. 'Stop! I don't want everyone stomping around in here,' he said. 'There're cables, pipes, and all sorts. Not to mention a couple of gas tanks full of highly flammable methane!'

Jenny and the rest of the search party halted in the doorway.

Walter panned his torch around again. 'Hannah! Hannah, love . . . are you hiding in here?'

It was completely silent.

'I really don't think she's here,' he said. 'I'll just take a quick look in the fermenting room. You lot stay there, please.'

He stepped across to the doorway leading to the next room. Jenny could hear Leona's trembling breath. Knowing what she was thinking; they were wasting precious time down here, she could be anywhere on the rigs, perhaps having tripped over the lip of a bulkhead, or fallen off the edge of a Portakabin and broken a bone on the deck below. A myriad of unforgiving hard and rusty metal edges for a child to come to grief on.

Jenny didn't want to even consider the most horrifying possibility; that she'd simply slipped over the side, despite the many railings and catch-nets and grids they'd built over the years for the benefit of the young ones; there were still gaps to be found.

Slipped over the side and gone for ever. Jenny shuddered and could only hope her daughter was not entertaining the same possibility just yet.

Walter emerged from the fermenting room; a quick shake of his jowly face told Jenny there was no sign of her. Then he stopped in his tracks. He aimed the torch beam at the generator.

Jenny took an involuntary step forward into the room and out of the passageway. 'What? Walter?'

He looked up at her, his face frozen.

'Walter?'

'Not another bloody step!' he hissed.

Behind her Jenny heard Leona cry. 'What is it?! Is she there? Hannah!'

Jenny ignored him and pushed forward through the doorway and into the generator room.

'No!!' Walter barked. 'Out!! Everyone stay the fuck out!!'

'Walter, is she there?'

'Get out!! Get out!!' he bellowed, stepping cautiously towards the doorway, plugged with Jenny's form, Leona trying to push her way in behind, the others craning their necks in the passageway.

'The feed pipe's been detached! It's on the floor!!' He reached Jenny and pushed her roughly back. 'Out, everyone out! No one goes in. I need to ventilate the room right now. There's gas everywhere!'

'But is she there?' asked Jenny.

He looked at her quickly and nodded.

Oh, God.

Leona spotted the subtle gesture, intended only for Jenny.

She suddenly screamed and pushed her mother out of the way to get through the narrow door and into the room.

'NO!' Walter grabbed her arm and wrestled her back out through the door into the passage. 'Somebody help me!'

Several pairs of hands restrained her as she struggled and screamed and kicked. 'No!! Let me SEE HER!!'

'Everyone get out! GET OUT!' yelled Walter. 'A spark could set the lot off!' He flapped his hands furiously at them, ushering them back down the passage. He expected Jenny to fall in beside him and assist in urging them towards the stairs at the end. Instead she slipped past him, wrenched the flash-light out of his hand and stepped into the room.

'Jenny! NO!' he barked. 'Get out!!'

She swung the light towards the generator and immediately spotted one of Hannah's bare feet protruding from behind the metal casing; a single sandal on the floor a few inches away.

Instinct overcame her and she rushed forward into the darkness to retrieve her granddaughter, not for one moment considering the risk of a spark of static, or the potential sudden disaster of anything metal hitting or scraping anything else metal; nor for one moment considering the foolishness of pumping the trigger on her wind-up torch to see her way inside as the bulb finally began to fade.

A tiny glimmer from the hand-held dynamo; a glow of light from the bulb, just enough for her to see the glassy-eyed face of her granddaughter lying amidst the cables and pipes of the generator. And just enough time for Jenny to scream as she scooped up Hannah's lifeless body, once more triggering the dynamo in her torch to look into the pale face for any possible sign of life.

Then things flashed white. That's all she remembered.

Chapter 20

Crash Day + 2 weeks

O2 Arena – 'Safety Zone 4',
London

This has to stop right now.

Alan Maxwell looked up from the numbers he'd been scribbling on the dull pink cover of the back of the emergency protocol manual. He looked out of the window of his temporary base of operations – a small office above the Starbucks, overlooking the dome's main entrance plaza. The floor was thick with lines of cots, most of them occupied. Hundreds of them. And there were hundreds more of them out of view, in the open area of the London Piazza, further round the dome's circumference.

We can't take in any more.

The figures, untidy but accurate, were telling him what he already knew. That stored below the dome's main central arena – where Kylie Minogue had performed only a few months ago, where Take That had been intending a reunion concert with Robbie Williams in a few weeks' time – on the endless low-ceilinged mezzanine floor, there was water and high-protein meal packs for sixty thousand civilians for twelve weeks.

Alan had been down there on the first day to inspect the floor. His first impression had been one of awe; that somebody, somewhere up the emergency authority's rickety chain of command, had actually made sure their job was done to the letter. It seemed that someone – God bless them – had actually been *ahead* of the game for once, making sure Safety Zone 4 had everything it needed to fulfil its role providing a safe haven to sixty thousand civilians. Pallets of cardboard boxes, plastic-wrapped and waiting, filled the floor as far as he could see. As well as food and water, there were four emergency generators, all of them running noisily, with enough diesel to run them day and night for three months.

A section of the mezzanine floor was filled with crates of medication, antibiotics, anti-inflammatories, refrigeration units, already plugged in and humming, filled with bags of blood and insulin. There was equipment enough, still boxed and waiting to be unpacked and assembled, to set up a dentist's surgery, even an operating theatre.

Alan had been amazed that in a bloody useless country such as this, a country that seemed to teeter on the brink of complete collapse every time more than a couple of inches of snow fell, so complete and thorough a job had been done at such incredibly short notice.

Heartwarming in a way, that when push came to shove, when it *really* mattered, there were civil servants who could tick the right boxes and make sure the job got done.

But that was a couple of weeks ago now.

That was back when he thought – as did everyone else – that this was going to be a disastrous, worldwide, three- or four-week Katrina-like event. An event that would shake the world. Rouse everyone from their complacency and remind the world's leaders and policy-makers that in the pursuit of endless economic growth and rising profit margins, the world had become a terribly fragile thing.

That's what he'd thought.

Four or five days of civil unrest, maybe a week of it; that's what he'd been expecting. Those civilians unable to seek refuge in one of the safety zones would be borderline malnourished, perhaps suffering from water-borne infections. And, yes, there'd be deaths . . . thousands of them most likely. Those caught up in the rioting. Those caught breaking curfew. Those caught red-handed looting. The streets of every UK city, town and village would be a horrendous mess that needed to be cleaned up. Every service stretched to breaking point as the country recovered. That was how bad he thought it would get.

Then there'd be years of litigation; years of pointing fingers and blaming the government for not seeing it coming, the oil industry for not ensuring some sort of redundancy in its supply chain. Then, of course, once the world was put back together again, the endless documentaries on TV hungrily picking over the finer details, examining what had gone wrong, and dramas reliving those few summer weeks, spinning out of the grislier details into stories to fill broadcast schedules. Alan had imagined TV channels would dine out on the oil crash for many, many years to come, as once they had on 9/11.

But he'd had all those thoughts two weeks ago.

Since then it had become patently clear to him, if not also to many of the emergency volunteer staff working for him, that this crash was far, far worse than a Katrina-like event. What made it worse, what made it a different order of event entirely, was the fact that it had hit *everyone*.

Where, with the victims living on the rooftops of New Orleans, or crammed into the Louisiana Superdome, there was an outside world ready to step in – albeit sluggishly – to drop supplies, to airlift those stranded, to roar in with convoys of National Guard troops to restore law and order, in this case, there was no one.

His eyes drifted across the cots, the orange-jacketed emergency workers dotted amongst them.

There's no one coming for us.

No one coming. He'd had a digitally encrypted communications line with GZ – Government Zone – in Cheltenham set up here in his Starbucks office. The emergency committee were based in GZ, complete with several senior echelons of civil servants, a sizeable garrison of troops and,

141

already, sixty thousand civilians within its compound receiving emergency rations and medical care. The first few days they'd been assuring him that extra troops and policemen were on their way. That he should calm down because SZ3 – Wembley Stadium – was doing just fine and they had *only* police holding their perimeter, no military personnel at all. They told him he just needed to hold tight, keep letting in those who turned up looking for safety, keep order, and stay calm. Yes, things were a complete bloody awful mess, but they would settle down by the end of the week and then there'd be the *real* work to do.

This morning, though, the line to GZ was jammed with competing calls coming in, and too few communications officers to deal with them. He finally got through to a harried-sounding junior emergency worker who admitted they were having some teething problems of their own. And this time, finally, acknowledging that, no – surprise, surprise – there weren't any military personnel spare to send over. The young man hadn't been particularly interested in his daily situation report either, suggesting that he write it up from now on and fax it over.

Alan was back on hold again, a whisper of crackling static and a digital tone that beeped every thirty seconds; been that way for the last hour.

The figures scribbled in front of him told him far more than he was getting out of GZ. So far, according to *his* people, they'd processed into the dome about two thousand civilians. Pretty much all of them in the first week, and merely a trickle in the second. The thick crowd pressing against the wire in week one had thinned out after word had spread amongst them that SZ3, SZ5 (Battersea) and SZ7 (Heathrow) were letting in far more people, far more quickly.

There were still a few every day. They usually seemed to turn up in the evenings as the sun settled and the distant sporadic noises of gunfire, isolated hoots and screams echoed out over the still, dark rooftops of south London as the night-time shenanigans began.

His workers let them in, no more than a dozen at a time, as per his standing orders, registered their details and listened with ashen faces to what they had to say.

Alan had sat in on a few of these faltering conversations, letting the orange-jacketed workers, usually professionals, care-workers, gently coax out their stories.

And, listening, it was increasingly obvious there was nothing beyond their spirals of wire, beyond the reach of their floodlights, nothing but a shambolic landscape of smouldering cars, smashed windows and cluttered streets, and small gangs of feral chavs happily getting by on what still sat on shelves in shops. There was nothing out there that was going to rebuild itself.

It's got to stop.

Alan had three thousand people inside the dome already. Three thousand mouths to feed. Far fewer than the sixty thousand he'd been instructed to allow in. But then, he tapped the pen against the pad in front of him . . .

But then those were my instructions when we thought we were going to be feeding them for only three months.

If he closed the door on any more civilians now, if it remained just three thousand mouths to feed, then the crates and boxes, stacked floor-to-ceiling on the mezzanine floor below, would keep them all going for roughly five years. More, probably, if he sent out his soldiers to scavenge, if he reduced the rations being handed out daily.

'Five years,' he uttered quietly. Just saying that sent a chill through him. If that's what he was considering – considering in terms of keeping things together here *for years* – then it really was a worldwide first-class fuck-up; a modern-day equivalent of the collapse of Rome, of Sodom and Gomorrah.

It really was all over, wasn't it? All over, except for isolated places like this.

The line went dead. Without thinking, he dialled GZ again and got the digital beep of a busy line once more.

He looked out at the cots, the slowly milling crowd gathered around a long row of benches where warmed breakfast rations were being doled out. He looked across the plaza, at the floodlights mounted on tall tripods beaming cold and clinical over them, despite the pale grey dawn seeping in through the wall of glass at the front. It was bright enough that those floods didn't need to be on. He thought of all four generators thudding away down on the mezzanine floor, eating slowly and surely into their stockpile of precious diesel.

'Shit,' he muttered, putting the phone down and standing up.

It was time for a major rethink.

Chapter 21

10 years AC

Dr Gupta watched the ceremony unfold in sombre silence, the north wind gusted mournfully through the spars and struts around the drilling deck, as Dennis, Howard and David carefully lowered the small wrapped parcel of Hannah's body towards the surging sea below, boiling with swirling white horses this morning.

Beside the opening in the deck – a grille pulled aside to allow them to lower her through, the very same grille they'd all been waltzing on just a week ago – Walter and Jacob stood, both spilling quiet tears into their hands.

The two people who should have been standing there, watching her go, were absent. Jenny, in the infirmary, drugged to the gills and fighting a fever.

And Leona.

She turned to look over her shoulder at the far-off accommodation platform, and yes, she could just about make her out; a forlorn, lonely figure standing on the helipad and watching the ceremony.

Poor, poor girl.

Jacob had tried talking her down. Tami had tried to talk her into coming down at least to see Hannah buried. She'd tried explaining that the healing of that awful pain in her chest could only begin with the saying of a proper goodbye. Leona, stubborn as her mother, simply refused to come down and remained up there as she had the last couple of days. All day long, a lonely vigil up there with only the swaying tomato

145

plants for company. As far as Tami knew, she'd not come down to sleep. The Sutherlands' cabin looked unchanged; Jenny's cut hair was still on the floor, Martha's hairdresser's scissors, comb and brush remained where they'd been dropped on the end of one of the cots.

Valérie Latoc offered a prayer as the bound corpse inched its way down. Martha stood beside him, her hands clasped, her dark cheeks shining with tears, her shoulders hitched.

'. . . such a precious spirit, a gift from God. An innocent who only knew this world and not the old one; not spoiled by the luxuries and privileges and distractions of that time. Here she found love, safety and happiness. And here she . . .'

Tami detected the grief in the man's voice. He too had been touched by Hannah; his nurse, his carer, his little guardian angel.

Oh, Leona, you should be down here.

The distant silhouette remained perfectly still, anorak flapping in the breeze. Tami could only imagine the poor girl's lonely torment. She needed to be right here, to see how many lives her daughter had touched; to see all the children in her class crying, to see the others, even the likes of Alice Harton, shedding genuine tears for her.

She was loved, Leona. Your daughter was loved by us all.

And she truly needed to witness her daughter's wrapped form slide into the water and fade into the depths. Closure; the way back to them, back from her lonely vigil up there, back to the land of the living – it could only begin with closure.

Tami could see, though, even from here, she could see it in her resolute stillness on the edge of the helipad. She'd seen it in the firm set of her jaw earlier; the lifeless gaze of her eyes and the calm, stubborn way she'd politely refused to come down for the ceremony.

Leona had no intention of coming back to them.

Tami suspected she knew how this ended. Tomorrow

morning, perhaps the morning after, Leona was simply going to be gone; at some point during the night, she was simply going to step out into the darkness and be gone.

Valérie Latoc finished his prayer and a solemn 'amen' rippled amongst those gathered around the hole in the deck. The old men lowered the linen bundle the last few yards towards the sea. A rolling wave rose up and soaked the cloth, rolled the body off its harness and took her away.

Jacob and Walter squatted down by the edge and together tossed a small plastic figurine after her. It tumbled and spun in the gusting wind between the platform's legs, pink and bright and finally lost amidst the grey froth.

Walter held Jacob closely as his shoulders heaved; more than a family friend – Walter was family. Tami wished Leona was down here, too, so she could hold her; let her open her heart onto her shoulder, soak her jumper with tears.

Oh, Leona . . .

She could see which way this was heading. It was touch and go with Jenny. There was a fair chance she might not pull through. And if she did pass away, young Jacob then would probably quietly leave. Then they'd *all* be gone; all the Sutherlands; the family who'd started this place.

Chapter 22

Crash Day + 27 weeks
5.45 a.m.

O2 Arena – 'Safety Zone 4',
London

Lieutenant Adam Brooks blew warm air into his cold hands as he stepped out through the dome's main entrance into the still-dark morning. Both guards saluted; Gunner Lawrence paired up with one of the Met officers. Lawrence made a better job of it as Adam acknowledged the salute and strode quickly past them beyond the pool of light.

His radio crackled again. 'Sir?'

'I'm on my way over,' replied Adam. 'How many of them did you say?'

Ahead he could see the faint glint of a torch beam flickering around in the darkness, picking out something beyond the wall of the barricade.

'Hard to say, sir. I guess . . . I dunno, several dozen of 'em. Maybe thirty or forty.'

That many? His pace quickened, standard-issue heels clicking noisily in the darkness. They'd not had a group that big turn up outside for months. These days they came in twos or threes, often alone; malnourished people who looked like scarecrows, faces rendered blank and immobile.

As he approached the guard point he snapped off his radio and called out. 'Lieutenant Brooks approaching!'

The torch beam that had been lancing out over the barricade wall swung his way momentarily and picked him out.

Adam winced and shaded his eyes. 'You say thirty to forty?' he called out to Gunner Huntley.

'Yes, sir. Looks about that.'

Adam jogged over to the base of the wall; six-foot-high panels of corrugated iron pilfered from the roof of the factory out in no-man's-land, welded together side by side, and topped with loops of razor wire. He climbed up onto a small crate and stood beside Huntley.

What he was about to say to these people he'd already said to hundreds of groups before. And the response was always the same; the desperate pleas to be let in, hopeless sobbing. Adam took the torch off Gunner Huntley and panned it down across the small crowd of pale oval faces – smudged with dirt, expressionless, eyes narrowed from the glare of torch-light, and all of them shivering from the cool night air.

'This is London Safety Zone Four,' he announced with tired formality, a cloud of his breath danced brightly across the torch beam. 'I'm afraid we can't take in any more people at this time, unless you have a special skill, in which case you can be admitted for a probationary period.'

There was an expected mewling of defeated voices amongst them.

'I'm sorry,' he replied, 'that's just the way it is.'

The voices raised in anger and frustration. Adam quickly counted. Forty-seven of them. He turned to Huntley. 'Better get Sergeant Walfield and a section of men up here, to be on the safe side.'

Huntley nodded, dropped heavily down off the crate, his webbing jangling, and scooted noisily off into the darkness towards the dome.

Adam turned back to them. 'Look, I'm sorry. We have barely enough supplies for the people already inside. We can't spread what we've got any further.'

Somebody's voice cut through the chorus of protesting voices. 'We've come from the Cheltenham safety zone.'

Cheltenham? GZ-C?

'Who said that?' he asked, panning his beam across their flinching faces.

A hand rose up. A woman; thin and dark-haired, her face almost as white as a ghost.

'I'm a government worker. One of the emergency workers.'

The others around her suddenly cast suspicious glances at her. Adam noticed a gap growing around the woman and a palpable sense of rage simmering amongst the others.

'Have you got ID on you?' he called down.

She fished inside her fleece top as a woman standing next to her spat in her direction. 'You fuckin' bitch,' she hissed, 'you're one of *them*?'

The woman produced her laminated ID badge, dangling from a chain. From where he stood it appeared to be legitimate, the same as that worn by the workers in SZ-4; Home Office logo, name and details, passport photo . . . although from here Adam couldn't really tell if that was the woman's mugshot.

'Okay, you better come in,' he said waving her forward.

Before the others rip you to pieces.

He nodded down at the soldier manning the gate to slip the bolt. 'Keep your shoulder against the door, though.' His torch beam swung across the others. 'The rest of you stay back!'

'Fucking bitch!' shouted a man. 'You're a guv'ment worker? And we shared our food with you!'

The woman eased herself through the snarling faces towards the door, grimacing as someone spat in her face; another man, barely more than a lad, mimicked headbutting her. So close, in fact, that Adam thought he'd actually done it as she recoiled, raising her hands to protect her face.

'Fucking fat-cat bastards like you an' the guv'ment left us outside to starve.'

'Taking care of their own, again.'

150

'Go on, then, fuck off . . . bitch!'

She reached the rough rusted metal of the gate and looked up at Adam. 'Please! Open the gate! They're going to kill me!'

Adam swung the assault rifle off his shoulder and cocked it noisily. 'Please, everyone, back off . . . right now. Or I *will* shoot.'

The crowd made some space, reluctantly drawing away from the base of the wall.

'Please! Let us in!' someone called out. 'It's dangerous out here.'

He ignored the voices. 'All right, open it,' he uttered down to the lad by the gate. It cracked open on thick rusty hinges that creaked noisily. The woman saw the gap and squeezed hastily through it, just as the others, yards away, instinctively stepped forward, some of them no doubt hoping to file through in her wake.

'I said stay back!' Adam shouted.

The woman was in and the soldier swiftly rammed the thick bolts back in place.

'The rest of you,' said Adam, 'should disperse. I'm sorry, there's nothing here for you.'

There was abuse hurled back. He could deal with the 'fuck-you's, the 'fascist bastard's . . . what he struggled with was those who desperately tried to appeal to his humanity.

'What do we do now?' an elderly woman asked. 'Please? I don't know what to do.'

'You should get out of London,' he replied. 'All of you! Get out whilst you're still fit and able enough. The city's dead space. You've got a chance out in the country.'

He heard the heavy clump of boots on tarmac and jangling webbing approaching. Sergeant Walfield and a section of their boys emerged from the dark.

'Everything all right up there, sir?' Walfield bellowed.

'You people really should go now,' he said to the others outside. 'We've got orders to fire upon civilians if they attempt to get over the barricade.'

The people drew a few steps back into the thick darkness; a pitiful mob that he suspected were all going to die sometime over the coming winter. If the cold or bad water didn't get them, then one of the many armed gangs would find them.

'Good luck,' he called out. Someone replied that he should go fuck himself.

Sergeant Walfield stood below him, eyeing the woman suspiciously. 'Don't we have standing orders to let *no one* in, sir?'

Adam stepped down off the crate to join them. He panned his torch across the woman's ID card again; the mugshot in the corner looked like her.

'Yes, Danny, but I think Mr Maxwell might be interested in talking to this one.'

Chapter 23

Crash Day + 27 weeks
6.15 a.m.

O2 Arena – 'Safety Zone 4',
London

Alan Maxwell stared impassively at the woman. The name on her ID card was Sinita Rajput.

'You say you're from GZ, Cheltenham?'

She nodded. 'Yes.'

He steepled his fingers beneath his bearded chin, deep in thought, his bushy brows locked together like two links of a heavy chain. The emergency contact line he'd had with them had finally failed eight weeks ago. If he tried dialling now he didn't even get the busy tone, just static. In the weeks leading up to that, his calls were only being answered with a pre-recorded message informing him that all communication officers were otherwise engaged and that he should call back at another time.

Maxwell offered her a warm smile by the light of the lamp on his desk. Its glow flickered slightly as the solitary generator hiccuped momentarily. Come dawn it was turned off. Daylight they got for free. For an hour in the early evening he allowed two of the four generators to turn over, giving them enough power for cooking and to run a couple of flat-screen TVs and DVD players. One of Lieutenant Brooks' foraging patrols had brought back a supermarket trolley full of DVDs from a ransacked HMV. It was something to keep his people distracted for a short period every day.

'So, Sinita, tell me what's going on over there.'

She looked up at him sitting behind his desk, flanked by

Brooks on one side and Morgan – Maxwell's deputy super-visor – on the other. Alan insisted they both remained on their feet when they had their daily briefing with him; a small thing really, just a gentle reminder that he was the one in charge here. The Chief . . . as it were.

'Things went bad there,' she said, after gathering her thoughts for a moment. 'I . . . I was one of the medical team. A ward nurse before the crash . . .'

'Good. That will be useful. Please . . . carry on,' said Alan patiently.

'We took in roughly sixty thousand at Cheltenham. Plus the thousand emergency workers, soldiers and government people. There was talk from the first day the safety zone started taking people in, that this . . . this crisis would blow itself out within a month. So they told us to distribute standard maintenance allowances—'

'How much?' Alan was intrigued.

'Fifteen hundred calories per adult female, two thousand calories for men. It was about nine weeks after the crash that my supervisor was telling the government people that it was better we started lowering the allowance.'

Alan nodded. His people had been on twelve hundred calories from day one.

'They agreed a while later,' she continued. 'But then it had to be a *big* cut. We were handing out eight-hundred-calorie nutrition packages for a month before they suddenly started rounding people up at . . . at gunpoint and removing them from the safety zone. They . . .'

She shook her head and closed her eyes, clearly willing herself not to cry, or appear weak in front of these strangers. Her jaw clenched. She took a moment before continuing. 'They . . . the soldiers were selecting non-essential workers. Old people, unskilled people. It was awful. Then, there was news from . . . from, I think it was Heathrow first, then Wembley.'

154

'What news?'

'The riots. Riots inside.'

Alan frowned. He'd heard rumours from several groups of people who'd tried their luck here. But nothing confirmed by GZ-C.

'They lost control in those places,' the woman continued. 'The soldiers were overrun by the refugees, the storage areas ransacked . . . completely gone in just a few minutes. The news made the government people at Cheltenham panic. One morning they started evicting the civilians that were left, just pushing them towards the exit. And then I think someone heard that all the other safe zones were rioting, and that news spread like wildfire . . .'

Her lips trembled, curled – her chin creased and dimpled.

'It's okay, Sinita,' said Alan. He got up, walked round and sat on the edge of the desk and patted her shoulder reassuringly.

She took a deep breath. 'It was a massacre. I saw hundreds of women, children, and boys and men . . . lying on top of each other. Those that didn't get killed . . . they ran.'

'And you?'

'I . . . I'm an essential worker,' she said with a humourless smile. 'I got to stay.'

She wiped her wet cheeks with the back of her hand. 'We lasted another two weeks, I suppose, on what was left. Then the soldiers turned on everyone else.'

'On the emergency authorities?'

'Oh, yes, the civilian emergency volunteers, the civil servants, the cabinet members . . . everyone not in their unit.' She looked up at Lieutenant Brooks, her wet eyes narrowing ever so slightly. She reached for her ID card and held it up. 'This piece of plastic didn't mean anything all of a sudden. Several other women I was working with were raped and . . .' Her words ground to a halt. 'I . . .' She started and faltered.

'It's okay, my dear, take your time.'

'So,' she wiped her nose on her sleeve, 'so, I left before they did the same to me.'

Alan stifled an urge to turn around and study Flight Lieutenant Brooks' expression. During the first few weeks he'd been haranguing Cheltenham to send him more soldiers to help guard the dome. Now he wondered whether he'd actually been fortunate not to have a regiment of troops sharing the dome with them. Too many men in uniform and a more senior ranking officer than Brooks might have been something for Alan to worry about if supplies eventually began to get tight here.

Not if . . . when . . . supplies become tight, Alan. When. They're not going to last for ever.

Maxwell shuffled uncomfortably. They had quite a few years' worth as things stood. But he wondered if Brooks and his two platoons of RAF gunners might one day decide to take matters into their own hands, decide who was essential and who wasn't.

Something to keep in mind.

Maxwell offered the woman a kindly smile – one he hoped was comforting, fatherly. 'Well, Ms Rajput, let me assure you that you'll be safe here.'

She nodded, eager to believe that, and then her face was in her hands, her shoulders shaking; her firm resolve to appear the strong woman in front of them had lasted as long as it could; she weakened and crumbled.

'There's food and water for you. We have an urn of heated water downstairs in the main piazza. Go down there and one of my people will sort you out a cup of tea.'

She stood up, pushing the chair back. 'Th-thank you,' she managed to sob. 'I . . . I . . . was—'

'That's all right, Ms Rajput. You go and sort yourself out now. Morgan here will show you down and take your details. Help you settle in.'

'You . . . you're a kind man,' she smiled weakly. 'But how . . . how have you . . . ?'

'Coped so well?'

She nodded. 'I heard . . . from someone . . . I think I heard, that every last one of our safe zones ended in a mess.' She managed a haunted smile of relief. 'I really thought it was all . . . all gone.'

'We've held out because difficult decisions were made early on.'

'What?'

Maxwell gazed out of the office window looking down onto the rows of cots below. Dawn had broken and pallid grey light slipped across the entrance plaza. The people were stirring, roused by the clatter of a ladle on a metal catering pan.

'Morgan will tell you,' he continued, 'I made the call to let in a lot fewer than I was told to.' He shook his head. 'Hardest decision I ever made, but I believe it was the right one.'

She nodded. 'Yes . . . yes, I suppose it was.'

Morgan led her out of the office. The door closed behind them leaving him alone with Brooks.

'My God,' uttered Brooks eventually. 'Then, what? It's just us now?'

Maxwell nodded. 'Us, and I suppose a few small groups here and there.' He laughed. 'The sort of survivalist nut jobs who've been hoping for something like this for years. I imagine they're like pigs in mud.'

'Jesus.'

'The thing is, Brooks, this dome, those people out there, *that* is the UK now. That's it. We're what's left of law and order, what's left of the chain of command.' He shrugged unhappily. 'And I suppose by default that's going to make me . . . well, that makes me the Prime Minister, doesn't it? The Big Cheese.'

Brooks looked down at him sharply but said nothing. He swallowed noisily, shuffled uncomfortably.

Maxwell stood up and stepped towards the window, looking down at Starbucks' outside seating area, at Morgan leading the woman through the chairs and tables. He sat her down on an unassigned cot, produced a clipboard and began asking her questions, scribbling down her answers.

If this is all there is now, just us – he shot a glance at Brooks – *then I need to think about the future. Who I can trust . . .*

'Brooks,' he said, 'I think I'm going to have to make some changes round here.'

The Journey

Chapter 24

10 years AC

Bracton

Jacob watched Walter silently scanning the horizon as he helmed the yacht, all the sails out and fluttering, the diesel engine chugging and spitting; turned on to make better time.

He knew the old man was desperate to find Leona; desperate to find her for Jenny. Behind the gruff mask he'd kept on his face since the explosion, Jacob knew he blamed himself for Hannah's death, for Jenny's injuries . . . and now, unless he could find her and persuade her to come home, he'd blame himself for Leona's departure, too.

Jacob returned his gaze to the sea. The small dinghy she'd taken had only a sixty-horsepower outboard motor on the back. With the sea as choppy as it was this morning she was going to make painfully slow progress. There was no knowing exactly when she'd set off, other than sometime before first light; so there was no knowing how much of a head start she had on them.

Nathan's eyes were far better than his. He stood on the foredeck beside him, probing the gently rolling sea for the telltale line of white trailing suds, or the dark outline of the small dinghy.

Jacob couldn't believe she could do this. Just up and leave him, leave Mum. He couldn't believe it, but had somehow half expected it. Hannah had always been her argument for not returning to the mainland yet. Hannah was the reason she wanted to make their life aboard the rigs. And she'd never needed to explain to Jacob why, because they both

161

remembered that winter morning the men came and did what they did.

But Hannah was gone now. Half, if not most, of her reason for staying gone.

But there's still me . . . and Mum, Leona.

It stung that she'd just bailed out on them.

'There's Bracton!' shouted Nathan; nothing more distinct than the pale, feathered silhouettes of rows of loading cranes, the outline of several small commercial freighters still securely moored at the quayside. William, Howard and Helen – those who'd hastily volunteered to come along and help Walter and the boys search for Leona – craned their necks port side to get a better view around the mast. There had been dozens more who'd offered to come, but Walter had been wary of overloading the boat with the well-intentioned and slowing it down.

'See any sign of her ahead?' shouted Walter.

Nathan squinted and shaded his eyes against the glare of the white sky. 'No.'

Half an hour later, they were tying up at their usual spot, right next to where the dinghy bobbed and bumped against the concrete, secured to a mooring cleat by a careless half hitch and a loop that would have unravelled itself eventually.

Jacob was the first onto the quay. 'LEONA!!' he shouted, his voice bouncing back at him off the warehouse walls across the way.

'LEONA!!' His echo filled the silent waterfront.

Walter stepped ashore. 'Right, there's six of us. We're not all splitting up and going in different bloody directions. Two groups of three, one gun each and we meet back here in one hour, all right?'

The others stepped ashore.

'Nathan, here you go,' he said passing him the army issue SA80. 'You and Jake and—'

'I'll go with them,' said Helen.

'All right.' He turned to the other two men. 'William, Howard and me then. Don't go any further than the commercial area; the warehouses, the loading points, the offices. Okay?'

Everyone nodded.

'And back here in precisely one hour. No later.'

Twenty minutes later they were out of sight of the others, walking amongst the low industrial units of the port authority buildings, when it occurred to Jacob he knew *exactly* where his sister was; or at least where she was heading.

'She's going home.'

'What?'

Jacob turned to look at Nathan and Helen. 'Going home. London.'

Helen's eyes widened. 'London?'

'Why'd she do that, Jay?'

Jacob shrugged. 'I don't know, just a feeling. She's talked about wanting to see our old house again.'

Both boys looked at each other in silence; an entire conversation within a glance. They'd discussed, fantasised many times about taking the opportunity one day. It was Nathan who spoke first. 'Jay, what about now? What if we go now?'

Helen had never been part of the plan though. He glanced at the girl. 'Nathan, we can't just leave her here, and she's too young to come with—'

'I know about it,' she cut him off.

'Know about what?'

'The lights,' she said. 'I know about the lights in London.'

'What? How?'

She glanced at Nathan. 'He told me.'

Nathan shrugged guiltily. 'Sorry, Jay, I know it was like a secret, but . . .'

'I bribed him,' she finished with a cunning smile. 'I let him have a feel-up.'

Nathan looked down at his feet, shamefaced. 'She knew somethin' was up.'

Jacob shook his head. 'Oh shit, Nathan!'

'Anyway,' continued Helen, 'I heard some of it, you two and Mr Latoc talking at the party. I know he seen something. I knew it. I knew he wasn't telling us everything he seen. I saw him telling you two, and I heard some of it.'

'Well it doesn't matter, you *can't* come, Helen,' said Jacob. 'It could be dangerous.'

She snorted derisively at him. 'Piss off, I can look after myself as well as you two idiots.'

'Look, man, are we really going to go, Jay?' asked Nathan. 'I mean, *really*? Right now?'

Jacob knew *he* was. He realised, for him, there was no choice in the matter. 'She's all I got, Nate. If Mum doesn't . . .' he bit his lip. 'If Mum doesn't make it, Leona's all I got left.' He turned and pointed towards the town. 'She's in there somewhere. Maybe she's already on the road. I have to go and see.'

'And then if we help you find her, we'll go down and see London, right?' asked Helen.

The boys looked at each other. 'Jake, man? You wanna do that?'

He realised he couldn't think of anything beyond finding his sister right now. As far as he was concerned he could promise them a trip to the moon, just as long as he found Leona first.

'Sure, all right,' he muttered.

Chapter 25

10 years AC

Outside Bracton,
Norfolk

An hour later, they were on the A road out of Bracton on bicycles they'd pulled out of a toyshop, at just about the same moment Walter must have found the scribbled note Helen had sneaked back and placed in the yacht's cockpit.

It was the only way Jacob could think she'd go, along the main road heading south-west, keeping herself to the middle of the road, and warily scanning the untidy gone-to-seed fields either side, the tall weeds and untamed bushes that threatened to encroach on the road from the crumbling hard shoulder.

He prayed she'd not been so lucky to find herself a bicycle to use, or if she had, that at least she wasn't pedalling as hard as they were. He kept finding himself drawing ahead of the others, desperate to eat up the road ahead of him and find her.

Mid-morning he'd stopped yet again to wait for the others to catch up and to take a swig from a bottle of water in his shoulder bag, when he thought he saw some movement up ahead.

He squinted, trying to make sense of the uncertain distant dark outline on the road; something low and round. Glancing back he could see the other two, broaching a low hill, struggling to catch him up. He put the bottle back in his bag, lifted his feet off the road and cautiously rode a little closer until his useless long vision gave him something more to work with.

A wooden chair in the middle of the road and someone slumped on it, back to him.

Even from this far he recognised the slope of her shoulders. 'Leona?'

She didn't stir.

Please no . . . please no . . .

He pedalled furiously forward. 'Leona!' he whimpered, finally clattering to a halt a dozen yards away and tossing the bike down at his feet. 'Leona?' he called out again softly. 'It's me! Jake!'

This time he thought he detected the slightest movement.

He was taking the last steps toward her when she slowly turned to look round at him. 'Hey,' was all she said.

Jacob was about to reach out for her when he saw one hand resting in her lap, holding a knife, and on the wrist of her other arm the light and unsuccessful scoring of the blade; nicks and scratches that told of squeamish attempts at a decisive incision.

She laughed humourlessly. 'You know me . . .'

He nodded.

'Chuck my guts at the first sight of blood.' She sighed and turned back to look at the road ahead, straight as a Roman highway. 'I thought I'd just wait here a while.'

He knelt down in front of her; her eyes were over the top of his head and they remained on the flat horizon.

'Lee,' he whispered, reaching out for the knife in her lap. 'Lee, can I have it?'

Her fingers tightened around the handle until her knuckles bulged white.

'Lee?' She was still far away. 'Lee!' Her eyes finally dropped down to look at him.

'Sis,' he squeezed her hand, 'I . . . I need your help.'

She said nothing, but a lethargic curiosity made her cock an eyebrow.

166

'I . . . my bike chain came off, Lee. Do you know how the shitting thing goes back on?'

She closed her eyes slowly and sighed. 'Jesus, Jake. Can't you do anything?'

He smiled and shook his head. 'No.'

She eased her grasp on the knife and he gently took it from her. 'Not without you, I can't. I'm rubbish without you.'

'Always a dork,' she uttered, and pressed out a wan smile.

He grinned, tears on his cheeks. 'And you were always a stroppy cow.'

'I know.'

Jacob glanced back up the road. Nathan and Helen had stopped their bikes a hundred yards short; sensibly figuring they ought to hold back for the moment.

'Lee, you were always the strong one. You were strong for me once, do you remember? Back in the house?'

She nodded.

Oh, yes . . . she remembered cowering in the darkness of their London home, the small suburban street outside dancing with the light of burning cars, several dozen kids drunk on what they'd looted from the off licence around the corner and on the end-of-the-world party atmosphere. For them it was the rave to end all raves. Fun and games. Looting and raping.

Then they'd decided to play treasure hunt and invade the homes one by one.

Leona still awoke at night reliving their desperate fight to keep the Bad Boys out of the house, hitting, swiping, scratching and biting through broken downstairs windows then finally running and hiding upstairs as they broke in through the barricaded front door. Hiding beneath the sink unit in the bedroom. Jacob, only eight then, trembling in her arms. They could hear the boys laughing, braying as they searched for their prize to rape, hunting for the 'smurfette' they knew was hiding somewhere inside.

We can sme-e-e-ell you-u-u-u . . . come out!

'Me, Nathan and Helen, we're going down to London.'

'Oh.'

'The lights have come on in London.'

She frowned. 'What?'

'Mr Latoc said he saw them . . . from a long way off. A big glow over the Thames.'

Leona stirred in the chair. 'He said that?'

'Yeah.'

'Across London?'

She missed the hesitation in his reply. 'All along it, all over, that's what he said.'

Some sense of *possibility* tingled inside her. An alternative to sitting here in the middle of the road until she could muster enough willpower to push that stupid blunt tip all the way into her wrist.

An alternative.

'They've been rebuilding quietly,' continued Jacob. 'Nathan reckons they wouldn't be radioing out and telling everyone that they're rebuilding things 'cause it might draw too many people at once. Swamp them, you know?'

Hannah loved the stories you told her of the past, didn't she? She loved the idea of shopping malls, ten-pin bowling, IMAX cinemas, fun fairs . . .

'That's why we haven't heard about it on the radios,' Jacob continued. 'It's a secret. They've been doing it bit by bit. Otherwise there'd be people coming across from other countries too, probably.'

. . . she liked the idea of Piccadilly Circus, the Trocadero, all glittering lights and neon signs; ice-skating at Queens and then a pizza afterwards; disco dancing to naff Abba songs till the early hours and then Ben and Jerry's ice cream for breakfast.

'It's one of those safe zones, I reckon, Lee. One of them that's come to life after all this time, and now it's rebuilding the city. It's remaking our home.'

Home. Hannah wants you to find home. The fairytale home, real home; not those five rusting platforms in the middle of the North Sea.

'What about Mum?'

Jacob was quiet for a few moments. 'Dr Gupta reckons she'll pull through. She's strong. We left a note. Telling them we're going to see what's happening in London. Then we'll come back.'

She could hear a lot more pain and conflict in his voice than he was prepared to own up to. As for herself, right now, Leona felt nothing for Mum but a dim sense of regret, clouded by blame and anger; some of it deserved, most of it not. Every ounce of grief she'd cried out in the last few days had been for Hannah. But then this kind of pain mostly flowed that way, didn't it? Downwards – mother to child. Mum knew that, she'd understand.

'If it's all getting fixed up, we can come back and get everyone to join us and return to London. How cool would that be?'

Leona nodded.

'Just a scouting trip,' he added. 'That's all. We're going to go find out and report back.'

London. Home.

Perhaps there'd be a chance to revisit their abandoned house in Shepherd's Bush. To lie on her old bed once more, look at the faded posters on her pink walls. And if this glistening promise of lights turned out to be an empty promise, a mirage that came to nothing, then she could think of far worse places to come to a fitting end than in her childhood room, snug beneath her quilt, and Dad – Andy Sutherland, oil engineer, father, husband – lying still in the next bedroom, undisturbed these last ten years.

Going home.

'Can I come along with you?' she found herself asking.

Jacob hugged her clumsily. He was always clumsy, her

little brother. He mumbled something into her shoulder. She stretched an arm out and hugged him tightly. Not just a sparrow-chested little dork any more, but a young man with broad shoulders. He was big enough that they could look after each other now.

'Thank you, Jake,' she whispered, planting a kiss on his head amidst the tousled hair.

'So,' he replied, letting her go and swiping at his face with the back of his hand, 'we need to find you a bike and stuff.'

Chapter 26

10 years AC

Jenny stared at him, sitting on the end of her cot. His face was still young, still thirty-nine, still carrying that tan he'd picked up last time he'd returned from a contract abroad; his fine buzz-cut strawberry-blond hair, a goatee beard and several days of stubble catching it up: Andy Sutherland, her dead husband, exactly as she remembered him.

You did well, Jenny, he said, a smile tugging his lips. *I'm so proud of you.*

'Oh, God, Andy,' she cried, knowing he couldn't really be sitting here. Knowing, at best, this was her fevered mind playing games with her. But it didn't matter. It was a good, lucid hallucination. Right now she was happy to have that.

'I've missed you so much,' her voice cracked painfully.

I've missed you, too. His voice, his soft Kiwi accent . . . but she knew they were *her* words. She reached out for his hand, wincing at the pain from the burns up her arm and across her shoulders, her neck.

Don't, Jenny.

She knew he was right, her mind – or perhaps it was the drugs – had given her this much. She should be thankful for that.

'Andy, your granddaughter . . . Hannah, she was beautiful.' Her voice failed, leaving just a whisper. 'You should have seen her.'

She was a pickle, wasn't she?

'She was. Just like Leona was at her age.'

171

Andy smiled. *Yes. Stubborn.*

In her dream, she could feel tears rolling down her cheeks. The saltiness stung her left cheek where the skin was open and raw and trying desperately to knit.

Andy looked so young; thirty-nine still.

'I feel old, Andy. Since you died it's been so bloody hard. So many days that I've wanted to curl up somewhere with a bottle of pills and just admit defeat.'

Survival is a hard business, Jenny. We got lucky over the last century and a half. Like a lottery winner, we all grew fat and lazy. You know what I'm talking about.

We. He was talking about mankind, talking about oil – the subject had obsessed him over the final years of their marriage. He'd become a Cassandra on the subject. An engineer who could see the fracture marks in the engine casing; the lookout who could see the approaching iceberg where no one else could, or even wanted to.

Andy had once told her that the twentieth century was the oil century; every major event, every war, every political decision had oil behind it. A century of jockeying for position, musical chairs to see who ended up sitting on the biggest reserves when the music stopped.

I could have done more, he said. *I could have warned more people.*

'We knew, and what did we do?' They'd talked about moving out of London, as far from a population centre as possible, but they never did. It ended up being just talk.

You did well to survive the crash, he said. *Got our children through the worst of it alive. You'll never know how much I love you for that.*

'But they're gone, Andy,' she whispered. 'Gone. I heard Walter and Tami discussing it over my bed.' They must have thought she wasn't hearing them. But she had, and many other harried conversations between them, filtered and disordered by the drugs, the fever, until it was almost impossible to untangle and make sense of. But this she knew – her children had left her.

He leant forward, close enough that if she dared dispel the illusion, she could have reached out and touched his tanned face.

They're grown up now, Jen. Not children any more, but strong young adults. They know how to survive, Jenny, because you showed them how to do that. Out there now, on the mainland it's just deer and dogs, and survivors like them.

Survivors, not scavengers. People who'd carved sustainability from the ruins around them. People like that minded their own, kept themselves hidden away. Good people essentially. Andy was right, there were no more bands of uniformed scavengers, or migrating hordes of city folk. They were long gone.

'Maybe . . . maybe *I* can't survive without *them*,' she said.

You have to, love. The people out here rely on you. You've made this place work. You've built a safe haven. It's sane here, there's fairness, kindness; it's like an extended family. That's a projection of you, Jenny, of your personality; firm and fair, just like you were with the kids. Somebody who could never stand that corporate arse-talk at work, any kind of bullshit, injustice, prejudice. He grinned. *That's why we got it together at college. You remember? You stopped me talking bullshit.*

Jenny managed a wheezy laugh – little more than a weak rattling hiss and a half-smile.

Don't give up, Jenny. They need you here.

'No they don't, they're fed up with me in charge. Anyway, I've had enough—'

Don't let someone else take over, Jenny. Don't let someone who wants to be in charge take over. You know where that leads.

Andy had always hated politicians. He'd always joked that the best way to filter out the bad seeds was to place a job ad

173

for Prime Minister in a national newspaper and all those that applied would be automatically disqualified. The bad seeds — those were the ones who were going to be jockeying for position whilst she lay here in the infirmary drugged to the eyeballs.

Don't let anyone else take over, Jen. I'm serious. You've made something good here. Don't let someone turn it into something else.

'But, Andy, I can't do it any more.'

Fight for it, Jenny, fight for it. Don't give up.

Then he was gone. Just like that. Gone. Conjured up and magicked away just as easily by her mind.

'Andy?' She reached out with a hand, wincing as taut healing skin stretched across her shoulder blades, and felt the cot where he'd been sitting. She wanted her hallucination back.

'Andy, please . . . I need you,' she whispered, settling her head back against the pillow, exhausted, dizzy, spent. 'Please . . . come . . . back . . .'

Chapter 27

10 years AC

Norfolk

'I'm glad we didn't set up camp in there,' said Helen, nodding towards the slip road with its diner and petrol station alongside it. 'It just feels wrong, sort of like it's a . . . I don't know, like it's some sort of museum.'

Jacob, Leona and Nathan finished assembling the tents, the kind that required little more than threading thin flexible plastic rods through several vinyl sleeves. They'd picked them up at a camping store along with a small camping trailer designed to attach to a car's bumper, that they were towing behind their bikes on the end of several lengths of nylon rope.

'Like one of those little thingies set up in a whatcha-call-it to show you what a typical street looked like in olden times.'

'A diorama?' said Jacob.

'What?'

'Diorama? Where they sort of make a scene of exhibits and stuff from the past.'

Helen smiled dizzily. 'Yeah, one of them things.' Her pale brow knotted momentarily. 'I think me mum took me to one of those once. All dark streets at night and flickery gas lamps. Must've been four or five then.' She glanced across at the empty buildings. Although some of the smaller windows were still intact, it was clear that both the diner and the petrol station had long ago been thoroughly picked clean.

'Anyway, glad we're camping out here on the road, really. I hate going in buildings and finding you know . . . *stuff*.'

She let the rest of her words go. Didn't need saying. They

knew what she meant; the dried and leathered husks of people.

'Jay, catch!'

Jacob looked up as Nathan tossed him a sealed tub of freeze-dried pasta. He caught it in both hands. Heavy. Something else they'd managed to find at the same retail park outside Bracton in the camping supplies warehouse. There were gallon tubs of this stuff in storage at the back; freeze-dried 'meal solutions' that required only cold water to metamorphose what looked like flakes of dust and nuggets of gravel into a palatable meal. Jacob noticed on the plastic lids covering the foil seal a 'best by' date of 2039. This stuff, kept dry, lasted decades. They'd piled a dozen tubs onto the back of the tow cart. Enough food to keep them going for weeks. Certainly enough to get them to London and back.

He scooped out four portions using the plastic ladle inside and poured in four pints of water from a plastic jug; stirring the savoury porridge until the desiccated flakes of pasta and nuggets of ham and vegetable began to swell. Before his eyes the sludge-like mixture began to look almost like food.

Half an hour later, the sludge was bubbling in a pan over a campfire. Helen dumped an armful of things to burn that she'd gathered from the diner: vinyl seat cushions, fading menu cards promising an all-day breakfast for £5.75, lace curtain trim from the windows, the pine legs from half a dozen stools.

Although the day had been bright and dry, it was getting much cooler out here in the middle of the road now the sun had gone down.

Nathan arrived with another load of flammable bric-a-brac; a stack of glossy magazines and A to Z road maps from the garage.

'But what I mean is,' said Helen, 'what I'm saying is . . . is . . . I just don't *get* it.'

Leona rolled her eyes tiredly. In the sputtering light of the campfire, no one seemed to notice.

'What's the bit you don't get, Helen?' asked Nathan.

Her bottom lip pouted and her eyebrows rumpled thoughtfully. 'Why . . . I guess . . . why it all happened so quickly.'

This subject was a floor-time discussion topic Leona had hosted during morning class on many an occasion. For children like Helen, who would have been only five at the time of the crash, and those younger, it seemed to be a bewildering piece of history; almost mysterious, like the mythical fall of Atlantis or the sudden collapse of the Roman Empire.

'Our dad knew it was going to happen,' said Jacob. 'He worked in the oil business, didn't he, Lee?'

She nodded in a vague way, eyes lost in the fire.

'Dad said the oil was running out quickly back then. He called it "peak oil". Said it was running out much faster than anyone wanted to admit.' Jacob had heard Mum and Leona discuss that week many times over. 'So, because there wasn't much of it, no one managed to build up reserves, no one had it *spare*. So when those bombs exploded in . . . in . . . those Arab countries and all those other oil places, and that big tanker thing blocked the important shipping channel over there and the oil completely stopped, there was nothing anyone could do. It was too late.'

He tossed several pages from a faded magazine onto the fire, producing a momentary flickering of green flame. 'There was no oil for anyone. That meant no fuel. No fuel meant nobody bringing food on ships and planes to England.'

Helen shook her head. 'So why weren't we growing our own food here?'

Jacob shrugged. 'It was cheaper to import it than grow it ourselves. Right, Lee?'

She nodded mutely. 'Economics. The finely tuned engine.'

'That's right,' said Jacob, 'the "Finely Tuned Engine".' He sighed.

Nathan shrugged. 'The fuck's that supposed to mean?'

'Something our dad used to say.'

Nathan and Helen stared at him, none the wiser.

'It's what Dad called the world,' he answered. 'It was one of his sayings, wasn't it, Lee?'

She nodded.

Jacob nodded at her. 'Go on, you can explain it better than me.'

She sighed. 'It was just one of his metaphors: the global economy was like a perfectly tuned engine, like a Formula One racing car; tuned to deliver the best possible performance and profit, but only under, like, *perfect* racing conditions.' She tossed a menu card on the fire. 'So, sure, it drives just fine on smooth dry tarmac. But not so good at coping with a pothole, or crossing a muddy bumpy field. That's what the world was − a finely tuned engine for churning out profit. That's all. Efficient, but very fragile. No money wasted on non-profit stuff like safety margins or back-up systems. No money wasted on tedious things like emergency storage or contingency supplies.'

She looked across the fire at them. 'For instance, no supermarket was ever going to bother wasting its profits on setting up expensive warehousing for storage when they could rely on a just-in-time distribution system. So this country only ever had about forty-eight hours' worth of food in it. It was always coming in on ships and trucks, refrigerated and as fresh as the day it was picked and packaged.'

'Dad used to say we'd be screwed in the UK if something serious ever happened,' added Jacob. 'More screwed than just about any other country in the world.'

'True, that,' Nathan nodded.

'There were no emergency stockpiles for us. No contingency planning,' said Leona. 'We were totally caught out.'

'Dad used to say the fuckwits who ran this country didn't have a clue between them.'

Leona smiled in the dark. He certainly did. She remembered him shaking his head in disgust at the TV, snorting at the dismissive platitudes offered by government suits when uttered by some talking-head.

The fire crackled in the silence. Jacob tossed some broken strips of chipboard onto the flames.

'It was only in the last year or so, when oil started getting *really* expensive, that the big important fuckwits at the top — the men in smart suits — began to realise their finely tuned engine was struggling to cope; that we were all gonna get caught out by something.'

'So why didn't they change things?' asked Helen.

Jacob shrugged. 'I don't know.'

Leona looked up. 'Because the fuckwits in suits were only thinking about the next financial quarter and their next big bonus, that's why.'

The others turned. It was the first real sign of life they'd had out of her all day.

'Too greedy for their own good.'

'Well, that's just silly,' said Helen. 'The men in charge should've fixed things if they knew they were all wrong.'

'Yeah, right,' muttered Leona. 'So, a pothole in the road finally turned up.'

'The bombs in those oil places?' said Helen.

Leona nodded. 'And our finely tuned engine just rattled and fell to pieces.'

'Within a single week,' added Jacob.

Leona tossed the wooden leg of a stool onto the fire, sending a small shower of sparks up into the sky, the flames momentarily flickering with renewed appetite. The dancing pool of amber light stretched a little further up and down the smooth tarmac of the motorway, picking out several abandoned cars along the hard shoulder, nestling amidst tufts of weeds that emerged between the deflated tyres and wheel arches.

'I suppose we all had it coming,' said Jacob after a while.

Leona nodded, her eyes glinting, reflecting the guttering flames. 'Dad was right,' she uttered quietly, before shuffling down on her side and zipping up her sleeping bag.

Chapter 28

10 years AC

'LeMan 49/25a' – ClarenCo Gas Rig Complex,
North Sea

Walter held her hand. He knew she wasn't hearing any of this, she was elsewhere, the place people go when they're dosed up on enough codeine to knock out a horse.

'The explosion shredded the feed pipes, it doubled back into the methane storage cylinder and blew that to pieces. The shards of that lacerated the other two of our three digesters. So, before we're going to have some power again, I'm going to need to find replacements for those as well.' He sighed. 'They were bloody well perfect for the job as well. I suppose if I can find another brewery nearby . . .'

Jenny lay still, her breathing deep and even. The right side of her face, her right shoulder and arm and her torso were bandaged. The burns from the flash of gas igniting had been third degree across her shoulder and arm, and second degree across her neck and the right side of her face. Dr Gupta had told him Jenny had something like fifteen to twenty per cent damage to her BSA – body surface area. A person could quite easily die from that amount of damage, she'd added.

An infection and a fever had threatened to complicate the matter. So there was little more she could do but dress the knitting skin and keep it as clean as she could and bombard her with antibiotics.

It looked as if the infections were clearing up and the fever lifting. Jenny's temperature was down, although the skin, where it had burned badly, still radiated an almost fever-like heat. Tami was still keeping Jenny out for the count; sedated and anaesthetised with a cocktail of drugs – as much as she dared use together.

'There'll be extensive scarring,' she had told Walter. 'This side of her face, her neck and her shoulder. There's a chance some of her hair may not grow back on the right side. For a woman that's, well, that's not easy to accept.'

The scars were always going to be there, across her cheek and neck where she could easily see them every time she faced a mirror; always reminding herself of the day she lost a granddaughter.

He sighed, squeezing her hand gently.

Life's a complete bastard, isn't it? A completely cruel malicious bastard.

Truth was, Hannah died because she was playing where she shouldn't, and had kicked the feed pipe by accident. That would do it, he realised. That would have been enough to dislodge the G-clamp.

But that's what they're saying, isn't it? He kept over-hearing mutterings that it was *his* shoddy workmanship that had killed the poor girl. Nasty spiteful assertions that the silly fool had cut too many corners, eager to hurry up and make electricity so he could impress Jenny – woo her into his cot with a spectacular display of his practical ingenuity.

Bitches.

And with Jenny out of the loop for now, for quite a few weeks, if not months, according to Dr Gupta, Walter was having to stand in as her replacement. No one seemed to be particularly happy with that idea. Certainly not that sour-faced bitch, Alice Harton, who seemed to be taking every opportunity to be canvassing support and stoking dissent.

Oh, yes, she sees herself as Jenny's replacement all right.

Without Jenny at his side he suddenly felt very lonely. Not even the other old boys, Howard and Dennis, were bothering to stand by him. David Cudmore, the chap Alice was bedding right now, must have talked them round for her. They all bunked together on the drilling platform, all thick as thieves.

And there was that Latoc fella, too. He was over there – he seemed to have attracted something of a following.

Groupies. That's what they were. His adoring bloody fan club.

Walter didn't have a cluster of people around him that could shore him up. If Jenny's kids hadn't buggered off and left him, he'd at least have had them gathered close and giving him some support. But instead, all he had was Tami, and perhaps Martha, although she seemed to be increasingly interested in spending time up the far end of the platforms.

Another bloody groupie probably.

Everyone else . . . they were carrying on with their duties as they were spelled out on the whiteboard and turning up for their correct meal sittings; doing their bit and politely nodding at Walter when he had to issue instructions. But that was hardly support.

'Jesus, Jenny, hurry up and get better,' he muttered.

She stirred in her sleep, her clogged voice calling softly for someone.

He wondered how much she was aware of things. Every day there were periods when her glassy eyes were open and she was groggy but awake; moments when she could manage a few muddled words through the fog of drugs, as she sipped carefully spooned tepid stew – not hot, that would hurt the raw skin around her lips. But those were snatched moments amidst a chemical haze. He wondered if she even knew Hannah was gone, that her children had deserted them.

Oh, Jesus.

Thing is, it would be down to him to tell her; news that was going to break her heart. Not now though – not now. If she really could hear him, then that was news she could do without knowing at this point in time.

He looked at her hand, strangely untouched by the

explosion, a lean and elegant hand. A grandmother's hand. A mother's hand . . . a beautiful hand. He raised it to his lips and kissed it gently, wishing he was twelve years younger and more her type; wishing he was a bit more like the husband she had lost in the crash. He knew she still mourned him, still spoke to him in quiet moments.

He sighed. Only with her like this, unconscious, did he have the courage to say what he'd yearned to say for a number of years now.

'I love you, Jenny,' he whispered. 'I'd do anything for you. You know that, don't you? Absolutely bloody anything.'

Chapter 29

10 years AC

Thetford,
Norfolk

It was far easier to replace Helen's bicycle than bother to fix the puncture. It went flat with an explosive *pfffft* just outside Thetford. Half a mile further along the road they rolled past a turning that promised them yet another retail park. Five minutes later the wheels of their bikes and the trailer rolled across a broad leaf-strewn parking forecourt. Untamed weeds pushed up in places, and the tarmac was lumpy where the roots of a row of decorative saplings were making a show of their spread down one side.

Like every other parking area they'd encountered, this one was more or less bereft of cars. Jacob remembered seeing roads clogged with vehicles in the week after the crash. It had seemed any car or van with at least a quarter of a tank of petrol had been pressed into service, packed with families desperately trying to get away from the chaotic anarchy of London.

But every artery out of the city had been sealed with a roadblock manned either by armed police and soldiers or 'emergency response workers' — civilians hastily pressed into service, armed and invariably supervised by a solitary police-man. They'd quickly discovered the civilian workers were a greater hazard, using the roadblocks as an opportunity to stop and shake down people for water and food supplies. Every major road and motorway out of London was now a grave-yard of cars, vans and trucks — a carpet of immobile metal rooftops, bubbling and blistering from the rust spreading beneath their paintwork. The frames of their windscreens dotted green with small islands of moss, anchored to the perishing rubber seals.

The retail park looked like the dozen others they'd passed by in the last couple of days; even damaged to the same degree, as if a tacit agreement had passed amongst the panicking people of Britain that IKEA, Mothercare, Pets World, B&Q and the ubiquitous McDonald's were to be ruthlessly targeted and plundered, and the likes of Currys, Carpetright and PC World were to be left well alone.

Leona told Jacob and Nathan to watch the trailer whilst she took the gun and led Helen inside Halfords to find a new bike for the girl.

Jacob watched them disappear into the dark interior then glanced back at the glass front of PC World. It looked utterly untouched. Not a single panel of glass broken, not even cracked. No lights on inside, of course. But, by the muted vanilla glow of late afternoon, he could just as well be in the past again; a Sunday morning before ten a.m. opening time, waiting for the first member of staff to turn up, yawning, nursing a hangover and unlocking the double doors for the first over-eager customer, impatient to get inside and replace an ink cartridge.

'You see PC World?' he said, pointing to it.

Nathan turned to look at the unbroken glass.

His eyebrows flickered up. 'Hey, cool. Ain't broken.'

Jacob realised that neither of them had seen an expanse of glass as large as this one still intact; not since *before*. Really quite an odd sight in a world where every window was a frame of snaggle-toothed shards, or snow-white granulated crystals.

Nathan bent down, fumbling for a lump of loose tarmac.

'What're you doing?'

He grinned. 'Gonna smash it.'

'What?'

'It's all ours, Jay. No one's did it in all this time. So it's, like, *ours* to smash.' He prised loose a crumbling chunk of parking lot which he tossed from one hand to the other with gleeful anticipation. 'Come on, Jay, we'll smash it together, on three.'

'No.'

'One . . . two . . .'

'I said NO,' Jacob barked, stepping away from his bike and letting it clatter to the ground noisily.

'. . . three—'

Jacob clumsily punched Nathan's shoulder and the tarmac dropped from his hand and clattered noisily to the ground.

'Hey! The fuck you do that for?'

'I don't want to smash it. I mean, why? Why break it? It's lasted this long.'

'It's a fucking window, man! That's all. Just a fuckin' window!'

Jacob's face hardened. 'It's just . . .'

'What? Just like it was before?' Nathan looked at him. 'Shit, Jay, what's the matter with you?'

'I just . . . I don't know . . . it's done so well to survive this far, you know? It just seems wrong.'

Nathan's scowl vanished and his faced creased with a bemused grin. 'Jesus, man. It's a piece of glass that didn't get broke. That's all it—'

He stopped and frowned.

Jacob turned to look towards the glass frontage they'd been discussing.

'Someone in there.'

Jacob saw it too. Movement in the dark interior beyond. The faint flicker of torchlight and the pale shape of a yellow T-shirt moving between the shelves and stacks of boxed printers and PCs.

'That one person you think?' asked Nathan. 'Or more?'

Jacob squinted. 'Dunno.'

A moment later the flicker of torchlight snapped off and then they saw the T-shirt grow more distinct as it approached the front of the store with the late afternoon light streaming in through the glass front. The pale T-shirt seemed to be carrying something in its darker arms. As it squeezed through a checkout and emerged through an open door that, once upon a time, would have slid aside with a compliant *whoosh*, they saw the T-shirt was on a man with pallid skin and a scruffy mop of long ginger hair who was whistling to himself cheerfully.

He was outside and in the sun when he stopped in his tracks, studying them intently. The whistling ceased.

'Leona!!' shouted Jacob. 'There's somebody out here!!'

'Hey!' barked Nathan. 'All right?' he said, taking several steps forwards.

The man in the yellow T-shirt lowered the boxes to the ground carefully – boxes with '5.1 Bose Surround Sound System' printed boldly on them. He reached up to his ears and pulled out a pair of small earphones, hissing music loudly in the stillness. His eyes warily appraised Nathan.

'Uh . . . look, I don't have any food,' he said, licking his lips nervously and shifting from one foot to the other. 'Honest, bro, I've got nothing you want. No food or water. I just—'

'Hey, don't worry,' said Jacob stepping forward to stand beside Nathan. 'It's all right, we're not going to rob you or anything.'

The man's eyes were drawn to movement from the Halfords' entrance.

'Who's there?' came Leona's voice across the car-park, echoing off the storefront like a gunshot.

'A man!!' Jacob yelled over his shoulder. He turned back to him. 'Are there other people with you?'

The man's face flickered anxiously. He looked relatively young, perhaps Leona's age; on his pallid face the meagre tufts of a trimmed ginger goatee. He pulled a Jesus-long cord of lank, greasy hair out of his eyes and tucked it behind one ear.

'No . . . uh . . . it's just me.'

Jacob offered him a friendly smile. 'Well that's all right then.'

The man watched Leona and Helen approach, his eyes on the gun she was holding.

'Hey! No need to shoot me. Look, I'm leaving!'

Jacob shook his head. 'Don't worry. It's okay.'

'You want this stuff? Fine, take it. There's loads more inside—'

Nathan shook his head. 'Relax, man.'

'Or jack my truck?'

'Shit. You got a workin' truck?' exclaimed Nathan.

He nodded, his eyes darting to a blue Ford Transit pick-up truck across the car-park.

'I've got a little diesel,' he replied cautiously, his eyes still on Leona; still on the gun in her hands. 'Not a lot. Just enough that I can run into town every now and then.'

Leona stepped past Nathan, discreetly lowering the barrel of the gun so that it wasn't levelled at the man any more.

'What's your name?' she asked.

'Raymond.'

'I'm Leona.'

She appraised him in much the same way she'd seen Mum silently judge newcomers. The man seemed well-fed and practically dressed with clothes either washed or recently pulled from a shop. He didn't appear to be a shambling loner draped with tattered rags and a dangerously haunted look in his eyes. He looked like he might have come from a community better furnished than theirs, actually. She noticed his earphones hissing music and dangling around his knees, wires snaking up to an iPod poking out of a hip pocket.

'How many of you?' Leona asked finally.

189

Raymond shrugged. 'Not many. Just me, actually.'

She pointed at his iPod. 'You've got electricity, right? I used to have one of those . . . they don't take batteries, you've got to recharge them.'

He nodded. 'Yeah, I've got a few things running at my place,' he conceded warily.

'But it's just you?' said Leona.

Raymond nodded. He studied them in silence for a while. 'You're all young. Just kids—'

'I'm twenty-nine,' she replied flatly. 'What's your point?'

'Sorry. Thought you were younger,' he replied. 'It's just that, occasionally, I come across groups of survivors. The younger groups, your age and younger, they're more dangerous. Well, to be honest, almost like wild animals sometimes. I try to steer clear of them.'

'We're good ones,' said Helen.

He nodded. 'Okay.'

'We're headed south to London,' said Leona. 'Apparently they're rebuilding things there. You heard anything about that?'

He shook his head. 'Nope.'

Helen took a step forward, entranced by the hissing still coming from Raymond's headphones. 'Is that . . . like, *proper* music?'

He shrugged. 'I got hip-hop, some garage, some rock . . . all sorts really. Just listening to a bit of Jay Dilla right now.'

Nathan cocked his head. 'Shit, I remember! My mate's brother had his stuff,' he uttered, approving. 'Dilla was well cool.'

'Yeah. I cleaned out a record shop and ripped all their CDs onto my hard drive. I've got pretty much everything, more or less.'

'Hard drive?' said Nathan. 'You got a computer?'

Raymond shrugged. 'Yeah, several, actually.'

'We have loads of spare food,' blurted Helen, 'could we come stay the night at your place?'

'Helen!' snapped Leona angrily.

The girl shut up, her face flushing crimson as Leona glared at her. She turned back to Raymond. He didn't look the dangerous schizo type; he had a slight build, looked like the kind of guy you'd see working in a comic store, or turning up at some Star Trek geek-a-thon, dressed as a Klingon.

'There's just you?'

He nodded.

Leona considered Helen's blurted suggestion quietly for a moment. 'All right then. Could we stay the night? Just one night, if we, you know, shared our food?'

Raymond's eyes darted from one to the other, warily returning to the gun dangling from her hands.

'Sure . . . uh . . . sure you're not going to rob me or something?'

'Would it help if I promised you we won't?'

He shrugged and wrinkled his nose. 'Okay,' he answered. 'Why not?'

Chapter 30

10 years AC

Thetford Forest,
Norfolk

Without any warning Raymond swung the pick-up truck off the road onto a gravel lay-by and put the brakes on.

'Why've we stopped?' asked Jacob.

'You'll see,' Raymond replied, climbing out of the truck and stepping across the gravel towards an overgrown cluster of blackberry bushes spilling out beneath the shadow of a mature oak tree.

'Maybe he needs a pee?' said Helen.

They watched him approach the brambles and fumble amongst the foliage. He stepped back and the bushes appeared to come with him.

'Uh?' gasped Helen.

'Oh, that's cool,' said Nathan. 'A disguised entrance.'

Raymond moved aside a six-foot panel of trellis through which the bushes had eagerly grown, twisting through the cross-hatches of plywood. Through the newly made gap they could see a faint track of twin ruts, running deep into the woods, dark beneath the thick summer-laden canopy of oak branches.

He rejoined them in the truck.

'Props, man,' grinned Nathan. 'Like the secret entrance to Batman's cave.'

Raymond smiled. 'Yup. Just like that.'

He drove the truck through the gap and got out to replace the trellis, sealing the entrance behind them. Back behind the wheel, they rolled down the track, bouncing uncomfortably where the ruts ran deep and puddles splashed muddy water in their wake.

Leona warily studied the shadowy trail ahead. The farmhouse they'd lived in for several years after the crash had been a bit like this, lost deep in the woods where one hoped never to be found. But, of course, they had been.

'How much further?' she asked.

'Just up here,' he replied.

She noticed a sliver of sky ahead, a break in the canopy, appearing, disappearing, appearing amidst the thick veil of leaves. Then, rounding a bend, dipping down through deep ruts, splashing droplets of muddy water on the side windows, she saw it.

Oh, God.

'Home,' he said casually as he rolled the truck up beside the service entrance to what appeared to be an enormous inflated geodesic dome.

It's so beautiful.

'Wow!' gasped Jacob, with wide-eyed amazement. 'It's like a space station!'

Raymond switched off the engine and they sat in silence, looking up at a web of triangular panels of semi-opaque plastic curving above them as the engine softly ticked.

'My humble castle,' announced Raymond with a casual twang that had more to do with a faint Scottish burr than any sense of arrogance. 'It's called The Emerald Oasis.'

Leona opened the door and stepped out of the truck, marvelling at the domed structure. Through the panels she could see tall dark forms inside.

'What's in there?'

He grinned. 'Paradise.'

He reached into the back of the truck for the Bose speakers he'd foraged from PC World and led the way in, pushing through the side entrance, a row of thick plastic flaps that slapped noisily to one side. 'Come in,' he beckoned to Leona, holding open a gap for her.

She led the way and immediately felt the warm moist air on her face. It reminded her of childhood holidays abroad – stepping out of the cool air-conditioned interior of a plane into the warmth of some simmering hot holiday location. Then her eyes registered the tall fronds of a host of exotic plants.

'My God, it's like a . . . like a rainforest in here,' she gasped.

'Well, actually, that's *exactly* what it is.'

The others entered behind her and the calming sound of chirruping insects, the gentle trickle of flowing water, the tap, tap, tap of moisture dripping from one broad waxy leaf down onto another was disturbed by a chorus of their muted voices, respectfully hushed to awed whispers.

'This place,' he said, leading them along a wood-chipped walkway, 'is, or I should say, *was*,' he corrected himself, 'an exclusive holiday spa.'

They passed a cluster of purple gourds above which several brightly coloured butterflies fluttered.

'Emerald Oasis. It's a temperature- and humidity-controlled one-acre bubble of tropical rainforest.' He stopped and turned towards them. 'Basically it was a bloody expensive version of Center Parcs.'

Leona looked at the others, they were grinning like simpletons. She supposed she would have been as well if, at the back of her mind, she hadn't also been wishing Hannah could be with them to see this too.

'It wasn't quite ready when the crash hit us that summer.' Raymond shrugged. 'Bad timing really. It was due to open for Christmas. They had celebrity guests booked in – a whole waiting-list of celebrities actually.'

The woodchip pathway curved past a luxury swimming pool and, beside it, a whirlpool spa.

'I keep fish in there now.'

He led them through another curtain of plastic flaps into a pinewood cabin. It was cooler here, the same temperature as outside. She could feel the moisture that had settled on her skin walking through Raymond's paradise begin to chill.

'There are eight chalets like this one, each sleeping a family of four. You lot can share this one, or spread out and use the others if you want. Up to you.'

Leona smiled. 'This is good, thank you.'

Raymond shrugged, a self-effacing gesture across his narrow shoulders that reminded her of a comedy actor Mum used to like. Woody someone.

'Okay, then,' he said. 'You want to get your stuff out of the back of the truck? Meanwhile . . .' he grinned at his Bose speakers, 'I just want to wire up these little fellas to my sound system.'

He turned and left, pushing his way through the flaps.

They turned to each other. Helen ended the wide-eyed silence. 'I so-o-o-o want to live here.'

The smell of freeze-dried tomato and pasta meals being heated up in the microwave attracted everyone from exploring different corners of the intriguingly landscaped jungle floor. Raymond brought out a large steaming bowl and placed it on a picnic table set out on wooden decking that overlooked the pool and soon they were all seated, hungrily tucking into their dinner.

'So you've got 'lectric, too?' said Helen blowing on her spoon.

Nathan shook his head and laughed. 'Duh . . . you finally noticed then?' Jacob snorted, and both boys began cackling.

'Hey, piss off!' she replied, dismissing them with a flick of her wrist. 'Children.'

'Sorry, Bubbles.'

She flicked Nathan her finger. 'I'm not as stupid and immature as you two.'

When all three of them had been younger and in Leona's class, Bubbles had been her nickname – short for Bubblehead.

Nathan and Jacob guffawed. Leona noticed Raymond smiling at the exchange, bemused and amused at the same time.

'You lot, pack it in,' said Leona. They did, but only after a few more muttered digs at each other.

'We got 'lectric, too,' said Helen, returning to her conversational gambit.

'Yeah?' Raymond sipped on a spoon of steaming pasta. 'What're you running, turbines or cells?'

Helen made a face, shrugged and looked at the others for help. 'Poo, I think?'

The boys laughed again.

'What about you?' asked Leona.

His bamboo chair creaked as he sat back. 'The whole spa was set up to be completely carbon neutral and off the grid. The enviro-dome has photovoltaic cells at the top.' He grinned. 'See, that's how this place was marketed. The entire thing was billed as an exclusive luxury destination with an absolute *zero* carbon footprint. The electricity used to heat the dome completely derived from our own renewable sources. The food served to guests was to be from local farmers. Total carbon-neutral stamp of compliance on everything.'

'Oh, yes, that's good,' said Helen, pretending she was up to speed on what he meant by that.

'The brochure even claimed to make a carbon-offset donation to cover the journey miles made by customers from their home to here; so they could enjoy their stay totally guilt-free.' He shook his head. 'All just a gimmick really. A load of crap. No such thing as a zero footprint. Any case, the cells on the roof were backed up by a diesel generator before the crash. Half of them weren't even wired in.'

'You're still running the diesel generator?' asked Leona.

'Shit, no. I've kept the diesel for the truck. The power's mostly coming from half a dozen household wind turbines I pinched from B&Q – the ones they started stocking a couple of summers before the crash, you know, when oil was shooting up?'

She nodded.

'Pretty good things those. Reliable.'

Jacob leant forward. 'So did you work here before the crash?'

'Yeah. I was the technical manager. Basically they poached me from Disneyland to come here and run this place.'

'Shit! *Disneyland!* Seriously?'

Leona wasn't surprised to see Jacob's mouth drop open. Mum and Dad had taken them both to EuroDisney back in 2008. Jacob had been about five then and was fascinated by the animatronics on the Pirates of the Caribbean ride. He must have dragged them from the exit back round to the entrance half a dozen times.

'Yup. Disneyland in Florida. I was chief oompah-loompah for one of their bigger rides.'

Helen's fair eyebrows locked together. 'What the hell's an oompah-loompah?'

He grinned. 'That's what the "cast" called us backroom nerds. Very funny, or at least they thought so. Mind you, we used to get our own back on them . . .'

Raymond talked all the way through dinner. Leona guessed he hadn't had any company for quite some time and now, feeling more at ease with them than he had been earlier at the retail park, he seemed to enjoy opening up, giving them a glimpse of his past life in the old world. His pasta must have been cold by the time he finally got round to finishing it. But she enjoyed listening to him, hearing references to the past, to places she would have *liked* to have seen and places she *had* seen.

Raymond Campbell; an engineering graduate from Edinburgh University, he'd bummed around in India and Goa for a while before getting work in London. Then, later on, he got to work on some prestigious development projects in Dubai and then Disney in Florida before finally getting the job to run this place.

'I suppose I've always been a bit of a tech-geek. I love fiddling with stuff, optimising systems, you know?'

Helen cocked her head and pursed her lips. 'Do you mean making things run better?'

Raymond smiled at her. 'That's exactly it. There isn't anything you can't make run a little better, a little faster, a little smoother, if you take the time to analyse it and component-split the processes,' he replied, his eyes remaining on the young girl – eye contact that lingered between them for a few charged seconds.

Leona stepped into the moment. 'So, Raymond, what's your crash-story?'

He knew what she meant by that, everyone had *their story*; how they survived the crash, what the first day, the first week, the first month was like for them, how they managed to get through it.

Helen played at being *hausfrau*, stacking up the bowls in the gathering darkness as he settled back in his chair again. It creaked in the stillness.

'We were preparing to open the Oasis back then. Our first guests were already booked in for the middle of December. If I remember right, it was some footballer and his fashion-model wife and their extended family. There were a dozen staff here and a couple of builders finishing up work on the chalets when it all started. Those bombs went off in Saudi, kicking off the Middle-Eastern troubles. The bombs in the big refineries and that tanker exploded in the Gulf blocking the shipping routes, and the Prime Minister came on . . . my God, do you remember that?'

They did. Everyone, except Helen.

'He stood in that press room, ripped up what he was meant to say, and told us we were all as good as screwed.'

Helen was too young to remember that so clearly, nonetheless, she'd heard the story many times over.

'So anyway, I was co-managing this place with a lady called Tanya – she was a botanist, in charge of the plants and bugs and stuff. Anyway, we dismissed all the others so they could get home to their families. We stayed, though; someone had to keep things running here.

'We thought it was a scare that would blow over in a few days. Like everyone else. We just thought the Prime Minister had panicked, had a nervous breakdown on camera or something. We assumed the government had a handle on it. We assumed there were oil reserves, food reserves and some sort of contingency plan for this kind of a crisis. But then, of course, it got out of hand so quickly. We watched on the news as the riots spread right across London. When the BBC stopped broadcasting, I guess we realised at that point that this was worse than we thought. Really bad.'

'We were in London then,' said Jacob quietly. 'Me and Leona, during those riots.'

Raymond looked at him. 'It must have been frightening.'

'It was,' replied Leona. 'Very.'

'Go on,' urged Nathan, 'you was saying, Ray.'

'So Tanya and me stayed on here. She continued to look after the tropical ecosystem, I kept the generators going and we sat it out, listening to the radio; FM for the first week or two, then medium wave then finally long wave as British stations stopped broadcasting. We heard about the safe zones in London and elsewhere collapsing a few months after the

199

crash. We heard brief reports on the short wars, Russia and Georgia, India and Pakistan, Israel and Syria, Palestine.'

'Yeah, we heard about those too,' said Jacob.

'I heard a Cuban radio station about three years ago talking about the way things are in America. They had it almost as bad as us here; pretty rough first few years. Federal authority disappeared overnight almost. It collapsed down to state authorities. Some fared a lot better than others. East coast: New York, New Jersey, Delaware, those ones, all ended up like Europe did, totally screwed. But further south, the gulf states like Florida and Texas seemed to do better – they had some oil reserves to play with. Apparently they've teamed up and there's some sort of order there. I think they said something about the President being based there.'

'Do you think they'll come over here?' asked Helen. 'And you know, help us?'

'I doubt it. Not for a while. They've got their own country to fix.'

'You not heard any more?' asked Leona.

Raymond shrugged. 'The station switched from English to Cuban. You can still pick it up, several Cuban stations actually. I think that country coped a lot better than just about anyone else.

'Funny though,' he continued, shaking his head, 'I never thought that just stopping the oil would fuck the world up quite so much. I understand now, of course. I understand why so many died, in this country at least. Perhaps if we'd all been given six months' warning, maybe even just a week's warning – enough time to learn how to grow some kind of a basic survival crop, buy the seeds and stick 'em in the ground . . . you know? But by the time the Prime Minister— what was his name?' Raymond looked around at the teenagers at the picnic table.

None of them could actually remember.

'Well, by the time that idiot blew his whistle it was already too late to do anything.'

He fell silent and the evening was filled with the creaking and chirruping of foreign-sounding insects, and the soft rustle of running water.

'Was Tanya your girlfriend?' asked Helen.

Raymond stirred. 'God, no. We were just colleagues, workmates, that's all.'

'What happened to her?' asked Jacob.

'She vanished.'

'Vanished?'

'A while back. One day we drove the truck into Thetford to forage for essentials. We thought it was safe to split up, we hadn't seen any drifters for a while.' He looked down at his hands, twisting the corner of his yellow T-shirt. 'She never came back to the truck. I called for her, for hours. Looked for her around the town. I returned to the Oasis, then went back the next day and tried again. I never found her. She just vanished.'

'Oh, God, that's awful,' offered Helen.

'Yeah . . . yes, it was. I figure she was taken by someone. Or perhaps an accident, fallen somewhere, injured or killed.' He shook his head silently. 'It nearly pushed me over the edge really. I didn't realise how close we'd got over the years.'

Leona stirred. 'How long ago was this?'

He shook his head. 'Happened, I guess, four years ago?'

Leona looked at him with pity. 'My God, you've been all alone since?'

'Uh-huh. Minding the trees and the bugs, keeping this place going, keeping myself busy.'

'Do you miss her?' asked Helen. Leona detected something in her young voice and the way that Raymond addressed her questions so attentively; there was a little chemistry going on there in the dark. The thought made her grimace ever so slightly. Helen was only fifteen and although

Raymond seemed quite boyish, he had to be in his mid-thirties; old enough to be her father.

'It was just the two of us for six years,' replied Raymond, 'just the two of us. So, yeah, of course I miss her.'

Helen began gently quizzing Raymond about Tanya, about his past life. He talked about that, about Disneyland, and the other three listened intently. Helen cooed dotingly, giggled too readily at his anecdotes.

Leona sighed at Helen's obviousness. She wondered whether her instinctive distaste at the thought of Raymond and Helen *as an item* was a hangover from the past, from the world before. She remembered curling her lip in disgust at a story in the newspapers: an aging rock star in his sixties bedding a sixteen-year-old Russian bar girl. An old tabloid story from a different world where such a relationship was a horrendous notion. She wondered though, how much those sorts of moral values had changed in this new world.

A different story now, perhaps, she figured. In this new world, a man a decade or more older would have a wider experience and knowledge base, better honed survival skills, better able to care for a younger partner than some sleek young strip of a lad.

All very tribal, very Darwinian. But it made sense.

She looked at the dark outlines of the others around the table; at Jacob, laughing, fidgeting in his bamboo chair, so full of hope that things were on the cusp of getting better, that London was waiting for him. Nathan too. And Helen flirting shamelessly with Raymond, distancing herself from the boys, pretending to be so much more grown up, clearly rather keen to make an impression on Raymond.

We've all got our little goals, and none of them involve returning to the North Sea.

She smiled, knowing no one would see her face in the fading light of dusk and ask her what she was thinking. Leona hoped they'd all find what they'd come along for. Most of all, she hoped her little brother would find what he wanted in London. His street lights.

Chapter 31

10 years AC

'LeMan 49/25a' – ClarenCo Gas Rig Complex, North Sea

'How is she this morning?' asked Walter.

Dr Gupta sipped on her breakfast chowder. 'The infections are clearing up. The dressings are coming off dry. I cannot tell you how relieved I am about that.'

Walter nodded. So was he.

'Basically, she has finished fighting off secondary problems, now she is busy healing.' Dr Gupta made a face. 'There will be a lot of scarring, however. She will have it up her neck and across her right cheek. I just wish we'd had a few pressure wraps to minimise the hypertrophic scarring on her face. Stupid really, in all our trips ashore for medical supplies I never really thought there would be a need for me to treat burns.'

He nodded and glanced around the mess. It was mostly empty now, most of the third sitting had finished and left for their morning chores to make way for the fourth sitting and the four long tables were empty save for five small children still eating at the far end, urged to get a move on by an exasperated mother. Walter knew them all by name, but since they'd only joined the community seven months ago, he'd yet to get to know them well. That was something Jenny was much better at – finding time to sit down and talk to people.

Walter knew he wasn't a popular choice of stand-in leader. Tami would probably have been more welcomed in the role.

She was looking at him as he thought that; reading his face

like a book. 'You know, Walter, no one can really blame you for that explosion,' she replied. 'That is not fair.'

'But they are, aren't they? I've heard what's being said.'

He sometimes even wondered himself whether he *was* to blame. Even something as simple as those £30 cooking stoves you used to be able to buy at any camping store had a bayonet fitting as well as a screw valve. Safety should have been more on his mind than *haste*; haste to get something up and running for Jenny. And his allowing Jenny to bring Hannah down into the generator's back room with those methane digesters, when no children, under any circumstances, should have ever been allowed in there . . .

Stupid. Stupid.

What was Hannah doing down there on her own, though? She knew she shouldn't play there, she knew that very well. So why? And the feed pipe lying on the floor, the G-clamp lying beside it.

Did Hannah do that? Did she pull it loose by accident?

There'd only been a fleeting few seconds down there in that dark room before the explosion. He'd caught the briefest glimpse of her feet protruding from behind the generator and the rubber hose dangling from the roof softly hissing gas. That's it. That's all he saw. But she would have had to have been climbing over the top of the casing to pull that hose free, surely? If she'd had an urge to climb on something, for crying out loud, there were plenty of other places she could have done that. It just didn't make sense. Hannah was a good girl. She knew she'd have been out of bounds. She knew the generator was dangerous; not a climbing frame. It just didn't make sense to him.

Dr Gupta interrupted his wool-gathering. 'So, what are you going to do with Mr Latoc?' she asked quietly. 'Is he staying or going?' She slurped a spoon of chowder. 'You cannot leave the question unanswered for much longer, you know?'

'I know, I know.'

Walter would ask Jenny what she wanted to do about him, but she was still out of it, either half asleep, or half-cut on those knock-out-a-horse painkillers she was taking.

Walter wanted the man gone. Valérie Latoc was trouble brewing. He had the people living over on the drilling platform in thrall to him. Every time he caught sight of the man, it was with a row of people sitting patiently, listening to him talking.

What the hell does he gabble on about?

Of course it was women listening, mostly.

What is it with women? Give them a coffee-skinned man and they go weak at the bloody knees.

But he'd also noticed David Cudmore and Kevin in one of Latoc's little audiences. It always seemed to look like a prayer group; a sermon on the mount kind of thing.

'He's some sort of preacher, I think,' said Walter.

'I know. Jenny would not be happy with him if she knew.'

Much as he'd like to, he couldn't just kick the man off the rigs. Jenny had said he could stay on probation and, given that she was slowly getting better and would hopefully be able to take the helm again one day soon, it was her decision. Not his. If she woke and found Latoc gone, she'd think he'd booted him off out of petty jealousy. In fact, everyone would say that, wouldn't they?

Walter didn't like the fact that Valérie was more popular. More attractive. Younger. He didn't like that at all so you know what he did? The bitter old bastard kicked poor Valérie out to fend for himself. God knows if he's still alive out there . . . I hope he is . . .

Even if he tried to have the man removed, Walter suspected it wouldn't be allowed to happen. There'd be an uproar amongst his fan club.

'Oh, speak of the devil,' said Dr Gupta.

Latoc entered the mess followed by three women. Walter knew them quite well, they were bunked on the main compression platform. He hadn't spotted them before amongst Latoc's regular drilling platform crowd. Keisha, Desirae and Kara. The first two were sisters who'd once lived in north London. Kara was originally from Nottingham. Together, the three of them were normally an infectiously cheerful group, filling any room they were in with loud and cheerful bingo-hall banter frequently peppered with high-pitched and raucous belly-laughs.

New recruits. It seemed that Latoc's brand of charm was spreading like a bloody virus to the other platforms now. They grabbed plastic bowls from the galley's counter and were served a ladle of steaming broth each and then sat together at one of the other long tables.

Valérie Latoc extended his hands across the table and they reached out for them. His head bowed, as did theirs, and he began to utter, quite loudly, a prayer of thanksgiving. Walter knew Jenny would be on her feet already, on her way over to ask him to do this quietly or take it outside. This space was communal, shared not only by non-believers but by so many others of different faiths, who were equally asked to keep their faith a personal thing.

Jenny was strict on this. No public prayers, not here, not in the mess. Otherwise the door would be opened to all sorts of petitions: people wanting to eat on single-faith tables, people wanting the men to eat separately from the women, people insisting on fasting, people insisting on eating before sun up or after sun down.

Tami tapped Walter's arm and nodded towards them. He shot a glance over his shoulder at them and then turned back round to face her, reluctant to meet her eyes.

'You know Jenny would not accept this?'

He nodded.

'If you let this happen, it will happen again.'

'I know . . . I . . .'

A dozen more people entered the canteen; the start of the

fourth sitting, children chatting noisily to each other, hungry and too energetic for the mums shuffling in with them. One or two of them eyed Valérie and the others curiously.

'You cannot let this happen and not say something, Walter. People see this and there'll be others who will want their particular faith blessings before each meal.'

'Yes, yes,' he whispered. 'Okay . . . let me just think how I'm going to say—'

But then it was done. Valérie, and the ladies sitting with him, chorused 'amen', released each other's hands and the canteen was almost immediately filled with their high-spirited chatter and good-natured laughter.

Walter bit on his lip and made a face. 'Maybe if he does it again . . . I'll, uh . . . I'll have a quiet word.'

Dr Gupta looked at him and shook her head, tutting. 'Not good,' she muttered. 'Not good.'

Chapter 32

10 years AC

Thetford Forest,
Norfolk

'I turned this little bit of the oasis over to, well, you can see,' said Raymond, pointing towards rows of runner bean and pea vines, 'to climbers mainly – vertical crops. You get a much better space-to-yield return.'

Leona nodded. 'We've done the same on the rigs.'

'It must be tight for space on there.'

'We manage. There's a surprising amount of surface on which to grow all sorts of things; every ledge, every walk-way, every deck, we have things in pots.'

He chuckled. 'What about sea salt? It's in the air. That must make it hard to grow things.'

'Where we are it's not so bad as say someone trying to grow vegetables in a garden on the seafront, where the wind whips up spray and spoils everything. We're high up. The upper decks where everything is growing . . . it's like a hundred feet above the sea.' Leona silently appraised Raymond's vegetable plot. 'Do you grow enough to get by on?'

'The tomatoes, the peppers, the oranges I showed you earlier, it's enough to sustain two adults. Tanya had it properly balanced to feed the pair of us indefinitely without taking up too much of the space. She didn't have the heart to uproot all these tropical plants and replace them with food plants. So, it turned out we had enough space to keep our rain forest ecosystem, and still grow enough fruit and veg to tide us over. I just follow the plans and planting schedule she drew up. Anyway,' he said, 'at a push I could grow stuff outside the dome in the woods, or pick mushrooms, berries . . . even trap rabbits. The forest is crawling with them.' He grinned. 'And it's not as if I've got anyone else to share the woods with.'

She looked out through the foggy perspex at the dark outline of trees. Raymond was right. He had little to worry about on that score. Thetford forest seemed to be all his.

'I often wonder how many people are alive out there,' she said after a while.

'In the UK?'

She nodded.

He sucked in a breath. 'I did the maths once. I reckoned on about two to five million now . . . roughly five to ten per cent of the population was my guess.'

'That many? It doesn't seem like there's anywhere *near* that many people around.'

'Oh, yeah,' he said. 'I think it's possible so many survived because the die-off here in the UK was so rapid. A slower attrition rate would have meant those small groups that have survived to today would have had more competition for resources. Think about how much is still out there. You can still find edible canned and packet food if you know where to look. If the die-off had been slower, those harder-to-find things would have been picked clean by now by those who were hanging on. You'd have nothing left now. So, ironically, I think if we'd coped slightly better and more people had managed to hang on and last longer, it would be harder for the survivors today.'

Leona frowned doubtfully. 'So where'd you suppose these two to five million people are then? We've seen no one really, not since we left.'

'Of course not. You've been on the road all the way, haven't you? Think about it, any groups struggling to survive within eyesight of a road would have long ago been paid a visit by a starving mob. Picked clean and wiped out.'

'They're all hiding then?'

'Basically. Tucked away in woods and forests, nestled discreetly in Welsh valleys, remote farms. Shit, I could even imagine city centre rooftop communities, as long as they were careful . . . the top of an office block with all that roof space? The top floors with all those large office windows would make a perfect greenhouse.' Raymond seemed tempted to sit down and plan out the viability of such an existence, then stopped himself. 'The point is, those who managed to lie low long enough to outlive the . . . the . . . the *unprepared*, until there were too few to present a problem, it's those people that are alive today, just hidden away somewhere. Trust me. There's plenty more people out there than you think.'

They could hear the sound of splashing and laughter. The others were messing about in the jacuzzi. There were no jets or bubbles, of course, and the water in there was murky with algae, but it was tepid.

'I think they'd rather stay here than head on down to London,' she said.

Raymond shrugged. 'You guys can stay as long as you want but since we're eating up *your* freeze-dried rations, eventually, I'll have to ask you to bring in some more food or . . .'

'Or leave.'

'Basically.' He offered an apologetic smile. 'It's lovely to have company but I really can't afford to feed you. It sounds shit of me to say that, but it totally unbalances my food system.'

She nodded. 'We have to go, anyway. The sooner the better. If we find there's nothing in London, those tubs of freeze-dried pasta crap have got to last long enough to see them safely back.'

He turned to look at her. '*Them*? Not you?'

Silently, she cursed her slip.

211

He looked at her. 'I . . . uh . . . I know about your little girl,' he said. 'Helen told me last night.'

'It's not her business to blab like that.'

'I think she just didn't want me saying anything clumsy. She was thinking of you.'

Leona looked away, tight lipped. 'Whatever we find, I won't be going back.'

'If you find nothing, and you don't go back to your rigs, then what?'

She shrugged. The gesture spelled it out all too clearly.

'You're going home . . . going home to end it, aren't you?'

She said nothing. She said nothing for far too long. Her fingers twisted and wrestled uncomfortably with each other. She could've blurted a 'no', but it would have rung false.

'That's it?' pressed Raymond. 'Going home to die?'

Eventually she looked up from her hands. 'Yes.'

Raymond nodded. 'I thought I saw that.'

'Saw what?'

'Sort of . . . a *calm*. You've made your bed and you're ready to go and sleep in it. If I'm honest with you I think I saw that in Tanya. She didn't leave a note or anything, just a whole load of planting charts and notes. Didn't want to leave me in the lurch. That's what I think happened to her. She just walked out on me, wanted to go home.'

Leona nodded. 'That's . . . what I want. I'm tired.'

'That surprises me.'

'Why?'

'You don't strike me as the giving-up type.'

She took a deep breath, looked around at the towering leaves above them, the shafts of light from a floodlight above lancing down into the micro jungle. 'Hannah was why I bothered. It's different now. I suppose it's easier in a way. I know that sounds shit, but it's easier. I suppose I see a way home now,' she replied. 'I see a way back to her, to my dad, to others I lost during the crash.'

'And you don't strike me as the expecting-a-lovely-pastoral-afterlife type, either.'

'Who knows? Maybe they're there, maybe not. But either way, I guess I'm all done in, Raymond, tired of the struggle. It just goes on and on and all you get every day for the hours of effort is enough food and water to keep you going for another day. That's not life. That's just—'

'Actually, it is. It's what *life* has been for more than half a billion years. The basic struggle to find enough protein to last another day.'

'Yeah?' she sighed. 'Well, you make it sound so wonderfully appealing.'

They both laughed, a dry mirthless chuckle that quickly petered out. 'Truth is, I'm not sure I can cope with another fifty or sixty years of eating boiled fish and potatoes, of longing for a steaming hot bath, longing for a million little luxuries that I'm never going to enjoy again.' She nodded at the others playing in the pool. 'They were all young children back then. They barely remember how wonderful life was, how much we had, how happy we all were.'

'Were we?'

'Shit, I was.'

'Hmm . . . I remember how it was becoming normal to talk of a failing society. You remember that? No community, no sense of belonging, no one looking out for each other any more.'

'*I* was happy, Raymond.'

'Then perhaps you were an exception.'

'Maybe I was.' She looked down at the vegetable garden. 'But I *do* know that I can't be arsed with this any more, grubbing around in the dirt for my protein.' She smiled. 'I know it sounds sad, lazy even, but I'm happy in a way. I know what I want to do, and I'm on my way there.'

'So the others . . . ?'

'Don't know. I'll take them to London to see if we can find

these lights. If it's all a waste of time, then I'll point them in the right direction to get back home. They're big boys and girls now. They don't need me to hold their hands.' She sighed. 'And then I'll find my way home.' She looked up at Raymond. 'Do please keep this to yourself.'

'Sure, all right.'

'I mean it. Most of all, I don't want Jacob to know.' Her voice faltered slightly. 'He wants to live on. You can see it. He's so young. Him and Nathan, they're so hungry for life, to fight on and to make things better again. You know? To rebuild things and have all those cool things we once had again.'

'And you don't?'

'I feel like an old woman. I feel like I'm sixty-five.'

'You're younger than me, aren't you?'

'Doesn't matter. It's how I feel. Life just isn't fucking well worth the struggle.'

'That's a shame. Particularly in someone like you.'

'Why?'

'Here you are, you made it through the worst of it. Ten years on, you're alive, you're not malnourished, you're healthy and fit. You made it this far. Why give up now?'

She looked at him. 'We're different people. I'm just a . . . I'm just a normal girl who'd have been perfectly happy working in an office Monday to Friday and kicking back at the weekends. You, on the other hand, strike me as the kind of survival nut who gets a buzz out of making a go of it. The challenge of it.'

She looked up at the pale plastic sky. 'I mean this is great. You've created a survival bubble and you'll be just fine. But it's a world for you,' she glanced at the others, 'and one guest. A little capsule for two. Meanwhile outside, the world is slowly being overgrown and buildings gradually crumbling and falling in. And there's us eating fish chowder every day

214

and getting all excited just because, for a couple of hours a night, we can turn on some light-bulbs.'

She pursed her lips. 'Like I said, without Hannah, I suppose I have the luxury of saying, stuff it. You know?'

Chapter 33

10 years AC

Thetford Forest,
Norfolk

'I want to stay,' said Helen adamantly. 'I know he fancies me and that's really okay, despite the age thing, because I think he's nice, too.'

Leona rested a hand on her arm. 'I'm not leaving you here.'

She pulled her arm away angrily. 'I'm not a *child* any more.' She looked up at Leona. 'And you're not, like, my teacher any more. Okay?'

Outside the chalet they could hear the boys laughing, talking. And music. Raymond was playing tracks from his favourite-artists playlist over the newly installed speakers; attempting to educate Nathan and Jacob that the *really* old stuff — Nirvana, Chili Peppers, Zeppelin — was better than the plastic pop they'd been exposed to in their childhood. Part of Leona wanted to rush outside and argue the case for the Goo Goo Dolls but there was a more pressing matter right now.

'Helen, you can't just stay here. You *are* still a child. And Raymond's a grown man.'

'He's just a few years older than you! And anyway I'm fifteen, nearly sixteen. And I really like it here.'

That was perfectly understandable. Perhaps under different circumstances, Leona wondered whether she might have batted her eyelids at Raymond a few times and earned that one spare space he'd hinted existed here in this finely balanced ecosystem.

Probably not. This was nice, it was comfortable . . . but it was a bubble. It wasn't the beginning of a new future, the start of Britain rebuilding; it was an isolated chamber that could never change, grow, develop, expand; a little kingdom for two people and several thousand butterflies and insects, that's all it could ever be – a time capsule in which Raymond was comfortably living. Waiting for the world outside to get a move on and fix itself; happy with his library of music and DVDs, and tending his acre of rain forest and his various vegetable plots.

'I'm grown up enough to make my own decisions,' said Helen firmly.

Think about it, she told herself, just a few months older in the world before and she'd be old enough to get herself pregnant, to be given her own council flat and cohabit with whomever the hell she chose.

What difference does a few months make now?

'If we leave you here, Helen, it'll be for good. You know you'd be stuck here?'

She nodded.

'And if it doesn't work out between you . . . what then? Returning home on your own – making your way to Bracton, and the rigs, by yourself – you know how dangerous that could be?'

'But it *will* work. I know he fancies me. And he's got such cool things here. This is everything I've ever wanted. I'll never get bored here.'

Bored? Leona shook her head imperceptibly; *bored*, as if that was the most important thing for Helen to be taking into consideration.

A thought occurred to her. 'So, have you asked him if he wants you to stay?'

She nodded. 'Last night. He said he'd like that.'

Leona couldn't recall a quiet moment with the two of them alone long enough to move onto a conversation like that. They'd all been out in the middle at the table by the pool until long after the sun had gone down and the lights had automatically clicked on, illuminating the large fronds above with soft ambient green spotlights. They'd all been together until they'd decided to turn in for the evening.

She must have sneaked across to his chalet during the night.

Leona didn't like the fact that Raymond had not mentioned something was going on. Perhaps the two of them had slept together. That felt wrong. But then she realised that was a judgement from another time. Different values then. Way different.

'Helen, I'm not happy leaving you here. Not on your own.'

Her face hardened. 'You can't exactly drag me along with you, can you?'

Her question rang off the wooden walls of the cabin until it was silent. Through the chalet door she could hear the thud of a drumbeat, a base line and Raymond singing tunelessly along to lyrics she vaguely recognised.

Helen was right, though, they couldn't drag her along.

'All right,' she said eventually, 'all right, stay if you want.'

Her face brightened, the sulky curl in her lip straightening. 'Thank you, Lee. I knew you'd see it my way.'

Leona offered a tight smile. 'I hope it works out for you both.'

They stayed a second night, which pleased Helen, giving her another try-before-you-buy session with Raymond. But Raymond seemed less engaged with the rest of them, distracted as if the novelty of their company had finally worn off and he was keen to get back to whatever routine he maintained, albeit now with his newly acquired partner.

Leona couldn't shake off the feeling that she'd handed over a child bride to a man old enough to be her father. Sure, Raymond looked much younger than his thirty-five years, but the age gap existed.

The boys weren't entirely surprised when she told them Helen was staying. Jacob was perhaps the most affected, surprisingly. He and Helen routinely poked and prodded each other with playground insults, but deep down, Leona realised, there'd been a tender sibling-like bond there.

The next day they packed their things aboard their trailer, still sitting on the back of the truck with their bikes, and Raymond drove them all to the junction beyond Thetford. An old army blockade of rusting loops of wire and flaking concrete barriers still stretched across the slip road leading onto the A-road. The road blockades were one of the measures put in place by the government, trying to restrict the mass movement of people by locking down the transport systems; railways, airports, block the motorways and A-roads to prevent logjams of traffic. It was the last thing they managed to do before the chain of command began to falter and they lost control of the situation.

Their last folly.

Jacob and Nathan hefted the trailer off the back of the truck between them, hooked their bikes up to it and made ready to lead the trailer around the blockade. Then there were tearful hugs between the boys and Helen as Leona stepped aside to talk with Raymond.

'You'll look after her, won't you?'

He nodded. 'I will.'

'And what if it doesn't work out? What if you two find out you don't get on?' she asked, realising she sounded like the mother of the bride cross-examining a potential suitor.

'Different rules now. This is the Make-Do world, Leona. You make sure things work. There really is no alternative.'

She shrugged. It was probably the best answer he could have given. Perhaps Raymond would drum some common sense into that woolly young head of Helen's.

She offered a hand and he took it.

'You know,' he said softly, 'don't get me wrong, but I

actually hope you *don't* find what you're after. You know? Your home, your way out.'

Her smile was tired and worn down to a lifeless curve.

They watched the others for a moment. Helen was sobbing like a baby as she hugged the boys. They in turn were firm-lipped, competing with each other to hold back tears in as manly a way as possible.

'Take good care of her,' she said again, squeezing Raymond's hand. 'If the boys decide to return to the rigs after London, they'll be sure to drop by and say hello . . . if that's all right with you?' There was gentle caution in her voice.

He pushed a lank tress of hair our of his face. 'Of course. And they'd be most welcome. They're a nice pair of lads. A good laugh.'

'They are.'

'And I'll look forward to seeing you along with them,' he added.

'Bye,' she said, letting go of his hand, turning and starting towards the others.

'Leona?'

She stopped and looked back at him.

He grinned awkwardly, looking like a child about to play a prank. 'I left you a present in the trailer.'

'What?'

'No big deal, just a little something.'

She cocked her head curiously. 'Uhh, okay . . . well, thanks.'

'I hope it makes a difference,' he said. 'Changes your mind.'

Her brows arched curiously and a half smile momentarily stretched her mouth. She turned back round and joined the others, grabbing the handlebar of her bike and lifting it up off the hard shoulder.

'Come on you two,' she said, wheeling the bike forward

until the tow rope pulled taut on the trailer. 'I'm not pulling this bugger on my own.'

They joined her swiftly; the three of them pushing their bikes forward, the trailer rolling behind as they curved round the edge of the blockade, past the small jumble of abandoned cars and vans that had been brought to a sudden cluttered standstill ten years ago. Some were still loaded with family keepsakes, photo albums, birth certificates and passports – slowly fading and yellowing.

Leona looked back and saw Raymond and Helen standing side by side at the back of his truck. She waved at them. Raymond offered a coy nod before turning away, rounding the truck and climbing back into the cab.

Helen stood where she was a moment longer, watching their progress up the slip road towards the A11. Then she, too, turned away.

Chapter 34

10 years AC

'LeMan 49/25a' – ClarenCo Gas Rig Complex, North Sea

'It's all right, I know, Walter,' said Jenny, her voice croaked weakly. 'I know Hannah's gone.' She licked her lips, they were cracked and dry.

'Jenny . . . I'm so, so, sorry,' he said.

'Water please, Walter.'

'It . . . it . . . was an awful bloody accident. I just—'

'Walter, please, get me some water.'

He stopped bumbling and reached for the tumbler beside her cot, gently tilting her head as she sipped from it. She winced painfully as he let her head back down on to the pillow.

'Who . . . who told you?' he asked.

'I overheard you and Tami talking,' she replied. 'Some time ago, I think, not long after you brought me in from the explosion. I've known for a while.'

She could have told Walter that some time during the last few feverish weeks her dead husband Andy had come to tell her; sat down on the bucket chair beside her cot, just where Walter was sitting now, and explained to her that Hannah had died in the blast, and her son and daughter had decided to leave. But she knew how that would sound. Fever or not, hallucination or not, she knew all those things and she didn't need to hear Walter's fumbling, heavy-handed attempt at breaking the news; she *really* didn't need to hear a stream of tear-soaked apologies from him right now. She knew what she needed to know. That's all.

She grimaced and whimpered as she adjusted position slightly; the tight and raw skin on her shoulder and neck stabbed at her mercilessly.

'How's the pain?'

'It's manageable,' she said, 'when I don't move.'

'Dr Gupta's lowering the dose,' he said. 'She's worried about giving you too much.'

'A little more,' she said wincing, 'a little more than she's giving me now would be good.'

'I'll tell her.'

Pressing matters, Jenny, pressing matters – the community . . .

'So, how are things?'

Walter's face instantly darkened. 'Things are getting messy.'

'*Messy?* What does that mean?'

'Morale is low. The explosion, the generator not working, no lights. And the schedule is beginning to break down. People aren't doing their jobs properly. The kids sneaking off after Leona . . . I suppose there's a feeling amongst people that they're rats leaving a sinking ship.' Walter shook his head unhappily. 'It's been very difficult trying to run this place whilst you've been ill. People haven't really taken to the idea of me being in charge. I've had Alice mouthing off all sorts of things about me . . . about you, too. And then, I think we've also got a problem with Mr Latoc.'

For a moment the name meant nothing to her. Vaguely familiar, that's all.

'The Belgian man? Valérie Latoc? We might have a problem with him.'

Then it came back to her. She'd forgotten completely about him. 'He's still here?'

'He's still officially on probation, but it's been, what? six weeks since he arrived?'

More woolly memories came back to her. She remembered

confiding in Martha, having her hair cut, wanting to look good. And she'd looked so much better, so much younger, for all of five minutes. Jenny had caught sight of her reflection yesterday and could have cried. Her hair was gone on the right side of her head, as if someone had taken clippers to her and walked away leaving the job half done. A fine pale fuzz was already growing back, but there was no knowing how it would look; it could end up as patchy, pitiful tufts that she'd forever more feel self-conscious about, cover with scarves or some floppy cap.

Her skin, livid red and as raw as tenderised meat all the way down one side of her face, down her neck and across her shoulder, would always be scarred, criss-crossed with star-bursts of pale ribbed flesh.

'Jenny, Valérie Latoc, it appears, is some sort of faith preacher.'

She looked back at Walter. 'Preaching *what*, exactly?'

'Well, from the bits I've overheard, it's a jumble of things; part Christian, part Islamic, mostly mumbo-jumbo. Dr Gupta tells me that he's started holding prayer meetings in the evenings in the mess.'

'What?'

'And his people now hold some sort of blessing before each meal. It's getting—'

'*His people?* For fuck's sake, Walter!' she snapped. Her face and neck stabbed her in retaliation for moving. 'Walter, what's going on?'

He shook his head. 'I couldn't really stop it, Jenny. There's so many of them who want to do it now. I can't just order them to stop it.'

'How many?'

'I'd say thirty, maybe forty of them.'

Jenny cursed silently. She guessed she might have had a problem with Alice spreading mischief in her absence. There were quite a number of people who actually bothered to listen

224

to her griping and agreed with her that the community was large enough that it was time to think about whether its leader should be democratically selected. But this bubbling under-current of dissent had been, at least before the explosion, something Jenny had been able to keep a lid on. Alice might have been voicing aloud an opinion that was beginning to gain traction, but she was also her own worst enemy, unpopu-lar because all she seemed to do was bitch and moan and make catty asides that seemed to get under everyone's skin.

But Latoc . . . she hadn't thought for one moment the softly-spoken man she'd interviewed — what seemed like a lifetime ago now — was going to be a problem. And he certainly hadn't come across as some sort of firebrand.

'Mealtime blessings?' she uttered. 'You let him start doing that? Did you explain it was one of our rules?'

'I . . . I spoke to him about it.'

'And?'

'He said it was not for us to make those kind of rules. You know, Jenny, do you remember? I thought he was trouble.'

She sighed. She remembered, but then she'd put it down to the old boy being a little jealous. 'Right,' she winced as she shifted position again, 'well, I think I need to have a chat with him, and soon.'

Walter nodded. 'Be careful.'

Jenny studied him for a moment. 'Why? What about?'

'He's become quite popular. Everyone seems to like him.' There was a note of bitterness in his voice. 'We really ought to get rid of him.'

'There's nothing wrong with him being *liked*, Walter. I can't . . . I won't, send someone off these rigs because they're popular. That's just, you know, life. Some people make friends more easily than—'

'But what if—' Walter clamped his mouth shut, perhaps realising he sounded churlish and paranoid.

'But what?'

'What if people here decide they want him to be in charge?'

She tried a smile. The scabs on her cheek crackled and split like brittle parchment. It hurt. 'Well that's fine, they can if they want. But he and his fans will have to go somewhere else. This is *our* home, you and me and the others that came here *first*.' Jenny felt anger bubbling up inside her.

This is our home. That's why there weren't bloody elections here.

It would be like having friends to stay in your house only for them to turn round later on and decide they didn't like the wallpaper and were going to redecorate.

'I'm not letting someone else take over our home, Walter.' She reached out and patted his shoulder. 'Don't worry. I'll talk to him about this. If he really wants to start doing missionary work, then he's going to have to leave and do it somewhere else.'

Walter nodded. 'I'm sorry, Jenny. I screwed up whilst you were sick. I suppose I'm just . . .' he shook his head, frustrated and angry with himself. 'I'm just not a people-person. Not like you. I—'

Jenny squeezed his arm. 'Don't worry.'

He sighed. 'I'm so glad you're beginning to feel better again.'

She looked at him. She'd have laughed if she could do it without moving. Laughed bitterly. *Feeling better? Better? Oh, yeah, I'm feeling great.*

What she wanted to do right now was just go back to sleep; take a triple dose of whatever horse tranquillisers Tami had been administering to her, and just leave . . . check out for good. Let someone else pick up the baton and look after this miserable island of lost souls.

But instead she smiled again, feeling the taut skin across her face wrinkle painfully. 'Yes, Walter, I'm feeling a lot better.'

Chapter 35

10 years AC

Suffolk

Raymond's present, as it happened, did make a difference. A huge difference.

She'd forgotten all about it as they got under way, sliding onto the saddles of their bikes and pedalling along the flat road south towards London. Heading through East Anglia, mercifully free of any steep inclines, just a long, straight and empty road, flanked on either side by untamed farmland that had gone to seed; fields of maize and rape that had quite happily propagated in partnership with the bees year on year without the need of any human husbandry or heavy duty machinery.

The trailer rolled obediently behind them on thick rubber tyres that crackled over ten years of wind-borne debris that had blown across the empty road; twigs, leaves, grit and gravel.

They stopped for a rest at midday, sweating from the warmth of the sun diffused by a thin veil of combed-out clouds. All of a sudden she had remembered Raymond's present and found an HMV carrier bag in the back of the trailer. Inside she found an iPod and – very handy – a wind-up charger to go with it. There was a note with them.

Leona,
I filled it up with a load of stuff from my library. Sixty gigabytes of music. It's fully charged, and the charger will sort you out thereafter. It's not the greatest hand

charger in the world – ten minutes of winding seems to give you about half a dozen songs' worth of power.

Music got me through several years of being alone. There were quite a few days when I guess I also thought 'why bother' . . . and it was the heavier stuff, like Zeppelin and Metallica, played bloody loud, that got me off my arse.

Seriously, I hope this somehow makes you change your mind. The world will be a poorer place without you in it.

Raymond.

PS: Yes, I will take good care of her.

Leona screwed the note up and discreetly tossed it into a pile of rubbish and dried leaves that had pooled against the kerb of the hard shoulder. Glad Jacob hadn't found the bag and read the note.

On the other side of the trailer the boys were both bitching about their saddle sores, Jacob nagging Nathan to swap because his saddle looked more padded.

She held the iPod in her hand, still smooth and unscratched, box-new in fact. Her thumb remembered how to switch it on. The small screen flickered, glowing weakly in the afternoon light. She stared down at the small screen in the palm of her hand, a menu that, once upon a time, had been so familiar to her. She must have scrolled up and down through it a million times back in the old world . . .

Music
Photos
Videos
Extras
Settings
Shuffle Songs

She imagined herself a nineteen-year-old degree student again. If her gaze could just remain within that two-inch backlit display she could pretend the world beyond it was as it once was; that the last ten years had been nothing more than a very lucid and very long dream. That it was an ordinary Monday morning once more, a lecture to get dressed for and hurry along to and not be late for, the bustle of other students around her in a shared kitchen, the hiss of a kettle, the tinkle of teaspoons in mugs, the radio blaring in the corner . . .

She held the iPod right up close to her face until the words blurred.

If I could just jump through the screen into the past.

'Hey, Lee? What you got there?'

It was Jacob. The fantasy evaporated and she realised her cheeks were wet. She quickly rubbed them dry.

'What is it, Lee?'

'A gift from Raymond,' she replied.

An hour later, back on their bikes coasting effortlessly down a gentle incline that seemed to have been going on for miles, she understood what Raymond had said in his note. Music pumping through the earphones, songs she half-remembered, favourites she'd never forgotten. A bit of rock music played deafeningly loud was as good a tonic as anything else.

On the flat horizon ahead of them she could see the grey outskirts of Cambridge and the late afternoon sun already beginning to make arrangements to settle for the night.

So should we.

Up ahead of them, off a slip road, was a short row of roadside terraced council houses, the front lawns littered with rotting rubbish and overgrown with grass gone to seed. Out front, a dozen cars, parked half on, half off the kerb were quietly rusting away, several of them blackened and twisted with fire damage from long ago.

A road sign informed them that Cambridge was five miles further up the road. It was as good a place as any to park up for the night. She pulled the earphones out and told the boys to steer up the slip road.

A few moments later, the bicycles braked with a hiss and skittering of dislodged gravel. They dismounted outside the row of houses and their cluttered overgrown front yards. Picking the emptiest garden they set about clearing some space, stamping down the tall grass and weeds and tossing aside enough of the garden toys tangled beneath to set down their tents and build a cooking fire between them. Leona sent Jacob into the nearest house to forage for firewood whilst she helped Nathan assemble the tents. She pulled a tub of their freeze-dried food out from beneath the trailer's tarpaulin and measured enough out for the three of them, whistling as she did so.

Jacob stepped cautiously through the open front door, pushing it in with a creak of rusted hinges and the rattle of a loose glass panel nestled in a weather-warped frame. The dim interior beyond had once been a small front room; a flat-screen TV, the glass cracked in one corner, a fireplace. Above that was a school portrait of a boy in his uniform, hair cropped short on a bullet-shaped head and grinning mischievously. On the mantelpiece beside the photo sat an attendance certificate for *Jamie Conner – Year 5* proudly framed. Jacob eased himself past a single sofa and an armchair, both rotting from damp and the rain that had blown in through the open door over the last ten winters.

He stepped across the lounge and into the kitchen and found a pine breakfast table and chairs that they could use for firewood. Several cheap kitchen units had rotted from their brackets and collapsed from the wall, spilling mismatched crockery and favourite tea-stained mugs across the counter and onto the linoleum-covered floor. A single weed grew proudly through the broken frosted glass of a back door leading onto a modest rear yard with a trampoline in it.

A narrow and steep stairway that creaked underfoot took him up to a bathroom and two other rooms with doors ajar. One was a boy's bedroom wallpapered with a pattern of footballs and goalposts and peppered with Blu-Tacked glossy pullouts of Ronaldinho. Through the other door he saw the end of a double bed and the tented bumps of something beneath a fading quilt. He didn't need to step forward to know what was in there. Jacob had seen this hundreds of times already over the years; the beds of families who had opted for the easy way out rather than fight to survive, beneath the faded quilt the pitiful twisted leather carcasses embracing each other, empty pill bottles on the bedside table.

He headed quickly back downstairs, content that the rotting kitchen units and the pine table and chairs were more than they needed to keep a fire going tonight. No need to come up and disturb young Jamie Conner and his parents again.

'South,' said Nathan looking at the others. 'South from here. Right? That'll take us down towards the Dartford Tunnel?'

Leona studied the scuffed road atlas by the flickering light of the campfire. She'd pulled it from the rack of a garage several days ago and already it looked thumbed enough to have belonged to a well-travelled sales rep. Flipping from one page to the next she muttered under her breath.

'I never could read bloody road maps.'

Nathan sighed impatiently. 'If we just head south, man, we'll, like, hit the Thames, right? S'all we need to do.'

Leona shook her head. 'Heading south from here won't take us to London.' Her finger brushed down the page from Bishops Stortford. 'We'll be going more towards the east of London and then we'll have to turn right to head in along the

Thames estuary. That's a lot longer.' She looked up at him and Jacob. 'We should just follow the road into London. It takes us right into the centre. That's far quicker.'

And Shepherd's Bush would be a couple of hours from there. Nearly journey's end.

Jacob frowned. 'But we might miss the lights Mr Latoc saw . . . we might go past them.'

'You told me he said the sky was glowing, Jake. Right?'

Jacob nodded.

'Well, if he was telling the truth, then you'll see them for miles. I'm sure we won't miss them.'

'He was crossing the river. He said he saw them to the east.'

'Yeah, Jake, but where was he crossing?'

Jacob shrugged. 'He just said it was somewhere near Big Ben.'

He looked down at the map, recognising the familiar blue loops of the Thames. 'We should head down to the river and just follow it.'

She looked again at the map. 'That means,' she said running her finger across the page, 'we'll come off the M11 onto the M25 until the Dartford Tunnel . . .'

Nathan nodded. 'S'right, then turn right an' follow the river into London. Easy, man.'

'We won't get lost,' said Jacob, 'if we just follow the river.'

The idea of keeping to the Thames certainly felt a little more appealing than heading into the bowels of the city, which might still be – most probably was – a ghostly necropolis of dark and abandoned office blocks and shopping malls. To have the open river to their left would offer some reassurance. A less direct route though and it would probably add another day to their journey, given the sluggish pace they were making towing the heavy trailer behind them.

Another day won't hurt, will it? She could hang on another day. She realised she wasn't in quite the same hurry to get home and pop a bottle of pills as she had been a few days ago.

'All right, then,' she sighed and shared a quick conciliatory smile with the boys. 'Along the river it is.'

Jacob placed a hand on her shoulder. 'Hey, maybe, if it's not too far we could drop by our old home. See how it is.'

Leona wondered if Jacob was probing; had somehow sensed her resolve to go home for good. 'I don't think so. Best we leave Dad in peace, eh?'

He looked up at her. 'I miss him.'

'I know, but he's not really there, Jake. It's just a body now. Just like all the others.'

They'd seen the desiccated remains that had once been dads and sons, mums and daughters, still clad in football strips, jumpers, summer blouses and teen fashion tops. And Dad was going to look just the same; a dried husk in clothes stained a dark sepia.

'All right,' he said eventually.

She reached out and squeezed his hand. 'Let's just head towards Dartford and see if those lights are there somewhere along the Thames, eh? Just like Mr Latoc said.'

Both of them nodded.

She folded the page of the road map over and then snuggled down into her sleeping bag, watching the flames dance and sparks flutter into the night sky. She fell asleep listening to Jacob and Nathan discussing comic book super-heroes.

Chapter 36

10 years AC

Jenny caught herself absent-mindedly tugging the tattered drape partially across her cabin porthole to dim the room slightly. She could hear the clack of feet on the metal steps up to her floor and then the softer tap on linoleum as they approached her door. She chided herself for fretting about how she looked. There were more important matters at hand.

She heard the rap of a knuckle on the door.

'Mrs Sutherland?'

It was Valérie Latoc.

'You can come in,' she said, pulling herself up on the cot to a comfortable sitting position.

He stepped tentatively into the cabin and offered her a warm and friendly smile. It seemed like an eternity since she'd last seen his face; another lifetime. In fact, just a month and a half had passed. She remembered wanting to look good for him because she'd found him attractive. Right now she felt painfully self-conscious of the livid ripples of healing skin on her face and her hair now clipped uniformly all over to a less than feminine short dark fuzz.

'You are much better?' he inquired.

'I'm mending, thank you.'

There was someone else behind him. Martha stepped into the room in his wake, her eyes lighting up with joy at the sight of her. 'Jenny!'

'Martha?'

Jenny hadn't asked for her to come up. In fact, she

expressly asked Walter to tell Valérie she wished to speak with him *alone*. The woman stepped around him and towards the cot, her broad dark face beaming kindly, genuinely relieved to see her friend awake and getting well.

'Oh, Jenny, love, I've been so worried for you,' she said, extending arms to embrace her.

'Please . . . don't!' she said holding up a hand to stay Martha. 'My skin hurts.'

Martha froze where she was. Her full vibrant voice faltered. 'Oh, love, I'm so, so sorry about Hannah. She was such a wonderful little—'

Jenny reached out and grasped one of her hands. This wasn't the conversation she wanted to have right now although she was learning to accept that everyone who'd so far been allowed to see her insisted on opening with an awkwardly offered condolence; genuinely heartfelt, of course, but always awkward and faltering. Each time for Jenny, behind her weary smile of gratitude, it was another painful tug on the stitching of her broken heart.

'I know . . . she was,' she replied. 'Thank you, Martha. I know you were fond of her.'

Martha's eyes filled as she nodded silently. 'One of God's little angels,' she whimpered. 'She's in a better place now, Jenny, love. So much better.'

Valérie nodded. 'Yes. We prayed for her soul. And yours . . . and that you would heal very quickly.'

Jenny grimaced. She felt that a 'thank you' was perhaps the right thing to say under the circumstances, but then, *prayers* − that was exactly what she'd wanted to talk to Valérie about, alone.

'Yes, and look, that's why I wanted to see you. I've been informed, Mr Latoc, that mealtimes in the mess have become an opportunity for an open prayer meeting.'

Valérie made no attempt to deny it. 'Yes, I have been saying a prayer before meals, this is correct.'

235

'Are you aware that it's one of the few things I ask people in this community *not* to do?'

His eyebrows arched, his smooth voice rose in surprise. 'To pray?'

'To pray aloud in a shared space like the mess room, yes.'

'It is just a blessing,' he smiled. 'That is all; a thanks to God for feeding us.'

Jenny was surprised by the sudden jab of irritation she felt. 'No, well you see it isn't God that has to shovel human shit onto our potatoes every day, is it? He doesn't water them every day with rainwater we've carefully collected or fetched by tug from Bracton, does he? He doesn't do any of the things we all have to do each and every day to survive.'

'We are here, alive and well,' he replied calmly, 'because He wills it. A little thank you at mealtimes, is this so much to ask?'

She stared at him, then at Martha who was nodding silently. She knew Martha had faith, was a Baptist, prayed every day and every night, but it was nothing she'd ever tried to press on Jenny. It was a personal faith, between her and her God.

'He *wills* it?'

Valérie smiled as he nodded.

'Jenny,' cut in Martha, her voice still trembling with emotion, 'I love you like a sister and it breaks my heart to think how much pain you're going through, love. Hannah, Leona and Jacob all gone. My boy, Nathan, left with them. I spend every night worryin' after them.' Her cheeks shone with tears. 'But it helps, love. It helps if you'll accept Him into your heart. His love will make things right for you again. His love—'

'Martha,' she raised her hand again, wincing from the pull on her tight skin, 'Martha, please.'

She hushed, clasping her hands together in front of her face.

Jenny could feel the salty sting of a tear rolling down her own tender right cheek.

Dammit. She didn't want Valérie to see her crying. She didn't need him to see her weak like this. It was only going to embolden him.

'God *isn't* going to bring back Hannah,' she said, struggling hard to keep her voice even. 'She died because a single fastening clamp came off the generator. It wasn't attached tightly enough and it came off. She died because we overlooked safety—'

'No. It was because He wanted her with Him, away from this dark world,' cut in Valérie.

'She died, Mr Latoc, because there should have been a fucking lock on the door, or a more secure clamp holding the feed pipe!' Her voice croaked unpleasantly. If she'd been stronger, it would have snapped a brittle angry bark. 'That's it. It was shitty, bad luck!' She felt her voice warbling, her throat painful. 'Just plain . . . shit luck.'

'Accept His love,' he urged her, 'accept God into your life, Jennifer. It's what everyone here needs now. God sent me here—'

'Now stop right there!'

It was quiet in her cabin except for the far-off bustle of activity coming from the canteen downstairs, the rattle of cutlery in a washing-up bowl full of saltwater, the nattering voices of those on galley duty this morning.

'There's a very good reason why I don't allow prayers over meals, why I'd rather we don't have organised prayer meetings on any of the platforms.' She sipped some water, taking the time to steady herself. 'We've got . . . shit, I don't know how many different faiths on these rigs. Catholics, Protestants, Jews, Muslims . . . at least half a dozen Hindus that I'm aware of. I say "yes" to one, I have to say "yes" to all. Then you know what'll happen?'

Valérie narrowed his eyes.

'Whatever weak glue it is that's just about managing to hold us together will dissolve and before you know it we'll have a Christian-only platform. A Muslim-only platform. There'll be people up here petitioning me for segregated mealtimes for different faiths, for periods of fasting, for calls to prayer at all times of the day. This community won't work that way. It'll fall apart.'

'Jennifer,' said Valérie, 'we will *all* be so much stronger unified by Him. The message I bring from God is for *everyone* to hear—'

'No!'

She wished she'd arranged to have this meeting with either Tami or Walter beside her. Just for a little back-up. 'No! I'm absolutely not having this! You want to pray, to thank God for your daily hot meal, well okay that's fine, but you can do it privately in your head. Or out loud in your own space before you come over here. If He's so bloody well omnipotent then I'm sure He'll hear you there just as easily as in the mess.'

'Oh, Jenny,' said Martha shaking her head sadly.

She turned her attention to her friend. 'Martha, I'm sorry, but that's the way it has to be. We've got by very well these last few years without ringing bells and calls to prayer.'

'Valérie has opened my eyes, love,' she replied. 'The crash . . . the end of the old world. It was the Lord making a brand new start. The End Times, just like He promised would come. It was the Rapture, love. And this place is our ark!'

Jenny glanced back at the man.

Ark? Just what the hell has he been preaching?

She realised Walter was right. Valérie Latoc was trouble.

'Martha, it was an oil crash. Oil was on its way to running out and the supply choked. That's what happened. You know that.'

'Or it is God's punishment for the sin of greed?' said

Valérie. 'Allah's condemnation for our arrogance? Jehovah's damnation for—'

'Will you shut up!'

Valérie did, but then he shook his head with pity. 'I am sorry, Jennifer, but I am here for a purpose. There is much work for me to do here. Please, I ask you to open your heart before it is too late.'

She wondered if there was an implied threat in that.

She shook her head and waved for them to get out. 'All right, we're done. You know my feelings on this. I don't want any more food blessings in the canteen, that's stopping right now!'

'Jenny?' pleaded Martha.

'I mean it! No more.' She turned her hard eyes on Valérie. 'You're still here on probation, Mr Latoc. Do you understand?'

For a moment she considered whether to revoke his probation right here, right now. But then realised Latoc would probably simply refuse. And then he'd have to be forcibly evicted. She wondered how many people would rally round him. Thirty? Forty? And other than Walter armed with a gun, who would rally on her side? A confrontation might be exactly what he's after; an opportunity to portray her as some sort of out-of-touch tyrant. An opportunity to discuss whether the time had come for someone else to lead them.

A stern warning for now, then. I need to get up and about and see how far he's got his little hooks into the people.

'I am seriously considering asking you to leave, Mr Latoc. If this continues, then I'm going to be forced to do that. It's one of the *few* rules we have, and you're breaking it. Do you understand?'

'Time is running out,' he replied. 'Do you know right now God is judging this place?'

'Please leave now!' she barked, pointing to the door.

They turned and stepped away obediently, Martha glanced

239

back over her shoulder at her as she left. It wasn't defiance or anger on her face, just sadness and, perhaps, pity.

As Jenny listened to the soft sound of their feet retreating down the passageway towards the stairwell, she realised that she'd achieved nothing more than to harden the man's resolve. She needed to get herself back on her feet, and do that quickly. To talk with Tami and Walter and the one or two others she trusted. In fact, she'd have counted Martha amongst them if she hadn't turned up alongside Valérie Latoc.

This isn't good.

Chapter 37

10 years AC

M25 Motorway,
London

The motorway took them clockwise around London in a south-easterly direction. They cruised along the wide, empty motorway, all eyes cast to their right examining the distant grey urban skyline for any signs of life.

On the approach to each slip road they'd become accustomed to the familiar pattern of a build-up of abandoned vehicles, trailing back down the exit run and out onto the motorway clogging all three lanes. Each time their progress was entirely blocked they were forced to unload the trailer and lift it over the central barrier between them and proceed along the oncoming lanes until they too, became impassable, then it was back over to the other side again. It seemed like every vehicle in London had ended up becoming ensnared on this motorway, caught bumper to bumper at every exit point.

Finally they came off at a junction that would take them into the city and, eventually, down to the Thames. There had been a frustrating half an hour trying to ease the trailer through a logjam of vehicles and around a barricade; once more having to unload the trailer, lift it over and repack it. But since then the ride had been almost effortless; the gentle coasting whirr of their bicycle wheels along the empty road, the occasional clatter of chains shifting gear and catching, the crackle of glass granules beneath their tyres and the rustle of dried leaves wind-borne and stirring.

And every now and then, when she decided it was her turn

with the iPod, she would get utterly lost in the soundtrack of her younger, happier days.

She grinned as she cycled; felt almost *good* – the music made the past feel tangible. For some reason it made some sort of a future feel almost possible. She began to ask herself what she was going to do if they really did see lights; whether she'd still want to part with the boys and head home.

Sunlight shone into her eyes, finding gaps through the thin veil of clouds; not too hot as they pedalled, but still T-shirt-warm when they occasionally stopped to catch their breath.

By early afternoon they took the next exit which, like all the others, was plugged with abandoned vehicles, on to another A-road heading west, roughly parallel to the Thames ten miles further south of them, into central London.

They soon discovered, though, that progress from this point on wasn't going to be quite so easy. Although the road wasn't so blocked that they needed to dismount and negotiate their trailer over or around any obstacles, there were enough cars and trucks left on the hard shoulder or skewed across one lane or another that it was a relentless weaving slalom for them.

By four in the afternoon, they were passing through a lifeless outer London, still and silent; terraced houses and three-storey blocks of flats lined both sides of the road, every last window smashed leaving dark eye-sockets out of which tattered net curtains fluttered.

Leona noticed how quiet the boys had become, particularly Jacob. The spirited chattering about computer games and comics had dropped down a notch as they'd left the motor-way. Now they pedalled in sombre silence, listening to the soft whisper of a breeze whistle tunelessly through empty office windows. They exchanged wary glances every now and then when they heard the clatter of loose things caught by eddies inside.

They crossed a bridge over a wide estuary, watching the

afternoon sun emerge to sprinkle dazzling shards of light across the still water. Tugs and barges lay askew on mud flats either side, gulls and terns stepping delicately between them across the silt looking for an evening meal. Over the bridge, the road dipped south bringing them ever closer to the Thames which they would have been able to see by now if it wasn't for the buildings on their left: shopfronts with floors of office space perched on top and riverside warehousing.

As they rattled and weaved along the road, the office blocks either side of them grew taller and more claustrophobic, pressing in on the road and towering over a seemingly endless parade of gutted newsagents, pubs, pawnbrokers and bookmakers. The sun was hidden by the tall buildings, every now and then a winking amber eye staring at them through first-floor windows, across the offices of abandoned call-centre desks and cubicle partitions.

'Hang on,' said Leona quietly. She stopped and pulled out her road map once more, orienting it to match the direction they faced.

Nathan looked around, frowning as he did so. 'Hey, I think I know this. This is, like, right near that big exhibition place.'

Leona nodded, her eyes on the map. 'The ExCel Centre?'

'That's the one.'

'What's the *eck-sell*?' asked Jacob.

She looked up at the junction they'd stopped at. Like every other, it was littered with all manner of pilfered junk, dragged out, examined and dumped some time during the last decade; tall weeds poking opportunistically up through gutter grilles, cracks and bulges in the crumbling tarmac road. Amongst the debris, the occasional small bundles of stained and sun-faded clothes, from which dark leathery twigs and tufted scarecrow heads protruded.

She spotted a rust-peppered street sign above a KFC. 'Prince Regent Lane.' She checked her map again. 'The exhibition centre is just down at the end of this road.'

Jacob squinted. 'Maybe that's where the lights were coming from?'

Nathan nodded. 'Could be. It's a big-huge place, Jay, right on the Thames.'

'They did those big exhibition things there,' added Leona. 'Ideal Home exhibition, a boating thing . . . it's enormous. It might have been used for one of the safe zones.'

The three of them stared down the street.

Jacob looking from one to the other. 'So, we should go and see, right?'

Leona debated whether, with the daylight they had left, they should settle themselves in for the night. They hadn't seen a single soul since entering London, yet she felt the urge to find somewhere secure, somewhere they could barricade themselves in. Even if there were no people around she'd seen plenty of dogs of all shapes and sizes scattering nervously away at the sound of their approach and watching them warily from dark doorways as they passed. She certainly didn't fancy camping out in the middle of the street tonight.

Looking at the others, neither did they.

On the other hand, she felt a burning urge to go take a look-see. According to the map the exhibition centre wasn't far away, perhaps another ten or fifteen minutes down the road. And then they'd be there, right on the bank of the Thames, with a clear line of sight up and down the river for miles. If it wasn't the ExCel building Mr Latoc had seen glowing at night, it could possibly be the O2 Arena, or perhaps one or other of the towers of Canary Wharf? Whichever building it was, if somebody was generating light enough to reflect off an overcast night sky, surely, from there, right on that famous bend in the Thames, they'd have the best chance of seeing it.

It was quite possible that they could be sleeping beneath powered lights tonight.

'All right,' she said. 'We've got time to go check out the ExCel. It's not that far from here.'

They climbed back on their bicycles and turned left into Prince Regent Lane. It reminded her of the main road near their home in Shepherd's Bush; a party-mix of shops either side: halal butchers, Caribbean takeaways, a shop selling saris, another selling hijabs, a snooker club, a small open-air market with rows of empty wooden stalls, a video store, a supermarket, mosques and several off-licences elbowing each other for space.

Moments later, halfway down Prince Regent Lane, they caught sight of the top of the giant exhibition building above a squat row of two-storey shops; they could see sprigs of white support poles protruding above a long pale roof. Beside it they could see the tops of several quayside cranes that had, once upon a time, serviced the busy barges pulling into Victoria Docks.

It was still light, the combed-out cloudy veil now lit from below by a setting sun; a beautiful vanilla skyline of ripples and veins staining the world with a rich sepia warmth. Although Leona had secretly doubted they were going to find anything at all in London, doubted the city was busy rebuilding itself on the quiet, she found herself desperately hoping the waning light of day would trigger an automatic lights-on response from somewhere nearby. She almost began to believe that the pale roof of the exhibition centre was going to flicker to life at any second, bathed in the clinical glare of a dozen roof-mounted floodlights.

Their pace quickened.

Towards the end of the road the squat buildings gave way to flat open ground, a scruffy little playground full of waist-high grass and brambles growing up the rusting A-frame of a child's swing. Beyond it was a railway track with a pedestrian bridge over the top that would lead them down rickety steps onto a large riverside parking area at the rear of the giant, warehouse-like ExCel Centre.

'Oh, fuck!' gasped Jacob. 'It's huge! I never seen a building this big!'

Leona remembered coming here once before, as a girl; she must have been ten or eleven, Jacob hadn't even been born then. Mum and Dad had taken her along to some sort of horse and pony expo – to see whether she really did want to 'get into horses' or whether it was just another of her many passing fads.

'We should leave the bikes and the trailer here,' she said, 'if we're going over the bridge to get a closer look.'

'I'll get the gun,' said Jacob. 'Just to be safe.'

He retrieved it from the back of the trailer.

'Give it to Nathan,' Leona said. Jacob sighed before he handed it over.

'Here.'

Nathan cocked it and slung the strap over his shoulder.

'Okay?' she said.

The others nodded silently, quickly kicking their bike stands down. As their feet rang noisily up the metal steps of the overpass she looked along the railway line below, sleepers lost beneath a carpet of tangled green, and at the small Docklands Light Railway station several hundred yards away. She recalled stepping out onto the platform down there, excited by the sight of the giant white building towering over her and the convergence of so many other mums and daughters looking forward to their day inside.

So quiet now, though. No bustle and hubbub of expectant young voices, just the soft rumpling of a gentle breeze and the distant tap-tap-tapping of cables against the white flagpoles above the ExCel roof. They crossed over the train track and down the steps on the far side and into the parking area – another deserted expanse of failing concrete divided by flaking lines of yellow paint.

Leona nodded at the looming, featureless rear wall of the centre. 'This must be the service entrance.'

Across the car-park their eyes drifted towards a quay with a safety rail running along it and beyond that the water of Victoria Docks, subdued and calm. Dazzling golden shards rippling across the still surface reflected the bedding sun, fat, orange and undulating like the hot wax of a lava lamp, looking to settle for the night.

Jacob nodded towards the quayside rail. 'Race you, Nate.'

The boys cut across the car-park, finally clattering against the railing on the far side, whooping with delight, claims of victory and counter-claims bouncing back at them from the rear of the ExCel Centre.

She joined them a moment later, gazing out across at the docks. On the far side, a row of antiquated cranes stood tall and aloof; an industrial-age silhouette of spars and counterweights, swaying rigging chains and the vaulted roofs of dock warehouses that cast a long deep shadow across the water towards them.

From where they stood, panting and resting against the railings, they had an uninterrupted view of the skyline of the city, looking east along the curving Thames and west towards the mirror-smooth towers of Canary Wharf, glistening crimson from the glare of the setting sun.

Leona cupped her eyes as she took it all in, suddenly aware she was holding her breath in anticipation as she intently scanned the urban horizon for any signs of life.

London looked beautiful. She realised her heart ached for this place to come alive once more. For quayside street lamps to glisten proudly along the waterfront, for expensive dockside flats to once more cast smug balcony spotlights down onto even more expensive yachts. But instead, the three of them were staring at a darkening, lifeless, horizon.

There's nothing here.

247

Not a single light amongst the gathering gloom. Not even a torch beam or a candle or a campfire.

Jacob turned to his right to look at the exhibition centre. 'Looks just as dead as everywhere else,' he said, his voice carrying the weight of disappointment they all felt.

'Perhaps the man lied to you two,' she replied. 'Told you what you wanted to hear.'

'Great,' grunted Nathan flatly.

The boys continued their vigil in silence. Still looking, still hoping. The reflection of the almost-gone sun glinted off a far away window, teasing them for a moment.

'I'm sorry,' she added softly. 'If the city centre was recovering I'm sure we'd have seen something from here.'

Jacob's lips clamped angrily. 'Shit!' He suddenly screamed, banging the rail with his hands. 'Shitshitshit!!' His voice echoed across the car-park.

She put an arm around his lean shoulders; they were shaking, trembling with rage.

'Why?' His voice broke as tears rolled down his cheeks. No longer the fresh baritone voice of a young man, but the heartbroken cry of a boy. 'Why not by *now*, Lee? Why not? It's been ten years!'

She shook her head. 'I don't know, Jake. Maybe there just isn't anyone left in London now.'

They'd not spotted a single telltale sign of life all day; no rooftop vegetable gardens, no parks turned into allotments that Leona had half expected to find, no smudges of smoke in the sky, no give-away odour of woodsmoke or burning rubber – the kind of smell that can travel for miles and miles.

Nothing.

'Maybe we could go and take a look inside the ExCel,' she said, squeezing his shoulder gently. 'There may be some things we can forage for. Then, we should find someplace for tonight.'

'What about tomorrow?' asked Nathan. 'What we goin' to do?'

Jacob angrily wiped his cheeks dry and steadied himself with a deep breath. He turned to Nathan and they exchanged a wordless acknowledgment of defeat, their faces both lifeless and spent; the naive energy that had driven them to race each other across the car-park felt stupid now.

'We head back home, I suppose,' said Jacob.

Leona nodded and smiled sadly. 'Yes, home.'

Chapter 38

10 years AC

ExCel Centre – Docklands, London

Along the bottom of the rear wall was a large sliding delivery-bay door that rattled loudly as they pulled it to one side; a delivery entrance that opened onto a storage bay. The dark space inside was filled with crates and boxes.

Leona pulled a wind-up torch out of her rucksack and quickly cranked the dynamo. The others followed suit. Between their glowing and fading bulbs they had enough light to step further into the gloom.

A quick examination of the nearest crate revealed nothing edible, nothing to drink; just a container of plywood and fibreglass display plinths. Leona pulled open another box and found it filled with the components of a lighting rig and endless loops of electrical flex. They pulled open several more crates and cardboard boxes to find a number of PCs, ethernet cards and network connection cables.

They moved through the storage bays, finding nothing of use to them until her torch picked out a door marked 'main hall entrance'.

'Let's try inside. Maybe there was a cafe or restaurant set up.' She looked at the others and shrugged. 'We might get lucky.'

Jacob stepped forward and pushed the door gently. It clicked open – a cavernous reverberating click echoed back. 'The Mines of Moria,' he whispered.

Nathan's deep voice chuckled nervously. 'This isn't a mine, it's a tomb.'

It was almost pitch black. The last faint glow of daylight struggled to reach down from several skylight windows in the roof high above. Jacob swung his torch ahead of them, picking out faded corporate-blue cord carpeting on the floor, damp in patches and stained where it appeared to be dry, and the smooth plastic walls of cubicles and display stands coated in a fine layer of dust.

'Shit,' whispered Nathan.

'What?'

'I remember now.'

'What?' Jacob repeated impatiently.

Nathan smiled. 'Computer and Video Game Expo! I remember it was on in London the week of the crash. I wanted me dad to take me along.' His quiet whisper bounced and hissed across the enormity of the central hall. 'They was launching the new Wii controller thing an' the new games an' stuff. And the new PlayStation. It was going to be *well-props*!' He flicked his wrist and clacked his fingers.

Jacob grinned in the dark. He loved it when Nathan did that finger-flick thing – all hip-hop street and cool. Back on the rigs Martha told him off every time she saw him do that; said his wrist would snap one day and his hand fly off into the sea.

'It was goin' to be well solid,' Nathan continued, muttering to himself. 'The crash could of waited another fucking week.'

Jacob's torch suddenly played across large plastic-moulded faces grinning down at them. Side by side, gurning cheerfully, Super Mario and Luigi, both ten feet tall, emerged from the gloom, standing guard either side of a Nintendo display stand.

'Shit, man! Jay, you recognise?' Nathan asked.

'Yeah! Oh crap,' he replied. 'Mar-i-i-i-o-o-o!' he chirruped in a squeaky singsong voice.

'Lui-i-i-g-i-i-i!' Nathan's voice squeaked back.

'Come on, you morons,' said Leona, 'we're not here to geek out.'

Jacob cast a sidelong glance at his sister, struck by the fact that she seemed to be coming back to them, rejoining them from the dark place she'd been for the past few weeks. The last two days he'd noticed her change. She seemed to be less withdrawn, bossy again just like she used to be. Not that he'd ever tell her this, but the sound of her haughtily issuing orders was a reassuring sound.

'Right, let's be quick about this,' she announced. 'We'll also need to find somewhere to camp tonight before it gets too dark.'

He grinned proudly at her; so proud of her strength, her confidence. But glad, too, that it was dark enough that she couldn't see him and ask why the hell he was smiling like a twit.

She wound her torch again as the bulb began to fade. 'The time Mum and Dad took me here I remember there were cafés and restaurants off along the sides of the main hall. Let's try down the left side first, okay?' Her hushed voice echoed through the cavernous darkness.

Both boys nodded.

Leona led the way, her torch beam picking out the still bright colours of exhibition placards, fantastic-looking characters, spacemen, monsters, aliens, demons. Although some rain and damp had found a way inside and soiled the cord carpet in dark patches, everything else looked almost pristine.

'I bet you're loving this, aren't you, Jake?' said Leona softly.

He nodded. 'It would have been good.'

She panned her torch around. 'I can't believe how untouched it all looks. As if this was all set up just, like, yesterday.'

'I remember some of the games,' he replied. 'I remember

the ads on the TV.' He looked at her. 'Did you watch much TV at college?'

'University.' She shrugged. 'A little. I remember it being mostly rubbish.'

Jacob stroked the tuft of bristles on his chin thoughtfully. 'Yeah, mostly rubbish.'

Their torches picked out different things simultaneously. Jacob's eyes were drawn to an elaborate and enormous dungeon diorama; ten-foot-high walls of fibreglass stone blocks, dripping with paint-blood, dangling chains and stocks.

'Nate, look!'

'Oh, man, cool!'

It reminded Jacob of a picture-book story he'd flipped through. One of the books they kept in the classroom's modest library back on the rigs; an ogre, a princess and a talk-too-much donkey. He loved that story.

Leona's torch was pointed the other way, lighting up a coffee and bagel bar.

'Ahh, maybe there's some bottled water over there?'

Jacob tapped her arm. 'Can I go look at that?' he asked, jabbing a finger at the dungeon diorama across ten yards of carpeted walkway.

She sighed. 'Fine, don't wander off, though.'

'Me, too?' asked Nathan.

She sighed. 'Oh for fuck's sake . . . go on.'

They jogged across, stepping inside through a 'stone' archway and into an enclosed area. They panned their torches around. The walls inside were more dripping stone, more blood, more chains. Across the vaulted roof were large plastic wooden beams that stretched from one side to the other from which goofy-looking plastic skeletons dangled with cartoon grins.

Jacob shook his head at the illogicality of it.

Duh. As if skellys can actually smile.

There was a smell in here, too, not unlike Walter's stinky rooms. No, in fact the odour was more like the one that came out of the composters they kept on the tomato deck – rotting food. He nodded with approving admiration at the guys who'd made this set; the stink cleverly added to the spooky atmosphere, the realism of the place.

Here and there set into the dungeon walls were large TV screens that reflected back his torch beam. He smiled. He liked the idea of that – modern-times TVs sunk into an ancient-times stone wall.

'Fucking super-coolio,' he whispered admiringly. 'Isn't it?'

'True.'

Not for the first time he wished he'd been just a few years older before the world had decided to go and destroy itself; to have been able to play a few more of these games, to have been more familiar with them, the characters, the worlds.

He panned his torch across the floor of the interior; more of that ubiquitous blue cord carpet, but in here it was scuffed and splattered with dark pools of dried blood, smear, splatter and drag marks across it that fitted so cleverly with the dungeon theme. He smiled at that . . . although it would have been cooler if the floor had been like the walls; made to look like ancient worn flagstones.

Ahead of him, in the middle of the floor, was a realistic pile of bones; a waist-high pyramid of skulls, and long arm and leg bones, with nice detailing, like tattered pink strands of flesh and dark clots of almost black blood in the creases and cracks of bone.

'Check out the bones,' he said.

'Just a sec.' Nathan was across the room, admiring a life-sized plastic mould of an orc, leering out of the darkness.

Jacob took several steps towards the pile of bones and squatted down in front of it. There were skulls in there that ranged from what he guessed were rat-sized to skulls that could have belonged to a large dog. He noticed a human skull nestled in the pile and nodded with admiration at how realistic the detailing was. He reached out to touch the plastic. His finger traced along the top of the cranium and it shifted with a heavy creak. Dislodged, it rolled down from the pile and clattered on to the floor with a thump.

Heavier than he'd expected.

He leaned over to inspect it more closely. Placing his torch on the floor he picked the skull up with both hands. That smell, the clever realistic smell, was so much stronger. As he drew the skull closer to his face, he realised where the odour was coming from. He could feel tickling tufts of hair on the top. He felt the cool flap of a tatter of skin flop from the lower jaw across his wrist.

His stomach suddenly lurched and a sense of disorienting dizziness enfolded him at the same moment that it occurred to him that he wasn't holding a plastic prop . . . instead he was holding the real thing.

Leona squatted down behind the small counter in what had once aspired to call itself the Quayside Breeze Restaurant. It was little more than a partitioned-off seating area of two dozen tables and bucket chairs, and a long glass counter which presumably had once held pastries and sandwiches. Her torch beam probed an empty refrigeration unit and several empty storage cupboards beneath the counter. Nothing. Not that she'd held out much hope. But since the exhibition hall appeared to be surprisingly untouched, she'd thought perhaps they might find a few sealed bottles of water.

It was then she heard Jacob's voice calling.

She rushed out from behind the counter, picking her way quickly through the tables and chairs before jogging across the open area towards that dungeon-like display both boys had seemed so taken by.

She heard his voice again, coming from inside.

255

'Lee!!'

'Coming!'

She stepped in through the stone archway and immediately caught sight of him and Nathan standing over the mound in the middle of the floor. 'What the hell is it?' she snapped.

He pointed silently at the mound.

'Jake? What?'

'Th-they're . . . *real*.'

She didn't understand what he meant by that, nor the significance of the mound his shaking finger was pointing at. She took a dozen steps towards him.

'What's real?'

She was now close enough to see quite clearly; the light of her torch picking out long femurs, curled ribs, the instantly recognisable oyster-shell outline of several pelvis bones . . . and the human skull, lying on the floor beside the pile.

Oh, Christ.

Jacob nodded silently, as if reading her mind. 'They're real. I . . . I touched one. I touched one of the—'

She instantly put her fingers to her lips to hush his too-loud voice.

'Shit,' hissed Nathan. 'Does that mean there's some canni—?'

Leona didn't want to say the word out loud. Somehow that would make it more real if she did. 'We should leave,' she whispered, 'leave right now.'

Both of them nodded.

'Whoever did this could be—' She clamped her mouth shut. She didn't want to think about who or what had stacked these bones carefully into a pile. She stepped cautiously back the way she'd come, wildly panning the fading beam of her torch across the faux stone walls and the dangling plastic skeletons above.

They were approaching the arched doorway when they heard the sound of movement; shuffling of feet, whispering of lowered voices. She pumped the dynamo trigger several times, and the faint glow from her torch pulsed brightly, picking out a startled wall of pale faces glaring back at them.

'Oh shit!' she gasped. She turned to the other two. 'Run!'

They stumbled out of the dungeon and turned right, running along a broad strip of uncluttered carpet. She turned to look over her shoulder to see only darkness. There were noises coming from back there; the slapping of feet.

Oh shit, oh shit.

'Fuck!!' bellowed Nathan.

She glanced forward to see more pale faces blocking the way ahead. She jabbed her hand right. 'This way!' They scrambled up onto a Microsoft display plinth and across a cluttered press-only marquee, weaving their way through rows of plastic chairs arranged in front of a large projector screen.

'Come on!' she screamed after the other two, deftly and quickly picking her way through and exiting the marquee on the far side. A moment later she was clambering over a length of velvet rope and stepping down off a plinth onto cord carpet again. Her torch faded to darkness and she decided to leave it that way, rather than attract attention.

She could hear Jacob and Nathan stumbling and cursing in the marquee. Not far behind her. They must have got tangled in the chairs. They were making too much fucking noise.

'Come on!' she called out.

'Which way did you go?' she heard Jacob's muted voice. Further away now. The morons were heading the wrong way.

'Over here!' she called.

Chairs clattered. She could also hear the growing noise of footfalls, and an awful keening cry, like a host of mewling babies all teething.

'Jacob! Nathan! Over here!' she hissed as loud as she dared to. Those things – children, that's what they'd looked like, children in rags, with long hair and dirty faces – they were *very* close . . . closer than the other two.

Don't call out again, stupid.

In the darkness she could just make out her immediate environment and found a dark nook behind a tall placard and a rubbish bin. She hunched down between the two as quietly as she could. A moment later the darkness in front of her was full of the sound of feet and plimsolls on carpet, gasping laboured breath, mewling and crying. She even heard slurred baby-words uttered between them. And the smell: an awful smell of human faeces and stale urine.

A moment later it was quiet. Her eyes, accustomed now to the dark, picked out the last small silhouettes passing her by; shambling little forms that could have been nursery-aged children.

The last of them gone, she eased herself out of the nook. It was then that she noticed the cold of her damp trousers against her legs and realised she'd pissed herself.

The hall echoed with the sounds of the chase still going on; the clattering of things knocked over; that mewling raised in pitch to a frustrated howling that sent a shiver down her back.

Oh fuck.

She had no idea at all which way was out now. She'd completely lost her bearings in the panic. She couldn't even tell from which direction the echoing noises of pursuit were coming. All she knew was that the pack of feral kids that had just rushed past her were to her left.

She turned right.

Chapter 39

10 years AC

ExCel Centre – Docklands, London

Dozens of them, picked out in the flickering beam of his torch; children, pale and gaunt, faces smudged with ages-old dirt beneath long greasy tresses of hair.

'Shit! They're all around us!' yelled Nathan.

Both of them backed up against a smooth curved wall of an Electronic Arts stand. Jacob pumped the trigger on his torch. The dim LED bulb brightened again, revealing more of them poised in a wary semicircle in the darkness, watching them intently.

Nathan held the gun up, sweeping it slowly across them, his finger resting on the trigger. 'Stay back!'

'Look! We're . . . we were just leaving, okay?' said Jacob.

The things stared back in silence. He realised then that they were just children. He guessed they ranged in age from five to early teens. It was difficult to judge – they could have been another year or two older than they appeared, but prolonged malnutrition might have stunted their growth. Their eyes, wide, stared back at them through tangled fringes of long matted dreadlocks.

'Look, we . . . we didn't know this place was y-yours,' Jacob continued. 'So, we'll just go, okay?'

He stepped sideways along the wall, his back sliding against the smooth curved wall of the stand. He tugged Nathan's sleeve gently to come with him.

'Yeah,' said Nathan, 'we're leaving now.'

The children remained perfectly still, silent, watching them shuffle along. They reminded him of the orphans in Oliver, lost, smudged faces in ill-fitting clothes. Girls and boys — although amongst the younger ones he struggled to determine which were which.

The wall disappeared behind them, and they found themselves taking a backwards step up onto a courtesy stand of stools and small round metal coffee tables.

The children advanced on them cautiously.

'Stay back, motherfuckers! I got a gun here!' Nathan shouted, as if it needed saying.

One of the children, a painfully thin boy — or it could well have been a girl — stepped ahead of the others and extended a slender hand.

'Ve-weee fuck-in hung-weee,' it piped in a small mucus-choked voice.

Both of them looked at each other, confused.

'Hung-wee. You foooo?'

Then they understood. 'We don't h-have any food on us.' He looked at Nathan. 'Do we?'

Nathan shook his head silently.

Another child stirred, stepped forward and extended both hands. 'Pwee gee wee.'

Jacob shook his head, struggling to understand.

'Pwee gee wee foo,' it said again, taking another eager step forward.

It was like listening to a baby's first words; toddler-talk. It would be *aww*-cute coming from the mouth of some chubby-faced infant in a buggy, but from these children bordering on teen years it was wrong. Tragically wrong.

His torch began to dim again. He pumped the trigger several times, quickly setting the dynamo whirring in the silence. The children all edged several steps closer encouraged by the momentary fading of light.

'Woah! Stay fuckin' back!' shouted Nathan.

More dirty palms extended — a growing sea of them. 'Foo . . . pwee. Foo, pwee!'

'I'm s-sorry,' said Jacob, 'I'm SORRY! WE DON'T HAVE ANY!!'

Then he saw a taller child pushing forward. A boy dressed in dark-stained corduroy trousers and what looked like the tattered remains of a blue secondary school blazer. Dark curls draped down across his bone-thin face. The first soft downy hairs of a moustache curled around the edge of his lips.

'We fuckin' hung-wee, *init*,' he barked in a wavering voice that sounded like the recently broken timbre of a pubescent boy. 'You go' sum fuckin' foo or whoh?'

'Not with us,' said Jacob, patting himself. 'Really.'

The boy's eyes rested on the assault rifle. 'Cool gun. Gimme tha'.'

Jacob followed his gaze. 'You want our *gun*?'

'Yeh, gimme tha'.'

'Not fuckin' having it!' snapped Nathan.

'*My* gun now,' said the boy. 'Gimme, a' you ca' fu' off.'

Jacob glanced at Nathan.

'No fuckin' way,' he replied. 'S'only one we got.'

And there was no guarantee that, on handing it over, the boy wouldn't want to try it out on them.

The boy took another step forward. 'Gimme a' gun so me ca' hun' dogs.'

Jacob swallowed. 'You eat . . . *dogs*?'

The boy was now only a yard away from them, his eyes on the glinting gun-metal grey. He suddenly made an impulsive lunge towards it, grabbing the end of the rifle's barrel in both hands. Instinctively Nathan fired. The child's dirty school blazer fluttered like a sail as he rocked back on his feet, pawing at the jagged wound in his stomach.

'Oh shit man! I'm . . . s-sorry . . . I'm sor—' said Nathan.

The other children surged forward, edging around the staggering boy; a forest of pale palms and dirty jagged nails

261

reaching out and clawing at them. Amongst the hands and arms, Nathan thought he saw the glint of several knives.

'Oh fuck, run, Jay!!' he screamed.

Jacob turned on his heels, clattering across the stools, tangling with the tables. Nathan fired a second shot into the air just above the children's heads — they recoiled for a moment.

He turned and ran through the wake of overturned stools and tables doing his best not to tangle with the upended legs as he followed the bobbing glow of Jacob's torch ahead. Dropping down off the far side of the stand's courtesy platform, he sprinted twenty yards down a broad concourse, flanked on either side by dark silhouettes of gaming mascots and cardboard cut-out superheroes and supervillains.

'Wait for me!' he shouted after him.

Jacob stopped, turned and beckoned him on. 'This way!' he shouted.

Nathan quickly caught up with him. Looking back into the darkness behind him he could hear the smack of hundreds of feet on the stand's floor, the clatter of metal tables and stools being kicked aside and a growing cacophony of shrill voices clamouring for them to stop.

'What about Leona?' gasped Jacob.

He shook his head. 'Dunno, I dunno. We got to run right now!' He looked at Jacob. 'Jay, which way do we go?'

The drumming of feet grew louder, coming up the concourse towards them. There was only one way they could go. They resumed running up the concourse, Jacob leading the way, dodging an increasing amount of clutter across the carpet; computers pulled out and smashed; wires and circuit boards splayed across the floor like eviscerated organs. This end of the main hall, more than the other, appeared to be the children's playground. A life-size fake potted palm tree had been kicked over and lay across their path. Jacob vaulted over the trunk. Nathan joined him a moment later, his big feet tangling with the stiff plastic fronds.

'Hurry!' hissed Jacob, pumping his torch trigger and turning the beam back down the concourse. Thirty yards back he could see them.

Nathan fired another shot back in their direction. The children ducked and froze for the briefest moment, like a game of grandmother's footsteps, then resumed.

'Go! Jay! Go! GO!!' urged Nathan as he yanked his feet clear of the palm tree's leaves.

Jacob swung his torch back up the concourse to pick out the way ahead. The pallid wide-eyed face of a child loomed out of the darkness in front of him.

'Whuh—'

A blur of movement and a dull crack, like willow on leather. The torch danced into the air, spun and bounced on the ground. Jacob flopped down lifelessly beside it, blood already spilling out of his long scruffy hair and across his forehead.

Nathan fired a shot into the darkness sending the flailing child – boy or girl, he had no idea – into a spinning rack of DVD cases.

He stepped forward, dropped down to his knees and picked up the torch.

'Jake?'

He shone the light down at his friend's face, now almost entirely smothered with blood.

'Oh, shit. Jake?'

He pushed a blood-soaked tress of hair out of his face to see that his eyes were open but glassy, fluttering and rolling. Nathan could hear the sound of approaching feet, shrill-pitched screams.

'Jake!! Get up, man! GET UP!!'

He remained still.

Leaving Jacob was the—

No.

He grabbed one of Jacob's hands and began dragging him along the carpet, away from the torch left lying on the floor, leaving a smeared trail of blood behind.

'Come on. Come on!!' he hissed. 'GET UP!!'

The plastic palm tree creaked and rustled. The children were clambering over it and coming.

No. No. No . . . Too fucking slow.

Nathan let his friend's hand flop to the floor and grasped the assault rifle in both hands. The thundering of pounding feet suddenly ceased and the darkness around him was filled with the wheeze and rattle of their laboured breathing.

A pair of tattered trainers stepped into the pool of torch light on the floor. The light rose, spun round and flashed blindingly into his eyes.

Nathan screwed his face up, aiming down the length of the rifle at it. 'Fuck off and leave us alone!!' he screamed.

'Foo . . . foo . . .' a young child's voice implored. 'You give foo . . .'

He pulled the trigger and the gun *clacked* uselessly. A child behind him giggled mischievously.

Oh, please, no.

A whimper escaped Nathan's throat. 'Please . . . please . . .'

Leona saw it; a faint grey outline. She realised it had to be the doorway leading back out onto the service bay – the way they'd come in. Dark forms fluttered through it like bats into a cave; children, more of them.

She heard gunshots again, echoing across the hall's roof.

Dozens of them flitting past her. She could hear barked voices and shrill girlish screams, excited caterwauling and boisterous jeering; like Dante's version of a school playground. She wondered where they'd all come from. Perhaps a boarding school? Or maybe they were children from a hundred different places, drawn to each other for the safety of numbers.

Not children any more, though. Just wild animals.

Jacob. Her heart thumped in her chest. *You can't leave him in there.*

The doorway was clear now, the last of the children drawn through inside and following the noise of the chase on the far side of the hall.

The boys knew where to head to, she told herself, they had the gun. Furthermore, she was going to achieve nothing cowering here. If they made it out, and then didn't find her beside the parked bikes, they might be stupid enough to come back in for her.

Go. Now!

She got to her feet and scooted quickly in the darkness across the floor to the open bay door. Resting against the cool breeze-block wall, she heard several more shots in the distance and the playground voices rising to a crescendo.

She quickly popped her head around the door, examined the loading bay. It appeared to be empty. She hesitated a moment, listening to the distant noises, trying to read them, trying to understand if those shrill voices were screaming in frustration at their lost quarry, or were the excited celebration of a kill.

Unable to decide whether to flee or go back and find Jacob, she lingered on another moment, until she thought she heard the soft patter of feet nearby inside. No choice; she slipped through the doorway and threaded through packing crates and cardboard boxes out towards the main sliding door of the loading bay. The muted peach glow of the after-sunset sky streamed in from outside, across the concrete floor.

Once again she hesitated a moment in the shadows as she scanned the empty acre of car-park outside. There was no one to be seen. She sprinted across the weed-tufted tarmac towards the steps of the pedestrian bridge over the railway, stepping as lightly as she could, but the metal steps rang far too loudly in the still night for comfort. She sprinted across the overpass to the far side.

At the top of the steps leading down to the playground she could see the trailer and their bicycles still parked below. And there she remained, looking back across the car-park at the open delivery bay, hoping, pleading silently to see – any second now – the dark shapes of Jacob and Nathan pegging it towards her as if the devil himself were in hot pursuit.

The last vanilla light of day was gone and the sky was now a deep evening blue, stars scattered across it. No moon yet. She could only just make out the rear entrance.

'They'll be out any second now,' she told herself. 'Any second now.'

Chapter 40

10 years AC

ExCel Centre – Docklands, London

The children scattered at the sound of approaching boots and jangling belt buckles. Nathan saw torches bobbing up the concourse and voices calling out to each other.

Then they were standing over him. Half a dozen young lads wearing neon orange vests that made them look like a highways maintenance crew; except, that is, for the guns they were each brandishing.

'Go on, piss off, you wankers!!' shouted one of them, firing a few rounds indiscriminately into the stampeding mass of children. He watched them go, tumbling over the plastic palm tree and disappearing down avenues between the corporate stands before finally shining a flashlight down at Nathan.

'You all right, bro?'

Nathan looked up. A young black man, he looked older than him; at a guess mid-twenties. Long thick dreadlocks cascaded from beneath a red Nike bandanna and a chunky gold chain glistening around his neck.

Nathan managed a hasty nod. He glanced back down at Jacob's body on the floor. 'My friend's . . . they . . . I think he's hurt badly.'

The black guy stooped down to the floor and flicked his flashlight across the prone form. 'He with you?' he asked.

Nathan nodded silently, his mouth hung open, still in shock at the last minute reprieve.

'Lemmesee,' the young man said. His hand flicked a blood-soaked lock of Jacob's hair out of the way and reached around under his jawline as if he was attempting to throttle him. He fumbled for a moment, adjusted his grip around the neck several times, narrowing his eyes in concentration as he felt for a pulse.

'Ain't dead, bro,' he said after a while. He turned round. 'Jay-zee, get him on to the cart.'

A tall black lad barked an order at two younger boys. They passed their guns to a colleague, stepped forward and scooped Jacob's body up between them.

'We takin' him home, Snoop?' asked one of them, a white kid who looked several years younger than the one with the bandanna — clearly their leader. He also sported a thick gold choke chain.

Snoop nodded. 'Yuh, Tricky, we takin' him back. We take him to get the doc' see to him.'

He turned to Nathan. 'You comin', too.'

Not a request, it seemed. An order. He looked down at the assault rifle still clutched tightly in Nathan's hands. 'Hey, nice gun, bro. Lemmesee it.'

Nathan passed it up to him, looking over his shoulder as he stood up. The other two were hefting Jacob away between them up the concourse.

The black guy nodded approvingly at the weapon. 'Army gun. Kept nice an' clean. This your piece?'

Nathan nodded.

'Good gun-care, bro. May be that the Chief will wanna make you a praetorian.' He flicked his head. 'Come.'

Nathan's gaze returned to him. 'Who . . . who are you?'

'Me?' he grinned. 'You call me Snoop — the *top dog*. You?'

'Nathan Williams.'

'What about the white kid?'

'Jacob Sutherland.'

Snoop shrugged. 'Okay, Nathan Williams, we're goin'

before them wild fuckin' rugrats return. Like fuckin' mosqui-toes way they keep comin' back here.'

He followed after the others, walking backwards swinging his torch to and fro and keeping a wary eye out for the feral children.

'Where we goin'?' asked Nathan, stepping smartly to keep pace with them.

'Take you back to the Zee.'

'The *Zee*?'

'Yuh. Zee . . . the *Zone*. Whcrc we live. Ain't far.'

'Jay . . . Jacob, my friend, he's going to be all right, isn't he?'

Snoop shrugged. 'Fucked if I know. Doc'll look him over when we get back.'

They stepped out of the main hall, down several wide steps into a foyer lined with registration desks and turnstiles and across a floor littered with glass granules that crackled under-foot. They pushed their way out through a row of rotating door frames, the panels cracked and lined with shards of glass.

It was almost completely dark now. Waiting patiently just outside the doors, beneath an entrance awning of canvas that stretched off down a long, covered approach promenade, were a pair of ponies harnessed to an improvised cart; the four wheels and a chassis of a car, with a flatbed of planks laid across.

'We was inside there with someone else,' said Nathan quickly.

Snoop shrugged again. 'Well, shit, they're dead or they run by now. Ain't my business.' He barked orders at the others. 'Get him on the cart.'

The other boys in orange vests eased Jacob onto the cart then clambered on themselves. He turned to Nathan im-patiently. 'Well, get on, unless you want wait around for the rats to come back.'

Nathan cast one last glance back at the dark interior of the ExCel Centre, desperately hoping to see Leona come stumbling out of the gloom, barking at them not to go and leave her behind.

'What you waitin' for? Get on, fool, or we'll go leave you behind.'

Nathan did as he was told, clambered onto the planks and settled down beside Jacob.

Shit. He shook his head and looked down at his friend's face, criss-crossed with rivulets of tacky drying blood, his breath rattled out though clogged nostrils.

Shit, Jay . . . please don't die on me, man.

Snoop hopped on the front of the cart and barked an order at one of the other lads. With a shrill whistle and the crack of a stick on their haunches, the ponies lurched forward and the cart spun out from beneath the awning and across the approach. Above them the last stain of dusk's amber was gone and stars had begun to dimly pepper the night sky.

Nathan clenched his lips, thankful it was dark enough that none of the others sitting beside him were going to notice the silent tumble of tears on his cheeks as he squeezed one of Jacob's clammy hands.

Please, mate.

Lee, what're you going to do?

She remained where she was, silent, her hands grasped the overpass railing, her eyes locked on the building, scanning the empty car-park for any possible shadows of movement coming her way.

An hour might have passed. She had no idea. It could have been longer. In that time a yellow, sickly three-quarter moon had risen and arced some of its way across the night sky. Its wan light glinted off the water of Victoria Docks, smooth and sullen, and every now and then a soft sigh of warm summer breeze stirred through the saplings on the railway bankings below her.

The only thing she knew for certain was that she couldn't walk away not knowing what had happened to them.

Maybe they've escaped out the other end?

In which case, they'd try and make their way back here. That's what she would do. The trailer parked at the bottom of the steps was all there was for food. They'd have no other choice than try and find their way back to the bridge.

Please not Jacob, too.

First Hannah . . . now Jacob. This shitty world seemed fully intent on taking away absolutely *everyone* she'd ever cared for; taken from her one by one so she could *really* savour the pain of each loss . . . get to squeeze every last ounce of hurt out before the next one could be snatched away.

Stupidly, for a while yesterday, listening to Take That, the Kaiser Chiefs, the Chili Peppers, even Abba, she'd allowed the gloom to shift ever so slightly. She'd allowed herself to wonder whether she really did want to go home to her old bedroom, snuggle up in whatever was left of her duvet and call it quits. Raymond's 'fight-on' spirit had managed to touch her for a few hours.

I can't lose Jacob, too.

Something was telling her she hadn't lost him . . . yet. That he was alive. But she might be wasting valuable time standing here looking at the back of the building.

Go back in?

The thought terrified her. Those bones . . . and the horrible look of those things, she could barely think of them as children; they were like wraiths, lost souls. No, running in there and getting taken by those feral children wasn't going to help anyone. She realised the only sensible thing she could do was to stay where she was and watch and wait for the boys' return.

Come first light, Lee, what if they've not returned? What then?

She had no idea. No plan.

Can't stay here for ever.

She stood in silence on the bridge, holding on to the handrail, listening to the soft rustle of trees below.

'Maybe I'll find him at home?'

Chapter 41

10 years AC

'LeMan 49/25a' – ClarenCo Gas Rig Complex, North Sea

Valérie Latoc watched the women moving amongst the terraces and walkways of the drilling platform, watering the plants from cans, taking care not to waste a single drop of fresh water. It was quieter here. Fewer people to break the soothing murmur of the sea below. Quiet enough to hear himself think.

Whilst Jennifer Sutherland had been unconscious, in the grip of a chemically induced stupor, he'd noticed how quickly things had begun to unravel under the stewardship of that poor old fool, Walter. His manner was clumsy and unappealing. He patronised people when he spoke to them. He was gruff and irritable, and when he did attempt some good-natured humour, it was usually ill-judged and fell uncomfortably into a silence.

No one seemed to like the poor man. He'd heard the ladies mutter about him. How his little rheumy pink eyes darted where they were not invited. How they hated it when he accompanied Jennifer on her tours of the rigs. The bunking areas in particular. His 'little ferret eyes' – that's what that woman, Alice Harton called them – always seemed to be hunting for a tantalising glimpse of someone half-dressed, according to her, lingering too long on items of underwear that dangled from washing lines strung from handrail to handrail. How he seemed too close to Jennifer and her family; how he'd been too close to poor young Hannah . . . always there, hanging around their personal quarters.

The superficial unity of this community had very quickly begun to unwind with Walter in charge of things. Without Jennifer Sutherland's forceful personality keeping things ticking over, they were drifting, breaking apart.

That's why I ended up here. Their compass is spinning. They're lost.

What they needed to know was what he fully understood. That their being gathered here on this remote, windy, damp artificial island wasn't just random happenstance. There was a purpose to it. Something far more important than mere 'making do' day after day.

Valérie knew deep down it wasn't mere chance that had driven him east out of London up to this remote rump of England. He was needed here. These people, these hard-working, these *wonderful* people, who'd managed to create something that vaguely resembled a little Garden of Eden on these ugly rusting platforms, they needed to hear that they were all alive and fed and safe and living in this remote place for a very specific reason.

God has plans for you.

Valérie could see what these platforms were; true they didn't have a keel or a rudder, or a hull – they stood on solid base rock instead of floating on the sea, but those details withstanding, undeniably, this was an ark for those God had determined should survive.

He understood now that God – Jehovah, Allah, Jahmeh . . . whatever people chose to call Him – had a sense of irony, a sense of humour even. He could have gone Old Testament on the old world and flooded it once again with globally-warmed ice water from the polar caps. But, instead, He'd chosen a very modern way to show His displeasure; He'd chosen to strangle man with his own arrogance. All that technology, all those power stations, all those convenient machines that mankind so relied on, were stilled

274

in one night when the oil was stopped from flowing through pipes from the Middle East.

Valérie shook his head. *Who would have expected God to be so modern-minded?*

He watched a dozen people making their way across the long walkway from the production platform. He recognised some of their faces from the last prayer meeting he'd held, and there were some new faces that they'd brought along with them. Word was spreading amongst the others that he had something to say worth hearing. That God wanted to talk to *all* of them – whatever faith they'd been clinging to in the past – and explain His plans. Here, on this sea-borne Garden of Eden, right here, was where the future could be written. And Valérie could feel the tug of destiny, the obligation to step into Jennifer Sutherland's shoes before things fell apart completely and lead these people to a place where he suspected Jennifer had already, gently been coaxing them; away from old material values towards a simpler, *sustainable* life.

The only thing she'd forgotten to add to the mix was God's merciful message. It was the knowledge that they were special, *chosen*, that would bind them together, and they certainly needed that.

Martha Williams appeared in the doorway across the deck from him. She waved to catch his eye. 'They're ready below,' she said.

He nodded. 'I will come along in a minute.' He watched her turn and step back inside. The woman had become his most helpful ally. Although Alice Harton had been one of his first converts, she wasn't a popular woman. Martha, on the other hand, everyone seemed to warm to, and trust. The fact that she'd recently gathered up her few belongings and moved across from the accommodation platform to be with him on the drilling platform had helped his cause immensely.

Others were coming now. Several more fresh faces each and every day.

Things were gently sliding Valérie's way. Walter was doing a fair job of alienating almost everyone he interacted with, and the more he sensed authority slipping through his fingers, the more stressed and harried he seemed to become.

When Jennifer finally recovered enough to climb out of her cot, he hoped she would be sensible enough, and selfless enough, to hand over the burden of leadership to him. These people needed what he had to offer. Needed it so badly. It would be damaging for everyone's morale if there was some sort of an unsightly power struggle between them.

For now, though, the longer she stayed in bed, the longer Walter had to really screw things up, the longer Valérie had to build his congregation, the better it would eventually be for all of them.

An idea occurred to him.

An idea to help speed things along. Many of the women already viewed Walter with a little suspicion; clucked amongst themselves at how close he'd always been to the Sutherlands, particularly Leona . . . particularly Hannah. Hadn't there been something about his almost constant proximity to the little girl that had looked a little inappropriate . . . *needy* even?

Didn't he just look the part, too? Old and unappealing, bushy eyebrows that shadowed furtive eyes and opportunistic glances and a Captain Birdseye beard on those florid cheeks, thick enough to hide the subtle leer of a pervert.

Just a suggestion. That's all. A question or two about Walter. What do we know about his life before the crash? Did he have some kind of . . . 'form'? Had he ever been on some sort of a 'register'? Perhaps? Who's to know, eh?

And that shrew of a woman, Alice, seemed the perfect person for him to ask.

After all, that's all it took — just *asking* the question — to

276

taint an unappealing old man like Walter with the lingering smell of that kind of a suggestion.

Once branded, always branded. It's how that kind of thing worked.

Chapter 42

10 years AC

Shepherd's Bush,
London

Home was almost as Leona remembered it. St Stephen's Avenue, Shepherd's Bush – a leafy suburban cul-de-sac flanked on either side by a row of modest terraced family homes fronted by modest gardens gone to seed.

They'd left this place a decade ago; the morning after Dad had died . . . in the aftermath of the riots. London's skyline had been smudged with columns of smoke, the roads and streets cluttered with things pulled out from homes and shops; like some bizarre end-of-the-world street party left for someone else to clean up. And it had been strangely quiet the day they had set off to escape London for good.

Ten summers and winters appeared to have changed little here; last autumn's leaves lay in small, wind-gathered mounds against the kerb and around the bases of tree trunks lining both sides of the narrow avenue. The front gardens were lost beneath waist-high grass and weeds. She noticed a tile had slipped here and there on one or two of the roofs.

She brought her bicycle to a halt with the squeak of brakes outside one of the houses.

She climbed off the bike, pushed open the garden gate with a creak and stared at the small front garden – liquor bottles and crumpled cans of lager nestled in the tall grass.

Hannah asked her once about their home and the crash. *Was there fighting, Leona?*

'Yes, there was fighting,' she replied. She still had night-mares about that week – ones that woke her with a scream in her mouth. 'There was a gang of boys that hung around outside. Boys, fourteen, fifteen, sixteen years of age having a party just outside our house every night of that first week.' Leona spotted the fading peak of a Nike baseball cap and the rusting blade of a flick knife tangled in the long grass.

'Then finally they got brave enough to start breaking into the houses one after the other. Stealing things, doing horrible things to the poor people inside.'

It must have been frightening.

'It was, love. Me and Jake did all right. Better than others. We survived it.'

She pushed her way through the stalks of grass, up the short gravel path to the front door. She examined it. It was closed and locked, just as they'd left it a decade ago. It looked like it hadn't been forced.

It meant he hadn't beaten her home. Her heart sank. *Jake's not here.*

He would have had to force the front door.

She fumbled for something she'd kept on a chain around her neck all these years, never really knowing why, and produced a worn and scuffed latch key that jangled against a brass ankh pendant as she pulled it out of her top. The key slotted into the lock and clicked effortlessly. She pushed the door open and stepped inside.

'Jacob?' she called out hopefully. Perhaps he'd forced the back door.

It smelled faintly of damp, of mildew, just like every other building did nowadays. But unlike so many other homes, at least it wasn't gutted, it wasn't a mess of things pulled out, inspected and tossed aside or broken; walls sprayed with graffiti. It still looked like a place in which people once lived — just dusty and in need of an airing.

To her left the doorway leading to Dad's study, to the right the door to the kitchen. There were cardboard boxes on the floor in the hallway, Mum's handwriting on them: 'Jenny's

CDs', 'Andy's DVDs'. She knew they'd been considering a trial separation at the time the crash happened. They hadn't been getting on for a while.

She shook her head sadly. It had taken the end of the world to bring the pair of them back to their senses. At least they'd had a chance to say to each other what needed to be said before . . .

Her eyes stung and she wiped the tears away.

She checked the back door, that too was still locked and unforced. Jacob hadn't come here last night. Which meant . . .

She closed her mind to what exactly that meant. She didn't need to do that right now. Not now.

Lee? Hannah's insistent voice in her head again. *What you going to do now?*

She looked up the stairwell in the hallway. Up there were their bedrooms, Mum and Dad's room, and presumably Dad's body at rest beneath a rotting quilt. She slumped down on the bottom step in the dark hallway and gazed out at the overgrown front garden, the open gate and the quiet leaf-filled street beyond. The morning sun dappled the brick walls of the house opposite. Quite pretty really, poppies in their front garden and cherry blossoms on the tree.

'I don't know. I guess I'll just wait here for a while.'

Chapter 43

10 years AC

'LeMan 49/25a' - ClarenCo Gas Rig Complex,
North Sea

Walter stared at the scorched interior of the generator room. The rubber pipes had ignited in the blast, then burned and melted. So had the digesters, leaving pools of hardened plastic on the ground. The generator itself was largely undamaged but it had been knocked off its mounting by the blast and the casing was dented in several places.

It had taken him a couple of years of tinkering, foraging and learning to build them a methane-fuelled generator. All that could be done again. At least he'd know better what he was doing second time around. Jenny said she wanted them to have power again. Said it was a beacon of hope for the people; a sign of progress. Something they really needed to see.

He surveyed the mess around him. It was going to take quite some time to get things fixed up again. He needed to find another small brewery with similar sized incubators or . . . he scratched his beard in thought, or he could link up a series of smaller beer-brewing bins, each feeding into the methane tanks independently. Either way, there was a lot of foraging work that needed to be done, a lot of back-and-forth between the rigs and shore. He wasn't sure he liked the idea of leaving Jenny alone so much. She was still weak and vulnerable and although she could get about a bit, shuffling painfully as her mending skin stretched and pulled uncomfortably, she wasn't strong enough to get much further than the stairs down to the mess room.

Down there she had a chance to chat with people as they came in for breakfast and evening meals, and she was determined to do that; to show her face, to show everyone it was going to be business as usual.

But it's not, is it?

That bastard Latoc was slowly pulling more and more people across to his platform to listen to his bloody sermons. He watched them traipsing across the walkway towards the drilling platform four or five times a day. Women mostly, some of them taking their children with them.

He wondered what Latoc's appeal was. *Is it his accent? Is it his looks?*

The man was slender and his lean face chiselled in a way that made him look both enigmatic and a little vulnerable. He imagined the older ladies wanted to mother him, the younger ones to bed him. But there were also some of the men amongst his followers; David Cudmore, Ronnie, Howard and one or two others. Whatever Latoc's phony spiritual message, it seemed to have got through to them as well.

Idiots.

He cursed himself for not having the balls to throw the foreign bastard off the rigs the first time he'd caught him offering prayers in the mess.

Jenny's support from those not yet under Latoc's spell was ambivalent at best. They were happy to go along with the routines as they stood: after all, everyone needed to eat. But there were many amongst them who longed for the community to relocate ashore. Others who just wanted to have a greater say in how things were run. They may not have been buying into Latoc's bullshit, but they certainly didn't seem to want to loyally rally around Jenny.

Ungrateful bastards.

After all she'd done. The least they could do was show a little support now she needed them.

As he surveyed the burned-out room, muttering his

thoughts and grumbles aloud, he heard, through the metal ceiling, the scrape of feet entering the chicken deck above. Feeding time.

The muted murmur of the hens' stupid cooing rose in pitch and persistence as they realised food was coming their way. The ceiling clicked with the sound of scurrying claws across the floor above as the birds scrambled to get close to those feeding them.

Several feathers and flakes of rust floated down from the ceiling, disturbed by the fluster of hungry birds. There were holes here and there; small ones. Patches of rust pecked at and worked on by the birds. Nothing so big that one of them could escape through, though. Not yet, anyway.

He returned his mind to the task of cataloguing the things he was going to need to acquire from shore. Trips he could try and combine with shore runs for fresh water and the periodical 'shopping trip' in order to conserve the marina's dwindling store of diesel.

We really can't stay on these platforms for ever.

As if in answer to his thoughts, another few flakes of dark rust and some more feathers fluttered down.

He heard one of the people above talking; recognised her voice. It was Alice Harton. She had the kind of voice that always seemed to carry. Before the crash she was a manager in a retirement home, which seemed to fit. Walter could imagine the hard-faced cow doing the rounds through a crowded day room, queen of all she surveyed, speaking deliberately loudly, patronisingly slowly, as if talking to a room full of children.

A loud, piercing voice.

Someone else answered, much quieter, murmuring something he couldn't quite make out.

'That's what she said,' replied Alice. 'And when I think about it . . . he was quite creepy with them all. Always hanging around them. Not just Jenny, but Leona . . . and Hannah.'

The mousy voice had something to say, again too soft to discern. Walter found himself stepping lightly across the floor, careful not to kick any of the snaking cables. He looked up through a narrow triangular crack, framed by the serrated edges of the rusting floor. Light flickered as someone stepped over him and a feather fluttered down onto his forehead.

'Well he did, though, didn't he? Do you remember? He told everyone *not* to go and look down there for her, didn't he? Said he'd go look for her *himself*.'

The softer voice replied with something.

'Oh, I dunno. I always thought he was a creepy old bastard myself. Hangin' round the Sutherlands like a fly on a dog turd. Knocking on their quarters at all times. I bet you he was just trying to catch a glimpse of them. Of Hannah.'

Walter's jaw sagged open with disbelief.

The other woman said something.

'Oh, yeah, dirty kiddy-fiddler. But he was always all over her, wasn't he? Holding her hand, hugging her and stuff. It's not like he was her dad. I'm sorry, but that's just creepy.'

The quieter woman spoke again.

'Well that's what we all thought, wasn't it? That he was just soppy over Jenny. But now I think about it, I reckon he was just using her and Leona to get closer to the poor little girl, wasn't he? It all makes sense when you think about it.'

Walter felt his blood run cold. He was half tempted to shout up through the crack that he'd heard what Alice had just said. That she was a dirty-minded bitch and he was coming up there to tell her as much to her face.

'Oh, yeah,' said Alice in response to the other woman. 'Oh, yeah, more I think about it, yeah. It's possible, isn't it? He took her down there and maybe this time he did something to her she didn't like. He went too far. So he panicked and killed her. So, then when the search party came down to the generator room and Jenny found her, he just flipped, didn't he? Made the generator blow up to cover his tracks.'

The other woman spoke.

'Or that, yes. Maybe he did pull it off and was waiting for it to blow. All I know is that he was acting very odd about the whole thing.'

Walter felt his heart pounding in his chest. He felt light-headed with panic.

Oh, Christ, is that what people are thinking?

The light through the crack flickered and reappeared as the two women above moved slowly across the floor amidst the chickens.

'Oooh, that's a really big egg, look,' said Alice. 'Anyway,' she continued a moment later. 'If I had kids, I certainly wouldn't let the dirty bastard near my little ones. No way.'

The other woman said something about Jenny.

'Well that's right. Someone should. But she's such a stubborn bitch. She probably give you a bollocking and throw you off the rigs for spreading rumours. Bloody Jenny's Law,' said Alice sarcastically. 'Bloody Jenny's *Law*. Who does she think she is, anyway?'

The other woman stepped across the deck as she spoke quietly.

'True,' Alice replied. 'Maybe he will. He *should* be in charge. I never really did the church thing before, but you know what he says seems to make so much sense. When I think about it, it was all so messed up . . . and . . . and, wrong. You know? I could imagine God was furious with us. Why not? Why not wipe the slate clean and start again?'

The other woman chuckled as she said something.

'Oh, but, he is, isn't he? I think if I was just a little younger . . .'

The two women giggled like schoolgirls as they finally finished feeding the chickens. He heard the wire mesh door to the chicken deck grate across the crap-covered floor and rattle shut behind them.

Walter felt a cold twist in his chest as he imagined others all over the platforms having this kind of conversation. He replayed in his mind every exchange he'd heard this morning, doing the rounds for Jenny, issuing the work tasks. All of sudden every reply, every half-smile offered to him, seemed to be tainted with the slightest hint of distaste.

Is that it? Is everyone saying that I'm a pervert?

But worse than that, if Alice was to be believed. Far worse than that.

Saying I killed Hannah?

Chapter 44

10 years AC

O2 Arena – 'Safety Zone 4',
London

'Jay? Jay, man. Wake up.'

Jacob felt fists pummelling the side of his head; the knuckles of some playground bully needling his soft temple. He winced from the pain, groaned and slowly opened his eyes and squinted at the foggy shape leaning over him.

'Jake, man.' It was Nathan. 'How's the head feelin'?'

His mouth was tacky and dry, his lips stuck together. With a little tug of effort they parted. 'My . . . head . . . really hurts.'

Nathan laughed, not unkindly. 'You got whacked well-hard.'

His eyes were focusing – not entirely, it was never going to be 20-20 without a new pair of glasses and he'd lost those long ago. Nathan's face, grinning down at him, sharpened. Over his shoulder Jacob could see a pale milky white sky . . . no, not a sky. He saw a stretching arc of material. Like sail canvas taut with a strong breeze.

'Where are we?'

'The O2 Arena.'

Jacob's eyes narrowed. For a moment that meant absolutely nothing to him.

'The Millennium Dome, Jay?'

Dome?

Then he remembered . . . the dome. One of the safety zones.

He struggled up onto his elbows, wincing from the

thudding pain in his head. Around him, across an open floor, he could see a dozen or so mattresses; several of them occupied. Surrounding them, a wall of neck-high partitions just like ones you'd find in an open-plan office; businesslike cream cord material surface, perfect for tacking-on Dilbert cartoons and cute kitty calendars.

'This is the infirmary,' said Nathan.

Jacob's hand wandered up to the side of his head to caress his needled temple, only to find cotton wadding and a bandage wrapped around his forehead.

'You had a real big bump on your head, like a tennis ball. And a nasty cut.'

It felt like a hangover. He'd had only one of those before — one time in Bracton when Walter had found a crate of Glenfiddich and they'd all toasted each other in the yacht's cockpit into the early hours.

'Where's Leona?'

Nathan hesitated.

'Nathan?'

'I think she . . . escaped.'

Jacob only had a hazy memory of what preceded his world going black. A large exhibition hall full of computer games. And . . . and pale, long-haired children, a whole crowd of them chasing them through the dark.

'We were rescued by some people from this place. They were nearby an' heard our gunshots.'

Gunshots . . . yes, Jacob definitely remembered gunshots.

'There was a bit of a fight an' stuff and they rescued us,' said Nathan, helping Jacob to sit up. 'And Leona . . . she, well I reckon she escaped out the other way.'

Jacob closed his eyes for a moment. Relieved. 'Are you sure?'

'Yup,' Nathan replied quickly. 'She's probably halfway home to let your mum know. Thing is, she'll be okay, right?'

He grinned again. 'Anyway, Jake, man, you really, really gotta get up an' *see* this place.'

'Yeah?'

'Oh, yeah. It's the fucking business. Got lights and 'lectric and everything. And there's like, thousands of people. You feel like gettin' up yet?'

Jacob nodded eagerly. His head hurt like a bugger and he felt nauseous enough to hurl. But sitting up on the mattress he felt a little better . . . and excited.

Nathan offered him a hand and pulled him up off the cot. 'Wanna try stand?'

Jacob grasped his hand and slowly got to his feet. 'So, what are the people like?'

'They're friendly,' replied Nathan. 'You know, we could stay if we wanted? They already said that's okay.'

He led Jacob towards a gap in the partition wall and stepped out onto a wide concourse. Jacob's jaw dropped at the sight of a nearby suspension arc rising up from the ground, tethered by an apron of thick iron cables, to converge with two dozen more arcs at the apex of the dome's canvas roof. To his right, he could see a long curving boulevard of shopfronts, cafés and restaurants, just like a real high street; like an indoor town.

The open space before him, though, was busy with people: men and women pushing trolleys of fresh vegetables, heading up the boulevard with gardening tools in their hands. A man, pulling along several five-gallon drums of water on a trolley, nodded politely at them. Although they all wore their own clothes, many patched and faded, they also all seemed to be wearing a turquoise armband.

'Why they wearing those?'

Nathan shrugged. 'It's, like, to show they belong here. You have to earn a band to live here. Guess it's like a passport or something.'

Jacob quietly observed the activity all around them.

'A work day,' said Nathan. 'Just like back home. Everyone's gotta get their hands dirty outside.'

He led the way. Most of the cafés and restaurants were closed. One of them, however, was being used as a canteen and groups of workers sat outside around the tables and slurped at warm steaming bowls of food.

At the end of the boulevard they stepped into an open area, a vast foyer, where Nathan led Jacob out of the large glass-fronted doors of the dome's main entrance.

The morning sun beamed brightly down onto the approach plaza, warming the smooth ground beneath his feet. Spread out in front of them across what was once a wide apron of car-parking reserved for coaches, he could see endless rows of greenery sprouting waist-high from neat rows of long grow-trays. Further along, workers carrying buckets emerged and disappeared down a maze of head-high walls of runner beans and pea vines, climbing frames of bamboo and plastic webbing.

'It's one huge farm,' said Nathan. 'Much better than ours. They got all sorts of food growing out there.' He waved his hand to their right. 'And the Thames is just over there. It's clean now. They say it's so clean you can drink it straight out of the river.' Nathan shook his head. 'Fuckin' awesome.'

Jacob nodded. 'Yeah, this is cool.'

He could imagine Mum approving of this. This is what she'd been trying to set up, somewhere that could sustain itself, feed everyone without having to rely on whatever could still be foraged from forgotten storerooms or over-looked depots. That's what it looked like they'd managed to achieve here.

Staring out at the rustling sea of leaves before them, he could see this place had so much more potential than their hanging gardens of Babylon out in the North Sea. There was much more growing here than there was back home. Their effort paled by comparison.

If Leona was on her way back to the rigs to tell Mum what had happened to them, then maybe she saw that they were rescued, maybe she saw a hint of the dome, perhaps she understood there was something here worthwhile.

Mum needs to know about this place. Mum needs to bring them all here.

He looked at Nathan. 'This is so cool.'

'Yeah.'

Jacob had been hoping to find a bustling city, street lamps aglow and – shit, why not? – maybe even one or two buses picking their way through the centre of London once again. But he realised now that was pitifully naive. A dream like that was still years away. But this . . . he realised with a growing certainty as he watched hundreds of people at work, the slashes of turquoise armbands flickering and moving dutifully amongst an undulating carpet of green . . . this, was where that *bustling* future was going to start. This place, the Millennium Dome of all the odd places, was going to be ground zero of a new United Kingdom.

He found himself laughing with excitement. Nathan joined him.

'This is it, isn't it?' he asked his friend. 'This is really *it*.'

Nathan nodded, knowing exactly what he meant by that half-question.

It. This was definitely *it*.

Chapter 45

10 years AC

Shepherd's Bush,
London

Leona gazed out of the small study window at the cherry tree swaying gently in next door's front garden, caught in the morning sun, the blossoms seeming to glow from within. A lovely view. She'd seen Dad a million times sitting in his office chair gazing out of the window.

Probably loving that same tree.

She smiled. It almost felt like he was there in the room with her somehow. Not the body upstairs in Mum and Dad's old room . . . not that. That wasn't Dad any more, it was just the fossilised remains of a cadaver beneath a rotting quilt. No, sitting here, at his desk, looking at the faded Post-It notes stuck to the side of his monitor, the walls, a year planner with jobs and contracts penned in and still yet to do, articles from oil industry magazines, charts and graphs pinned to the cork board, a Gary Larson calendar on the desk; one fresh cartoon for every day. It was still on Monday 4 July – the day he left here for his last job over in Iraq just a few days before the crash happened.

This study, the room itself, was Dad.

Nanna said Grandad was the one who discovered the oil was all running out?

Leona smiled at the memory of Hannah's voice.

Was he a famous science man?

'No, just a geologist and an engineer,' she said aloud. She shook her head. 'And no, he didn't *discover* that. Everyone knew, they just weren't bothered about doing anything.'

The whole oil business knew it was running out. Dad just wrote the report about how bad it could get and how easily the entire industry could be disabled by taking out no more than a dozen distribution nodes.

'He just wrote a report about it.' Hearing her own voice deadened by the walls of Dad's book-lined study was strangely reassuring. 'He wrote this big essay about it. A big chunky thing. Wrote it way back just before the new millennium, when I was just nine. And he warned what might happen. How someone could make oil stop with just, like, a few bombs in all the right places. They paid him a lot of money for it.'

She shrugged. 'And then ten years later it happened. It happened exactly as he'd written it down. Bomb after bomb . . . as if he'd predicted the future.'

Wow! Was Grandad a wizard?

Leona laughed. 'No, not a wizard, Hannah.' Her gaze drifted back to the window, the glowing cherry blossoms outside, her mind a million miles away. 'My mum never told you kids when she did the peak oil class, though – never told *anyone*, in fact – that the people Dad wrote the report for were the same people that made those bombs happen.'

She laughed again, bitterly this time. 'In a way, you could say the end of the world all started right here, in this little room. Dad – he sort of wrote the plans for it. Showed how it could be done.'

People . . . bad people?

'Yes, bad people.' She shook her head vaguely. 'Never really knew for sure who they were. Dad thought they were oil people. I guess they weren't.'

Evil terror-men?

'We'll never know. Doesn't really matter who it was now, does it? Or why they'd want to do it. It doesn't matter any more. They're all gone. It's history now.'

Something skittered across the floor above; it could have

been a rat, or a wild cat chasing a rat. Their home's new tenant, mother nature, was clearly impatient to move in.

How long?

Not Hannah's voice any more, just her own.

How long?

She opened her mouth to answer her own question and realised she honestly didn't know. 'Jacob and Nathan might yet come,' she uttered softly. She didn't want her little brother coming home and finding her, like Dad, tucked up and dead. Because, yes, he must have made it out of there. He must have. So, maybe the boys had found their lights and new friends and a future, or if not, were well on their way back home.

So how long?

How long indeed. There was food in the trailer outside, and water. Enough to keep her going for weeks, if not months. But that wasn't the plan.

'I'm home,' she whispered.

And that was good enough for now. Her eyes drifted back to the shifting cherry tree outside.

Chapter 46

10 years AC

O2 Arena – 'Safety Zone 4',
London

Jacob looked up at the young man, flanked on either side by two others. All three of them wore tatty neon orange waist-coats with the word 'staff' stencilled across them in fading white. He'd seen others like them walking in pairs around the edge of the huge plantation outside, observing the people tending the crops.

'Security,' Nathan had said; the Zone's 'police' keeping the peace.

'My name's Snoop,' said the middle one. His smile revealed a gold tooth. 'Heard you was up and walkin' about. So the Chief wants to talk with you.'

'Right now?' asked Nathan.

Snoop nodded. 'Now.'

They were led out of the infirmary and along the boule-vard. The canvas 'sky' above was beginning to dim as the sun outside set and the tall, high-street façades on either side cast a deep violet shadow between them.

'Lights should be comin' on any sec,' said Snoop.

They were entering the open area of the entrance foyer when a distant chugging sound started up and almost im-mediately a floodlight atop a tall tripod kicked in, bathing the floor with a cold clinical glare.

'This way,' said Snoop.

To their left was the main entrance. Through the glass front wall Jacob could see the acres of green outside and an approaching stream of workers coming in for the evening.

To their right – the direction they were being led – a large sign invited them to enter the O2 Arena. Nathan had pointed that out to him earlier today and told him the central stadium area of the dome was off limits to everyone but staff – the guys wearing orange jackets. Jacob had asked why and Nathan had shrugged, saying he guessed it was where all the supplies, medicines and guns were kept.

They entered an archway and pushed through a turnstile that clacked noisily as it admitted each one of them in turn. Jacob could hear – actually *feel* – the steady bass thump of something coming from ahead of them. They climbed a short flight of steps and found themselves emerging onto an aisle between endless rows of pale blue flip-down auditorium seats that arced in both directions around a circular stage ahead of them.

Both Jacob and Nathan gasped at the sight. The stage at the centre of the O2 Arena was an Aladdin's cave of flickering, pulsating lights and jangling noise. The floor covered with criss-crossing nests of power cables, pinball and arcade machines.

Above the stage, on a circular lighting rig, spotlights of different colours spun and flashed on and off.

Nathan shook his head, his jaw hanging loose from a thread. 'Oh, man, you're shittin' me!'

Snoop turned back to look at them both, amused by their reaction. 'Fuckin' wicked, uh? Tonight's Party Night. Chief puts the light show and arcade on for us one night every two weeks.'

Jacob watched as dozens of boys played the machines, moving from one to another in lively groups, laughing giddily, popping to the bass-heavy music pumping out over the sound system.

'Come on,' said Snoop. 'Can't keep the Chief waiting.'

He led them down the central aisle towards the stage, around the bottom of it towards the rear, both Jacob and

Nathan's eyes glued on the fun and games going on around them. Finally they came to an entrance beyond the last block of seats and a ramp leading down to double doors with the words 'Back' on one and 'Stage' stencilled on the other.

Beside the doors stood another young lad in an orange staff vest. Snoop casually raised his fist and knuckle-kissed.

'Hey, Trix, we good to go in?'

The boy nodded deferentially to Snoop. He pushed through the heavy doors into a dimly lit area beyond. Burgundy carpet lined the walls and dim recessed spotlights in the ceiling reminded Jacob of a plush cinema he once went to as a kid.

'Chief!' called out Snoop. 'I got here the newbs we picked up.'

'Thank you, Edward, you and your boys can go join the party if you want whilst I have a chat with them.'

Snoop made a face. Jacob guessed he preferred to be called Snoop rather than Edward. He turned nonchalantly on his heels, casually flicking his wrists at the other two to follow him. They turned and left, pushing through the heavy, acoustically shielded doors which let in a momentary cacophony of jangling arcade bells and pumping dance music before swinging shut and muting the noise to little more than a muffled rhythmic thud.

Stepping into the pool of light cast from a spot in the ceiling, a white man in his late fifties emerged; stocky and short, a face like a grizzled East-End barrow boy, pockmarked skin barely covered by a silver and grey close-clipped beard that was never going to look anything other than patchy.

'All right?' He extended a hand. 'I'm Alan Maxwell.'

He sounded just like he looked: like an ill-tempered sales manager.

Nathan grabbed his hand and shook it. 'I'm Nathan Williams and this is Jacob Sutherland.'

Jacob smiled as they shook. 'I just want to thank you very much for taking us both in—'

Maxwell waved him silent impatiently. 'Sit down. I want to have a chat with you.'

Both boys did as they were told at once. There was something about his gruff commanding voice that told them he didn't stand on ceremony, he didn't swallow bullshit, nor did he take 'no' for an answer.

'So? You like the place so far?'

'You kidding?' Jacob grinned. 'It's amazing. All those games machines and the disco lights and everything. It's brilliant!'

Nathan just nodded. Playing it cool.

'Safety Zone Four. One of twenty-seven regional emergency rallying points in the UK,' said Maxwell. 'And the only one to survive.' They nodded silently. Maxwell tidied away a folder of papers he'd been scribbling notes on when they'd entered.

'It survived because I made a deliberate choice to disobey the emergency authorities' instructions during the crash. This place should have taken in about sixty thousand civilians and provided them with food and water for twelve weeks.' A dry half-smile on his lips. 'Twelve weeks . . . that's a bloody laugh. That's how long they reckoned it would take to tidy the streets and get everything back the way it was.'

He looked at them both, locking them down, in turn, with a long uncomfortable stare. 'I allowed in just under two thousand lucky people. Then I stopped.' He shrugged. 'I suppose the other fifty-eight thousand I *should* have let in are all probably dead somewhere. But I'm okay with that. I sleep all right.'

He shrugged. 'Sounds harsh but that's the way it is. Bottom line . . . I turned out to be right. The world *didn't* fix itself. The supplies in the other safety zones ran out and they ended up in a complete bloody mess.'

He stroked his clipped salt-and-pepper beard thoughtfully. 'Anyway that explains why we're still here. I asked Edward to bring you over so we can talk. I do this with any new waifs and strays we take in nowadays. It doesn't happen quite so often.'

'There are still people out there,' said Jacob. 'In fact there's dozens of kids living in that exhibition place across the river.'

'Them? Oh, they're feral,' said Maxwell. 'No more than wild bloody animals now.' He looked at the expression on their faces. 'Don't feel sorry for them. Most of them can barely talk. Many of them were small children when it happened and they still are in a way.'

'I don't feel sorry,' said Nathan. 'They nearly killed us.'

Maxwell nodded. 'Every now and then we come across packs of them and have to scare 'em away. Otherwise they'd be trying to get in. Anyway,' he continued, 'the pair of you clearly haven't gone feral so I'm guessing you've come from somewhere else that's managed to sort itself out.'

'Yeah,' said Jacob. 'But not as big or as cool as this place.'

Maxwell shrugged. 'Unfortunately, that's what I suspect – that this is probably, by far, the largest going concern in the country. Where've you two come from?'

'Norfolk,' said Nathan. 'A place in Norfolk.'

'You walked down?'

'No we got some bicycles.'

'What's it like out there? Did you come across many people?'

Jacob made a face. 'Nothing really. It's just lots of empty towns.'

'Yeah, we was hoping we'd see other groups an' things. But it was just a load of rotting buildings an' stuff,' added Nathan.

'So, what about where you came from in Norfolk?'

'Well actually it's off the north-east coast,' said Jacob. 'On a bunch of gas rigs.'

Maxwell's frown lifted ever so slightly. 'Really?'

Nathan nodded. 'But it's rubbish up there. It's always wet and cold, ain't it?'

Jacob nodded.

'Shit,' nodded Maxwell, 'it must get *very* cold out there.'

'Oh, but we got heaters in some places,' said Jacob. 'And the gas gives us some electric anyway.'

'How many people living there?'

They looked at each other. 'I think it's about four hundred and fifty now, isn't it?' said Jacob.

Nathan shrugged. 'About that.'

Maxwell's eyebrows arched. Impressed.

'So, where'd you get all *your* 'lectric from?' asked Nathan, nodding towards the double doors and the soft, insistent pump of a dance beat from beyond.

'Ahh, well we have a sizeable reserve of diesel here and four emergency generators. I put all the lights and the arcade machines on for my boys once a fortnight. It keeps them happy.'

Jacob frowned. *My boys?*

Maxwell noted that. 'The staff . . . the ones in orange vests? They like to call themselves praetorians.'

'Pry-tory . . . ?'

'Praetorians, like the Roman soldiers that used to guard the emperor,' said Maxwell. 'They think of themselves as my bodyguards. I suppose they're sort of that. But they're also the security here. The zone's police, if you want.'

'But they're . . . some of them look young. I mean, younger even than me and Nathan.'

'Yes . . . yes, I suppose some of them are.'

Nathan cocked his head. 'You got *kids* in charge here?'

'Bollocks to that,' Maxwell huffed. The closest, it seemed, he was going to come to a laugh. 'No, *I'm* in charge here. But they're my police force. And in exchange for the work they get special privileges.'

'Privileges?'

'You know, I treat 'em.'

'Like the arcade machines outside?' asked Jacob.

'Yeah. We've got all sorts of things for my boys; arcade machines, Xboxes and PlayStations, a little cinema. Other treats. Every other Saturday night I crank up the second and third generators and they get all that.'

Jacob and Nathan exchanged a glance.

Maxwell's lips stretched far enough to almost call it a smile. 'If you're a good pair of lads then you might be able to join them. I'm always after boys I can trust. Young lads I can rely on.'

They both grinned. 'We'd like that,' said Jacob.

'Well, we'll see. For now you can stay on probation until I'm sure you're not going to be troublemakers.'

'Oh, we ain't troublemakers,' said Nathan. 'We came looking for something exactly like this. That's why we came to London, isn't it, Jay?'

He nodded eagerly.

'We just *knew* there had to be something like this here. Somebody getting things sorted. A new beginning an' stuff.'

'Yeah and we were—'

Maxwell silenced them both with a hand. 'You'll be on probation. And I'll talk to Edward about you . . . see what he thinks. See if you've got the stuff to make it as praetorians.'

Both boys grinned.

'But for now you'll remain with the civilians outside. Edward will find you somewhere to sleep and assign you to a work group.' He waved a hand towards the doors. 'Off you go then. We'll talk again soon, I'm sure.'

Jacob and Nathan rose from the seats.

'Thank you,' said Jacob again.

'Yes, all right,' said Maxwell impatiently. 'Go find Edward, he'll take you back to the workers' area.'

Chapter 47

10 years AC

Maxwell watched the doors swing to, shutting out the annoying din coming from the arena. The noise reminded him of the cheap seaside camping holidays his parents used to take him on when he was a boy; amusement arcades, slot machines, bumper cars, two-penny-push machines. The incessant blinging and flashing lights; simpletons all around him quite happy with that.

He shook his head. The world was full of simpletons.

Although somewhat less full now.

He returned to the task at hand. An audit of the supplies left downstairs on the mezzanine floor. That floor had been full once. Now the subterranean space was mostly bare green linoleum, dotted with islands of pallets of goods; shrinking islands.

Day to day life for Alan Maxwell had become a precarious balancing game; a very complicated game, the principal goal of which was to eke out what was left downstairs as long as possible without his people realising how little of it was left.

So far he'd played the game very well; lasted much longer than he thought they would. Some food was being grown outside; the basics, dreary vegetables of one kind or another, some fruits too. But nowhere near enough to keep over two thousand people alive indefinitely. What it was doing was helping to pad out the supplies of tinned foods, making what they had go a lot further.

Most mealtimes his people were served thick broths and

soups, of which their freshly unearthed vegetables constituted most of the volume. The few dozen tins of corned beef added to the mix made it almost palatable. This summer's crop had been better than last, but come winter, when there was very little left to dig out of the troughs of earth outside, they were going to be once again wholly reliant on these dwindling islands of canned food.

Month on month, year on year, the game he played was about reducing the amount of stored food he handed out. An accountant's game of allocating calories per head; lowering the calorie count in a carefully controlled way. Giving less to those deemed least useful to the community; managing everyone's expectations and morale . . . keeping the sinking boat as steady as possible.

Because sink was what it was eventually going to do.

The Zone simply wasn't capable of being turned into a giant farmstead capable of producing forty thousand calories of food every single day. The workers – two thousand men and women of all ages and a hundred or so children – were eventually going to starve very slowly. Not this winter. Maybe not even the next. But it was going to happen eventually.

Maxwell's job had become one thing; managing the decline.

Keeping order on the decks as the good ship slowly slid under. The boys – the praetorians – were going to be his rearguard. As long as there was fuel for the generators so they could play their games and have their noisy music and flashing lights once a fortnight, as long as he had a store cupboard of privileges to offer them, as long as he kept them on his side . . . they'd do absolutely anything for him.

One day soon he was going to have to rely on them to evict large numbers of the workers, to make that food downstairs last a while longer. And then again, eventually, he'd have to rely on the boys he most trusted to evict other boys. Until one day, it was just going to be him and Edward 'Snoop' Tindall. Then he'd ask Edward to leave. And finally alone here in Safety Zone 4, he'd pull out that rather fine bottle of Bordeaux he'd liberated from the basement of Harrods, kick his shoes off and get comfortable on one of these leather couches. He'd take his time, make sure he enjoyed the entire bottle before blowing his brains out.

See, that was the long game. Divide and conquer, and divide again. Until he was the last man standing.

But now . . . the glimmer of an interesting plan B existed.

He pushed aside the paperwork on the coffee table.

He had allowed himself a little fantasy. A fantasy in which some going concern existed, a going concern big enough to sustain most of his people. In his fantasy, he'd imagined some castle or stately mansion in the countryside outside London. Surrounded by a network of cultivated fields, and farm animals – all that difficult set-up work already done for them. There just for the taking. He'd even managed to gild that little fantasy by casting himself as some sort of jovial medieval baron in his keep surrounded by bountiful fields and dutiful peasants working them for him.

There'd been patrols around London, around the outskirts of London, even into the countryside, but they'd found nothing that could support a wholesale relocation. Just a few small family-sized farms that had been barely coping. Farms they'd stripped clean, of course.

So that's what it remained, his fantasy. No medieval fiefdom. No Baron Maxwell.

But those boys . . .

Those two *well-fed* boys and their four hundred-and-something community living on . . . what did they say? An oil rig? And they had power, too?

He sat back and pinched his bristly chin gently between thumb and forefinger.

Chapter 48

10 years AC

Shepherd's Bush,
London

Leona had lost count of the days. She guessed maybe four-teen or fifteen of them had gone by. Obviously Jacob and Nathan weren't coming. Obviously, they hadn't made it.

It's time.

She'd decided that this morning was going to be her last, but had spent the day in a fog of ridiculous procrastination, pondering how best to do it. Pills in bed had been the plan. But then an awful thought had occurred to her that she might not do it right; not enough to kill her outright, but leave her alive with a failing organ, or paralysed. In any case, the chemist on the corner of Uxbridge Road had been stripped of every single medicine.

She'd found a knife and had a trial run at seeing whether she'd have the courage to push it through her skin, all the way so that it severed an artery. Just like last time, she'd baulked at doing it, heaving several times, her forearm marked and scratched with a dozen aborted attempts.

As the afternoon waned into evening she realised the only certain way of doing this was a drop. A drop high enough to ensure she wasn't left dying in agony with ruptured organs and shattered bones.

She knew a good place.

One last trip upstairs to say goodbye to their bedrooms. Leona had always considered a person's bedroom to be the 'negative space' they left behind, like an impression of a coin in a blob of Blu-Tack – it was them, or at least a negative of them, and it was the closest thing she had to saying goodbye in person.

Jacob's room, north-facing, was dim. She smiled at the wallpaper of pirate ships, the shelves still stacked with Playmobil and Games Workshop figures, and books and rubber-banded packs of trading cards.

She whispered a farewell.

Out on the landing, dark but cut by a golden lance of sunlight across the floor, she hesitated beside the only closed door. She didn't need to open it again. She'd done that several days ago and wished she hadn't. Several panes of glass had smashed, leaves were dusted across the room and piled up in one corner. A bramble of some kind was growing on the bed, taking root in the quilt and feeding off nutrients that had long ago soaked into the mattress. Feeding off her dad. She'd angrily wrenched the damned thing off the bed and tossed it out through the window and not been back in since.

Bye bye, Dad.

Then she was down the stairs, tiptoeing across the hall. She opened the front door and stepped outside. A quiet still suburban street. She realised how beautiful the world could look on an evening like this; the russet and green leaves of the horse-chestnut trees on fire in the sunlight, red poppies in the opposite garden like discarded M&Ms. The summer green of tree branches almost meeting each other now across the narrow street, sweeping and hissing in the breeze and the broken tarmac road, dappled with shifting light.

Really quite pretty.

Jacob and Nathan watched the dome from the outside. It was warm enough that they sat out in T-shirts on the edge of the vegetable plantation, on the quayside overlooking the Thames.

In the middle of the dome's canvas roof, multicoloured

lights marbled the surface from inside, and out of the very apex, twin spotlights lanced up into the night sky. They could just about hear the gentle thud of music drifting across the rustle of leaves, and the murmuring of quiet conversations from groups of people nearby.

'It looks amazing, doesn't it?' said Jacob.

Nathan nodded. This was the first time they'd come outside to watch the lights. Better than staying inside the dome, where the pounding music made it impossible to sleep anyway. Pretty much all the workers spent Party Night outside, some dragging their bedding with them, happy to sleep outside until dawn.

A fortnight ago, as Snoop had escorted them out of the central arena, he'd told them that Party Night normally lasted into the early hours. He'd not been wrong. As well as the machines, he'd said, there was alcohol . . . and *the girl-friends*, too. He'd winked at them both as he shooed them down the stairs and out through the turnstile. 'Play your cards right and you bros be joinin' the fun soon enough.'

'It's going to be cool,' said Jacob.

'Yeah.'

He imagined it was going to be a bit like the rock festivals Leona used to go to. She always used to say she had a well-bangin' time at them. After-gig parties that lasted until dawn in a field somewhere. People still dancing hypnotically as the sun came up. Others zonked out in tents or eagerly discussing the meaning of life in hushed voices around smouldering campfires. She told him once, before the crash, that he had all of that to look forward to at college; parties, music, stage-diving, girlfriends, his first proper hangover, his first joint . . . all the cool things she was enjoying . . . between occasional essays, lectures and course work.

Except, of course, she'd been wrong.

His teen years had been spent watching the North Sea pound relentlessly at the rigs' support-legs; watching migrating Vs of birds and every few weeks – a special treat – picking through warehouses and cargo containers on Bracton's freight storage quay.

'We're going to stay here, then?' asked Jacob.

'Shit, I know *I* am.'

He nodded after a moment's consideration. 'Me, too.'

Maybe he'd give it a year or so then check with Mr Maxwell that it was all right for him to go back home and pay the rigs a visit. Maxwell seemed like a decent enough bloke from what he saw. A bit grumpy, but somehow that was reassuring; like they were seeing him warts and all. No pretence. Far better than somebody, all smiles at first, that you just knew was going to turn out to be someone else entirely later on.

He watched as the dancing spotlight beams panned across each other, producing a giant X in the sky. He lay back on his elbows and looked up at the stars.

He'd go back and tell Mum, and Leona, and Walter about their time here. How good they'd got things at the Safety Zone. Maybe he'd even be able to persuade them to come back with him and see for themselves; merge the communities together. There was certainly space enough for everyone here.

'Hey, Nate?'

'Uhh?'

'You reckon being one of these praetorians is a bit like being a soldier?'

Nathan gave it some thought. 'S'pose. More like being a policeman, I think.'

'But they get guns.' He'd seen them patrolling outside in pairs, watching the workers, guns slung over their shoulders.

'They gotta have guns, mate. I mean, them wild kids that attacked us? They're out there, Jay. Reckon they've got to patrol the perimeters like border guards or somethin'.'

On patrol . . . just like for-real soldiers. A uniform as well.

Jacob looked around and saw a cluster of men watching them silently from a dozen yards away. He'd noticed an undercurrent of resentment from some of the workers towards the praetorians. He decided to lower his voice a little.

'I hope Maxwell *does* take us on.'

Nathan settled back on his elbows and joined him looking up at the stars.

'Me, too. It's gonna be props, man.'

'Yeah, really props.' Jacob sighed. It always sounded naff when he tried using some of Nathan's cool words.

'It's going to be good.'

The one thing Leona feared the most was not doing it properly. She wanted a clean drop, one impact and it was all over. Dying slowly, dying painfully; the thought of that terrified her. Which is why she wanted somewhere high enough to be absolutely certain.

She pushed the maintenance access door open and stepped out onto the roof of the Westfield shopping mall. It stretched out before her like a football pitch, criss-crossed here and there with pipes that ended with AC outlets. At the far end was a spiked brush of antennae and satellite dishes.

By moonlight the pale weathered surface reminded her of the helipad back home. An island alone in a dark sky. With the stars scattered above, she could just as well have been standing on a platform in the middle of space, drifting through the universe for eternity.

She made her way across the broad expanse, seeing her dark moon shadow cast before her. As she neared the edge she saw it was rimmed by a safety rail – not enough to put off someone determined but enough to protect a hapless worker from an unfortunate tumble. She ducked down and climbed between the bars and then gasped as she caught sight of the sheer drop below.

All of a sudden she felt dizzy, her legs wobbled beneath

her and she quickly sat down, wrapping one arm around the rail. Her stomach churned, she wanted to throw up – her body's reaction. It had finally woken up and realised what she was intending to do and was now doing everything in its power to convince her otherwise.

She cursed herself for being a weak, silly cow. Cursed whatever deeply-bedded survival instinct was making this last task so bloody difficult for her, making her hand clutch the rail tightly.

'Just a little jump,' she whispered. 'And then we're all done.'

Her body remained unconvinced.

'Just another step,' she urged. 'And then . . .'

She imagined letting go and leaning forward; just five seconds of air whistling past her ears, chilling her face.

Please don't jump.

Leona looked up at the sound of the little voice and saw Hannah, chin resting on the railing, a leg swinging impatiently, scuffing the tarmac with the tip of her sandals.

She smiled at her daughter. 'Hello again, trouble.'

Hannah rolled her eyes and offered a long-suffering smile. The gesture was so her. Leona laughed softly at the vision of her daughter, hanging on the railing and gazing out at the dark horizon. She could quite happily indulge this fantasy for a minute or two.

Please don't be a silly gonk, said Hannah.

'I'm tired, Hannah, love. Tired of struggling along.'

She frowned. *Why be so tired?*

It was hard to explain to a child who'd never known anything other than life on the rigs. Hard to explain how difficult it was to get up each and every day and work ceaselessly to squeeze such a meagre payback out of life. When once upon a time it was effortless; a meal was the mere opening of a fridge door, the three-minute wait for a microwave. Warmth was the flick of a switch. Skin-tingling luxury, the twist of a hot water tap.

'I'm just tired,' she replied. 'I miss the way things were.'

Was the old times really that good?

'Yes, they were.'

She remembered there were those who moaned about how materialistic and selfish the world had become; people on late-night TV chat shows, people who wrote columns in newspapers. She wondered how many of them were still alive today, getting on with practising what they'd preached. And for those of them who were still alive, she wondered what they'd happily trade for just one steaming hot shower, for a freshly grilled cheese-on-toast, for an ice-cold beer.

The small things.

It's still very silly, said Hannah thoughtfully. *I didn't need all those things that you miss so much.*

Leona was about to mutter something about it being better to never have had than to have had and lost, but it seemed unkind and dismissive. She wasn't sure how much longer it would take to convince her hand to let go. And there were things to say.

'I love you, Hannah. I'm sorry I was a crap mum.'

Mum. Leona felt her aching heart tighten. Why hadn't she insisted Hannah call her that instead of Leona? Something in the word, in the bond that it implied. She'd missed out on that. They'd been more like sisters than mother and child.

Leona wiped her damp cheek on her shoulder.

Another regret. Something else to ponder on her way down.

I don't think you should . . . not yet.

Leona laughed weakly. Her fantasy Hannah, it seemed, was every bit as bossy as her real one had been. 'But I'm ready now. I want to.' Her hand loosened its grip on the rail.

Not yet.

'Why?'

Look.

Leona turned to gaze out across the still, dark skyline of London. There was nothing to see.

Jacob was right.

'What?'

Just look, silly.

She looked again. Dark. Nothing. Dead dark London, that was all.

Lights.

Leona so far had seen nothing. But then the faintest flicker. A beam visible for an instant, gone the next.

'Oh, God!' she whispered. She saw the beam again, so faint, like the solitary thread of a spider's web catching sunlight from an angle, then gone.

Go and see.

Leona's eyes had lost the beam. She looked to the left a little and her peripheral vision detected the faint lancing movement once more, but turning to look at it directly, it was lost. It was east of Shepherd's Bush, quite possibly along the river as the boys had suggested; Canary Wharf, perhaps the O2 Arena.

You have to go see.

The shimmering lance of light seemed to have gone now.

She turned to look at Hannah but she, too, had gone. Where she'd stood the pale roof remained unscuffed. A soft breeze whispered along the dark street below teasing a pile of dry leaves to race each other along the kerb, and a shutter somewhere creaked on rusty hinges, clattering against a frame.

Chapter 49

10 years AC

O2 Arena – 'Safety Zone 4', London

It was midday when Leona finally approached the dome. She emerged from the Blackwall Tunnel, leaving her bicycle behind in the darkness and picking her way through a barricade of razor-wire hoops long ago abandoned and left to sag and rust. She crossed an empty dual-carriageway and walked up a shallow grass embankment towards the giant blister of vanilla canvas crowned with its distinct ring of canary-yellow support spars.

It was at the top of the embankment that she noticed a perimeter of corrugated iron panels six feet high, topped with spools of more of that hatefully sharp razor wire; a cobbled together Hadrian's wall that stretched left and right in front of her.

The faint spotlights she'd seen had to have come from here; this was the right direction, east of Shepherd's Bush, easily nine or ten miles away. She emerged from the overgrown grass embankment and slowly approached the perimeter wall's main gate, wondering one more time whether Jacob and Nathan were already somewhere inside. It was a hope.

Dizz-ee watched the workers as he slurped lukewarm river water from a scuffed old Evian bottle and relaxed in the deckchair in front of the gatehouse. Although the boys called it the gatehouse, it was nothing more than an IKEA garden shed erected for those on duty on a rainy day to shelter inside.

This afternoon felt like it was going to be a really hot one; first proper summer's day of the year. He cursed his misfortune at being given this morning's perimeter guard duty rather than the afternoon shift. Apart from the fact that he and his guard posse had to rise early with the workers – and most of his boys were still nursing sore heads from last night – this afternoon, outside, it was going to be lovely. Inside, on the afternoon rota, standing guard on the entrance turnstiles to the central arena, the praetorians' and Chief's quarters, it was going to be hot and stuffy.

Snoop, being the completely selfish shit that he was, liked his lie in, especially after party nights. Privilege of rank. So he made his number two dog get up and take the morning shift instead. Dizz-ee could quite happily have passed the job onto the third dog, Jay-zee, but he was already assigned to the canteen watch.

Dizz-ee screwed the cap back on his water bottle.

Fuck him.

He was stuck at being second dog. Stuck for ever, or stuck until Snoop screwed up somehow and pissed off the Chief enough. Maybe that was going to happen eventually. He knew Snoop saw himself as being the Chief one day; fancied the idea of no longer taking orders from the wrinkled old snowflake bastard.

That ate at Snoop. Said it was old-world racism all over again that some rich, middle-aged *white* fuck should rule the roost once again. *They had their go*, Snoop kept saying. *Had their go and they fucked the world up. Should be a brother runnin' the shit here.*

Mind you, Dizz-ee could see his point even though he was white; even though Snoop was an arrogant fuck that he'd like to see screw up badly. Maxwell looked just like all those stiff old farts who'd collectively fucked-up the world between them: bankers, politicians, government types . . . *suits*. It didn't sit well with him either that some suited old twat should be in charge. It should be someone younger.

It wasn't about race; black, white, didn't mean shit to him. Rankled with Snoop though. Stupid arrogant fucker was bound to challenge the Chief head-on one day. Snoop could go and do that if he wanted. And see what happened. Chief would probably win out.

And then I'll be top dog.

It was going to happen one day. Snoop's temper was going to get the better of him sooner or later. Serve the selfish lazy bastard right.

His ill-tempered gaze returned to the swaying rows of plants, and the workers toiling quietly amongst them. They were all *oldies* – twenty-five and older. No babies, no kids amongst them. Chief Maxwell forbid that; making babies. It was one of his emergency laws. The bloke might once have been a rich white fat-cat, but he was smart enough. No baby mouths to feed. Not for the foreseeable. Girls got themselves pregnant? They just forced it and got rid of the baby-gunk that came out. Far better that than eviction.

He watched the workers. Some of the boys called the workers 'dome-niggers'. Seemed about right, they slouched about with sullen slave-faces. Good for nothing more than digging, planting, picking and muttering.

Dizz-ee called them 'serfs'. There was a picture book he'd once read: *Look Inside A Medieval Castle*. It had excellent cut-away illustrations showing all the things that went on inside, little labels and explanations on everything. He remembered there was a king, or a duke or baron in the middle of the castle. And then in the great hall, his knights, there to protect him in times of battle and in return for that a share of the king's privileges. And outside in the fields . . . the serfs.

He liked the idea that he was a bit like one of those knights of old. If he ever became top dog – shit, *when* he became top dog – he fancied the idea of coming up with a logo or a coat

315

of arms or something that the praetorians would all have to wear on their jackets. They'd all have to pick a knight name, like Sir Kill-a-lot, or Sir Frag-enstein.

About a billion times cooler than walking around with rapper names and the word 'staff' stencilled on them.

'Yo! Dizz-ee!'

Dizz-ee turned to Flav, standing a dozen yards away and jabbing a finger towards the ground beyond the perimeter wall.

'What?'

'Over there . . . girl coming over.'

Dizz-ee turned round, shaded his eyes. He was right. Striding towards them, a teenaged girl. She didn't move like the wildies, all furtive and edgy, ready to break and scamper like startled rabbits at the sound of a single gunshot. She looked clean, scrubbed and well fed, too.

Dizz-ee waved at Flav to follow him and jogged across to the gate section of the barricade. He pulled open the wire gate, just wide enough to step outside. Twenty yards away the girl stopped and stared at the gun he had levelled at her.

'So, what d'you want?'

'I saw the lights of this place, last night,' said the girl. 'You got power?'

Dizz-ee silently appraised her. She looked more presentable than most of the girls in the 'cattle shed'; many of them were looking the worse for wear, skin purple and mottled from bruising, most of them unpleasantly thin and malnourished. There hadn't been any new girls in the pen for quite some time. Some fresh ass would be sweet.

Keep her for myself.

'Hey, Dizz-ee. What do we do?' asked Flav quietly.

Thing is, he knew Snoop would bag the girl for himself just as soon as he clapped eyes on her. The selfish shit-fuck would pull rank on him and have her himself.

'Shall I go tell Snoop we got a girl coming in?'

316

Dizz-ee shook his head. 'No, hang on. I'll take her in myself,' he replied under his breath.

Flav looked at him uncertainly. 'You know Snoop'll want the girl,' he whispered.

'Fuck him. We'll put her in the cattle shed with the others. He don't go there much now, since they all looking so rough. I'm having her myself.'

The girl was watching them whispering from twenty yards out. 'Can I come in?' she called across.

She sounds well posh.

'So, what about me, Dizz? Do I get a piece of her?'

'Maybe, when I'm all done.'

Flav considered that for a moment. 'A'ight,' he said, smiling.

Dizz-ee winked at the younger lad and then pulled the gate wider. 'Yeah, sure,' he called to the girl waving her forward. 'You better come in.'

She hesitated. Dizz-ee cocked his head at the girl. 'Come in,' he smiled. 'It's safer inside than out. Safe zone, this.'

The girl stared at him for a moment. 'Okay,' she said and stepped slowly forward through the gap in the barrier, her eyes darting warily between Dizz-ee and Flav, the guns in their hands and their official-looking orange jackets.

'Bit *young* aren't you?' she said to Flav. 'To be . . . like, "staff"?'

Flav stiffened and for a moment she thought the young lad was going to slap her in the face. Dizz-ee didn't want his fresh meat all puckered and purple on the first night, so he stepped forward. 'Oh, Flav's man enough,' said Dizz-ee, 'bro's thirteen, aren't you?'

Flav nodded.

'Come on.' Dizz-ee smiled warmly, offering her a hand. 'Come, I'll show you round.'

Chapter 50

10 years AC

'LeMan 49/25a' – ClarenCo Gas Rig Complex, North Sea

'If I'd known he was some sort of bloody preacher,' said Jenny.

Dr Gupta nodded as she replaced the dressing on her shoulder. 'He does seem very good at it.'

A gusty day today; wind moaned softy at the porthole of her cabin, anxious to be let in. Clouds scudded across the blue sky. The dark-grey sea below them was frosted with lively white horses.

'Five times a day now he holds prayer meetings over there,' said Walter, nodding through the glass at the outline of the drilling platform. 'You can see when it's prayer time, the north walkway's thick with his groupies making their way over.'

'I should have evicted him,' uttered Jenny, wincing as Dr Gupta gently rubbed some antiseptic cream onto her shoulder and neck. She should have realised then, when he'd turned up at her request to discuss the matter of prayers at mealtime, that the only way to sort the problem out was promptly returning him to shore with a bag of supplies to help him on his way.

She hadn't realised how quickly support for him was going to grow. It looked like fifty to sixty people were part of his 'church' already. Every time she heard that football whistle being blown from the far platform she turned to see which of her people started to put down their tools and make their way over; more every day, it seemed.

'Yes,' said Walter quietly. 'He's nothing but trouble.'

'The problem is, Jenny, people want their faith,' said Dr Gupta. 'And that's what he's offering them.'

Jenny nodded. Tami was right. She'd worked so hard to ensure that there was nothing divisive such as *religion* to add to the numerous difficulties with living out here. She remembered back in the early days, in the first few years after the crash when things were at their darkest, all manner of bastardised, radicalised hybrid faiths had begun to emerge. Faiths that justified the most brutal treatment of those who begged to differ, brutal treatment of strangers or people who just didn't look or sound right.

Even the community they'd been living with deep in the woods outside Newark had begun to develop its own twisted version of Church of England Christianity. There was an ex-parish vicar who opened their community meetings with a sermon and a prayer. The prayer Jenny could even go along with, occasionally murmuring the words with everyone else. But the sermons were gradually becoming more and more hate-filled and poisonous; blaming the Taliban, al-Qaeda and some pan-Arabic, pan-Islamic plot to destroy the decadent West. The words were beginning to make sense to some of the people there. It gave them someone to blame, an ethnicity to universally despise and a justification to turn away many of the faces who emerged from the woods asking for food and shelter.

Jenny had vowed to keep this place just as free of that kind of bigotry as she had of vulture-eyed young men who might want to turn this refuge into their own personal harem. So, there were the rules. *Jenny's Laws.* No public prayers, no preachers, no organised faith and no prayer room, to list but a few of them. Those who needed to commune with God were at liberty to do so, but quietly and privately.

Dr Gupta was right, though. She never realised how many of the people here wanted to hear Latoc's Old Testament nonsense; needed some sort of spiritual guidance. Someone to tell them once a week that God was smiling on them, that they were doing the right thing, pleasing Him, that everything, one day, was going to be all right. They wanted to be reassured that the loved ones they'd lost in the chaos, the riots, the fights for supplies, or died from drinking bad water or spoiled food, were in a better place now and would one day be reunited with them.

This was a shit world everyone had inherited. Completely shit. Every day a tedious and repetitive grind for survival. The lights that Walter had managed to power with his generator had been their *only* luxury – a glimpse of the wonderful past and a promise from her, and Walter, that the future was going to get better.

It's no wonder they were turning to someone like Valérie Latoc. From what she'd heard second-hand, he was telling them all the things they craved to hear; that this was all for a reason, part of a bigger plan and they were a big part of this bigger plan. If she'd been a little smarter about things, she could have done the same; moulded some version of a faith to suit their ends. Just enough to give them all some comfort and certainty that they were right to be out here, struggling together for some future goal and that God was jolly pleased with them. And, of course, that God was quite content with the community being run by Jennifer Sutherland.

That's all she'd have had to do. But she'd have felt like a fraud.

Instead, like a stupid tyrant, she'd laid down the law, and now someone had arrived who was feeding on that need like a hungry mosquito on a bare forearm.

'So why don't we just say his probation is over, Jenny?' asked Walter. 'Tell him his time's up and you've decided to let him go.'

Jenny shook her head. 'I'm not sure I can now, Walter. I think if I told him to go we'd have a riot on our hands.'

'So what can we do?'

She looked out of the window at the far platform. Perhaps there'd be a cap to this? So what if near on sixty, or even a hundred, members of their community appeared to be regulars now at Latoc's prayer service? There were over four hundred and fifty people here. He still only had a minority. Provided his church-goers continued to do their bit on the work rota and there were no silly dictums from the man that said women had to shroud themselves from head to foot, or they could only eat fish on a Friday, or some other bizarre and illogical article of faith, then perhaps they might not need to turn this into a confrontation.

Maybe the novelty would wear off. Maybe Valérie Latoc wasn't as polished a preacher as he thought and his turnout would eventually begin to wane. It was early days yet.

'I don't think there's anything we can do other than see how this goes,' she said finally. 'If he's a whacko, some kind of radical nut, then he'll trip himself up eventually. He'll end up preaching something that someone doesn't like. They'll fall out over it and then I'll have to step in to soothe some egos. Far better that, than I appear like some sort of brutal bitch dictator that they can all rally against. Right?'

'And if he's not?'

'Not a religious whacko?' Jenny shrugged. 'Then we don't have a problem, do we? As long as we're all getting on nicely then I suppose we have a manageable problem.'

Dr Gupta nodded slowly. Walter was tight-lipped.

It was a plan of sorts, but not one she was entirely sure about.

Chapter 51

10 years AC

O2 Arena – 'Safety Zone 4',
London

Maxwell paced slowly along the base of the perimeter wall, looking inward across the endless rows of plants. His modest kingdom, tended by hundreds of workers dutifully wearing their turquoise armbands. Under other circumstances, in a different time, some might have called this a work camp . . . perhaps even a concentration camp. But then, Maxwell mused, they'd have missed the point and judged it unfairly. This wasn't a place to punish people or to annihilate a subset of the population. It was what the ruthless bloody business of survival tended to look like; some had to work the fields, some had to guard the walls, and some had to administrate.

Get used to it.

He shook his head.

'So anyway,' he said, aware that both the boys had been walking with him a while and were still none the wiser as to why he'd had them brought out here to tour the perimeter with him. 'I've been doing some thinking since I spoke to you last. When was that? Two, three weeks ago?'

Jacob and Nathan looked at each other. They'd lost track of how many days they'd been here. Maxwell smiled; the Zone had that effect. He squatted down and examined a small bed of late-sprouting rhubarb stalks that they were experimenting with.

'So you lads were telling me about your journey to London. That you didn't see a great deal going on out there?'

'We didn't see no one, really, did we, Jay?'

Jacob shook his head. 'Not really. Nothing anything like this size. There was a guy called Raymond . . . and those wild kids.'

Maxwell stroked his chin. 'Hmm. See, I hoped there would be plenty of other groups like ours. After ten years, you know, I was hoping some of the smaller groups of survivors might have pooled together. That we'd start seeing village-sized groups emerging out there.'

Both boys shook their head. 'Ain't nothing like that,' said Nathan.

Maxwell shook his head sadly. 'What a complete balls-up we made of things, eh?'

The boys looked at each other. Neither seemed to know what to say.

'Well, it's not *your* fault,' sighed Maxwell, running a hand through the tight grey curls on his head. 'You were just small boys back then. No, it was *my* bloody generation, we're the ones that ballsed everything up. We got too busy chasing money . . . pffft.'

He let the stalk of rhubarb go and stood up. 'Anyway,' he continued, 'so that got me thinking about the place you came from? On those gas rigs? It would make a great deal of sense for both our groups to hook up. To share resources, skills . . . that kind of thing. I mean, it seems like all we've got left is each other. Right?'

'That's right, Mr Maxwell,' said Jacob.

'You two seem like decent enough lads to me. You've behaved yourself over the last few weeks. Pulled your weight on the chores you've been given. You're both bright lads, nice an' polite. So I'm guessing you've been brought up by decent enough people. Not a bunch of crazies. Am I right?'

Nathan nodded his head. 'They're really nice people.'

'All — what was it? — three hundred-and-whatever? Good men and women are they? Peaceful lot?'

'Four hundred and fifty . . . or thereabout.'

323

'Actually there's hardly any men at all,' added Jacob. 'Mostly women and old people.'

'Yeah,' Nathan laughed self-consciously, 's'pose we was sort of the men, weren't we, Jay?'

Maxwell nodded thoughtfully. 'And who's in charge there? Do you have some government official? An ex-Member of Parliament or something? I'm sort of hoping there's something left of the government that I can hand over the reins to.' Maxwell sighed and smiled wearily at the boys. 'What I wouldn't give to be able to take a break and let someone else take charge for a while.'

'There's my mum,' said Jacob. 'Jenny Sutherland.' He made a face. 'I'm afraid she's not a member of any government, though.'

'She's pretty cool,' added Nathan. 'She's in charge. Runs things pretty much on her own. But she's, like, totally fair.'

'So why the hell are they stuck out on a gas rig of all places?'

'Safety, mainly,' replied Jacob. 'We moved about five or six years ago. There were bands of scavengers making it too dangerous on the mainland.'

Maxwell looked at Nathan. 'It must have been bloody hard, moving, starting again from scratch.'

Nathan shrugged. 'I dunno . . . I guess. Me an' my mum joined them a year after.'

'It was hard at first,' added Jacob. 'But we were lucky. The nearby town was a freight port. There was loads of ware-houses full of shipping containers of supplies. We wouldn't have managed otherwise. We had a couple of boats and we were ferrying stuff from there nearly every day at first. Wasn't a big deal ferrying stuff. I mean the rigs are just off the coast. You can just about see them from Bracton. Maybe fifteen miles out, wouldn't you say, Nate?'

He nodded.

Maxwell cocked his head. 'Bracton?'

'Yeah. It was a port and a gas refinery. All the underwater pipes from the rigs came into there.'

'Whereabouts is that?'

Both boys looked at each other for a moment. Not a shared glance of suspicion; more wondering how best to explain. 'Sort of north-east curve of East Anglia,' replied Jacob.

'It's down a bit,' said Nathan. 'South of Great Yarmouth.'

Maxwell nodded, he knew where they meant. He'd spent his youth living in Southend. He'd even visited Great Yarmouth for a camping holiday with his grandparents in the early eighties. Alan remembered it being pretty grim then during the height of the recession; a cheap and not too cheerful holiday resort, a wet summer that year and an incessant chilly offshore breeze that swept across the deck of the town's dismal pier. And miserable-looking, cold, grey-skinned families holidaying on the cheap; all beer, fags and arcades.

'All right,' he said, 'I'm going to send some of my boys up there to introduce themselves, say "hi" and see if we can arrange a talk with your mum. And, given we're all a little wary of strangers these days, I'd like you two to lead them up there and make the introductions.' He cocked a dark eyebrow. 'What do you think of that?'

Both of them grinned.

'You're right, Mr Maxwell,' said Nathan. 'Better if we go along. Mrs Sutherland won't lower no ladders for a bunch of blokes she don't know, not with guns. No way. Ain't that right, Jay?'

He nodded. 'She's sort of very suspicious of strangers.'

'Quite right,' said Maxwell. 'As she well should.' He stopped walking and turned round to look at them. 'Okay, well here's what we're going to do – we're going to initiate you as praetorians. That is . . . if you want.'

'Shit, yeah,' smiled Nathan.

Jacob nodded eagerly.

'Good. I've already spoken to Edward "Snoop" Tindall.' Maxwell shook his head and laughed drily. '*Snoop* . . . ridiculous bloody nicknames they've given themselves. Anyway, I've spoken to him and he thinks you're a pair of good guys and he's happy to have you aboard.'

'Cool.'

Maxwell took half a step forward. 'It's all about *trust*, lads. By my letting you join them, I'm trusting you. Snoop and his boys are trusting you. Just like being in the army, your fellow squaddies rely on you, and you on them. If there was a fight, if outsiders came here to take what we've got, those boys would be asked to fight for us, to lay down their lives if they had to to protect these people out here,' he said, indicating the workers amongst the rows of plants.

'Right,' said Jacob nodding solemnly.

'That's why I give the boys their little treats; their Saturday nights, the music, those bloody noisy arcade machines.'

'What about the others?' asked Jacob. 'These people?'

Maxwell tightened his lips, looked away for a moment. 'We keep them safe, we keep them fed. I'm sure they'd much rather be here in the Zone than out there.'

'So,' Jacob frowned, 'they're *never* allowed in the arena?'

'No. Not at any time. Staff only.'

'But, uh . . . why is—?'

Nathan subtly tugged at his friend's arm. 'Hey, Jay? Doesn't matter, right?'

Maxwell realised these two boys needed a little more explanation. Needed to understand the way things worked here. 'It's all right,' he smiled. 'You need to know how it is.'

He pinched his chin for a moment. 'Order,' he said breaking the silence. 'To keep things in order. I keep the boys separate from the others because they need to be able to *police* them, even to *punish* if it comes to it. Do you understand?'

Jacob looked at Nathan. 'I guess.'

326

'You sound doubtful?'

He shrugged. 'It just . . . it seems—'

'Look, I know it probably doesn't sound all nice and fluffy and democratic, but it's how I've managed to keep two thousand people alive all this time – we've kept going while every other safety zone crashed and turned on itself. They're very young, I know, but that's for a reason. They don't come with all the old prejudices, all the old pre-crash attitudes and baggage. They're good boys. And what's more, I trust 'em. They do as I ask of thcm, and they keep order for me.'

He tried a flat smile. 'Obviously, I'm not going to force you. If you don't want to become—'

'Shit, man, yeah!' blurted Nathan. 'I mean . . . really sorry, I mean, yeah.'

Maxwell waved dismissively. 'Jacob?'

'O-okay,' said Jacob. 'I *do* want to be a praetorian.'

'Good.' He clasped his hands together. 'Because I'm hoping your mum's people will want to partner with us,' he continued. 'And I'm happy to work with her and see what we can do to make life a little better for everyone.' He shrugged. 'She bossy . . . your mum? She going to have me running circles round her?'

Jacob laughed. 'She can be a bit bossy.'

Maxwell joined him. 'Good! She'll whip me into shape, I'm sure.' His face straightened. 'Seriously, we need each other. It looks like we're all that's left of Great Britain. And if things work out, I think the pair of you would make good lieutenants. I like to have people around me who ask questions. Keep me on my toes.'

The boys grinned.

'Trust,' he winked. 'It's all about trust.'

'You can trust us,' said Nathan.

'Excellent. Well, then, this Saturday night, we'll initiate the pair of you. You'll get your orange jackets, be eligible for all privileges. And I'm sure Edward will come up with a couple of ridiculous bloody nicknames for you.'

They laughed.

'And then,' he said to Jacob, 'we'll sort out paying your mum a visit, eh?'

'Yes,' he nodded. 'Thanks, Mr Maxwell.'

He pursed his lips. 'Once you're initiated you'll have to call me "Chief", though. Just like being in the proper army, eh?'

Jacob grinned.

'Right,' said Maxwell. 'We're done here. I've got things to attend to. I'm sure you've both got work groups to rejoin. Off you go.'

The boys both nodded politely, thanked him and turned on their heels.

He watched them go.

Trust? He looked at the pair of orange-jacketed praetorians following him dutifully a dozen yards behind. Alan didn't trust any of his boys as far as he could throw the little buggers. As long as they had their treats, their Party Night, their grog, their sex slaves . . . they were as obedient as well-trained Yorkshire terriers. That's the simplistic level on which those brutal little thugs worked.

The young . . . so malleable.

These two, though. Maybe they'd turn out to be as easy to influence as the others once they began to enjoy the extras.

He was pretty sure there wasn't a young man born who'd willingly walk away from perks like those.

He suspected he was going to need them on-side. Not that he had anything that he'd dignify with the label 'plan' just yet. But, there were ways and means. The home these boys had come from – a gas rig with a population of women, kids and old people and a nearby port full of pickings. An easy target, and quite possibly the plan B he'd been hoping for all these years.

Ways and means?

There were the three barges tied up at the rear of the dome. One would be more than enough to transport his boys. Another filled up with all that was left of the supplies on the mezzanine floor. The third barge to pack in a couple of hundred or so workers.

Those left behind?

Well, not to put too fine a point on it . . . sod 'em. They were doomed here eventually anyway. This place wasn't the future, it was a waiting room. One gigantic departure lounge.

Everything that counted could be packed onto those three barges, and the river tugboat parked up in Victoria Docks just across the water should be able to tow them. He estimated that if they took it carefully, hugged the coastline and hoped for calm weather, the barges would make it down the Thames, out of the Thames estuary and up the coastline of East Anglia to Bracton in what? . . . three . . . four days?

The alternative was to wait on here and oversee the gradual, systematic and orderly starvation of two thousand people.

He resumed his morning tour, nodding and smiling at the familiar faces he passed. He spotted the man who'd once been an officer in the RAF regiment, still wearing the tattered remnants of his khaki greens.

'Morning, Brooks.'

The man looked up and nodded politely. 'Morning, Chief.'

Maxwell had rather liked the young man but leading up to the 'change of guard', he'd begun to ask too many bloody questions. And he'd heard murmurs amongst the young Flight Lieutenant's men that they should be in charge.

It had been a necessary move, kicking them out and replacing them with the boys. His lads, his praetorians, never asked questions. They just got on with what they were asked to do.

Without his platoon Brooks was no longer a threat. Good worker, too.

Chapter 52

10 years AC

O2 Arena – 'Safety Zone 4',
London

Adam watched Maxwell go. He could quite happily stab that self-serving bastard in the eye. That regal fucking nod, the pompous way he acknowledged his people; once a mid-level civil servant, now the absolute ruler of his own little kingdom.

And he'd made damn sure there was no one going to challenge the way of things here, hadn't he? Damn sure.

Adam hadn't seen it coming.

The school Maxwell had set up had made perfect sense at the time; there'd been over a hundred boys in the camp of schooling age. Another hundred or so girls as well. And Maxwell, being an ex-teacher, his pre-crash job something to do with a regional education board, it made sense that he'd want to see the kids get some sort of schooling.

It didn't even to occur to him that Maxwell was playing some kind of long game when he announced he wanted to school the boys separately. It just happened. Anyway, there'd been too many other things on his mind. He and the lads of his squadron were out patrolling almost daily, foraging, looking for survivors in the aftermath, looking for signs of any other communities hanging on.

That bastard was clever about it, too. Moved the boys into the middle of the dome for their classes. The young lad, Edward Tindall, the oldest boy in the camp, was about seventeen when the crash happened. He became Maxwell's

331

'head boy'. All the other lads looked up to Edward; all urban-cool, hip.

Adam resumed his work, kneeling down and potting onion bulbs.

Maybe it was how the Cheltenham safe zone went down; the army finally turning on the civil authorities. Or maybe Maxwell had caught wind of Adam's men grumbling. Whatever it was, at some point the bastard had made up his mind that he didn't want thirty trained soldiers and another twenty-seven police officer auxiliaries hanging around the dome.

How it happened, the 'changing of the guard', was pure bloody Maxwell. One of the girls was found raped and shot dead just outside the zone. Enough evidence had been strewn around to indicate it had been one of Adam's lads. The same night Maxwell instructed Adam to order his men to hand in their guns so they could be inspected to identify which one had been fired.

And that's what he'd done. Naively, stupidly – followed the bastard's orders.

In the early hours Edward Tindall and his boys, all armed with those same fucking guns, had turfed the lads out of their bunks and out of the camp.

Oh yeah, they'd picked out one man to make an example of; said it was him who'd raped the girl and murdered her. Gunner Simon Lawrence. The soldiers were kicked out but Adam and the three other platoon NCOs were allowed to stay. Maxwell's intention communicated quite clearly to the men as they were escorted out; try breaking back in or causing any mischief and your officers will suffer.

Next morning Maxwell had gathered everyone together in the dome's entrance foyer and made his big 'Year One' speech – new order and all that. His students, his boys, were now functioning as the zone's security personnel. The time had come for them to prepare for the future, no one was coming to rescue them, so now it was time to start growing their own food . . . and so on and so on; there were going to be work groups, task assignments; everybody was going to have to contribute something to their long-term survival.

And then, to clarify the point that this really was Day One of a new regime, Gunner Simon Lawrence was brought out and executed for the rape and murder of the girl.

Adam looked up and watched the backs of the two praetorians walking dutifully a dozen yards behind Maxwell, guns slung casually on their shoulders.

He'd even decided to choose the youngest of his boys to pull the trigger. A little pyschotic fucker who swaggered around under the name 'Notor-ius' these days.

The two praetorians and Maxwell slowly patrolled the edge of the field, heading towards the guards standing around the hut at the front gate.

You're a shrewd cunning bastard, I'll give you that.

Maxwell knew his recent history; of course he did, he was once a history teacher an' all.

Child soldiers.

Always the most ruthless. Always the most biddable.

Leona heard movement outside her room. It was a small stifling space, the walls concrete breeze-blocks painted a hospital mint green, above her a fizzing strip light, the cold cement floor beneath her feet covered by a scuffed black rubber mat. There was a mattress on the floor and a bucket in the corner. It was meant for her to use as a toilet. She'd held off using it for as long as she could, but in the end she'd had to. Now the smell of it was thick inside this place, almost as bad as the slurry room back home on the rigs.

She heard a girl's voice coming from the room next door, muffled through the wall. She sounded compliant, single grunted syllables. Another voice, a boy's voice, young enough that it sounded as if it had yet to break and deepen. He was giving her instructions and she sounded as if she was obeying. It was quiet for a minute or two, a solitary bump against the wall, then she heard the boy's voice once again; a short shrill yell that sounded painful.

She wanted to think the girl had hurt him, kneed him in the balls, jabbed his eye with a fingernail. But she knew it wasn't that. He'd got what he came for.

Her eavesdropping was interrupted by the sound of a key in her door. She took several quick steps from the wall and backed up into the corner of the room beside the toilet bucket.

She knew who it was before the door swung open. It was the boy who treated her like a caged pet – his own little plaything. It was the boy who had ushered her into the camp, the short stocky runt with his one shaved eyebrow, his neck weighed down with bling, with his peaked white Nike baseball cap and that we're-going-to-play-some-more twinkle in his eyes.

'Hey, honey! Dizz-ee's home!' he sing-songed. 'Sup? How's my bitch. A'ight?'

'Fuck off,' said Leona through swollen lips.

'Fuck off is it, eh?' He stepped into the room, closing the door behind him and locking it. 'We're goin' to try again, love. An' this time you're going to be a good little bitch, right?'

He was about Nathan's age, maybe a year older – nineteen, twenty. A short little runt but surprisingly strong. Much stronger than her. She'd managed to keep him at bay last time with her nails and bared teeth, earning a livid bruise and swollen mouth for her efforts. But the time before, he'd managed to wrestle her down to the mattress and nearly managed to get inside her. But she thrashed and wriggled and slapped so much that he lost his concentration. She paid for the struggling that time with a swift hard kick to the stomach. He left her doubled over, struggling for breath and retching bile onto the floor.

Leona had lost count how many nights she'd been in here,

how many times she'd had to wrestle the evil little bastard off her. But she knew she was running out of time, running out of fight, and he knew it, too. Soon he was going to be coming in here and she was going to be like the girl next door, mutely nodding, lifting the torn rags of her shirt and letting him get what he came for.

But not tonight, she wasn't giving up tonight. 'You touch me again and I'll rip your thing right off.'

Dizz-ee laughed. '*Thing*?'

He stepped into the middle of the small room, removed his orange jacket and his faded Nike cap and tossed them both on to the mattress.

'See now, you goin' to give me it tonight, a'ight? You gonna cotch with me? Or do I have to break your face again?'

'Fuck off.'

He shook his head and tutted. 'We got off to a bad start. You didn't know the rules. Maybe I should've explained them to you instead of slappin' you. So lemme tell you how it is before we get goin'.'

He squatted down in front of her, wrinkling his nose for a moment at the smell coming from her bucket.

'We're all living in Medieval England now. That's what it is. We've got new rules for everyone. New roles, new classes.' He offered her a broad, friendly smile. 'Now take me. I'm what we call a "praetorian guard". We're like the Chief's bodyguard.'

He settled down on the floor in front of her. 'At school, know what my favourite subject was?'

She said nothing.

'History. I loved that subject. I had a great teacher. Mr Harwood, a great teacher. He sort of inspired me.'

Leona noticed how easily the 'street' had slipped out of his voice.

'He made history come alive for me, you know? One of the periods of history we studied with Mr Harwood was medieval

335

history, you know? All that cool feudal stuff; barons and dukes and princes. Little kingdoms within kingdoms . . .'

Dizz-ee's voice drifted further away from what she'd become used to; now no longer some wannabe wigger trying to out-black everyone else, but instead . . . very different.

'And there were very clear classes, right? People born into a duty they were destined to perform for the rest of their lives. Almost like . . . no . . . *exactly* like the social structure of an ant or termite colony. Fighter ants, worker ants, yeah?'

She said nothing.

'You see, the old world was different, wasn't it? I remember some of it. I remember teachers telling us anybody could become anything they want if they put their mind to it.' He laughed. 'But that was then. A different world now.' He shrugged. 'It's a medieval world now, and we're back to clear social classes.'

Leona looked up at him. 'You sound different.'

Dizz-ee seemed to wince at that.

'Us praetorians're like King Arthur's knights. There's trouble? If there's bad guys come into the neighbourhood threatening an' shit? Then we're the ones gonna go out protect you. And, we're not scared of any shit. Trust me. We'll die for the King. Die for his people if need be.' He nodded at her. 'Die for a skanky little bitch like *you*, even. That's what makes us knights . . . *special*, see. We the first and last line of defence for the Zee.'

Leona laughed at him. 'You sound so stupid.'

'Uh?'

'When you pretend to be some kind of gangster.'

'What?' He slapped her face hard. 'Fuck you!'

She curled up on the floor, protecting her bruised face from another blow.

'Say that shit again and I will fuckin' kill you! Do you understand?'

It was quiet for a moment. She could hear him breathing,

hear footfall across the ceiling, hear the muted sound of the girl next door acquiescing to another boy.

'That was my old life,' said Dizz-ee after a while. 'Fucking grammar school shit. Now I'm a soldier. A fucking knight.' He took a deep breath.

'So, like I was saying . . . in this medieval world of ours, we got the workers – the *serfs*, them old people who work out in the field and grow our food. They feed us an' stuff, keep us goin' in exchange for us protectin' and watchin' out for 'em.'

She could hear the middle-class white boy was gone from his voice.

'Now *you* . . . well see, you got a special place. You're sort of in between knights and serfs. You can't be no knight 'cause you can't fight, but you can be better than the serfs and get some of the privileges an' shit that we get. You get to have the nice food outta the tins from down below, you know? You get to have the grog, the dope, all the smokes you want. What you are, girl, is a *girlfriend*. An' all you really got to do is play along. You know? Just open up like a good girl every once in a while. The more you do for the knights, the more treats you gonna get. It's that simple.'

He shuffled a little further forward, leaning over her. 'Other girls in the cattle shed see the sense in that. They don't want to go back to being with the serfs. That would be kinda stupid, right? 'Cause they get nothing. No privileges. See how it works?'

He stretched a hand out towards her. 'So why don't we try it again tonight . . . and this time it'll be cool. No need for me to smack you like last time. No need for you to get all scratchy and bitey like you did. What do you say?'

His hand rested lightly on one of her knees, pushing it gently apart from the other. 'Shit, you might even enjoy having a piece of me in you.'

Angry. She told herself. *Not frightened, Leona, don't sound frightened. Be fucking angry.*

She reached out for his hand and twisted his thumb back sharply. 'I'm not your bitch or your "ho"' . . . So FUCK OFF!!'

He recoiled slightly, looking bemused by her outburst, as her voice echoed off the hard walls.

'You're so pathetic,' she added under her breath. 'You know that?'

'I said don't—!'

'Why . . . why do you even talk like that? Trying to talk like a gangsta? You're not even black.' She sneered. 'We used to laugh at wannabes like you. All that bling, the swagger, the stupid fake American accent—'

'PISS OFF!!'

All of a sudden she was seeing stars and feeling her cheek throb warmly before she realised he'd just backhanded her again. Much harder this time. Her eyes back on him, she could see he was done explaining himself to her. He was peeling his tracksuit bottoms off, past his bare knees and preparing to roll them over his large white trainers.

Instinctively she reached for the toilet bucket beside her and hurled its contents – a cloudy mixture of faecal matter and urine – at him.

He froze for a second, his eyes closed, lips clamped as the rancid slurry dribbled down his face, and dripped onto his bare thighs. He retched, a thin stream of vomit on to the black mat, then dry heaved once more.

'You are so fucking dead!' he hissed, pulling his tracksuit bottoms up and backing towards the door. 'Fucking dead!' he said again, wiping the muck from his face and reaching for the handle of the door behind him.

His urge to rape her had evaporated. Now all he seemed to want to do was beat a retreat. 'I'm fuckin' done with you, bitch. Gonna' put you out for the rest of da boys to 'ave.' He unlocked the door and opened it. 'They'll gang-bang your ass to pieces.' He slammed the door shut behind him, the noise reverberating endlessly off the hard walls, making the small room sound like a cavern.

Leona sat perfectly still with her hand on her cheek, already feeling it begin to swell along the jawline. She heard voices through the wall again; the compliant mumble of the girl, followed moments later by the rhythmic grunting of a youth. She wondered if the girl was really there out of choice – because she got treated to a little alcohol, a little dope every now and then. Or spreading her legs, simply because the fight had been beaten out of her.

From another room, further along, she faintly heard another female voice, whimpering painfully.

Her eyes drifted to the soup of rancid faeces splashed across the floor, and up at the cold blue bar of the fizzing strip light in the ceiling and realised, if she had a decent enough sharp edge to work with, she could do far better than a few aborted scratches right now.

Chapter 53

10 years AC

O2 Arena – 'Safety Zone 4',
London

Snoop watched the boys working over the man. The fool had been caught red-handed this morning trying to steal some canned fruit from one of the boys' tents in the central arena. How the fuck he'd managed to get in was a conversation he needed to have later on with SouljaBoy; the stupid little idiot must have walked off from his post on the entrance turnstile.

They were whipping him with bike chains; digging bloody divots out of his skin, but not breaking any bones. They needed him working again as soon as possible, not laid up in the infirmary for months in a cast. Just enough of a lesson learned that he wasn't going to try it again any time soon.

Snoop watched not because there was any sport in it, but because those boys could get a little out of hand if he didn't. They didn't need a cadaver, just someone whupped enough to know better and pass that on.

The sun was setting out here, settling across the river. Snoop liked it out the back; the rear entrance to the dome. Quieter. Away from the shuffling workers, the clack of spades on soil. He settled back in the deckchair, silently watching the lashing chains for another minute before he raised a hand.

'A'ight! That's all!'

Three of them stopped, Ceebay carried on lashing out another couple of times.

'Shit, I said stop!' barked Snoop. The boy relented after another swift kick.

'Now take him to the infirmary. Get him seen to.'

The four boys carried the man back across the quay and into the dome, leaving Snoop alone with his sunset. He listened to the sound of the barges bumping and nuzzling the quayside. Barges they'd not used for a while; not since they'd last tried foraging up and down the Thames.

He sighed. Ceebay, just like Dizz-ee, just like Notor-ius; all hotheads that needed watching. Mind you, at their age he remembered himself being no different; wanting to prove himself to be the hardest, meanest. Prove that he could be much more than just a runner, or a spotter; that he could be a top-fucking-dog and run a den.

Old days, those . . . back when there was a business, when money actually meant something.

He was top dog now, right? No longer a foot soldier but a general.

True.

Ten years ago, being a general would've meant controlling most of the corners of a postcode; would have meant a thirty per cent cut on the takings. Not bad. But here, now, it was a very different kind of power to, say, having money. It was absolute fucking power.

Maxwell had set things up well here; a rigid hierarchy that worked efficiently. The workers kept safe and fed, the girls in the cattle shed with their extra privileges as long as they played along, the praetorians keeping an eye on things, then of course Snoop as top dog . . . and Maxwell, the Chief, at the very top. Everyone with a role, everyone with a place and absolutely no misunderstandings.

The system had worked just fine for the last three years, since the boys had kicked out those soldiers. Everybody got something out of it . . . all right, some more than others. And it would carry on working for as long as there was food for everyone to eat, and treats for the boys.

But there's the thing, a'ight?

341

Snoop knew just as well as Maxwell that all the shit they had down below in storage wasn't going to last them for ever.

Whilst the Chief was an arrogant pale-ass fucker, all suit and bullshit, he was smart. Very smart. The man knew his history, had taught a little to Snoop and the other boys. Made them see how everyone from Roman emperors to Anglo-Saxon kings, even East African warlords, all kept house the same way: a warrior elite at the top of the pile kept sweet and well-paid.

The Chief was shrewd and he knew, despite all the stuff they were growing out front, that their supplies were running out. He had a plan. He must have a plan. Snoop was sure the wily old bastard was sitting on something clever. Because the alternative – fun though it was for the boys – was what? To sit right here until it all ran out?

Then what?

He watched the Thames glistening calmly, the gentle slap and murmur of water against the base of the quay. The Chief had some kind of long game going. He was certain of it.

Jacob lurched in his cot and his eyes snapped open. He found himself staring up at the tangle of their camouflage netting, and beyond that at the pale canopy of the dome's canvas.

It was still dark.

In the cot beside his own he could hear Nathan's deep and easy breathing, fast asleep and untroubled . . . as he always seemed to be. Nathan never appeared to be anything other than untroubled, it was his default demeanour. His un-flappable cruise control. Mr Laid-back calmly accepting the *whatever-comes-next* that life throws at you like some good-natured diner casually awaiting the next course of a mystery banquet.

Jacob so envied that about him.

The last few weeks had seen them pulling long hours outside amongst the workers; learning a whole new way of life, new rules. Then that all changed again when Mr Maxwell said they could grab their belongings and move up into the central arena. Nathan accepted both vastly differing regimes with an effortless shrug of his shoulders.

They now slept on immeasurably more comfortable beds than those mattresses outside. They had their own tent of sorts – a camouflage net draped across an 'A' frame of metal rods. It was perched on a stretch of terrace between two large sections of arena seating. Other tents, similar to theirs, were clustered in groups around the vast stadium, in spaces where rows of plastic bucket seats had been pulled out.

They'd only been awarded this privileged level of comfort and privacy a few days ago, after Maxwell had said they could join the praetorians. So far the nights had been noisier than outside with the boys trash-talking each other, calling out crude exchanges across the cavernous stadium from one tent to another. All good natured, and usually things quietened down when the night lights were dimmed.

Tonight, though, he'd been awoken by something going on.

Noises had percolated into his sleep and become part of his dream – the one he often had. Too often. Him and Leona in a dark house at night, lit up by the flames of a burning car outside. The shifting silhouettes of intoxicated teenage boys larking around, jeering and laughing at the families hiding in their homes down St Stephen's Avenue.

'Oooo are ya? Oooo are ya?' several of them chanting like supporters at a football match.

'Weeee comin' to part-eeeee!!' another voice sing-songing over the top.

Jacob shook away the last tendrils of sleep and the nightmare. He could feel the coolness of sweat drying on his bare skin. Another stuffy night inside. Even though the dome's roof was an opaque canvas, when the sun was shining much

of its energy permeated through and built up inside through-
out the day.

He heard the noises again. Voices in the distance; voices
that had taken part in his dream. He sat up and looked out
through the drape of netting. Between the gaps in the webbing, down across the endless sloping rows of bucket chairs,
on the arena's stage, he could see a couple of torch beams
flickering around amongst the dark and silent outlines of the
arcade machines. Some of the praetorians were down there,
messing about.

He could hear their banter, hee-hawing laughter as several
of them pretended the NASCAR machines were switched on
and that they were mid-race. They sat in bucket seats and
yanked their steering wheels one way then the other as they
stared up at the large blank screens in front of them. A scuffle
broke out between a couple of boys watching, both wanting
to sit in the same booth. It was no more than pushing, shoving
and posturing and snarled words exchanged. Jacob settled
back in his cot, once more looking up at the webbing and the
distant dark pall of the dome's canvas, and found himself
wondering whether he could really fit in as one of them; they
all seemed so aggressive and intimidating.

Tough talk. That's what Snoop called it. Because the boys
were so young, they had to appear to be tougher, meaner,
than they were for the adult workers to accept them being in
charge.

It's mostly just hot-air bullshit, Snoop had said with a grin.
They're good boys.

Jacob desperately wanted to be a praetorian. He'd caught a
glimpse of party night: the arcade machines; they had a
cinema room with a big projection screen and a library of
DVDs; there was another room full of Xboxes and plasma
screens all linked up and playing 'Call of Duty'. And the big
light show from the lighting rig above . . .

If heaven was powered by electricity, this had to be it.

344

You've got to learn to act like they do.

He closed his eyes, trying to get back to sleep, but his mind restlessly hopped from one thing to another.

Not only did he not think he'd make a very good praetorian, he had a sneaking suspicion the other boys didn't think too much of him. Oh, yes, they put up with him because he was Nathan's mate. They liked Nathan because he made them laugh. Like he could everyone else. Been here a few weeks now and *all* the other boys let on to him as they passed by with a grin and pressing of fists.

Jacob barely got a nod from them.

Why? Because I'm not funny enough?

The injustice of that skewered him painfully. Why did popularity amongst these younger boys boil down to the simple ability to tell a joke? It's not as if Nathan actually told jokes anyway, he just had a cool way of chuckling; a sort of yuk-yuk-yukking that was inexplicably infectious. That, and his calm manner, and the cool street talk he could easily slip into at a moment's notice.

A cold doubt stirred deep down inside him; the thought that his old friend was going to get fed up with him and move on . . . too busy enjoying his celebrity status.

And then you'll be right on your own, Jake.

Chapter 54

10 years AC

'LeMan 49/25a' – ClarenCo Gas Rig Complex, North Sea

Jenny looked up, shading her eyes from the sun. 'He's what?'

'Evicting us,' said William Laithwaite nodding vigorously. The bent out of shape specs on the bridge of his nose wobbled precariously. 'He said all the rest of us who aren't in his *church* have got to move off his platform this afternoon and find space on one of the other platforms. It's not right!'

Jenny stood up slowly, emerging from amongst the fruit-laden stalks of the tomato plants. She'd been busy securing the weaker branches of the more wind-battered plants to the cane support frames with lengths of twine. She liked working up here on the roof of the accommodation module and up the steps on the helipad, particularly on such a nice day. One hundred and sixty feet above the sea, it was the highest usable surface amongst the platforms; the highest and most peaceful place to work. It took her mind away from the gnawing concerns of the world below.

'All right, that's enough,' sighed Jenny wearily. 'I'm not having this. Where's Walter?'

William pointed down at the empty davit arms below. 'He's taken the yacht ashore again. Said he needed to find some more bits and pieces.'

Damn.

He seemed to be trekking ashore more and more often in the last few weeks. He kept coming up with excuses to bugger off; components he needed to source in Bracton for the generator mark II. She really could have done with him

346

being here right now, though. He had the keys to the gun locker.

That thought stopped her in her tracks for a moment.

My God, really? I'm thinking of taking a gun with me?

She realised that's exactly what she'd love to do. Something small and discreet tucked into the waistband of her khakis. Something she could whip out and level at him whilst she told him she'd had enough of his divisive preaching.

For a while after their last confrontation, Jenny had allowed herself to believe some sort of an uneasy status quo had been established. That Latoc would keep his prayers and sermons to the drilling rig and that the hundred or so followers he'd attracted might have reached its natural cap. But the son of a bitch had recently insisted on segregated mealtimes – one breakfast and evening meal sitting for his followers.

And what had she done about that?

Nothing.

She'd excused herself from confronting him directly about it because it hadn't caused the disruption she'd anticipated. But also because she'd noticed the mealtimes were fast becoming a recruitment opportunity for *them*; every sit-down session peppered with pockets of his followers coaxing the others to come along to a meeting and listen to Valérie talk.

Then, last week, he'd decided to move across to the compression platform – against her express wishes, given that he was technically speaking still on probation. And again, she'd argued herself out of confronting him head-on because, even though it was relatively crowded over there, yes, there were still spaces on that platform. What's more, Latoc had made a private arrangement with Hillary Glossop – one of his flock of course – to swap places. People fancied a change of scenery, or found a neighbour's personal habits irritating, swapsies like that happened quite often. Provided both parties were happy, Jenny had no obvious excuse to refuse that, since Hillary was quite happy to change places.

But this? Evicting people from there?

'What are you going to do?' asked William.

I've had enough of this.

'Going to talk to him,' she sighed, pulling on her cardigan. 'He's gone too bloody far this time.' She stepped across the roof and grabbed the handrails of the steps down to the module's third floor gantry.

'He wouldn't listen to us!' William called after her. 'We told him he couldn't just kick us out . . . that's our home for Christ's sake!'

Across the void between platforms she spotted the laundry group scrubbing clothes in a long trough of soapy seawater on the cooler deck of the smaller compression platform. Lines of brightly coloured clothes flapped like a coalition of national flags across the sun-bleached deck. Amongst the laundry team she spotted Sophie Yun, the eldest of four Korean sisters. Sophie had told Jenny a couple of days ago that she and her sisters were moving off the large compression platform. She'd said the prayer meetings were now becoming too noisy and they were beginning to feel unwelcome amongst all the Latoc-faithful.

Jenny shook her head as she descended a third flight of steps down to the bottom of the module and onto the platform's main deck. She winced with a stab of pain as her taut skin pulled under the dressings.

Segregation.

This is exactly what she'd hoped to avoid, border lines developing between a notion of Them and Us. Before too long, she was sure, it was no longer going to be known as the primary compression platform, instead 'Latoc-Land' or 'New Jerusalem', or something equally ridiculous.

Jenny cursed herself for letting the man stay in the first place. Cursed herself for finding him just a little attractive and fantasising that there was a frisson there that was going to lead somewhere. Cursed herself for being such a stupid bitch.

She'd let things inch slowly Valérie's way because his people were still dutifully attending their various work groups and getting on with what needed to be done, and the children were still attending the classes being held by Rebecca. Jenny had been prepared to let things continue because the alternative was unthinkable; two separate *tribes*, each living on their own platform and eyeing each other suspiciously down the length of a one hundred foot long suspended walkway.

Us and Them was not how this place was going to survive.

She crossed the main deck and stepped onto the long walkway leading to the main compression platform. At the far end she could see a cluster of *his* people watching her coming over. She picked out some of their faces. Denise, Alice, Laura and baby Tom in her arms, the youngest member of the community at six months old. Jenny smiled and called across a 'good morning' to them. Nods back. That's all. A wary nod from each of them. They stood at the end of the walkway's long creaking wire cage like guards at a border crossing.

Trying to appear *reasonable*. That was her big mistake. So far she'd realised her only strong suit was to make a big thing of appearing unfalteringly reasonable, whilst quietly hoping that Valérie's embarrassingly Old Testament shtick was going to start unravelling and sounding ridiculous.

The old 'give him enough rope' strategy.

But instead, since making his bed over here, it appeared that his congregation was growing in size again; a lot more ears for him to bend. And ridiculous-sounding tales of floods and Noah's Arks and God's plan seemed to be exactly what people wanted to listen to in the candlelit gloom of an evening.

349

At the other end of the walkway, she stepped out of the cage and beamed a friendly smile at the women.

'Where's Valérie?'

Alice Harton's eyes narrowed ever so slightly as she took a step forward. 'Why?'

'I need to talk to him about some accommodation issues.'

Alice made a show of giving it *her* consideration. Finally she shrugged and shuffled a half step back, as if she was giving Jenny permission to step on board.

'All right. He's up on the top deck near the scrubbers.'

Jenny's smile was thin and utterly insincere. 'Thank you, Alice.'

She pushed past them and used the external flight of stairs up the side of the tall compression module. Jenny realised she'd not actually seen any of those ladies for days. Not since the segregated meal sittings had started taking place.

In fact, she'd not seen Martha for several days either. Last time she'd seen her they'd passed each other on a walkway. She'd been talking animatedly with Kaisha and Hamarra, talking evangelically about the wonderful future, filling the wire cage with her sunny voice. Her face had lit up at the sight of Jenny, a genuinely friendly smile and a little wave as they passed each other. Jenny thought she saw a ghost of sadness in Martha's eyes that she couldn't talk her friend into joining them.

Jenny missed Martha. Really missed her.

Not for the first time, she wondered how easy it would be to do that – to join her, let Martha talk her round. She could announce she was standing down and someone else could run things. Perhaps she'd sit in on one of Valérie's sermons. There might be comfort in that, finding faith . . . allowing herself to believe that Andy and Hannah were somewhere wonderful waiting for her, to believe she might see them again one day.

Better still, to have faith that God was looking down on

Jacob and Leona, keeping them safe and well on the mainland and would one day soon lead them back home to her.

Her tired knees creaked on the second deck landing as a fresh gust of wind toyed with her cardigan and tickled the untidy tufts of her shorn hair.

Shit, that would be so easy.

She could hand the reins over to Valérie Latoc, let him organise things from now on; assign, rotate and shuffle the work schedules so that everyone was kept happy, the sleeping arrangements, the water runs, arbitrate over all the petty disputes and squabbles, make sure everyone was turning up each mealtime and getting a fair food allocation, as well as taking his turn shovelling human shit, scooping up bird poop, carrying heavy water butts from one terrace to the next, endlessly watering and nurturing their valuable crops.

Let him do all that.

She grabbed the guard rail and pulled her way to the top of the final flight of steps, stepping onto the top deck, cluttered with snaking lube-oil pipes, sump tanks and the flat-topped cooler units; a lunar landscape of blistered white paint and seam lines of rust. He was on the flat top of one of the cooler units, using it like a small stage. He was standing in the shadow of one of the towering twin vent stacks, the breeze playing with his long dark ringlets as he engaged an audience of listeners, perched amongst fat pipes, exhaust outlets and gauge panel cabinets, hanging onto his every word.

My God . . .

She realised it could be a scene from the Bible; that's how the wily bastard was staging it. She was reminded of some old movie; a sermon on the mount, a young Robert Powell as an implausibly photogenic Jesus promising the meek that they'd inherit the whole shebang. She recognised young Edward amongst the audience, perfectly cast as the meek, smiling contentedly, perhaps even understanding some of what Latoc was saying.

351

So easy . . . to just give up and join them. How about it? You in?

But the scene transformed into satire as she recalled one of Andy's favourite movies: *The Life of Brian*. She recalled one of the Pythons in the audience mis-hearing the phrase 'peace-makers', and asking what was so bloody special about the 'cheese-makers'. Why the heck *they* should inherit the earth.

She looked again at Valérie Latoc and this time he didn't look like Jesus. In fact he looked no more like a prophet than any number of orange-tanned television evangelists she'd seen on cable. No more like a prophet than any number of self-improvement gurus peddling their own brand of psychological snake oil. No more like a prophet than some oily timeshare or kitchen salesman.

'Mr Latoc,' she called out, her words whipped from her mouth by the stiff breeze.

Heads turned to look at her. So many familiar faces she was used to being greeted by, now distant and guarded – strangers to her.

He shaded his eyes from the sun as he turned to look at her.

'Jennifer,' he smiled pleasantly. 'I presume you've come to discuss the sleeping plans?'

'You're damned right I have.'

Chapter 55

10 years AC

'LeMan 49/25a' – ClarenCo Gas Rig Complex, North Sea

Valérie stared at her across the pile of blankets and cushions. He'd only been using these rooms on the top deck for the last few days, but had already managed to make some grubby rooms that had once been labelled the 'System Monitoring Suite' into a space that looked comfortable, inviting even – almost like some Bedouin tent.

'We need the room,' he replied. 'There were too many coming to pray with me on that small rig where you were keeping me. Here we have room for as many as want to come, yes?'

She suspected his calm, even voice and that supercilious smile was his attempt to goad her.

'Yes. But you're kicking people off this platform, you can't do that. Where people are bunked is down to me. And the way I do it, is to consult with them. See who wants to be where and—'

'Those who need my guidance, *need to be right here*, Jennifer. And those who don't, well . . .' he spread his hands, 'there is lots of room elsewhere, yes?'

Jenny could quite easily have slapped that face. No, not slapped, she'd bunch her hand first and hope to knock out a couple of teeth.

Calm, Jenny.

She took a breath. 'The thing is, that's *their* choice. I'm not having you throw out people you don't want around you and moving in those you do.' Despite her best intentions, she could hear anger creeping into her voice. 'I'm not having that, do you understand?'

He smiled. 'The thing is, Jennifer, you are losing them.'

'What?'

'These people. They need a spiritual direction, a guide. They are lost and frightened.'

'What? They're not *frightened*! Look, I came here, I led my family and others here because it's safe. No one's bloody well frightened here.'

'Yes, you did that. You made them safe, and trust me when I say God is grateful for all you have done for—'

'Oh, for fuck's sake, cut that crap!' she snapped. 'Don't give me the God thing, because I just don't buy it.'

'I am sorry,' he sighed. Silent for a moment, his eyes studied her intently. 'The truth is they need more than this. More than safety, more than food. They need purpose.'

'They have a purpose!'

'No, what they have is just existence. They eat, they drink, they sleep. That is all. No one can live on that for ever. I have seen other people on my travels, Jennifer. Other communities like yours . . . maybe not so large. People who did not allow God in.' He shook his head sadly. 'Eventually, they wither and die.'

She thought she saw the glint of a tear on one of his cheeks and wondered if he was so deluded that it was actually genuine.

'If it was my choice,' he continued, 'perhaps God should have come and spoken to *you*, not me. After all, it was you worked so hard to create this safe haven, in fairness it should be *you* that leads the people. But I am afraid this is how it is, God chose me.'

'God *spoke* to you, huh?'

He ignored her. 'Your people are beginning to understand this place is . . . is *special*. That it fits into a grander plan.'

'Right. Which is what?'

354

'The crash, the end of the oil age, the wars, the riots, the starvation, ten years of darkness – it was all part of God's scheme. To clear away the old and start again.'

She laughed. 'Valérie, you know and I know that's bull-shit. Shall I tell you what I think?'

He spread his hands. 'Please.'

'I think you came on to these rigs and you saw an opportunity. You saw a safe and isolated environment. You saw that we could feed ourselves indefinitely, and that there aren't a lot of other men, are there? Not a lot of competition? You've seen a lot of vulnerable women looking for some-thing more . . . you've seen all that and decided to make the most of it.'

He shook his head. 'You have me wrong, Jennifer.'

'I think I've got you just about right. I don't fucking trust you!'

'Trust?' He smiled. 'If you want someone *not* to trust I have heard things about your Walter that concern me.'

That threw her. She wasn't expecting that. 'What?'

'Walter,' he said again.

'What's— What about Walter?'

'He has always been very close to you, yes?'

'Since I first met him,' she replied. 'Not that it's any of your business.'

'Close to you . . . close to your daughter. Close to *Hannah*.'

Jenny angrily snatched a cushion in one hand, wondering what she was going to do with it. Throw it at him?

'What? What's *Hannah* got to do with anything?!'

'You remember the day she was missing?' continued Valérie. 'You remember he did not want anyone to search that generator room, yes?'

All of a sudden she could see where he was going with that. 'Don't you dare say another fucking word! Don't you even think of trying that with me. Do you hear?'

355

Jenny dropped the cushion and took several steps towards the door, before turning to face him. 'Walter's a bloody good man. I've relied on him for years! He's done so much for us. Don't try and—'

'Jennifer, I am telling you what people are thinking. That is all.'

'I came here to discuss these evictions! And that, Valérie, is stopping right now!'

He said nothing.

'And the mealtimes will be sat according to work groups. Do you understand!' she added. 'We are not splitting this place up into your kingdom and mine!'

He shrugged. 'It's too late.'

She turned for the doorway.

'Jennifer,' Valérie called out after her.

She stopped in the corridor outside.

'You are going to lose these people to me, Jennifer . . . and to God. Then you will be alone. Just you and Walter.'

She turned round. 'There's four hundred and fifty people here. How many come to listen to you? A hundred?'

'More each day,' he replied almost apologetically. 'Soon it will be all.'

Jenny felt rage bubbling up and out of control. She knew it was going to come out as a shrill bark before she'd even opened her mouth. 'Right! That's it!! I want you off this rig, NOW!!'

He said nothing.

'I WANT YOU TO FUCKING LEAVE, NOW!!' Her voice rang off the metal walls beside her, down the passage-way and out into the space of the compression module's gutted main chamber.

His reply was measured and quiet. 'No. I have work to do here.'

She turned and headed down the passage and out onto a walkway that overlooked the cavernous interior of the module. She saw pale oval faces peering out from a jungle of hammocks and bunks, between washing lines strewn from one side to the other, from the floor, up three storeys to the ceiling. Eyes followed her as she followed the railed walkway to a door that led outside onto an external staircase.

They all heard that. Heard me lose control. Shit.

Chapter 56

10 years AC

O2 Arena – 'Safety Zone 4', London

Snoop sat down at Maxwell's beckon; the leather sofa creaking softly. Through the thick double doors of his quarters they could hear some of the boys whooping with delight as they scored a goal. They were kicking a football around on the arena's main floor. A game usually ended with a punch-up. So far, it seemed, they'd managed without it turning into a fight.

He could see there was something on the old man's mind. 'What's this about, Chief?'

Maxwell offered him a thin smile and steepled his fingers thoughtfully. 'The future, Edward. The future.'

Something flipped uncomfortably inside him. The last time he'd seen the old bastard looking like this was last year, when he'd awoken in the middle of the night and wandered into his quarters at the top of the arena, away from the boys. He'd ordered Snoop's girl to dress and leave immediately. Once alone, he'd casually wondered what Snoop's opinion on some sort of a collective suicide might be. Something potent stirred into the evening meal; no one need know.

He'd been drinking heavily that night. And it had been the first time Snoop's confidence in Maxwell had been shaken.

The old fucker had passed out shortly afterwards and he'd had the boys take him back down and put him to bed. Next morning, it was like the conversation had never happened.

'What you got in mind?' Snoop asked warily.

Maxwell looked across the coffee table at him. 'We're moving.'

'Moving?'

He nodded. 'You heard me right, Edward.'

'But . . . we got our shit sorted here, right, Chief?'

Maxwell shook his head. 'No, our shit here, I'm afraid, is not sorted.' He smiled. 'You know that, Edward. Come on. You're a smart lad, you know that just as well as me.'

'We growin' all types of shit out front and stuff.' Even as he blurted that, Snoop knew it was empty bluster. What they were growing was nowhere near enough to feed them all. It padded out the tasteless gunk that was served up each day; it was definitely slowing down the rate at which they were eating their way through the countless pallets of tinned and dried food packs, stored down on the mezzanine floor. But it wasn't enough to feed them.

'Edward, I did another stock take a fortnight ago. It's not good. We'll have to start evicting people soon.'

Snoop was silent for a moment. 'S'really *that* bad, man?'

Maxwell sighed. 'Edward, you've been downstairs with me. You know what it's like.'

Snoop nodded. A growing sea of empty wooden pallets, flattened cardboard boxes, tossed aside sheets of plastic wrapping. He hated going down there. He always emerged with a queasy sense of unease in his gut; as if the world's future was measured by how much of the floor was still occupied by squat towers of untapped polythene-wrapped supplies. He let the Chief do the number-crunching, the worrying. The man had a plan, right?

'We have about enough food to last into next year. Then we'll be left with whatever's being grown outside.'

'Shit.'

'Yes, shit. But that can't be such a big surprise for you, Edward?'

He stroked his chin. 'Didn't think it was *that* bad, tha's all.'

'It's not just the food; the fuel for the generators. It's nearly all gone, Edward. There won't be too many more party nights for our boys.'

'But we got fuel in them barges out back, yeah?'

'No, it's an entirely different grade of diesel. You can't pour that in, it'll clog everything up.'

Snoop folded his arms unhappily. 'Why the fuck I learnin' this shit now, man?'

Maxwell stared sharply at him. 'Talk to me like that again and you'll be out, Edward, do you understand?'

Snoop realised he was pushing his luck. He might be able to snap the man's old wattled neck without any real effort but that would leave him in charge; leave him holding the baby . . .

. . . just when it needs its shit cleaned up.

'Sorry, Chief.'

Through the double doors the boys roared. Someone must have scored again.

'Look,' said Maxwell, 'we knew this day would eventually come, Edward. We're lucky to have lasted this long. But here it is. And it will be bad. When the food and the generators run out, the boys will turn on you and I, then probably on each other. The workers will turn on the boys. We will end up like the other safety zones did. It won't end up particularly well for anyone.'

'The praetorians will be well angry, Chief. They believe you . . . you said the Zee was going to last for ever.'

'They're just fucking children. What do you expect? They can't think five minutes ahead, let alone worry about to-morrow, or next year.'

Snoop said nothing for a while. Maxwell was right. The boys were perfectly happy doing what they were told just as long as they had their smokes, their treats; just as long as they had access to the girls in their cattle shed. He tended not to venture down there much these days. It smelled of shit and stale sweat. More than that, he preferred to keep a little distance from the girls – the distance of authority; the cattle-shed girls were for his foot soldiers: the general got his pleasures elsewhere.

'So you got a plan, Chief?'

Maxwell grinned. 'Of course I do. When do I not have a plan, Edward?'

'What?'

'The new boys – Nathan and Jacob – they've come from a community that has access to fuel, Edward. Fuel on tap. They're living on drilling rigs for fuck's sake. Do you under-stand what that means?'

Snoop nodded. 'Sure, we can make more power.'

Maxwell smiled dismissively. 'It's much more than that. It's the life blood that flows through a *civilised* world. When the last of our little stockpile runs out, and the floodlights go dark here . . .' Maxwell shook his head. 'We'll all become cavemen again. It's that simple. Just like those wild chil-dren . . . fucking savages.'

Snoop didn't need him to say any more. He'd seen those pale feral wraiths up close enough times. He'd seen the remains of their eating: dogs, cats, rats . . . and on one occasion the tattered remains of a human cadaver.

'We're going to the rigs, then?'

Maxwell nodded.

'When?'

'As soon as possible,' replied Maxwell.

'How soon?'

'We should start preparing the day after tomorrow.'

Snoop's eyebrows shot up his forehead. 'What?'

'You heard me right, lad. We need to start preparing. I'd say we've got another month of reliable summer weather, hopefully, and if we're going to use those river barges, then we need the best weather we can get.'

'But . . . ain't those barge things just for rivers an' shit?'

'They'll float just as well on the North Sea, so long as we're not dealing with choppy weather. That's why we need to get a move on. Autumn's coming. We wait too much longer, then we'll have to do this next year.'

Snoop considered that for a moment. 'The boys won't be happy leavin' the dome behind. S'all they know.'

'Those little thugs will do as you tell them. Anyway,' he continued, 'I'll tell them the place we are heading to is tapping oil, that we'll have power that *will* last us for ever. And we'll bring along on the barges all the comforts the boys are used to – their games machines, the girls, the booze. There'll be space enough for those things. And when we get settled there, they'll be able to play the games and movies *every* night, not just once a fortnight.'

'Yeah? For real?'

Maxwell smiled. 'Yes, Edward, for real.'

Snoop grinned. 'My boys'll like that.'

'Of course they will. And we'll also have a smaller, more manageable population; a smaller kingdom, but at least one that doesn't have a sell-by date printed on the side. Also, with limitless fuel, it means we can forage much further. Up and down the coast. It gives us a lot more scope.'

'What about them workers, we leavin' them behind?'

'We'll take a few with us, yes. The rest? Well, if the poor buggers can survive here on their flippin' cabbages and onions, good for them, but they'll not be my concern any more. The important thing is that we load up and slip away without them finding out, all right?'

'Right.'

'We'll be nice and discreet. Don't want a panic or a riot on our hands as we leave. So, we'll load those barges up with the minimum of fuss. We don't need to take everything, just what we need. We can always come back here later and pick up whatever goodies we left behind.'

'Okay, Chief.'

362

'Maybe you can move some workers into the arena area to help with the loading, and those will be the ones we take along with us. We keep them in the arena until we go.'

'Y'know where these rigs are?'

'Yes, I checked it on the map. Just a dozen or so miles offshore from a seaside town called Bracton. Thing is, we know this place is on some rigs, right? I have no bloody idea how big they are, or how tall they are. We may need to forage some ladders and ropes and grappling hooks from a hardware store and—'

'We attackin' it?'

Maxwell shrugged. 'Ideally, we won't need to. I don't want us to have to storm these rigs. I don't want a bloody battle if it can be helped. I don't want to risk damaging these rigs. I just want us to arrive, say hello, come aboard and then once we're on, calmly evict those we don't want around. That's why those two new boys are so important. They're going to vouch for us . . . get us on so we don't have to fight our way on.'

'You think they'd do that?'

Maxwell shrugged. 'They might if we treat them good enough. Make a fuss of them. Treat them like celebrities. We're going to make them praetorians. So let's give them a great initiation party, give them some booze, give them some blow and make sure they have a good time.'

Snoop grinned.

'And, I think what we do is, we make them both your number twos. Give them some *authority* over the other praetorians.'

'Shit,' Snoop pulled a face. 'Some of me boys won't like that. Dizz-ee will fuckin' well throw a shoe, man.'

Maxwell shook his head. 'Which boy is that – Lawrence Bolland?'

'Yeah.'

'The boy's a big idiot. He's only your number two because he's the oldest, right?'

Snoop nodded. 'Fucking wigger. I can handle him if he gets shitty.'

'I'm sure you can. What about the rest of the lads?'

Snoop gave it some thought. 'Nathan they like. They think he's well-sick. But the other one? Jacob? His face don't fit so well.'

'What's wrong with him?'

Snoop shrugged. 'Way too quiet, man . . . a loner. The other boys think he's, like, stuck up.'

'Stuck up how? Too posh? Too nerdy? Too white?'

'He just don't fit.'

'Well, you'll just have to embrace him, Edward. Give him your official stamp of approval tomorrow night. The boys will follow your lead. Just give those two lads a bloody good time, all right? Make 'em a part of the family.'

'Sure.'

'And if you can, make sure they try a bit of junk. You know? Won't hurt if they start developing a bit of an appetite for that, too.'

'Right.'

'Okay, Edward, that's all for now. I need to do some planning, make a list of what we're taking along. You can talk to the troops and let them know about Nathan and Jacob. Party night can also be their initiation party. And why not sweeten the deal a bit. Let them know it's double booze and blow rations for all of them. That should soothe any ruffled feathers.'

Snoop got up and made his way towards the double doors, feeling a growing fizz of excitement in his stomach. The Chief had a fucking plan. The boys might grumble a bit at being uprooted, but he could keep them in line – even that twat Dizz-ee.

He was outside, walking up the sloping aisle to the arena

when he realised already he had questions in his head that he should have asked. Questions like, how could he know there was going to be enough fuel to last them for ever on those rigs? Hadn't that shit been running out or something? Wasn't that why the world got totally fucked in the first place?

He guessed Maxwell had a handle on that. The man certainly wasn't a fool.

Chapter 57

10 years AC

Bracton Harbour,
Norfolk

Walter listened to the gentle lapping of water against the quay and the boat's fibreglass hull. It was an altogether more relaxing sound than the thump and roll of the North Sea. That and the soft *tink* of the halyards against the mast.

Bracton was quiet and still as it always was. Earlier he'd heard the snapping and yipping of a pack of dogs disputing some small find, but since then nothing but the tide.

He could have headed back to the rigs before it got dark. He could have made it back in time. Instead he chose to overnight here and sail back some time tomorrow morning.

To be honest, he preferred the time away from the platforms. Things were getting unpleasant on there. Jenny refused to talk to Latoc any more and that bastard was carrying on as if he was now in charge. There were well over a hundred and fifty, maybe even two hundred of them now following the man. Too many, really, to all fit on the large compression platform. Since the accommodation platform was the one directly linked to his, Walter guessed he'd soon be insisting Jenny and the others currently bunked there vacate onto the next platform down so as to make way for his overspill.

The day that happened, Jenny might be better admitting she'd lost control of the rigs to him and prepare to gather up her things and those who wanted to go with her, and come ashore. The accommodation platform was the heart of the community, and surrendering that to Latoc was as good as losing it all.

There was another reason he preferred as much of his time as possible ashore, ostensibly scouring for bits. It was the staring. Everyone was doing it now and not just Latoc's loony followers; long icy stares as he passed by, not even a formal nod, or a half smile, or a limp wave.

Just the bloody staring.

He knew what it was. That silly rumour. Alice Harton's rumour, or whoever else she'd picked it up from. Just words. The rigs were full of words. In between chores it was all there was to do, gossip. But this . . . it was nasty. And there really was no verbal defence a man could make against that kind of innuendo. In fact, to bluster aloud that he'd never had any inappropriate thoughts about Hannah would seem to condemn him still further.

He protesteth too much!

Hannah, she was a lovely little girl. He was very fond of her, almost like a granddaughter to him. And yes, there'd been occasions he'd been in the Sutherlands' quarters when Leona was washing her hair or scrubbing her in a tin bath. But it was all innocent. For Christ's sake, this was the kind of environment – all of them living cheek-by-jowl – where people *were* going to catch each other half dressed occasionally. It happened all of the time. But this . . . this kind of suggestion made by someone out there, someone who presumably had an axe to grind, somebody whom he must have annoyed or upset at some point in the past, this kind of suggestion stuck fast and never shook off. It made every hug he'd given Hannah, every peck on the cheek and a million other innocent physical interactions since she was born, take on a sinister new meaning. And dammit, yes, it *could* make him look like some pervert if that's what someone wanted to see in him; a pervert carefully, patiently playing out some

367

long game, biding his time as he groomed the girl and earned Jenny's and Leona's implicit trust.

An idea like that, once planted . . . *Jesus* . . . any interaction with Hannah would appear suspect.

'Fuck!' Walter snapped suddenly, angrily punching the side of the yacht's cockpit. The fibreglass rang hollowly. He was angry enough he could throttle the vicious bitch, and he could start his guessing that it *was* Alice Harton who came up with that kind of poison.

The thought enraged him. The idea that everyone back on the rigs must actually now be wondering if he'd taken Hannah down there, done things to her . . . then killed her? That he was capable of that?

No. Jesus, No. Not *any* child . . . not anyone, in fact. And certainly not someone he'd known since she was born, grown to love as if she was his own flesh and blood, for Christ's sake. He'd been a friend of Jenny's and her family since before the rigs. He'd known them when they'd lived together outside Newark. They were bloody *family*.

The truth was, Hannah had been down there, where she *knew* she shouldn't be. Messing around amongst pipes that should have been more securely attached. And that . . . *that* was what he was guilty of. Carelessness. There should have been a lock on the door. There should have been adequate ventilation.

Unless, of course, that's what happened to her. That she was . . .

Latoc.

He slapped the cockpit once again. 'You fucking bastard!' he hissed. 'You fucking bastard!'

He'd seen the pair of them, as thick as thieves: Hannah and Latoc. The man helped around by Hannah, cared for, nursed by Hannah. His arm around her shoulders, his face so close to hers that their hair tangled, talking in hushed conspiratorial voices.

He almost laughed at the irony. Now the idea of Latoc being a pervert had taken hold in his head, every interaction of that Belgian bastard seemed to take on a sinister dimension.

Maybe that damned rumour had come from somewhere other than Alice's big flapping mouth. Maybe that sick twisted fuck, Latoc, had put the idea about somehow. Just made a veiled suggestion and let it evolve and transmit and grow as it spread like swine flu from one gossiping mouth to the next.

But why?

The first answer seemed obvious. He wanted to strip away Jenny's allies. Leave her isolated. He'd done a swift job of winning Martha over. Maybe Tami Gupta was next? If he couldn't woo the woman, maybe he'd start some nasty rumour about her as well?

Another thought occurred to him. Latoc didn't seem to like other men; didn't like them around him. Oh, yes, Valérie Latoc seemed very comfortable amongst women, but other men . . . ?

He sees us as a threat.

Perhaps the bastard wanted to make the rigs his own 'lady palace'; a procession of dutiful acolytes for him to choose from. Perhaps that was his game; getting rid of potential male challengers one at a time. They'd rescued him. He'd woken up in the infirmary and saw the place was mostly women and like a greedy little boy in a sweet shop decided he wanted it all for himself.

That made a hell of a lot of sense. Like a rogue lion coming across another pride and coveting it, the first order of business was removing from play the existing alpha male. Before the explosion, before the bastard had arrived, Walter knew he wasn't particularly popular, especially amongst the women-folk. He knew they found him rude and gruff and impatient. Maybe a little arrogant. He didn't suffer fools gladly. And maybe, yes . . . probably, he was a pompous old bastard. But he was tolerated and extended due courtesy because he was Jenny's right-hand man. Because he knew how to fix things up. Because he knew how to pilot the boats. Because he'd built a generator that gave them electricity and light after the sun had gone down.

They wouldn't have managed without him. *He* was the alpha male.

There were no rumours back then, were there? No icy stares.

Then Latoc came along.

Then the explosion.

Then people pointing fingers at him for allowing Hannah down there.

Now this — that he was some sort of a paedophile.

Latoc wants me off. Wants me out of the way.

A final thought occurred to him. There were other girls Hannah's age.

Fuck you, you bastard.

Tomorrow morning he was going back. Tomorrow morning he was going to stand right in front of Valérie Latoc, in front of as many people as possible, and he was going to accuse the son-of-a-bitch of molesting and killing Hannah. And if the obtuse foreign fucking bastard tried wriggling his way out of it, then he was going to take a swing at the shit.

From where he sat in the cockpit Walter could see faces lining the railings all the way up from the spider deck to the main deck. A welcoming committee. Every last person, it seemed.

He eased the yacht towards the support-leg beneath the dangling hooks of the lifeboat davits, dropping the sails so she slowly bobbed forward on the last of her momentum.

'Cranes, please!' he called up.

What's going on? What's happened?

370

The hooks inched down from the davits with a loud clacking as manual winches were turned. Walter gaffed the nearest with a pole and began securing the harness hooks to it.

Dennis and Howard climbed down a rope ladder from the spider deck and dropped onto the foredeck beside him.

'What's going on? What's this all about?' he asked them.

Howard eyed him coolly. 'Natasha Bingham went missing yesterday.'

Walter knew Natasha. She'd been one of Hannah's best friends. Same age, same frizzy hazel-coloured hair; they used to look like twin sisters from a distance. Tweedledum and Tweedledee.

'She's missing?'

Howard nodded. 'Yesterday morning, same time you left for shore,' he said. The implication was right there in his voice.

Walter felt his face pale. 'What?' He turned to look from one to the other. 'Howard? You're not saying . . . ?'

Neither man said anything. Then Howard relented. 'Sorry, Walter, we need to check.'

'YOU THINK I TOOK HER!?' he found himself screaming at them.

A shrill voice from the spider deck, twenty feet above him answered him. 'If you've touched her, we're going to kill you, you dirty old bastard!'

He looked up to see a row of faces, Alice Harton's snarling. Beside her the girl's young mother, Denise Bingham, her face mottled pink with grief and worry. Others either side of them, all of them grasping the rail, knuckles bulging.

'I didn't bloody take her! She's not on my bloody boat!'

From the deck above he heard Latoc shout down. 'Please check inside.'

Howard and Dennis stepped carefully along the side deck

and dropped down into the cockpit. Howard ducked down through the hatch into the small cabin below.

'There's nothing down there!' shouted Walter. 'I told you, she's not on my boat!' He squinted at the railings above, shading his eyes as he tried to make out where Latoc was standing. He spotted the man's dark ringlets fluttering in the breeze, sixty feet above him, and the outline of his dark, trimmed beard amongst a row of pale faces.

'You!' he shouted. 'Latoc! It's you! I . . . I worked it out last night!'

'Oh, we can guess what you were doing last night!' shouted Alice, from the deck beneath. 'You dirty old bastard!'

Walter ignored her. 'You made our generator blow up, Latoc! You did it! *You* killed Hannah and you covered it up with the explosion!'

Latoc shook his head. 'God have mercy on you, Walter, if we find you've hurt this girl . . . as well!'

'What?! You know I . . . I didn't touch *Hannah*! I never bloody touched her! I—'

'God have mercy on you if we find something, Walter, because I am certain none of these women will!'

Howard emerged from the cockpit, his face ashen and sombre. His rheumy pink eyes met Walter's. He shook his head. 'Jesus, Walt,' was all he could mutter as he held up a small sky-blue plimsoll in one hand.

Denise Bingham screamed at the sight of it. 'Oh, no!! Oh, God!!'

Walter stared at the plimsoll. It was Natasha's all right. Sky-blue with a butterfly on the strap. She always wore shoes that colour. Every time her feet had outgrown another pair, it was on the 'Needs and Wants' list: *Denise Bingham = pair of sky-blue shoes, plimsolls pref, trainers if not. Size 4 this time, please!*

He shook his head. 'I . . . I . . . don't know why . . . I . . .' he looked up at the rows of faces. He saw Denise's face crumpled, broken and red. Beside her Alice and others, jaws set rigid in condemnation. Sixty feet up on the cellar deck he saw Martha standing next to Latoc, shaking her head sadly and crying. And further off, a hundred feet up, leaning over the railings of the main deck he recognised Jenny. Her head dipped slowly into her hands and he thought he saw her shoulders heaving.

'I didn't do anything!' he called up to her. 'JENNY!! I DIDN'T FUCKING TOUCH HER!!'

Chapter 58

10 years AC

Jacob had been transported to another world; a world of neon lights rushing past his car on either side leaving lens-burn streaks of colour, pinks, electric blues, aquamarine greens. Vertical billboards glowed dancing Japanese characters, and streets thick with whizzing brand names he vaguely recognised: Sony, Atari, Panasonic, Mitsubishi.

Flashing yellow chevrons appeared in the corner of the wide plasma screen in front of him; an early warning of a sharp right-hand turn coming up ahead. He eased back on the arcade booth's accelerator pedal and prepared to make the turn as soon as he could make out where the turning was amongst the hectic whir of flashing graphics on-screen. It wasn't often he missed his old glasses, cracked, scuffed and discarded a lifetime ago, but he certainly missed them now.

Easing back further on his pedal, the engine noise, pumping out of the seat speakers either side of his head, dropped in timbre from a high-pitched Formula One scream to the throaty roar of a performance car. He picked out the turning ahead and was spinning the wheel in both white-knuckled hands when Nathan's glistening Lotus blurred past, shunting him into a barrier for good measure and leaving him in his wake as he accelerated up the dual-lane Tokyo highway. The boys gathered around Nathan's booth, leaning on the headrest, roaring with laughter, slapping his shoulders and urging him on.

Jacob struggled to reverse out of the barrier as other cars

barged past him knocking him back into it, one after the other. He could hear fresh choruses of laughter coming from the other player booths further along.

Yeah, everyone pick on me, why don't you?

He muttered under his breath, not concerned that anyone was actually going to hear him over the pumping beat of music and the mechanical whine of a dozen racing cars. There was no one gathered round *his* booth urging him on.

He was just about managing to disentangle himself once more from the barrier when the words RACE OVER punched their way out of the screen.

Everyone howled in unison as the results flashed up on-screen. He could see Nathan hadn't won, but had done well, fourth out of twelve. Jacob watched his friend, several booths along, clamber out of his seat casually knuckling and high-fiving the swarm of boys around him.

Jacob climbed out of his seat and was quickly replaced by another, smaller, boy lingering nearby, eager to get in on the next race.

A strobe on the large circular lighting rig above the stage kicked in amidst whirling spotlights that cast multicoloured beams down through the thin pall of cigarette smoke above. The strobe made everyone appear to move with a jerkiness that reminded him of one of those Victorian moving picture-show drums that played a looped animation you could view through a slit. He squinted. His eyes were already tired from concentrating on the race and stinging from the smoke. The strobe wasn't helping things.

He caught sight of Nathan's face over the heads and shoulders of his fan club. Eye contact for a brief moment. His friend nodded and winked at him as he took a pull on a long crinkly cigarette pressed into his hand by someone.

Jacob wasn't ready for that. Not for the dope. Not that anyone had bothered asking him yet.

Then Nathan was gone, whisked away by several boys,

shouting over each other, wanting to see how big a deal he was on 'StreetFighter'. Nathan said something that had them all roaring with laughter again as they bustled him away through the maze of machines.

Jacob slurped another mouthful from his can. The cider had tasted pretty good with the first bubbly mouthfuls. But now, running flat, he could taste the burn of alcohol. Not a particularly nice taste but at least the buzz he was beginning to get from it was making him feel a little better.

Another race had started and boys were cheering and jeering and trash-talking each other. Nathan was gone. He felt self-conscious standing amidst the carnival of flashing computer game colours and the press of sweaty bodies, pushing hurriedly past him from one group of arcade machines to the next. Holding on to his can of cider and looking for someone, anyone, to talk to, he felt conspicuously alone.

He wished Leona was here.

She'd be loving this, the lights and the pumping sound system. He imagined it was just like one of those rock festivals she used to go to. He looked around. He presumed there'd be more girls than he could see here, though, at a rock festival. Amongst the fifty or sixty boys at the party and not on duty, he'd counted only about a dozen girls. All of them about Helen's age or thereabouts, drinking and smoking, getting the occasional go on the pinball machines.

His eyes followed them, glancing at their bare midriffs, the odd enticing flash of a pale leg, the curve of a slender shoulder. Some of them wore make-up smudged on so thick they looked like the models he'd seen on faded advertising billboards; all charcoal dark eyes, ghost-pale cheeks and coral-pink lips.

He was beginning to feel a frustrating yearning in his groin; frustrating because the girls all seemed to be *taken*; chaperoned . . . led from one machine to the next, more often than not, with one or more male arms wrapped protectively around their necks or waists. Led like poodles being taken for a walk.

Even if there weren't other boys around – boys who looked like they'd knuckle his face if he even tried *looking* at their girl – he doubted he'd know what to say to one of them anyway. Although the cider was giving him a tingling urge and just a little courage, he was still about a million miles away from actually walking up to one of them and trying out a simple 'hello'.

He felt a heavy hand land on his shoulder. He turned round to see it was Snoop's second-in-command, Dizz-ee.

'A'ight?' he greeted him loudly.

Jacob nodded and cracked an awkward too-cheerful grin. 'Yeah, I'm fine.' He nodded. 'What a great party!'

Dizz-ee hunched his shoulders casually. 'Once a fortnight. S'what we got goin' on here. Right?'

Jacob nodded his head vigorously. 'Cool.'

'Praetorians play real hard. S'only 'cause we grind hard too, man. This time tomorrow you gonna be all sweared-in and wearing one of the orange jackets. Get dues from the others.'

Jacob's vacant smile told Dizz-ee he was falling behind.

'Get respect, bro . . . the jacket gets you respect.'

Jacob got the distinct impression Dizz-ee had been sent over to chat to him. There was something forced about his grin, the body language. As if he'd much rather be elsewhere.

Dizz-ee nodded at the racing booths. 'So, you play the games?'

'Yeah, they're excellent fun. I think I'm a bit rubbish, really. I—'

'What about them?' Dizz-ee said, tipping a nod towards a young girl nearby, watching the current race as she tottered unsteadily on heels too high for her. She pulled slowly on a long joint, trying to look grown up and sophisticated as she did so. The make-up, glittering rouge plastered on her cheeks and crimson lipstick smudged around her mouth, oddly made her look younger, like a child playing at dressing up in her mother's clothes.

'You like the look of our girlfriends?'

He watched as young male hands crawled over her like spiders; cupping, squeezing. The girl ignored the pawing, glassy-eyed and lost somewhere beyond the plasma screen in a cartoon Sega-world of golden rings and sprinting hedge-hogs.

'They're . . . sort of . . . yeah, very pretty.'

Dizz-ee found that funny, shook his head. '*Pretty?* Heh, that's the gayest sounding shit I heard today.' He slapped Jacob's shoulder again. A smile smeared too easily across his face.

He's laughing at me.

'Hey, jus' kidding, man. Listen, you ever *boned*, bro?'

'Boned?'

'You ever *do* a girl, Jake?'

He was about to ask what Dizz-ee meant by 'do', but then the penny finally dropped. He realised Dizz-ee was talking about shagging. No. He'd never. There were plenty of times he wished he'd had, though.

'No, I uh . . . never had a girlfriend. Not yet. I was—'

'Fuck!' Dizz-ee doubled over laughing. 'Come on, you shittin' me?'

'No . . . I'm not sh—'

'So, lemme go set you up with a girlfrien', bro. Right now.'

'What? No . . . I, no really I'm—'

Dizz-ee grabbed hold of both his shoulders firmly, spun him round and began pushing him forward, threading him across the crowded stage, past games booths, past clusters of turning heads, amused faces, some slyly smiling, others laughing openly. Jacob felt his face flush bright crimson, sensed he was being set up for some kind of a very public prank. He caught a glimpse of Nathan on the other side of the stage, playing a dancing game, a joint hanging from his mouth. Snoop was beside him cheering him on as he duelled deftly on a grid of glowing pads against some other boy.

'Where are you taking me?'

'Hey, be chill,' replied Dizz-ee.

In the middle of the arena's circular black stage was an opening that led down a short flight of stairs into darkness.

'What's down there?'

Dizz-ee, still steering his shoulders, pushed him forward down into the opening. 'We call it the cattle shed. Gonna get you some fresh pussy.'

As they made their way down the stairs, he noticed a sign stencilled on the wall beside him; 'Sound System Storage: Stage Hands Only'.

'What's down here?'

'You'll love it.'

'You got animals down here?'

Dizz-ee snorted and shook his head, laughing. 'Zoop-zoop!!' He flicked his wrist, clacking one finger against another. 'No, man, it's not cows an' donkeys an' shit. It's where we keep the girls.'

A row of spotlights, recessed into the low ceiling, cast muted light down on a short passageway off which two dozen black doors opened. On each of them were words stencilled in scuffed and peeling white paint: 'Amps', 'Spkrs', 'Cables', 'FX units', 'Lighting', 'Monitors', 'Props'. Like the Chief's backstage quarters, grey corded carpet lined the walls and deadened the sound. Unlike the Chief's quarters, though, across much of it the boys had left their mark, personalising it with livid-coloured graffiti tags and cartoon depictions of the dome, of London, fire, riots.

Most of the storage room doors were open. Jacob realised the girls he'd seen upstairs on the stage . . . these were their *bedrooms.* This backstage or, more precisely, *beneath*-stage, storage area had been converted into a dormitory of sorts. He noted sturdy-looking brass padlocks dangling from each door handle.

Dormitory? More like a prison.

'We got a new one down here. One that come in recently and needs some breakin' in.'

'I'm not sure I—'

'So, you serious? You never boned, right?'

Jacob shook his head as Dizz-ee guided him towards a closed door at the far end of the passage.

'What about a *bee-jay*, man? You ever been blown?'

Jacob shook his head, not really sure what he was being asked. He supposed he'd probably know if he'd ever been 'bee-jayed'.

'Shit . . . you ever even felt up a girl, bro? You know? Got a titty-squeeze or something?'

'No . . . I . . . I've never done a . . . a titty-squeeze.'

Dizz-ee shook his head again, incredulous. 'Where the fuck you been all these years? You ain't lived at all. *Sex* is the shit. Getting the poonie is *tight*. Better than getting all fuck-faced on that bodizzie, better than dope, man.'

Jacob felt the very first tickling of excitement. It felt wrong, but also unavoidably insistent.

The last time he'd felt like this had been the time he'd walked in on Anita and Claire; two middle-aged women who'd both put some 'wants' on the shopping list but failed to turn up at the canteen to collect. Pulling aside the beach towel 'door' to their quarters, he'd seen them entwined with each other; he'd seen absolutely everything. There'd been many other times, of course. The accidental revealing of flesh here and there; unavoidable really. There was even a stack of flesh magazines that he and Nathan had found in a shop ashore and shared between them. He'd found a little guilty relief with them over the years.

But nothing compared to the growing buzz of excitement he could feel right now.

'The girlfriends are the best. We've trained 'em up to do anything. I mean, you ask, man, and they'll do it for you. *Anything* you want.'

They stopped outside the closed door. 'New one's in here.' He let go of Jacob's shoulder and turned him round to face him. 'She's a newb. So you and me goin' to be in for a bit of bucking and tossing, a'ight? You gotta hang on to stay on, yeah?'

Dizz-ee pulled out a key ring that jangled noisily. 'You need me to hold her down for you? No problem. You need to do that for me, too.'

Hold her down.

There was something about that phrase that instantly deflated his hunger. Hold her down? Jacob had assumed there was a girl in there who might just *want* him – just like those ladies in their flesh magazines, with their come-and-get-me-now eyes and their legs spread wide.

'Hold her down?'

Dizz-ee grinned. 'Yeah, man. She's gonna buck and twist for you, bro. They always do first few times. S'what makes the new ones fun.'

'This girl,' Jacob nodded at the door in front of him, 'she . . . she won't *want* me?'

Dizz-ee cocked an eyebrow. 'You shittin' me, right? She's gonna buck and scream like a banshee.' He grinned. 'Like one of them cowboy rod-e-o rides. The harder they fight you off, better it is. Trust me.'

He slipped a key into the lock and turned it. The thick brass padlock sprung open with a heavy click. 'An' shit . . . if she don't want play along, you can slap her up. Just don't knock her out or nothing, okay? There's other boys I promised could cotch with her later on tonight.' He grinned again. 'Know what I mean?'

'I don't want to do this any more,' said Jacob.

Dizz-ee looked at him as if he'd spoken some foreign language. 'You don't want to get a fuck?'

Jacob shook his head.

'Shit, man, it's a perk of the fuckin' job. It's here on tap. You gotta take some pussy. It's like medicine. Rite of passage an' all that.'

He pulled the heavy door open.

Chapter 59

10 years AC

O2 Arena – 'Safety Zone 4', London

The first thing Jacob registered was the overwhelming stench of human shit.

A girl cowered in the corner of the room, bruised blue arms wrapped tightly around her pulled-up and clamped together knees. She was naked and every inch of her skin seemed to be covered in a mottled mark of one sort or another. The girl was whimpering at the sound of the door creaking open and at the first sight of Dizz-ee she buried her face in her knees.

'Sure she needs a bit of cleanin' up,' said Dizz-ee. 'I been busy on her last week, but reckon she's got to be shag-ready now.'

It was quiet in the room save for the soft fizzing of the strip light. The deep throbbing beat of music coming from the stage above was muted by the acoustic cushioning of the small room's walls.

'I can't do this,' said Jacob quietly. The wretched sight of the girl's narrow frame beaten black and blue was enough to completely kill off any residual desire for a sexual encounter.

The girl suddenly looked up sharply at the sound of his voice. One eye was swollen and purple and almost entirely closed. The other eye he vaguely recognised.

'Jacob?' she muttered.

Dizz-ee cocked his head curiously, still smiling amicably. 'Uh? She know you?'

Jacob found himself robbed of breath. 'She's my sister.'

Dizz-ee giggled. 'No way! You're shittin' me? Fuck. There's a crazy fucking coinciden—'

Jacob had swung his fist before he realised he was doing it. It was ill-aimed and glanced off Dizz-ee's cheek, knocking him back against the door frame. Not even close to knocking him down, though.

Dizz-ee clasped a hand to the side of his face. 'The fuck you do that for?'

'You did this to my sister?' asked Jacob, his voice quiet, fluttering with adrenalin.

Dizz-ee studied him. 'Yeah, she's *my* girl. Do what the fuck I like with—'

Jacob rushed forward, his hands grasped hold of Dizz-ee's shirt and, with strength he didn't know he had, he lifted the boy off the ground and threw him across the room against the wall beside Leona.

Dizz-ee bounced off the wall and landed heavily on his bottom.

'You fucker!!' screamed Jacob, stepping towards him. 'You bastard!!'

But he stopped short, staring down at the glinting blade pointed at him. He felt ice-water instantly pour through his veins.

A knife. Nothing terrified him quite so much as the sight of one held in a shaking, twitching hand.

'Gonna stab you up,' said Dizz-ee calmly. 'Gonna pop you, then gonna pop your sis.'

Leona scrambled away from him, over the mattress into the opposite corner of the room and pulled her legs up protectively.

Jacob's anger was held in check for the moment as his eyes studied the tip of the knife. Remembering a time long ago, when he was eight, the tip of a blade held against his throat, pushing so hard he thought the thing was actually already through the skin and inside him.

Dizz-ee laughed. 'You want to come again? You want to try it?'

Jacob remained poised, his hands clenched, unclenched, clenched.

'Snoop told me we're leaving this place. Gonna go live on your place. Cool, uh? Said your mum's the big boss there.'

Jacob said nothing. He and Nathan had been so stupid telling Mr Maxwell where they'd come from. Stupid. Too trusting. Stupid, stupid, stupid.

'First thing we gonna do when we get there is fuck your mum. Shit, man, reckon we'll *all* have a go at her.'

Jacob realised Dizz-ee was goading him. Trying to get him to lose control of himself and make an ill-judged lunge for him. His anger, the rage that had made him lash out, was fast ebbing now, being replaced with a growing sense of dread at the sight of the long blade angled towards him. He felt the trembling spread, grow more pronounced. Angry with himself that he wasn't able to hide his fear like other boys and men seemed able to do effortlessly.

'Awww,' said Dizz-ee, pouting a lip in mock sympathy. 'You all scared now?'

'No,' replied Jacob, his voice warbled uncontrollably.

'You're shittin' your pants, I can see that.'

In the corner, behind him, he could hear his sister whispering for him to back off . . . to be careful.

'You just a little fuckin' mummy's boy, eh?' said Dizz-ee, sliding up the wall slowly, getting to his feet. 'Little mummy-boy.'

Jacob stayed where he was, keeping an eye on the knife as Dizz-ee waved it slowly around like a wand. 'Or shit, maybe I was right. You a gay boy really?'

'Jake,' rasped Leona, 'come back . . . please come back.'

'No, Jake,' said Dizz-ee, 'come and get me.'

He's scared, too. Jacob could hear it in his voice. The slightest tremble.

'Oh, yeah, we're gonna' show your mum a good time on that lady rig.'

'Jacob,' whispered Leona. 'Jacob . . . please. Don't.'

So quiet in this small, hot fetid room. Nothing but the sound of all three of them breathing, and the gentle far-off thud of music.

'You comin', gay boy, or what?'

'Jake, it's all right,' said Leona. 'I'm all right.'

He lowered his hands slightly and took a small shuffled step backwards.

'Look . . . I'm sorry, Dizz-ee,' he uttered, his voice the gentle murmur of defeat. 'Really sorry for hitting you.'

Dizz-ee straightened up; taller and wider than Jacob, he looked down at him.

'You *are* a fuckin' gay boy.'

Jacob leapt for the knife and grasped it in both hands. Dizz-ee tried pulling it free and Jacob felt the blade slide along his fingers, knowing it was sliding deep. Both hands busy trying to keep hold on the knife, he used his head, smashing it forward into Dizz-ee's face.

Dizz-ee rocked back against the wall clutching at his crushed nose with his free hand and screaming in agony. Quickly Jacob let go of the knife with one hand, made a fist and punched Dizz-ee in the face again. The blow landed hard on the tip of his jaw. His legs buckled and he slid down the wall, still holding on to the knife, the blade slick with blood from Jacob's hand.

Jacob looked around for something else to use as a weapon.

He saw the metal bucket.

Grasping the handle he swung it high over his shoulder, surprised at how heavy it was despite being empty. He brought it down, aiming for the boy's head, but it glanced off his shoulder.

Jacob gave up on the idea of wrestling for the knife. He let go with his other hand and now, with two hands on the bucket's handle, he had better control of the heavy thing. Dizz-ee, still stunned by the last blow, flailed blindly with the knife. It glinted and flashed dangerously in the glow of the strip light above. But Jacob dodged it.

He swung the bucket up over his shoulder again and this time, with the strength of both arms, he brought it down hard.

The contact sounded thick and damaging; a metal rim contacting and cracking bone. Dizz-ee grunted and flopped forward onto the floor and the mattress in front of him.

'Jacob!' whimpered Leona.

He couldn't bring himself to stop. The bucket came down again on the back of the boy's head. Another dull crack of bone beneath the baseball cap. And again.

And again. This time the cap fell off, revealing the back of Dizz-ee's head. The scalp was split, and the skull beneath was dented; like a heavy thumb mark on a plasticine model.

He was about to swing it down again.

'Jake!!' Leona cried.

He stopped. Even to his inexperienced eyes it was obvious Dizz-ee was dead. Blood pooled from the dent in the back of his head, down across his neck and soaked into the mattress.

'Oh, Jacob . . .'

He looked down at his sister. She was reaching out for him, no longer caring to cover up her naked bruised body. Her hand pressed against the side of his torso and she was sobbing.

'It's okay, Lee,' he said. 'It's okay. I done him in.'

She shook her head.

'I'll get you out . . . me and Nathan'll get you . . .'

But she didn't seem to be listening to him.

He felt burned out from the exertion. Light-headed from the release. The adrenalin was spent and the rush suddenly gone. He wondered if this was how soldiers felt after a battle. Not so much exhausted by the blows they'd landed but from the sudden absence of whatever had coursed through their veins to give them courage. All of a sudden he wished there was a comfy armchair in this room for him to flop down into.

Leona's arms were around him as he settled down dizzily to his knees.

'You okay, Lee?' he slurred, wondering whether that was the cider finally catching up on him.

'I'm okay,' she whispered softly. 'I'm okay.'

He realised then that she was actually cradling him in her arms, her face overhanging his, looking down at him, her tears dropping onto his cheeks. She stroked his forehead, pushing lank twists of blond hair out of his eyes. It was then that he saw the crimson on her fingers and knew he'd messed up somehow.

Shit.

'Did the boy stab me?'

She nodded, her lips clamped, her chin dimpled and creased.

'Oh . . . right.'

The fizzing, flickering strip light on the low ceiling illuminated her hair like a scruffy halo, her face a darker silhouette that was leaking a steady river of fresh tears onto his cheeks.

He didn't remember feeling stabbed, didn't feel the blade at all. It wasn't as bad as he'd imagined it would be. 'Am I . . . bleeding quite a lot?'

She shook her head. He knew she was lying. She was rubbish at that. He could feel her body trembling, her shoulders heaving.

'Lee . . . ?' he said.

Her face came lower, closer. He could feel the puff of her fetid breath on his face. 'My poor little brother,' she whispered.

'Home,' he said. 'You got to go back home . . . warn them. They're coming.'

That annoying, fizzing light above them was too bright. He found himself squinting back the brightness, then feeling his eyelids so heavy he closed them to give his stinging, tired eyes a rest. 'Please don't let them hurt Mum, will you?' he murmured. 'Promise?'

'Promise,' she replied.

It's just you and Mum left now. He wasn't sure if he said that out loud or just thought it.

'I'll look after her, Jake.'

He had a dim memory of them carrying Dad upstairs. How heavy his body was, even between the three of them. He remembered them tucking him into bed, saying their good-byes to him. Remembered how proud he felt of him. Dad the hero. Dad who saved them from the bad man with the knife in their lounge. He wondered if Dad would've been proud of him too.

He figured he would.

He smiled. That was a good feeling.

Snoop felt an insistent, irritating tug on his arm. He was scoring high on the table; one of his better totals and still had another bonus ball to play.

'The fuck is it?' he snapped.

'We uh . . . we got a problem, Snoop.'

Snoop lowered his voice. Not that anyone was likely to hear them over the clatter of bells and the thud of music. 'What kind of problem we got, Deej?'

The small boy, one of the youngest, and white, looked as pale as a ghost. 'Fight down in the cattle shed, between Dizz and Jacob.'

Shit.

He looked around for Nathan and saw him across the stage, shooting zombies, badly, and looking drunk enough that he was ready to topple over.

He slapped a passing boy on the arm. 'Hey, take over. I got a chart score. Don't fuck it up for me,' he grinned.

He turned to Deejay. 'Let's go.'

Snoop led the way across the floor, threading through the crowded space between machines, doing his best to look easy, smiling and knuckling the boys he passed. Finally, at the top of the stairs down to the cattle shed, he caught the eye of one of the older boys.

'Yo, Roost!'

The lad ambled over. 'A'ight, Snoop?'

'The cattle shed's closed. No one's going down there until I say otherwise.'

'Okay.' Roost nodded. 'You gettin' some?'

Snoop ignored that. 'No one gets past, right?'

'Right.'

He led Deejay down the steps. 'So what the fuck's gone down?'

The boy swallowed nervously. 'You better see.'

Deejay led him towards the one storage door standing open, a shaft of flickering light spreading out across the corridor floor.

Then Snoop saw for himself. Dizz-ee splayed across a mattress, soaked dark brown around his oddly misshapen head. And on the rubber-mat floor, the white boy, Jacob, sprawled amidst a large pool of blood.

A naked girl was cradling him in her lap.

Jesus.

The room reeked of shit; overpowering, like a faecal force field. The room was sprayed with splatter dots of blood. But the girl . . . the girl looked like something out of the boys' collection of horror DVDs; her legs and belly and hands coated with the boy's blood. The pallid skin of hers that wasn't coated with blood was mottled with purples and browns, and her face . . . her jaw was a swollen grapefruit, one eye puffy and almost completely shut beneath a bulging eyelid that looked as full and glossy as a plum.

'Fuck's been going on here?'

Deejay shrugged. 'Dizz-ee's girl. He been working on her a while.'

Snoop stepped into the room and squatted down. A fucking mess. Dizz-ee was supposed to be in charge of the shed; the number two's responsibility. The girls, some of them needed tempting a little, some of them needed a bit of gentle coercion; a little dope, just enough to set up an appetite, usually did the trick. But this . . . the stupid violent bastard looked like he'd been systematically beating the crap out of her.

'Hey,' he said to the girl.

She didn't respond. He reached out, cupped her chin and lifted her face to get a better look at it. 'What the fuck happened here?'

She stared silently at him.

'They fight over you? That it?'

Her eyes locked on his. It could have been a defiant glare, it could have been that her mind was off elsewhere.

He turned to Deejay. 'Are there any other girls this fucked up?'

'No, Snoop. They all upstairs.'

It looked like this sorry thing had been a personal project.

'Go get her some clothes from one of the other rooms, and then take her out to the infirmary. She's all done here.'

Deejay disappeared.

He turned to look at her. 'This ain't right. The shit down here works on privileges,' he said, studying the bruising on her face. Some of it looked a week or two old, some of it looked today-fresh. 'That's the fucking system. Not . . . not this.'

He could've sworn there was a faint flicker of reaction in her one good eye.

Deejay was back with a fistful of clothes.

391

'Okay, clean her up, Deej, and dress her and get her out.'

He stood up and stepped back out of the room into the narrow hallway, relieved to breathe air less pungent. Now he had to figure out the mess with the dead boy. Like Maxwell said, if they were planning to approach those rigs as friendlies, they needed Nathan and Jacob to vouch for them.

Well one of them was fucking well dead, courtesy of that stupid asshole, Dizz-ee.

Great.

Chapter 60

10 years AC

O2 Arena – 'Safety Zone 4',
London

Nathan stirred on his cot feeling like his head had been wedged in a metal worker's vice overnight and something in his stomach was churning and flopping like a landed trout. Once upon a time, when he was eight, he'd gotten drunk slurping the slops out of glasses at a family wedding. He'd spent the night perched over a toilet bowl and the next day thinking he was going to die, his mum scolding him way too loudly, wagging a finger in his face; no sympathy whatsoever.

He'd felt very much then like he felt now.

He opened his eyes and saw the camouflage netting above him. It was a bright sunny morning outside, he could tell from the filtered light coming through the far-off canvas lid of their world.

The place was quieter than normal. Nothing more than the faint sounds of the workers outside the arena – the odd raised voice, the clatter of things being wheeled on trolleys, carried by the odd echoing acoustics of the dome.

With an unbelievable amount of effort he turned on his side to look out of the netting down at the stage below. By day, not a particularly impressive sight. Nothing more than a mess of black cabinets and a rats' nest of snaking power cables. In amongst them he noticed a couple of the boys sprawled amongst the arcade cabinets, curled up like pale foetuses. Clearly far too hammered from last night to find a way back to their cots.

'Oh, man,' groaned Nathan.

He eased himself onto his back again, gazing through bleary eyes at the silhouetted pattern of webbing against the bland brightness beyond. He remembered the first couple of hours of the evening; supper, then the whole stage powering up spectacularly. Playing the games, both he and Jacob running from one cabinet to the next like children in an adventure playground.

Then the booze and the dope clouded things a bit.

He remembered the pair of them separating. To be honest, he was finding Jacob a bit *clingy*, uncomfortable with all the attention and preferring to shy away and stay on the periphery. Whereas Nathan wanted so badly to party, to make up for too many lost teenage years. To have a complete blast. He wanted to chat to the girls, to enjoy the celebrity-like status of being the new-lad-in-the-hood, being the centre of attention.

It was a sad fact but Jacob was turning out to be a bit of a drag. Here they were, having found something that was, in all honesty, even better than Nathan could have hoped for, but instead of enjoying it, Jacob seemed to be hiding away from it. Withdrawing, not mixing and talking with the other boys. And shit . . . the boys, even though they were mostly younger, they were a laugh. It reminded him of the camaraderie he, Jay, and the other younger boys had enjoyed back home. Only it was even better; the booze . . . the smokes.

Oh, God, the music. It was a thousand miles away from singing along to an out-of-tune acoustic guitar; singing 'kumbaya' with the other children on the rigs – the height of an evening's entertainment.

Nathan didn't get it. Didn't understand what the hell was up with Jacob. The boys here may be a year or two younger than them but they had all the same interests . . . games and stuff. Shit, some of them even had Yu-Gi-Oh decks that Jacob could have traded with. And them being that little bit older and having come from some other place, the boys sort of looked up to them as wise and worldly travellers.

Like celebrities.

He just didn't get it. The pair of them were praetorians now. The elite. Getting every perk available. It just didn't get any better than that. And if what Snoop had been telling him earlier last night was true, that he was thinking of making them both his second-in-commands, then for fuck's sake what the hell did Jake have to *sulk* about?

Nathan wanted to shake Jacob by the shoulders and tell him to snap out of whatever had got into him. After wishing for something like this for so long, he wanted to remind his oldest friend that this was *it*.

And not to bloody well go and ruin it.

Sinking back into a head-pounding half sleep, he resolved to pull Jacob aside today, somewhere quiet, and warn him that if he kept this sulking up the other boys were going to notice it, maybe even start playing on it. And before long they'd be taking the piss out of him. There was no way Snoop could afford to let Jacob continue being a second-in-command if, behind his back, the rank and file were all razzing him.

'He's what?'

'Dead.'

Maxwell stared at Snoop. 'Dead?' His tone of voice demanded further explanation. Immediately.

'It looks like they had a fight, Chief. Had a fight over one of the girls. There was a new girl Dizz-ee was breaking in.'

'New girl?'

'I didn't recognise her, but then she was beat up quite bad. I suppose the white kid, Jacob, took a liking to her and Dizz got jealous.'

Maxwell shook his head angrily. 'You were meant to look after the *pair* of them.'

395

Snoop shuffled uncomfortably. 'I was. I was taking care of Nathan and . . .'

'And what? You decided to put that stupid moron Dizz-ee in charge of Jacob?'

Snoop could only nod.

'What the fuck were you thinking?'

He could have been honest; could have told Maxwell that he was up for a laugh last night and that Nathan seemed a whole lot more the party type than Jacob did. So, he delegated the boring one of the two to that fuckhead, Dizz-ee. But the old man would probably throw a hissy fit if he did.

Instead he lowered his gaze to the floor. 'Okay, I messed up.'

'Jesus Christ, not fucking half! Of the two of them,' said Maxwell softening his voice. 'Of the two of them, Jacob Sutherland was the one who could have given us the *most* leverage.'

'I know that, Chief,' Snoop mumbled.

Alan Maxwell ground his teeth with irritation. 'Well, it's done now. No point crying over spilled milk. Here's what you're going to have to do. Tell the other lad . . . Nathan . . . tell him that Dizz-ee got a little too out of his head and for some reason took a disliking to his friend. I'm sure you can come up with some plausible reason. Maybe he found out somehow that I wanted to make these two new lads second-in-commands and he didn't like the idea.'

Snoop nodded.

'You tell Nathan you found out what happened. In your anger you went down there and killed that moron, Dizz-ee. Understand?'

'Yes.'

'Hopefully Nathan will be grateful to you for that.'

Snoop nodded.

'Help yourself to a joint and a bottle of booze. You go and bond with him, commiserate with him, get pissed together and tell him you're really cut up about what happened. Tell him he's in our family now and we look after each other. Got it?'

'A'ight, Chief.'

'Now, what about the girl?'

'The girl?'

'Yes, the one they were fighting over.'

'Oh, yeah. She was worked over pretty bad. Dizz-ee was breaking her in personal. Not a pretty sight.'

'Could she tell a different story?'

Snoop could see what Maxwell was thinking; kick her out of the dome, or silence her.

'No, she was all beat up and stoned on some of our shit. Don't think she knows what planet she's on any more.'

'Where is she?'

'Out of the cattle shed now. I put her back with the workers.'

'Okay.' Maxwell nodded. 'Okay, that's that little crisis sorted then.' He turned to Snoop. 'You go keep Nathan on our side, all right? You and him are going to be like blood brothers from now on. And you're going to assure him that when we leave in a few days' time, it's a fucking peace envoy; a meeting of minds . . . a pooling of resources.'

'Okay.'

'You charm the fuck out of him, Edward. Because if he's not onside, then we may have to fight our way on. Do you understand?'

'Sure.'

'And I'd rather not have to. If there's a load of fuel-making going on there, we *do not* want to damage those rigs any more than is necessary to take them.'

Snoop bit down on his lip and balled his fists inside the pouch pocket of his hoodie.

'I know.'

'Right then, Edward, you know what you've got to do.'

Maxwell dismissed him with an angry waft of his hand. Snoop turned to go, then stopped.

'Chief?'

'What now?'

'We still going soon?'

Maxwell looked up from a pad of paper on which he was scribbling. 'Yes, of course. The sooner the better. I'm going to assemble the boys this evening.'

'What you goin' to tell 'em?'

'New beginning, Edward. A new home with enough electricity that every night they can watch their DVDs, play their games.' Maxwell smirked. 'Think they'll like the sound of that?'

Snoop nodded. He was certain the boys would love the sound of that. That was pretty much the level their minds operated on. 'Sure.'

'Right, well piss off and do what you've got to do.'

Snoop nodded and headed back towards the small north entrance. Maxwell watched him go before turning back to his pad and the list of supplies they needed to stow aboard those barges before they were ready to go.

The sooner we leave, the better.

The storage floor beneath the stadium might still contain enough stores of food to pad out their daily broth for another year, but it was the dwindling supply of twenty-litre jerrycans of diesel that concerned him. They went through two of those each time the boys had their party night. Maxwell had already experimented with reducing the nights to once every month, but the boys had begun to play up, taking their frustrations, their boredom, out on the workers. Instead, over the last few months, Maxwell had been starting up only one of the R16Cs instead of the normal two. It had meant losing some of the floodlights outside the arena, it had meant disabling some of the lighting system, it had meant pulling the plug on some of the least used arcade booths, but the boys, so far, hadn't noticed. Most of them were usually too pissed and too stoned to care.

His recurring nightmare, the one that woke him at least every other night in a cold sweat, was the one where he was standing on the stage in the middle of the boys and saying 'Sorry, lads, I'm afraid that's it. There's no more booze left, no more drugs, no more power for the arcade machines.'

Every time he had that nightmare it ended, for some reason, with him being tied to a hastily cobbled together crucifix and paraded along the boulevard outside the central arena, carried through the workers, screaming and spitting at him before being taken out of the dome and planted amidst a pyre of firewood. Why his nightmare took on a bizarre medieval theme he couldn't figure out; why young Edward Tindall seemed to be dressed like a member of the Inquisition, why the boys all looked like monks, baying for his blood as he squirmed on the cross and his skin bubbled and blistered in the flames . . . it really didn't matter. It scared the crap out of him.

The sooner they were settled in on that gas rig and up and running again, the better.

Maxwell sucked in a deep breath to settle his nerves. If those little thugs knew how much they actually frightened him . . .

Chapter 61

10 years AC

O2 Arena – 'Safety Zone 4', London

She opened her eyes at the sound of the voice. Soft and friendly. A man's voice. She saw a lean face half lost behind a dark beard.

'They made a mess of you, didn't they?'

She said nothing; her mouth was dry and sticky.

'Here,' he said, gently sliding a hand under her head and holding a plastic beaker to her lips. She sipped a mouthful and swallowed.

'They brought you in early this morning. You've come from the cattle shed, haven't you?'

She wasn't entirely sure where she'd come from. Just a room, somewhere. A room without a window.

'When they started up their brothel, there were quite a few girls ended up like you. Girls who weren't ready to play.' He studied her face a moment. 'They really went to town on you, didn't they?'

She sipped some more water.

'I'm Adam, by the way. Adam Brooks.'

Her lips were still too sore to try saying much, but she managed to croak her name.

'Fiona or Leona?'

She nodded at the second name.

His eyes narrowed. 'You're the girl that arrived at the gate several weeks ago, aren't you?' He seemed certain of that. 'Yeah, that's you. That little thug Dizz-ee let you in.'

She nodded. 'Dizz-ee . . . thash him.' Her top lip felt like a bloated slug lying across her teeth – slothful and heavy.

'He's a nasty piece of work, that boy.'

She could have told the man that the nasty piece of work was dead, but quite honestly it was too much work for her sore face, and there were a roomful of raw memories that would come with that effort.

Adam let her head gently back against the pillow. 'You rest. I'll go and get the duty nurse – there may still be some ibuprofen lying around.' She closed her eyes and remembered nothing else.

A couple of days later she felt recovered enough to make her way to the soup kitchen and join the sombre queue of workers waiting in line to be served. She was given a bowl filled with a watery and tasteless mush of cabbage and onions. She thought she spotted several baked beans floating in amongst the muddy liquid and a small sliver of something grey that might possibly have been meat.

Tasteless, but all the same she spooned it in automatically after she'd found an empty table on the edge of the seating area.

'Mind if I join you?'

She looked up and recognised the man she'd spoken to. Adam.

She nodded at him.

'How are you feeling, Leona?'

She shrugged. She felt nothing. Empty; just a human frame going through the necessary rotations of life: eating, shitting, sleeping.

'You're up already, though. That's good.'

There was something else, though. Something that was keeping her going. 'It's 'cause I want . . .' she held a hand to her jaw, feeling a painful twinge. One of her back teeth had been split when that bastard had backhanded her. The hot soup had found a way down to the tender root. 'I want to go . . . home.'

Adam looked up at her. 'Home?' He sat down at the table. 'Do you mind if I ask where the hell you came from? Because as far as I've seen, there's no one out there. No one, that is, apart from wild people in rags.'

She continued eating in silence, carefully spooning the hot broth into the side of her mouth less battered and bruised. 'A community,' she replied eventually.

'We patrolled all the way down the Thames estuary on a barge. All the way down to Canvey Island. That was a few years ago.' He shot a glance at a couple of boys standing watch over the queue, wearing their orange vests. 'Before Maxwell's coup. Never saw anything that came close to being called a community. We even took one of the trucks and half the platoon through London and out into the Sussex countryside. I suppose we were hoping to see something — woodsmoke, a tilled field, a horse and cart. You know? *Something*. Some eco-village, some government enclave still holding out. Somebody we could join with and leave this place behind. Not that I told Maxwell that's what we were hoping to do. But the lads and I found absolutely nothing.' He shook his head. 'Just fucking wilderness.'

He smiled sadly. 'Who'd have thought we'd all be so bloody crap at surviving?'

She looked up at him and saw in his lined, gaunt face, a man who was much younger than he appeared to be behind that dark beard.

She was tempted to tell him about Mum's community; to reassure him that there was someone else out there, but caution kept her silent.

Then she had a fleeting recall of something Dizz-ee had been saying to Jacob; goading him to attack. *Snoop told me we're leaving this place. Gonna go live on your place. Cool, uh? Said your mum's the big boss there.*

402

Oh, God.

First thing we gonna do when we get there is fuck your *mum. Shit, man, reckon we'll* all *have a go at her.*

They already knew about the rigs. Jacob must have told them.

'Look, Leona, are you anything to do with the two boys who were picked up last month?' asked Adam.

Two boys? Nathan must have survived the ExCel Centre as well.

'Black boy and a white boy. Only, apart from those two and you, the only people we've seen approach the zone in the last couple of years are those wild kids. Sometimes they come begging for scraps, you know, when they've run out of dogs to eat.'

Her eyes remained on the bowl in front of her.

They know.

'There's rumours floating around, Leona. Rumours of another big community like ours. That that's where you and the two boys came from?'

She knew her face was giving her away. 'Not true,' she said evenly.

Adam lowered his voice a little and leaned forward. 'But, if it *was* true then I would be very worried for them.'

'Why?'

'Especially if Maxwell and his boys knew where exactly they were.'

Her mouth was hurting. She'd already spoken more words today than her jaw wanted her to. 'Why?'

'Because we're dying here.'

Dying? She'd taken a look out at the acres of green in front of the dome; row upon ordered row of vegetable crops; a soup kitchen not unlike theirs back home. They seemed to have managed thus far on what they could produce.

'You grow food,' she replied.

Adam's lips curled with a derisory sneer. 'It's not enough.

403

Nowhere near enough. There are two thousand, two hundred and seventy-nine people living here. What we've managed to produce out there would sustain less than half that number. This is our third year of trying to grow our own stuff. Last summer was better than the first. This summer was worse than either. I don't know whether we're doing things all wrong; same crops in the same soil, or the soil's being over-used . . . there are no bloody horticulturists here.'

'Where . . . where do you get . . . ?'

'Where's the *rest* of the food coming from?'

She nodded.

'A stockpile. A rapidly shrinking stockpile.' He dipped his spoon into the murky broth in front of him and slurped a mouthful. 'Last time I had a look down there was over three years ago, and it was three-quarters gone even then. Maxwell's got us all out there every day, tending those plants, tilling the soil, turning the crap from the latrines into the earth to make it more fertile, but it's largely window dressing.'

He leant forward again, lowering his voice still further. 'It's for show, that's all it is. To keep everyone busy, to assure them there's a future here, that there'll always be food for everyone.'

He was almost whispering now. 'But there isn't. It's a fucking sham.' He looked down at his bowl. 'Only half of what's in there came from the vegetable garden out front — the rest is tinned goods.'

Leona looked down at her own bowl and studied the grey liquid.

'When we finally run out of what's stocked downstairs, then we're all going to be screwed. That's when things will turn fucking nasty here. Maxwell knows that. The bastard has known that for the last ten years.'

'Why . . .' She pursed her lips, and felt an ache course across her face. 'Why did he not . . . start growing . . . earlier?'

404

'I don't know. I suppose he started out thinking a decade's worth of supplies was enough to see us through. That some relief effort would have come to the rescue by now.'

Leona remembered a conversation with Dad from a long time ago; asking him why the world carried on using oil if they knew it was running out. That was just silly, wasn't it? He'd replied that people had a tendency to instinctively stick their heads in the sand; to expect to be rescued by someone or something else – technology, market forces, whatever.

Old habits: a hard thing to change.

'I think he's been expecting it all to fall apart at some point. His plan has been to delay that for as long as possible.' Adam laughed. 'A bit like the *Titanic*, really; assuring the second, third and steerage class passengers that all's well, meanwhile organising a life raft for himself and his thugs.'

She recalled Dizz-ee's grin again. *Shit, man, reckon we'll all have a go at her.*

'Leona, where's home? *Where* did you come from?'

Her eyes narrowed and she looked away.

'Look, I'm not spying. I'm not one of *them*. I'm too old.' He gestured at the two praetorians standing nearby, overseeing the long queues of workers, bowls in hand, waiting to be served from a steaming urn. 'Maxwell trusts only the young ones. He only recruits young lads because he knows exactly how to control them. That's how this whole fucking prison camp works. Those boys are being kept well fed, the rest of us he's gradually starving to death. Look at me.'

Adam pinched the back of one of his hands. The skin bunched like parchment, then slowly settled back. 'I really can't fake that. I'm starving, just like everyone else here. Another year, maybe two . . . all the workers are going to be dead. And those boys, and Maxwell, will be having a big party at your place.'

Shit, man, reckon we'll all have a go at her.

'Norfolk,' she said. 'We came . . . we came down from Norfolk.'

Adam stopped, smiled. 'Seriously?'

'What's funny?'

He shook his head. 'Not funny, just . . . just a coincidence. I used to be based in Suffolk, at least my regiment was. Up in Honington. You know it?'

She shook her head.

'Royal Air Force regiment,' he replied. 'Back when the crash happened we were assigned to this safety zone to guard it.'

Adam began talking about his old life, a tour in Afghanistan, but her mind was filled with a nightmare; she saw hordes of orcs raping and pillaging The Shire. She saw young boys glistening with bling in their neon-orange jackets in a tightly packed, cheering crowd, like boys around a schoolyard fight; each of them taking their turn on her mother, then Dr Gupta, then Martha . . . and all of them with Dizz-ee's leering, grinning face.

'Adam . . .'

He stopped talking.

'Can I . . . I . . . trust you?'

He stared at her silently for a moment. 'Can we trust each other?'

'I . . . have to leave. I have to . . . warn my mum. Those boys . . . I think they know where we came from.'

Chapter 62

10 years AC

'Please, Walter, please tell me you didn't do it,' said Jenny.

The old man was huddled on the floor of the paint store-room. The only light came from a small wire-grilled porthole at the top of one of the walls. One of the panels of glass had cracked and wind whistled through the gaps between shards and wire, playing a bitter melody for them both.

'Walter?'

She crouched down beside him. The wrinkled folds around his eyes matched the colour of his florid cheeks and his raspberry nose.

'I didn't do it,' he whispered. 'I didn't take Natasha.' He looked up at her, his face wet with tears. 'And I never hurt Hannah. I swear I—'

'What about her shoe?' she asked firmly. Her voice hard and accusing. 'How did it end up on your boat?'

He shook his head desperately. 'I . . . I don't know. I really don't know.'

She studied him a while longer. Looking into his face she could see the poor old man wasn't lying to her. Guile was something he completely fell flat on. Being utterly unable to say what was untruthful in situations where it might be appropriate or even diplomatic was one of the reasons he'd never been the most popular member of the community. Walter couldn't lie to save his life. He could do many things, but bullshit wasn't one of them. She put a finger to her lips to hush him. 'I believe you,' she said softly.

I just needed to look into your eyes as you said it.

The old man let out a strangled sob, his shoulders sagging with the release. 'I'd do anything to protect her . . . to protect you.'

She placed an arm around his wide frame and hugged him gently as his body shuddered with tears. She knew he was innocent.

The tears finally subsided and she let him go, settling on the floor beside him, leaning her back against the storeroom's cool wall. Outside the door, she could hear Howard shuffling on the stool in the hallway. On guard duty. The stool creaked under him as he moved, uncomfortable holding the weight of that shotgun in his old liver-spotted hands.

She'd been surprised when she'd first seen Howard on his way over to one of Latoc's sermons. Howard, Walter and Dennis, the three stooges, hunched over a cribbage board on many a dark evening. She'd found it hard to believe that those two old boys had taken on Latoc's nonsense; had turned on Walter.

'He's taken over,' she said.

Walter looked at her. 'What?'

'There was a public meeting this morning and he proposed a vote to remove me.' She sighed. 'The only person who objected out loud was Tami.'

The women had shouted her down. Quite an ugly scene. She was jostled as she spoke up from the crowd, and then baying voices had drowned her out. Valérie calmed them down to silence with a gentle wave of his hand and then Jenny had tried to speak.

'I told them it wasn't down to a bloody vote. I said this place was our home; you and me, the kids and the others that first set it up . . . our home. And that everyone else were guests that we'd allowed to stay. My house, my rules.' She laughed sourly. 'They just loved that, didn't they?'

The mess had erupted with angry cries, and Alice Harton's foghorn voice over the top calling her an 'arrogant bitch'.

'They voted Latoc as the leader. It's all over, Walter.'

'What's going to happen?'

'I think he's going to evict you. He'll probably evict us both. He won't want me around causing him trouble.'

Walter shook his head. 'He's going to turn this place bad. Ruin everything we've built.'

Jenny nodded tiredly. 'I know.'

'You can't let him do that.'

'I can't stop him, Walter. It's done. Everyone's chosen him to lead the community.'

I'm not sure I want to stop him either.

There was something quite appealing about the idea of taking a boat ride ashore and walking away from all of this. Just a long walk through Bracton and out the other side into the summer countryside and whatever overgrown silent villages and towns lay beyond. Find some nice quiet leafy meadow to lie down in and give up.

They sat in silence for a while, listening to the wind whistling through the crack, Howard shuffling outside, and the moronic clucking of the chickens a deck above. The smell from the slurry room, along the dark passage outside, was still strong, even though the melted plastic containers had been pulled out weeks ago.

'I think . . .' said Walter finally, 'I think it was Valérie Latoc who took Natasha.'

She turned to look at him.

Presented with the evidence of her shoe on Walter's boat, Jenny had allowed herself to believe, at least until now, that he was guilty. She'd turned her back on nearly seven years of trust between them. Seeing the truth in his eyes, she realised how stupid and unfair she'd been. Natasha could plausibly have been playing on his boat as it dangled from the davits, even though she knew she wasn't allowed on there. A strong gust would have set the boat swaying and she could quite easily have tumbled over the side.

But Latoc?

She was surprised the possibility had never even entered her mind.

'Latoc?'

'I think he killed her, Jenny. I think he killed her then put one of her shoes on my boat.'

She tried to see it in her mind. Tried to imagine his calm impassive face attached to a killer's hands. Tried to imagine where . . . how . . . he could do it. This small world of theirs was surely too crowded to do something like that. Especially on the compression rig where the majority of his people were camped up in that teeming maze of hammocks, bunks and laundry lines. A voice would carry; a voice crying out in pain or fear, it would reverberate around the hard metal walls of that module like a stone on a snare drum.

But he has those rooms at the top to himself, doesn't he?

The top floor, the monitoring suite.

And Natasha and her mother were amongst Latoc's faith-ful.

They'd trust him. Denise'd trust her daughter with him.

Jenny tried imagining again, and this time she could see him quietly enticing the little girl upstairs. In her mind's eye she could see everyone outside at work in the sun spread out on the walkways, on the decks, on the terraces of other platforms, and Valérie Latoc, encountering the girl alone in one dark corner of that large cathedral-like space. Natasha bunking class as she sometimes did. So wilful, just like Hannah used to be. Jenny could see him offering the girl a warm, friendly smile . . . and her smiling back. Absolutely nothing to be concerned about.

Mr Latoc is a good man. My mummy says so.

She could see him holding out his hand, her grasping it and him leading her up metal stairs past floors of hammocks and towels and rugs and dangling laundry. She could see him smiling down at her, the glint of a predator in those warm brown eyes as they headed along the walkway to his rooms.

This is my kingdom now, and these are my people. And yes, I shall do as I please.

'I think he killed her,' said Walter. 'And he tried to set me up at the same time.'

She looked at him.

'Two birds with one stone, Jenny. I'm in charge of the guns,' he said gesturing to his chest, a thatch of grey-white bristles where once locker-room keys had nestled on a chain. 'Or I was. He's got those guns now.'

God help us, Walter, you might just be right.

'Jenny.'

'What is it?'

'There's something else.'

'What?'

'Do you think Hannah was dead already when we arrived?'

Jenny tried to remember the last moments before the blast. It was at best a tangled jumble of images. A rising sense of panic . . . fear they were never going to find her because she'd disappeared into the surging sea below.

'I . . . I can't remember.'

'What if that was him, too?' he whispered. 'What if he took her there . . . did things . . . killed her, then pulled the methane pipe free to cover his tracks? He could have known something would set off the gas . . .'

He was talking some more, but she was no longer listening. She could see the scenario. She could actually see it because . . .

Hannah was very taken with him, wasn't she?

She remembered seeing Latoc with Hannah on quite a few occasions, him talking quietly to her. She'd visited him countless times in Dr Gupta's sick bay. Jenny wondered if those dark eyes she'd found so attractive had all the while been busy making plans from the moment he'd first come round.

'Jenny?'

Walter had been saying something to her.

'Jenny?'

She stood up. 'I have to go,' she told him.

'Where are you going?'

She knocked on the storeroom's door. 'Howard! I'm coming out now.'

A bolt slid noisily and the door creaked open. 'All done, Mrs Sutherland?'

She smiled at Howard standing in the dim corridor outside holding the shotgun uncertainly in both hands. Although Valérie Latoc was now in charge, the old boy still nodded deferentially at her.

Without thinking about it, she stepped swiftly out of the storeroom and snatched the gun out of his unready hands. He stared down, goggle-eyed at his empty palms. 'Uh, Mrs Sutherland, could I have the gun back, please?'

'In,' she said, nodding at the storeroom.

'In?'

'Yes, in there with Walter.'

He nodded and stepped inside.

'Jenny? What the hell are you doing?' called out Walter as she swung the door shut on both men. She rammed the bolt home, locking both of them in. She didn't need Walter trying to wrestle the gun off her. Trying to stop her.

'I'm going to kill the bastard,' she replied evenly.

Chapter 63

10 years AC

'Do you see? Once upon a time it was said that *money* was the root of all evil. Money was a bad thing, yes? But not as bad as the oil,' said Valérie, his voice carrying across the still assembly of faces and bouncing off the hard metal ceiling of the compression chamber thirty feet above them. The ideal place to address them all, his voice seemed amplified in here.

'Oil was the truly bad thing. It turned us into slaves, yes? We became lazy and greedy and selfish because of it. It allowed us to fill this world with too many people, to cover the land with endless cities, to fill the sky with poison and the sea with chemicals. You see, oil was a bounty we did not *earn* through hard work. It was merely *found*. It came to us as a free gift. A treasure we discovered in the ground. An offering from the Devil, you understand?'

They listened to him intently, all faces turned up to a gantry which served perfectly as a pulpit.

'So,' he continued, 'for a hundred years mankind has lived on the back of this free gift; learning how to be the lazy man, becoming fat, forgetting how to care for himself. We became like the drug addicts, dependent on our fix of heroin. Unable to do anything other than wait for the next fix.

'Then God made the painful decision. That the world was wrong. The Devil's offering was poisoned and the poison had spread into our veins and infected everyone. God really had no choice, you see? We should not be angry with Him.'

Valérie dipped his head in thought for a moment.

413

'When He stopped the flow of oil, the Lord knew that was to be the end for almost everyone. He knew that billions of people would starve, would turn on each other for whatever food could be scavenged. He knew that the powerful nations would fight over the places still producing oil until their fuel ran dry and they could fight no more. He knew all these things . . . and it hurt Him that He had to do these things.'

His audience considered that in silence.

'You know, I have seen London. I have seen Paris. I have seen Brussels. I have seen Berlin. I have travelled across much of Europe. I did this in the early days. And back then we all hoped that there would be places that survived and started to rebuild things, yes? I remember that I was heartbroken by what I saw. Burning cities, bodies everywhere. Roads thick with migrating people, all starving or sick with water-borne diseases.

'After a few years the world did finally become quiet. Most of the dying was done. Those that were left were the ones least poisoned by the evil oil. Farmers in far-off countries, uncivilised savages who could make life on a stretch of dust. And,' he gazed down at them, 'people like you.

'It was three years ago, walking through a city empty and crumbling, nothing but the wild dogs and cats. It was night time and completely dark. It was then that God spoke to me. He said to me, "Can you hear my voice now that it is still and silent?" I said "yes". He said, "Can you see the stars in the sky now that they are not drowned out by man's bright lights?" I said "yes". It was then that I realised that this . . . this crash, it was no disaster. But a new beginning. Like the flood, God was clearing away all that was wrong.

'Then He told me there was a special place, a place out at sea, an ark. And on this ark were good people who had survived and learned good habits and old ways. He told me these people . . .' he gestured with his hands, '*you people* were the ones He had chosen to rebuild the world.'

The audience stirred; he heard an 'amen' down there amongst the upturned faces.

'But,' he continued, 'you had started to make mistakes, to make the wrong decisions, to adopt old bad habits.'

He could hear some in his audience shuffle uncomfortably.

'Yes,' he said smiling patiently. 'Yes, the generator and the lights. A return to the habits of the oil world. This is why I was directed here. He told me to hurry, to make my way as quickly as possible. So, that is why I came. To lead you back to the correct path. The simple existence God wants for us. Not polluted with lights after dark. Not cluttered with a million metal and plastic things that flash and make noises.

'Come on,' he shook his head, 'come on . . . do you remember how unhappy we all were? How unsatisfied we all felt? Yes?'

A chorus of voices in his audience agreed with him. Thoughtful heads nodded.

'Children could not play outside because we did not trust one another. We all walked around in lonely little bubbles with headphones in our ears to block other people out. We could not talk to each other any more, instead we typed messages through computers. We were unhappy with the possessions we had because the television showed us people who had so much more. We were unhappy with ourselves because we did not seem to smile as much as the beautiful people we saw on the television. You understand?'

He lowered his voice, tempered with sadness. 'That was never what God wanted for us. That was not *living*. It was existing, nothing more—'

A door noisily squeaked on rusting hinges and a gust of wind stole into the cavernous chamber, setting the laundry lines aflutter. Valérie turned to his right and saw a blurred bar of daylight narrowing as the door swung shut again. He heard footsteps ringing out on the metal treads of the walkway, then, out of the dimness at one end and into a pool of daylight cast from a skylight far above, stepped Jennifer Sutherland.

'Jennifer.' He smiled warmly.

She stared at him in silence, her eyes lost in the shadows cast by her brow.

'Jennifer, have you finally come to join us?'

She pulled something out from beneath her cardigan. He recognised the dull metallic glint of a gun in her hands.

'You're a bastard,' she hissed under her breath.

He took a step backwards. 'Jennifer, I am very sorry about the vote this morn—'

'Shut up!' she snapped.

'You are still welcome amongst us. Welcome to join—'

'SHUT UP!' She shouldered the shotgun.

Valérie bit his lip and nodded. Several voices called up from below. Pleading voices.

'Jenny!' cried Martha. 'What're you doing?'

The side of her face scarred with a spiderweb of knitting skin gave nothing away. The other side, unblemished, hardened as her jaw clasped; lips tightened like purse strings. The gun wavered unsteadily in her hands.

'Jenny?' cried Martha again, 'please, put the gun down, love!'

'*You*,' she hissed at him. 'It was *you*, wasn't it?'

Valérie shook his head. 'I do not know what—'

'Natasha . . . and Hannah.'

'Those poor sweet girls,' replied Latoc. 'They are . . . they are in a far better place now, Jennifer. They sit with our L—'

'SHUT UP!!'

He slowly backed up another step. 'You know it was Walter who killed them. You know that . . . but I think you cannot accept that, no?'

She racked the gun. 'I know Walter! I *know* Walter. But you . . . I can see what you are now!'

416

Valérie smiled. 'I am what?'

'You're fucking dead,' she whispered. The chamber echoed with the deep boom of the shotgun.

Chapter 64

10 years AC

O2 Arena – 'Safety Zone 4',
London

'He's definitely up to something,' replied Adam Brooks quietly. 'I think he's getting ready to go. He'll take who he needs and be gone.'

Leona could see his face through the gaps in the shifting veil of leaves, fumbling amongst the bamboo canes and pea vines for the few remaining pods. He was in the next aisle going through the motions of working but actually keeping a lookout for any *jackets* walking the perimeter nearby, or any other workers inching their way along the aisle and getting close enough that they could listen in.

'When they leave,' Adam continued, 'things will fall apart quickly, Leona. No jackets around, it'll suddenly be everyone for themselves. Complete bloody chaos. And that bastard Maxwell, I'm certain, won't be leaving any food supplies behind for us. It'll turn ugly very quickly. This place will fold just like the other safety zones.'

'Then we should be sure our escape happens before that,' whispered Leona. 'I mean . . . as soon as we possibly can.'

Jacob's words haunted her. *Don't let them hurt Mum.*

'We have to get back home before they arrive there.' She reached through the leaves for a pod, wincing at the pain along her bruised arms and ribs as she stretched for it. 'Brooks, you told me there were one or two other soldiers like you?'

'Adam,' he smiled. 'You can call me Adam.'

Leona stared at him silently. 'The others?'

'Just the three of us now. They put us in different work groups, so we hardly see—'

'Would you trust them?'

'They're good men.'

'But do you *trust* them?'

Adam hesitated a moment. 'Yeah, I think so.'

Leona nodded. 'Then they can join us if they want. Could you go find them? Talk to them?'

'Sure. I think they're over the other side this morning, but I could arrange for us to meet somewhere at a break time.'

'Do that then,' she replied.

They continued working in silence. The air filled with the fidgeting of leaves and the trickle of water poured from watering cans nearby, the quiet murmur of conversations and the far-off echo of someone hammering.

Leona looked a lot worse than she felt. The swelling around her eye had gone down, now it was just a black eye, a shiner. The bruises over her arms and legs, mottled dark patches that only hurt if she pressed against them. And thankfully, no broken bones or internal damage, as far as she was aware. Her jaw still ached when she spoke at length, but that too was better than it had been.

Several days since those things happened. She'd lost track of exactly how many days. The time she'd spent in the cattle shed had felt like months at the time, years even. But since then, since meeting Brooks – *Adam*, she corrected herself – there'd been a surprising convergence of purpose, and with this man even a possibility of escape.

She had only one single goal; thoughts beyond that were just noise.

I have to warn her.

Adam was right. There was something going on in the middle of the dome. Yesterday they'd watched about a hundred workers, many of them work-group leaders – the ones who'd earned the Chief's trust and been awarded

419

McDonald's plastic name tags – being herded through the entry kiosks and up into the central arena. Panic rippled amongst those looking on as a rumour spread that this was some sort of an act of punishment, that one of the praetorians had been assaulted by a worker and an example was going to be made of them all. Beaten in batches. But no more people were herded through, and the young boys in jackets barked orders at them to go back to their jobs.

Today's rumour-mill was spinning with stories that the workers were building something in the middle. There were certainly noises coming out, of things being shifted and dismantled, the sound of scaffolding poles clattering heavily on the ground. The idea that something was being *built* seemed strangely reassuring to everyone else, but Leona knew it could only be the noise of approaching departure.

How soon, though, that was the question.

'We'll need a gun,' she said quietly. 'Can you get a gun?'

'The only way we'll get one is wrestling it out of the hands of one of those boys,' said Adam. 'What about food and water?'

'Water's not a problem. Any river or stream will do,' she replied. The waterways were no longer a thick soup of nitrates, heavy metals and used condoms. You could scoop a handful of water from the Thames now and drink it without doing yourself any harm. It tasted like pond life but it wasn't going to kill you. Best thing that could ever have happened to mother nature, she decided. Mankind screwing *himself* over for a change. There were canals and rivers up through Norfolk. They could easily find some plastic bottles, rinse them out and fill them with the Thames. Water wasn't a problem.

'If we can find some bicycles from somewhere,' she said, 'we could be back up in Norfolk in three or four days. We won't need food.'

Adam shook his head. 'We will. None of us have any fat to

burn. Seriously. A day or two without food and we won't be able to walk, never mind cycle.'

'We'll find something,' she replied. 'There's still food out there.'

'And what if your mum won't let me and my lads on? We'd be in poor shape to go anywhere else. We'd be fucked.'

'She will.'

'You're sure?'

'They're going to need you, aren't they? To fight off Maxwell's little army.' Leona dropped a handful of pods into his bucket. 'So how do you think they'll travel there? They got trucks?'

'The barges,' said Adam. 'Thames barges. We used them a few years back when—' He stopped talking for a moment as an elderly man came down his row, sprinkling water from a can into each grow trough. Adam let him pass by before continuing. 'There's a tugboat moored up on Thames Wharf with a nearly full tank of diesel. Hasn't been used since the last time. He'll use that to tow the three barges.' He looked at her through the leaves. 'That's how he'll get there.'

Leona caught his eyes. 'Can those barge things go out on the open sea?'

'If they hug the coastline and as long as the sea's calm, yeah, they can do it.'

'How long will it take them?'

Adam shrugged. 'I don't know. Your place – did you say it's off the north coast of Norfolk?'

'Not really. It's not far from Great Yarmouth. Do you know th—'

'I know Great Yarmouth. My grandparents used to live there.' Adam pinched his lips in thought. 'Lemmesee, that's what? A hundred and fifty . . . two hundred miles of coastline for them to follow?'

Leona shook her head. She had absolutely no idea.

421

'I don't know,' he continued. 'Maybe it'll take them a day or two if the weather stays good.'

She felt her heart quicken. 'Oh, God!' she whispered. 'I thought it might take weeks! Then . . . shit . . . then we have to go—'

'Don't say tonight.'

'Yes, tonight.'

He shook his head.

'Tonight, Adam. Can we arrange to go tonight?'

He bit his lip. 'Jesus. I . . . that's no time at all to—'

'They could leave at any time. *They* could be leaving tonight!'

He raised a hand to hush her down. 'Shhh! Okay, okay. Look, I'll see if I can find the lads this afternoon and arrange to meet at the evening meal break.'

'Please, do that,' she nodded. And then almost as an afterthought she smiled through the vines at him. 'And thank you.'

'Maybe we should be thanking you. The only reason nobody's yet bothered trying to sneak out of here is . . . well, we thought this place was it; all that was left.' He smiled. 'I'll try and get back to you before the mid-morning whistle goes, okay? With a time and place to meet the lads.'

She nodded but he was already gone. She resumed half-heartedly picking undeveloped pea pods, hardly even petits pois; food that would end up being thrown into whatever was being boiled to a watery pulp for this evening's meal.

For a moment she wondered where her strength was coming from to be doing this; she ached all over, she ached inside. She couldn't make sense of the calm detachment she was feeling; Jacob gone, Hannah gone, and she felt nothing.

Her eyes followed the arrogant swagger of two orange jackets patrolling along the perimeter wall, chatting animatedly, excited about something; both sporting matching white baseball caps perched on their heads at a jaunty angle. Their hands and fingers flicked with exaggerated street gestures they could only have picked up from films or from the older boys. Even the crotch-grabbing swagger both boys were attempting to pull off was a poor affectation of something they must have seen on a DVD or a computer game.

No, she did feel something; a determination, an *angry* determination, that those vicious little bastards weren't going to get on the platforms and have their fun. She was going to see those child-tyrants die before she allowed herself to shed another tear for Jacob, for Hannah, for Dad. They were no different to the White City gang who'd tried to break into their home and rape her ten years ago. Only some stupid bastard had decided to give this lot guns and tell them they were righteous in all that they did.

Before she shed another tear, she vowed, she was going to see them die, tumbling like lemmings into the North Sea.

Chapter 65

10 years AC

Nathan watched them loading up the second barge; a human chain of workers leading out of the dome's rear service entrance across twenty yards of gravel and weed to the concrete wharf. The barges bumped and scraped impatiently as the Thames stirred softly and a fresh breeze rustled through loose corners of cellophane half wrapped around catering packs of Fray Bentos corned beef and Heinz baked beans.

In his hands he held an army issue assault rifle; an SA80. The very same weapon the old man, Walter, had once allowed him to test fire briefly; a small piece of his old life. Around his waist, beneath the orange staff jacket, webbing dangled, pouches stuffed full of thirty-round clips of ammunition.

A real soldier now, eh?

Not for the first time he could feel the magical power that holding a weapon like this gave you. He remembered watching the news one night before the crash, when he was about eight or nine. Some American kid had ambled into his high school with a similar weapon and proceeded to kill every kid in his class. He'd asked Mum why the kid did it and she'd said it was because he was evil.

He knew why the kid had done it now.

It was that sense of invincibility, of immortality, one felt holding the cold steel weight of a weapon like this. One tiny pull on his trigger and he could mow down those workers like skittles at a bowling alley. It was almost God-like power and all of it contained within the impulsive twitch of one finger.

That's why, Snoop had quietly confided in him last night, only the *older* boys carried fully loaded guns on patrol. The younger ones were issued with the same weapons, but with an empty ammo clip.

It's the moment of pause, bro. That's what he'd said . . . the moment of pause.

The young ones had ammo in their pouches, of course, but the time it took to eject an empty clip, unbutton the pouch, pull out another clip and ram it home was the time a younger mind needed to decide whether it was actually necessary to shoot a worker or simply bark an order at them.

Killers, said Snoop, *they've been educated by me and Maxwell to kill without mercy. Child warriors, Nathan, the best in the world. Ruthless motherfuckers, bro, but they need grown-ups like you and me to lead them.*

There'd been something conspiratorial in the way he'd said that, softly spoken for his ears only. *You and me, bro.*

Snoop seemed to be trusting him implicitly. There was a growing bond between them. Last night, as they'd shared a joint and looked out across the moonlit Thames, he'd said, 'I'm so fuckin' sorry 'bout your friend, Natc.' Nathan knew he meant that. Word was when Snoop had discovered what had happened to Jacob, he'd killed Dizz-ee himself.

'I really liked Jacob,' Snoop had added. 'Three of us would've made a fucking good team.'

Nathan gazed out now at the barge being slowly loaded and felt a painful stab of guilt for shaking Jacob off at the party. He'd been so buzzed-up on the booze, the games, the smokes, the hero-worship . . . Jesus, the boys had been all but carrying him around on their shoulders. And the girls. He could see them making eyes at him – they all wanted to be girlfriend to the second dog; all wanted the kudos and the extra treats that go with that.

He remembered thinking, *me and Snoop are the fucking kings here.* He remembered feeling like some kind of God emperor, like a pharaoh, like Alexander the Great. Him and Snoop, all-conquering generals.

And then he'd caught Jacob's eye across the stage and he knew with absolute certainty that his best friend just wasn't going to fit in there; that Jacob wasn't going to be part of this dream. An unkind thought had sneaked in under cover of the booze.

Maybe it'd be better if he went back home?

He pulled on the cigarette, savoured the bitter burn in his throat and watched the smoke flicker out in front of him.

Well he's gone now ain't he? You got that.

Something inside him flipped over like a bed partner turning over to face away. Like he had bad breath. Like it was sick of the sight of him. It left him feeling queasy.

Self-consciously he thumbed the sunglasses up the bridge of his nose; an expensive pair of Moschinos that Snoop had given him.

Eyes are like fuckin' windows, bro. First rule of command, don't let the little people look in . . . know what I'm sayin'?

Nathan was glad to be wearing them now. This small scrubby path of quayside was busy with workers and praetorians. He didn't need anyone seeing his tears. He wiped his nose, hawked and spat on the ground.

'You a'ight?' asked Hammer. The boy standing guard with him was almost as tall. His head was bare, shaved down to the skin except for a zigzag of bristles that wrapped round the back of his bullet-like skull.

'S'fine,' Nathan slurred coolly. 'Sun's well bright, though.'

Hammer nodded, pulling on a cigarette and puffing out a ribbon of blue smoke. 'Hot.'

They watched the loading in silence for half an hour, and then Snoop joined them on the quay.

'S'up?'

Hammer nodded and offered Snoop one from his packet. Snoop pulled a cigarette out and took a light.

'Chief reckons on another day prepping-up before we go.'

Nathan nodded towards the barges. 'Are we taking all three of those?'

'Yeah.'

'Loaded with food and stuff?'

Snoop pulled, exhaled and shrugged. 'Chief's idea. We take along as much as we can get on there. No knowing what's left to forage on the way up, right?'

They nodded.

Hammer looked at Snoop. 'You gonna tell us more about this place we goin'? Coz I heard Jooz sayin' it was Alton Towers or somethin'.'

Snoop grinned at Nathan. *Kids, eh?*

The boys were being kept in the dark. It was easier than trying to explain to them all exactly what an oil rig was, what it looked like, what it did. That, and it kept them all busy guessing, making up their own rumours.

'Big surprise, Hammer.'

'Aw, shit, Snoop, c'mon, gimme a clue.'

'No. Now go an' help Rascal and the others with packin' the Toca Rally booths. I wanna talk some shit with Nathan.'

Hammer nodded and swung casually towards the dome's service entrance; he flicked his cigarette butt at one of the workers as he stepped inside.

'How you doin', Nate?' he asked.

'Yeah, I'm good, man.'

'You're okay with this, right? Us goin' to your old home an' stuff?'

Nathan nodded. 'Sure.'

'We'll treat 'em good, you know? Ain't gonna be like no pirate raid or nothing. This'll be our new home. All workin' together an' shit. Pooling what we got.'

'Yeah, I know.'

Snoop looked at him. A long hard look that suggested there was more that he wanted to say. 'Me and you, Nate. Know what I'm saying? Me and you.'

Nathan could hear that gently probing tone in Snoop's voice; a tone of voice that was asking whether he could be trusted, even if he wasn't using those words.

Nathan smiled uneasily. 'Sure.'

'One day . . . you know? Maxwell . . . he won't be around for ever.'

Nathan turned to look at him. Snoop grinned. He slapped his shoulder. 'Later. I gotta go see how much more shit we got to bring up from the mezz.'

Chapter 66

10 years AC

O2 Arena – 'Safety Zone 4',
London

They stood in silence amongst a cluster of several dozen large green plastic water butts. They were filled with human waste collected from the latrine cabanas inside the dome. The air above them seemed to shimmer with the warmth of fermentation. The odour of rancid shit was so powerful Leona felt like it was coating her tongue, the back of her throat, lining her lungs.

'Jesus, Brooksie, why the fuck d'you have to pick this place to meet?' said one of the men.

'Why do you think? We got a little privacy here. Just make it look like you're taking a leak.'

The men obediently circled around a pile of waste and pretended to fumble at their flies.

'Right then,' said Adam, 'let's start talking. We won't have long before the whistle goes.'

'So,' said Leona, trying to look like she had some purpose being here standing amongst four men supposedly taking a piss break. 'These guys were in your platoon?'

'All that's left of our unit,' replied Adam quietly. 'This is Sergeant Danny Walfield,' he said pointing at the man standing opposite her. Dark, almost black, hair, had been kept cropped relatively short, an untidy cut that looked as if shears had been used. On top it was going thin. He had a thick moustache curving down either side of his mouth, like the black neoprene-grip handlebars of a racing bike. She guessed he was in his mid-thirties.

'All right, love?' he grunted. She nodded back.

'And this is Lance Corporal Sean Davies. But everyone calls him Bushey.'

A slightly younger man with long curly ginger hair pulled back into a bulky ponytail and a scruffy, wispy goatee around his mouth. 'Hey,' he said with a small self-conscious wave.

'And Lance Corporal Davey Potter.'

Thinning a little at the temples, long brown frizzy hair swooped down either side of his narrow face to unite with a thick grizzly beard he'd clearly not bothered to tame in years. He pushed his round-framed glasses up his nose. 'They call me Harry,' he said in a tone of voice that sounded as if she ought to have already guessed that. She cocked her head, not sure what he was getting at.

'On account of the glasses and the surname. Potter? Remember them books?'

The books? Then she got it. She remembered them. Jacob hated those bloody books.

'Right, I get it.' She looked at his unruly hair. 'I'm surprised they don't call you Hagrid.'

He shrugged. 'Well, I had short back and sides back when I joined the platoon, didn't I?'

'And this,' Adam said to the three men, 'is Leona.'

They exchanged formal nods. Like Adam, like every other worker here, they were wiry-lean; every last ounce of surplus fat burned away years ago as a slow and steady downhill curve of calories in their diet was waging a war of attrition on their bodies; slowly but surely starving them to death.

'Right, so like I was saying lads,' he said, 'Leona's the one that came in last month, after those two boys. All three of them came down together from this other settlement in Norfolk.'

'Norfolk is it?' said Harry. 'That's where we was based.'

Adam carried on. 'Their settlement is a going concern, not

430

another crash 'n' burn. It's doing just fine and it's quite a big settlement, right?'

She nodded. 'About four hundred and fifty of us.'

The men looked at each other, stunned.

'That's right,' said Adam. 'And the thing is, lads, Leona says we'd be welcome there.'

'You got food . . . you know, like for ever?' asked Bushey.

Leona nodded. 'We've been self-sustaining for the last four years.'

'It's not just fucking vegetables?'

'We have fish, loads of fish. We have eggs too. And chicken occasionally.'

'Eggs!' Harry looked at Bushey. 'Did you say *eggs*?'

'Fuck that.' Bushey made a face. 'You said chicken? I'd sell me own grandma for a Kentucky Fried—'

'Quiet, you two,' said Walfield.

Adam nodded gratefully. 'But here's the thing, lads,' he continued. 'Maxwell and his soldier boys are planning on moving there themselves. They know about it, and they're going for it. That's what all that noise today has been about. That's why they grabbed a hundred workers earlier this morning and took them into the middle. They're packing up their stuff and leaving.'

Walfield nodded. 'Shit! That's what we were saying earlier, wasn't it? Thought they'd found someplace better, that this was them fucking off with the supplies.'

'Well, you were right,' said Leona.

'The thing is, gents,' said Adam, 'we have to beat Maxwell there and—'

'Oh, I get it,' said Bushey nodding slowly. He looked up at Leona. 'You want us to help fight those boys when they arrive?'

Adam looked at him and splayed his hands in guilty admission. 'Yes. We'd help Leona's people defend themselves. That's the price of admission.'

The men looked at each other. It was Walfield who spoke. 'I don't know, Brooksie, mate. They're all psyched-out in the head. It's Maxwell's doing. Last few years he's been brainwashing those little pricks into believing they're all fucking superhero warriors. That makes 'em dangerous.'

Harry nodded. 'They'll fight like bloody pit bull terriers. Maxwell will probably coke them out of their heads before he sends them in.'

'How many other men are there at your place?' asked Adam.

'Not many, I'm afraid. About a dozen grown men. Although most of them are pretty old.'

Walfield, Bushey and Harry glanced at each other unhappily.

'A dozen men and us. Sixteen effectives,' said Adam.

'Seventeen,' added Leona. They looked at her. 'And every other woman there who doesn't want to be raped by a gang of teenagers,' she added quietly.

The men nodded. Point taken.

'What about weapons?' asked Walfield. 'What have you got?'

'Some guns. Four or five, I think.'

'That's it?'

She nodded.

Bushey shook his head and turned to Adam. 'That's not good, sir.'

Sir? She looked at Adam and it occurred to her for the first time that he must have been their commanding officer. The deferential body language, the guarded familiarity hinted of old habits hard to kill off.

'What she hasn't told you fellas yet is *where* they're based.'

'It would need to be a bloody castle,' said Harry.

'It's better than that.' He turned to her. 'Isn't it, Leona?'

'Yes, I suppose it is. It's a gas rig on the North Sea.'

432

Their eyes widened in comedic unison.

'It's big,' she added, 'five separate, linked platforms all sitting on eighty-foot support-legs. It's hard enough climbing on when there's someone above giving you a helping hand. Trust me.'

'And a whole lot harder if there's several hundred people firing guns and throwing things down at you,' added Adam. 'Right?'

She nodded. 'That's right.'

The men continued to pretend to be pissing in silence.

Walfield spoke up again. 'We'd need more guns.'

'Well, we'll be getting two more when we take down the little fuckers guarding the gate.'

Bushey looked up. 'Rush them?'

Walfield smiled. 'I've got a shiv I keep under my cot. Would do the job nicely.'

'No way,' said Harry. 'They'd drop us before we could get close enough.'

Adam shook his head. 'I'm pretty sure they patrol with empty clips. Maxwell was worried about them wasting ammo unnecessarily. You remember? Limited ammo was a concern when he had us weapons-training them?'

They nodded.

'And no one's ever bothered to try and escape. Shit, most nights those boys aren't doing their job properly, anyway. They're too busy arsing around.'

'Or sleeping on the job,' added Walfield.

'It's the last thing those boys will expect,' said Adam. 'Even if they *are* packing loaded clips, I bet they'll still be fumbling for the safety by the time we're on them.'

Walfield grinned. 'Useless twats.'

Adam turned to Leona. 'Most of the boys were pretty crap at handling the SAs properly. All thumbs. You watch them. They hold them like movie gangsters.'

433

Harry nodded and smiled. 'Christ, we were shit drill instructors, weren't we?'

'So we're doing this? said Bushey, scratching at his ginger goatee.

Walfield nodded. Harry gave it a moment and nodded. 'I'm in.'

'Bushey?'

'Get away from this shit hole? Yeah, I'm in, sir.'

'Good. Then we're going for it tonight.'

'Tonight?'

'Yes. You've all heard the noises coming from the middle. They've been at it all day. They could be leaving at any time.'

'Are we sure that's them packing up?' asked Harry.

Walfield nodded. 'Someone in my work group got a look round the side of the dome. They've got the barges lined up there. They're loading stuff on.'

'If we don't get home first,' said Leona, 'if they get up onto the rigs before us, then it's all for nothing. We might as well stay here and just wait for things to fall apart.'

'How long'll it take Maxwell to float his way up?' asked Walfield.

'My guess, it might take him three or four days,' said Adam. 'Say, two days if the sea's millpond calm.'

'So how're we getting there?'

They heard the shrill scream of the work whistle in the distance.

'On foot,' said Leona. 'Bicycles if we can find some. Shouldn't be difficult – first retail park we come across there'll be a shop.'

'How long will that take us on bikes?'

'Two days,' she replied. Her eyes flickered towards Adam. 'Maybe three . . . four.'

'So,' said Adam, 'that's why we need to get away first.'

The whistle blew again.

'We're out of time, lads. So, tonight we're going for it. Okay?'

The other three men nodded as they pretended to shake off and tuck away.

Adam looked at them all. Very quietly he spoke, little more than a whisper. 'Right then. One hour *after* the bedtime whistle blows.'

'Where do we meet?' asked Walfield.

Adam thought about it. 'The rainwater pool.'

Leona knew where he meant. He was talking about the large family-sized paddling pool. It was to the left of the dome's main entrance, towards the river's edge.

'Got that, lads?' said Walfield. Both lance corporals nodded. 'Back to work then.'

Leona watched the three men turn and make their way through the cluster of stinking plastic butts towards the plantation, converging with all the other workers.

Adam stirred. 'All right, Leona? You okay with them?'

She knew what he was asking of them. 'They seem like good men.'

'They are. They're good fellas.'

'And you were, like, in charge of them?' she asked.

He shrugged awkwardly. 'Once upon a time, yeah. I was their CO.'

'Like an officer?' she asked.

'Exactly like an officer. Flight Lieutenant, to be precise.'

'That sounds impressive.'

Adam led the way through the butts back towards the aisles of beans where they'd been working this morning. 'It's not. I was a junior officer really. I was only twenty-five when the crash happened.'

'Flight Lieutenant . . . sounds like you ought to be flying a plane.'

'RAF regiment,' he sighed. 'Air Force grunts. I'm not a pilot, I'm afraid.'

'Oh,' she replied.

Adam laughed softly. 'And that's *exactly* the response I used to get from girls.'

'I'm sorry, that was rude of me.'

'Don't worry, doesn't mean anything now, does it? My work group's on root-crops the rest of today,' said Adam, pointing to the other side of the plantation, near the old boarded-up entrance to North Greenwich tube station. 'We're digging up whatever runty little potatoes and onions are left in the grow troughs. So, I'll see you later.'

She smiled. 'Later.'

'Enjoy the rest of the day,' he said.

'It's going to drag,' she replied.

He laughed and she thought she saw a smile under that dark beard that she could grow to like.

Chapter 67

10 years AC

'LeMan 49/25a' – ClarenCo Gas Rig Complex, North Sea

Valérie Latoc's jaw set in quiet deliberation for a moment. Finally he looked up across the table at everyone who had crowded into the mess to hear his judgment.

'God has not given me guidance on this,' he said caressing the bandaging wrapped around his right hand. Dark brown smudges of blood still showed through the layers of cotton and lint. Beneath the wadding his hand ached dreadfully.

He'd been incredibly lucky . . . *blessed* even. Jennifer's shot had been poorly aimed, kicking to one side as she'd pulled the trigger. Some of the pellets from the round had caught the hand he'd raised to protect his face. He'd lost his little finger, and the top half of the next finger along. The rest of the shotgun's pellets had whistled harmlessly past, rattling off the compression chamber's far wall.

'You should decide what is in *your* hearts,' he told them. 'And let that guide your decision,' he added sombrely.

There was a silence for only the briefest moment, then Alice Harton broke it. 'They should both be tossed over the side! She's a fucking psycho. She's bloody well dangerous. And Walter . . . he's . . . he's scum!'

Murmurs of approval from those standing behind her.

'Jennifer is a very distressed person,' said Valérie. 'And it is understandable. Surely it is also forgivable?'

'She went at you with a gun!' shouted someone at the back of the room.

'She shot you!' added Alice.

'Yet here I am alive and well. And that is as God wills it.'

'Praise be,' someone gasped.

'The Koran and the Bible teach us that forgiveness is what brings us closer to God.'

He gazed at their faces, wary that someone, somewhere, might just ask him to cite a passage from either. He knew a little of both books; he'd certainly had time enough to read them both in Prison D'Arlon. He could manage well enough with a street-corner debate . . . certainly not enough to fool a theological scholar, though. Mind you, it never ceased to amaze him how little those of faith seemed to actually know of their books. It was easy enough to invent theological-sounding passages, provided you used the right language. Most people presumed you were quoting something too obscure for them to recognise. It was more than his knowing a little scripture that made people listen to him, though. It was the confidence of utter conviction that he carried. He hadn't trained as a priest or a pastor, he had not studied as an imam. What he had was a far higher authority than that. What he had was the authority of a prophet.

God had picked him . . . despite his *weaknesses*; God had never judged him on that. In fact, Valérie realised, it was his weaknesses, the temptations of the flesh that goaded and teased and tempted him when his mind was still, that made him so perfectly suitable.

I am the lowest of the low. And yet, even in me, God has seen redemption.

Natasha.

Yes. God has forgiven me that moment of weakness. He really has.

He'd dreamt of her last night. Smiling beautifully, sitting at the Lord's side like a wonderful angel. And Hannah sat on the other side.

You have been forgiven, Valérie, God had told him. *They understand now that what you did was done in love.*

The girl's scream . . . that one scream he thought would bring dozens of people running inside and up the steps to his rooms — he'd smothered that scream so quickly with a cushion. And he'd prayed aloud for her soul as her small arms and legs thrashed beneath his weight, beating pitifully at his hands. He'd shed tears for her as the thrashing eased off; shed tears as he pulled the cushion away and saw her still face, lips already turning blue.

I am so sorry, he'd sobbed. *Please forgive me. I am weak.*

The mess was noisy with voices discussing the matter, shrill voices talking over each other with increasing volume.

'—after what he did?'

'—dirty bastard should go over.'

Dr Gupta cut in loudly. 'We don't know he did anything to Natasha! We found a shoe. That is all!'

She was shouted down by a wall of angry voices. Valérie raised his hands. 'Let the doctor speak!'

Tami Gupta nodded gratefully at him. She had the floor, the room was quiet. 'We found a shoe on his boat. That is all. *A shoe.* And that is all we have. And we are happy to see him dead because of just that? When you think of all he has done for us, that he has been amongst us for years and nothing like this ever happened—'

'There's always a first time!' someone shouted out.

'Yes . . . yes, but not Walter. I know it's not Walter.'

'How do we know it's not his first time anyway?' asked Alice. 'How do we know he wasn't a paedo before the crash? How do we know if he was ever convicted? Was on a sex offenders' register? Huh?'

Tami shook her head. 'We do not know. But then, we know nothing really about each other's lives before the crash, do we? Right? Only what people say about themselves.' She looked around. 'I am sure there are many more secrets in this room — things we did before the crash, things we did during the crash — that we feel shame for. That we keep to our-selves.'

She looked at Valérie. 'Even you, Mr Latoc. You could be anyone; have done anything and we do not know.'

Valérie smiled. 'And perhaps that is why this world is a new beginning. We have left our old selves behind and start with a clean slate.'

Tami nodded. 'Yes. So . . .' she looked at Alice, 'so we should only judge Walter on the person we know—'

'And we are. You've seen how he was with Hannah. He was all over her, the dirty pervert!'

Tami slapped her hand down on the table next to her. 'How dare you!' she all but screamed. 'How bloody dare you!' Her shrill voice bounced off the hard low ceiling. 'She was like his own, like his own flesh and blood. It was never like that . . . like you say!'

'But he was always in their rooms,' replied Alice, 'wasn't he? Always hanging around them, always poking his nose in.'

Heads nodded either side of her.

Tami shook her head. 'He was as good as a grandfather to her. I know you do not like him but I know he is a good man.'

'Oh, yeah!' Alice snorted sarcastically. 'Just like a scout leader, or an outreach worker. A good man until you go and find all the filth on their computer. That's how it usually—'

'Alice!' Tami snapped. She shook her head. 'You have a dirty, poisonous mind! I know why he was with the Sutherlands so much.'

'Why?'

'He is in love with Jenny.'

That silenced Alice for a moment.

'He loves her,' she continued. 'He . . . he worships her. *That* is why!'

'And that's exactly how manipulative people like him can be,' said Alice. 'Work through the mother to get to the child.'

Tami's face creased with exasperation. 'Why, Alice? Why do you hate him so much?'

'I just *know* men, Tami. You don't mix old men like Walter with young girls!'

'But he has never done *anything* like this. How can you say he did things to Hannah or Natasha!'

'Oh come on, you've seen him with Hannah. Carrying her, holding her . . . it's not right, it's not *appropriate*!'

'It is not *appropriate* to hold a child?' Tami looked incredulously at her. 'Not *appropriate* to hug a child? Where my family come from . . .' she paused a moment, 'where my family *came* from, it was natural for *all* the family, the aunties and the uncles, the cousins, everyone, to cherish the children, to show them love, to *hold* them.'

'Well that's *your* fucking country!' shouted someone from the back.

Tami lowered her eyes, infuriated. 'My country? My country!' She sighed, looking defeated. 'Yes, you're right, that's how it was in my country. But in my country, a good man like Walter would have been respected. He would be treated much better than this.'

'Oh,' Alice tutted. 'And that would probably explain a lot about your country.'

Valérie let them carry on, amused at how venomous some of them seemed to be regarding the old man. He almost felt sorry for Walter. The poor old fool's biggest crime was looking too much the part; old and ugly. Wasn't that how people liked their perverts to look? It made it so much easier to tear them to pieces.

Valérie could see his women were unanimous in wanting an example made of him. That much was obvious. They wanted a pound of flesh for Natasha Bingham. Nothing less would satisfy them. The matter of Jennifer Sutherland, though, that had yet to be addressed.

He raised a hand. It was enough to quickly halt the heated

debate. The women shushed each other until the mess was finally silent.

'I believe there is nothing more sacred than the innocence of a child. And I do believe it was Walter. What he must have done to the poor girl on that boat . . .' he shook his head. 'I cannot forgive him that.'

He could hear the muted sob of Mrs Bingham and murmurs of agreement.

'Walter will be cast out for that. And may God have mercy on his soul.' He rubbed his bandaged hand unconsciously. 'As for Jennifer, she is a person who has been through so very much. I do feel much sympathy for her. Not anger. She has lost all of her family. She lost that little girl. And she is angry at me because she believes I have stolen all of you away from her.'

'She's a fucking nut!' shouted someone.

'She had it coming, the fascist bitch!'

Valérie raised his good hand to quieten them down. 'No, she is not a . . . *nut*. And I do not think she should share the same fate as her friend. But,' he shrugged, 'I cannot trust her not to try and attack me again.'

'Kick her off!'

'She's got to go!'

He sighed. 'It may well be. I shall pray and consider. However, tomorrow the old man must be dealt with. It would be unkind to him to delay.'

Tami turned to him. 'No, you cannot do this!'

Valérie looked at her and smiled sadly. 'The judgment is not just mine. God has made His will known through our mouths, through this discussion.' He could see from the set of their faces that that was just what they needed to hear; that it would be someone else's call; blood – rightful blood – on the Lord's hands, not theirs.

'So then,' he continued. 'Let us pray.'

Chapter 68

10 years AC

O2 Arena – 'Safety Zone 4',
London

Time.

She quietly eased herself up off her mattress. It was almost completely dark inside the dome. Some light spilled up against the canvas roof from the arena; there were still floods on in there that provided just enough ambient light for her to make her way through the maze of partitioned clusters of beds.

The quietness around was filled with the steady metronome of deep breathing, the murmurs of uneasy dreams and distant echoing noises coming from the dome's centre, of young male voices and the clatter of activity.

They're still at work.

She made her way into the piazza, across the open floor and past the infirmary, a hundred yards down the curved boulevard towards the east entrance and waited for a while amidst a jam of parked-up flat-bed trolleys and wheelbarrows to check the whereabouts of tonight's guards.

There were usually three pairs of them; one pair always meant to be on the front gate, the other two pairs at different stages of walking a lap around the entire perimeter of the Zone. Adam had told her the boys were quite often guilty of shirking off. Either all six of them clustered around the gate and neglected to bother walking the perimeter at all, or only one pair would go for a perfunctory wander every now and then. Ironically, he said, it was that lack of consistency that made sneaking out that much harder; there was no knowing for sure how many would be on the gate. She sat and waited in silence for a moment, listening for the light scuff of trainers, the soft murmurs of conversation, watching for the bobbing glow of their cigarette tips.

She was travelling light; nothing more than a couple of scuffed old one-litre plastic bottles with screw caps. Water they could find as they went, but food . . . well, if they were lucky it was only going to take a few days to make their way back home.

No sign of any jackets nearby. Quietly, she slipped out of the dome through the main entrance.

She cursed the silver-blue light of an almost full moon, shining boldly down on the plantation. To her left, a hundred and fifty yards away, was the quayside and the Thames glittering beautifully. She could see the long low outline of the family-sized paddling pool over there, but no sign yet of Adam and the others waiting for her.

It's right out in the open.

Adam couldn't have picked a worse place for them to rally. There was no shade from the moonlight to hide in; anyone looking eastwards, across the plantation towards the river, was surely going to see their dark huddled forms beside the pool. Leona had been hoping there'd be clutter around it: shopping trolleys, wheelbarrows, buckets, watering cans . . . items they might have hidden amongst.

She looked towards the area of the plantation where she'd been working this afternoon; the tall rows of beans and peas, tall enough that she could hide down one of the leafy alleys. From cover there she could keep an eye on the pool and wait for the others to turn up.

She scooted low and quick across the open ground from the entrance, reaching the nearest grow troughs of kale and spinach leaves and hunkering down amongst them. These were barely three feet high and she was flat on her face to stay hidden amongst them.

She raised her head, chancing a hasty glance towards the front gate. It was almost impossible to pick anything out; there wasn't the glistening reflective backdrop like the Thames to silhouette against, instead, all she could make out was the long line of the encircling barricade and where the gate was, the low hump of the garden shed the boys sometimes played cards in.

Then she saw the faint tip of a cigarette move upwards and glow brightly for a moment. She followed the tip as it moved down again and then remained still. She thought she could hear the soft murmur of voices coming from there.

So there's at least two by the gate.

She crept along the aisles of kale and spinach, heading towards the taller aisles of peas and beans. Bent double, almost on her hands and knees, she loped a dozen yards at a time then dropped down to huddle amongst the grow troughs to check again on the whereabouts of the boys.

She wished she could have seen exactly how many were gathered at the front. She'd spotted only one cigarette glowing. That could mean anything; just one of them or all six of them over there. And if only one or two of them were on the gate, then the other four could be anywhere; patrolling the perimeter, or quite possibly hunkered down some place quiet and sheltered enjoying a discreet crap.

She made her way further along the low rows of rustling leaves until finally, with some relief, she was amongst the aisles of climbers. At last she could straighten her aching back.

Walking upright, but with careful deliberation, she made her way down the row. At the end of it she could see the Thames glittering like a tray of cheap diamonds. The far end was nearest the pool. If she waited there she'd be able to see Adam and the others coming.

She picked up her pace, walking swiftly between the narrow walls of swaying leaves. Their rippling movement was unsettling; stirred by the soft breeze rolling down the aisle, hissing and fluttering in unison, each time her peripheral vision screaming nervously that a shifting stalk was an arm reaching out to grab her.

She was too busy cursing the full moon's brightness and the state of her own jangling nerves to pick out the dark prone form stretched across in front of her and before she could stop herself she was splayed on the ground.

'Shit!' she hissed under her breath.

It was a body. For a moment she feared it was one of the boys sleeping on the job; perhaps stoned, drunk, passed out. She scrabbled away from it, expecting the confused murmur of someone waking. But there was no movement.

She stopped and gingerly crawled back until she was kneeling over the body. By the moonlight she could see a glistening black slick beneath the head.

Blood.

A moment later, a dark form emerged through the foliage, gently easing aside the bamboo supports. 'For fuck's sake, could you make any more noise?' whispered Walfield. She recognised the man's Manchester accent and the dark handlebars of his moustache.

'Did you kill the guard?' she asked.

Walfield looked down at the body and nodded. 'Stumbled on the bugger whacking off on the beans.'

That didn't seem right to her. 'You actually killed him whilst he was—'

He nodded, looking down at the body. 'That's Jay-D. Big piece of nasty shit he was. Don't shed any tears for him, love. If you knew how many women he's fucked up over the last couple of years . . . well.' He shrugged. 'It was shank the fucker or let him swing his rifle on me,' he continued matter-of-factly. 'Anyway, now we have a gun and a pouch full of clips.'

'Where are the others?'

'I dunno. We can wait for 'em here.' He sighed. 'Fuck knows why Brooksie decided the pool was the best place for us to rendezvous, it's right out in the bleedin' open.'

He gestured at her to hunker down and they waited, scanning the pale wall of the dome, almost luminous by the glare of the moon. Anyone running along the bottom of it towards the paddling pool would have stood out like shadow puppets on a cinema screen.

Five minutes passed before they finally heard the soft pad of approaching footsteps. She saw several dark shapes emerge from the gloom, coming up their aisle. They too nearly tripped over the body.

'What the—'

'Shhhh!' hissed Walfield. 'Lads – it's Danny here!'

'Shit. You do that?' asked one of them.

'Aye, nearly tripped over the little fucker having a wank.'

Either Bushey or Harry giggled.

Adam and the others joined them. 'Sorry we're late. There were four of them chilling out right outside the dome's main entrance. Buggers just wouldn't move on.'

Leona looked at the men. 'We're all here. So, let's go.'

Adam turned towards her, picking out her silhouette. 'We heard them talking about it. They're definitely headed towards your settlement.'

Bushey snorted drily. 'The stupid twats have no idea what it is, though.'

'They think they're going to some sort of bloody castle.'

'I heard one of them say *Alton Towers*, for fuck's sake.'

They were laughing, but it made sense. The jackets were children really, big children with guns, but children nonetheless. That's how Maxwell was treating them – telling them what they wanted to hear, letting them believe what they wanted to believe.

'They're planning to leave tomorrow night,' said Adam.

Her heart stuttered. 'Tomorrow night?'

'Yes.'

'Oh, God, then they'll get there first!'

'Not necessarily. If we leave now and push hard—'

'There's no time to waste,' she finished for him.

They looked at each other, quicksilver faces, eyes lost in dark shadows.

'Then let's go.'

Adam led the way up to the end of the aisle, taking them to the quayside and the river's edge. They turned right, staying close to the end of the plantation, all of them dropping down to a back-aching scooting run as the tall rows of pea and bean vines gave way to a waist-high field of tomato plants.

Finally, they arrived at the eastmost end of the barricade wall, where the patchwork sheets of corrugated iron overhung the quay and a spiral of razor wire looped over the edge and down onto a river bank of glistening silt.

Ahead of them, over the six foot high barricade, stretched a no-man's land of crumbling concrete and fading lines of paint marking out coach parking bays. Beyond that, the long dark warehouse outline of a building that had once been the Beckham Football Academy.

Adam spoke in a low murmur. 'All right. We could go over the wall here, and we're out or . . .'

'We need more guns,' said Leona.

The men looked at her.

'We need more guns,' she said again. She pointed along the wall, in the direction of the gate and the low hump of the garden shed.

Adam nodded. 'She's right.'

Harry jabbed a finger at the wall. 'Sir, we can be over this and gone in—'

'We need the guns,' replied Adam. 'And a hundred yards that way are five more we could grab.'

Walfield nodded. 'S'right.' He grinned. 'And a chance to give the little shits a farewell kicking.'

Chapter 69

10 years AC

O2 Arena – 'Safety Zone 4',
London

She stood up, emerging from between the rustling rows of leaves twenty yards away from the gate. She called out almost immediately, not wanting them to spot her and fire before she had a chance to talk.

'Hello?' Her voice carried across the stillness and she watched the five boys, standing in a circle in murmured conversation, suddenly spin on their heels. She heard the click and clatter of their guns, swung off shoulders and pointed in her direction.

'Please . . .' she said quickly, 'don't shoot. I just need to speak with you.'

There were two taller, older boys and three smaller ones. *Second Generation.* That's what Adam called the younger ones; boys more recently recruited and trained by the boys that he, Walfield and the other two had originally trained. The older two would be in charge. Leona took several slow steps forward, her hands instinctively raised. She addressed herself to the taller of them; a straggly-thin black boy wearing a bandanna on his head.

'I want to join the girlfriends,' she said. She felt a twist of nausea in her gut as she spoke.

Bandanna's posture subtly shifted, his head tilted over on one side, his shoulders squared as he puffed himself up. She recognised the body language; all the boys did it when they wanted to make a show of bravado in front of their comrades.

'You wan' join our girls?'

Leona nodded.

A torch snapped on. Instinctively she covered her face from the blinding light.

'Drop your hands, lemmesee yo' face,' said the boy with the bandanna.

She did so and heard from somewhere behind the glare of the torch one of the younger boys chuckle. 'Ahh, man, she's all beat up.'

'You ugly,' said one of the boys. 'Piss off back inside.'

The torch wavered off her face for a moment, down and up. 'Face ain't all that, love,' said Bandanna, 'but the rest looks tight. Show us your tits an' we'll see.'

'What?'

'You heard me. Show me your tits,' repeated Bandanna.

The other boys liked that, a ripple of giggles amongst them. 'Go on, make her show all the pooty,' one of the smaller boys egged him on.

Leona felt nausea inside turn quickly into a barely suppressed gag response. For a fleeting moment she thought she was going to chuck up this evening's gruel right there.

'I said show us the fucking tits!' snapped Bandanna.

She saw Dizz-ee's snarling face on his; an almost identical sneer.

Come on. Come on. They're distracted enough now, surely?

'We do like the old tell-ee-show *X Fat-ryy* on you, bitch,' said Bandanna. 'You give us all an *audition*, right? You show the pooty an' dance for us. An' I'll decide.'

A peal of excited laughter spread amongst them. The torch was off her face again and down on her chest, on her torso. She could see that Bandanna had slung his rifle on one shoulder. Although the other four were no longer pointing their guns at her, they still had them in their hands.

'Come on! You heard. Take your fuckin' clothes off!'

Bandanna took a step forward, one hand already down and

fiddling with his flies. He stopped and turned to the others. 'Forget the dance. Let's just do her. Me first, then it's Biggz' turn. Then you three can 'ave a go. 'Kay?'

The other boys nodded. She noted the other older boy — presumably Biggz — set his gun down on one of three plastic garden chairs by the gate, getting ready for his turn.

For God's sake. Come on!

Bandanna turned back to her and closed the distance between them. 'S'up? Why ain't you undressin', bitch?'

She smiled tightly. 'I'm a bit . . .' she nodded at the others. 'Not in front of everyone, please? We could go over th—'

'You wanna be a girlfriend, then you gonna do it anywhere we wan' it. Now show me some titties an' bush right now or I'll have to slap you up.'

Her hand slowly reached down for the hem of a tatty and faded purple sweatshirt that had been donated to her in the infirmary.

It was then she heard a scrape of feet on the ground and a stuttered breath drawn in surprise.

Bandanna flashed the torch over his shoulder back at the boys, just as Biggz's long legs began to slowly buckle, his eyes wide and rolling, his hands scrabbling at something sticking out of the side of his neck.

'What the f—?'

Movement. Bandanna swung the beam of his torch to the left, catching a last-moment blur — Adam Brooks and Bushey both racing towards him. They careered heavily into Bandanna, knocking him to the ground and sending the torch spinning into the air. She heard the three of them struggling and scraping on the floor. The boy let out a startled high-pitched scream that was quickly muffled as a hand clamped heavily over his mouth. She could still hear his gagged voice, screaming, and the *oooff* of exertion as either Adam or Bushey punched their knives into him.

451

She could hear the other three boys, clinking and rattling in the dark.

Loading their guns?

Someone scooped the torch off the ground and shone it in their direction.

'Drop your fucking guns!' snapped Walfield. The three younger boys, to Leona's eye, surely no more than thirteen, stared at the light, wide-eyed and startled like rabbits caught on a back road.

Huey, Dewey and Louie, she found herself thinking.

One of them shook himself out of the momentary stupor and resumed fumbling a clip out of his pouch, arrogantly certain by the determined look on his face that he could load, cock, aim and fire his assault rifle before some stupid old peasant.

Walfield didn't bother repeating his warning. The single shot cracked loudly, filling the torchlit space between them all with a billowing cloud of blue smoke. The boy slammed back against the barricade wall, rattling the wire at the top and loosing sheets of corrugate. He slid to the ground, already lifeless and bleeding out from what was left of the back of his head.

The scuffle on the floor with Bandanna was over now. Adam appeared within the loom of light from the torch, blood spattered in ribbons across his shirt.

'You boys drop your guns and webbing and go!' he snapped.

Dewey and Louie nodded vigorously, placing their guns quickly on the ground and sliding effortlessly out of the loose webbing designed for grown men. They stepped back uncertainly, their eyes glued to the gun in Walfield's hands.

'Now piss off!'

They turned and sprinted off into the dark, down a walkway between sections of the plantation towards the dome's main entrance, their feet slapping noisily in the darkness.

'We gotta go now, sir!' said Bushey. 'They'll all be coming this way!'

'The guns!' said Leona. 'And *all* the bullets. We need to gather them up.'

Adam nodded, scooping up the discarded orange jackets and several pouches of army webbing. 'Pick up everything they dropped, *everything*. We can sort through what's crap later.'

Harry appeared in the cone of light, carrying an armful of plastic bottles. 'You okay?'

She nodded. 'I'm . . . yeah, I'm okay.'

She bent down to scoop up the weapon that Bandanna had dropped. She saw the pale glow of his trainers sticking out of the darkness, and from the dancing light from the torch one of his hands palm up, fingers looped with chunky gold rings, slowly, reflexively curling open and closed as if beckoning her over.

She wondered why she felt nothing at all. Not for him, not for the other boys. She wondered if that made her as sick and empty inside as them. Impulsively, she stepped forward into the gloom and swung a leg at where she guessed his head was. She made contact, dull, cushioned and heavy.

'You bastard,' she spat through gritted teeth.

She swung another kick at him. And another.

You bastards.

She felt the bile in her throat, a stinging acid burn that threatened to bubble up and leave her retching.

'Come on, Leona,' said Harry softly, reaching for her and pulling her away from the body. 'He's dead now.'

'Right then,' Adam announced. 'That's everything. We should go.'

As if on cue a floodlight near the main entrance flickered on and she thought she saw a flurry of movement in the entrance foyer through the glass wall.

453

Adam swung the torch on her. She winced at the bright light.

'You good to go, Leona?'

'Yes,' she nodded, swinging the assault rifle onto her shoulder. 'I'm ready.'

Chapter 70

10 years AC

O2 Arena – 'Safety Zone 4', London

Maxwell watched the last of the workers being herded aboard the third barge – the end of the daisy chain; if it looked like they were running tight on fuel, or the load was simply burning too much diesel, they could easily just unhook the rearmost barge and let it drift. There were no supplies on that barge to lose, none at all; just a hundred of those malnourished scarecrows standing cheek by jowl in the hold. And if they had to cast them adrift it wouldn't be the end of the world, they'd be able to recruit more workers from amongst those people living on that rig.

Four hundred-and-something of them living on there, that's what the dead boy had said, wasn't it? Depending on how much food was being grown there – if there was only enough to sustain four hundred-and-something, then he'd have to jettison that sorry-looking lot in the third barge anyway.

Better they were all on the last barge anyway – those workers might take it into their heads to try overpowering the dozen or so praetorians he was going to put on there with them. Since the breakout the night before last of a group of them – that officer, Brooks, and his comrades – news had seemed to spread amongst the peasants that Maxwell and his boys were packing up and leaving. The scheduled work routines had broken down. This morning a worried crowd had amassed in the entrance foyer just in front of the turnstiles into the arena. Some of the workers had attempted to make their way around the outside of the dome along the narrow quayside towards the rear to see what was happening back there. His boys had fired their guns into them, leaving several dozen bodies and the rest scattering back the way they'd come.

More of the workers had managed to push their way into the arena and down to the mezzanine floor to help themselves to the last few stacks of supplies; pallets they'd not managed to find space for aboard the second barge.

Well, you're going to be disappointed, folks. There ain't a lot left.

It had been something of a hectic morning so far.

The tugboat's diesel engine chugged noisily, transmitting a thudding vibration that rattled through the small vessel's deck, through his feet. The tug bobbed on the choppy water like a stir-crazy dog on a leash as the last dozen workers shuffled across the boarding plank and down into the third barge's hold.

'That's it I think, Chief,' said Snoop.

'Thank you, Edward.'

The late-afternoon sun burned off the glass and steel sides of the distant office towers of Canary Wharf. He'd so very much wanted to get off at first light this morning without a fuss . . . without having to post cordons of guards, without having to waste valuable rounds of ammo keeping them back. And, of course, to make a day's travel whilst the weather looked so calm. But wheeling the last of the stacked pallets of food and supplies up from the mezzanine, and the comforts and gadgets and perks the boys enjoyed and expected to bring with them, had taken much, much longer than he'd anticipated.

'Your little trollops are all on?'

'Yeah, we got all our girls,' replied Snoop.

He spotted the last of his boys backing out of the north-east entrance, some personal possessions under their arms. Those that had been guarding the narrow quay around the sides doubled back swiftly, keen not to be left behind.

Snoop cocked an anxious eyebrow. 'Chief? We ready?'

'Yes. Let's not waste another bloody second.'

Snoop rapped the helm with his knuckles. 'Chief says go, Jeff.'

Jeff had once been a truck driver. Said he could handle boats, too. He'd piloted the tug up the Thames several years ago when Flight Lieutenant Brooks and his merry men had been sent to reconnoitre the river up to Kingston. He'd managed not to wrap the thing around a bridge support or end up stuck on a silt bank. Jeff seemed to know what he was doing.

'Right, here we go.' With a hand that was all knuckles, veins and fading tattoos, he eased the throttle forward.

The diesel engine dropped a note and the tug lurched subtly as the engine engaged. At first Maxwell wondered whether they'd overestimated what this small ugly vessel could pull as it seemed to make no headway at all, the weed-tufted concrete quay beside them showing no sign of receding.

The engine chugged laboriously for a moment, but slowly the tug began to move.

'Shit, thought we were stuck,' said Snoop.

With several feet of slapping water between them and the quay, Maxwell finally let slip a barely audible sigh of relief, just as several dozen of the more foolhardy workers emerged out of the rear entrance of the dome to stand on the quayside and watch them pull away. A couple of his boys fired off opportunistic shots in their direction and the emerging crowd dived to the ground amidst the weeds.

Maxwell gave Snoop a glance. 'Tell those fucking idiots not to waste their ammo.'

Snoop nodded and promptly left the cockpit.

As the tug strained and groaned and the train of one tug

and three barges slowly eased away from the quay, Maxwell smiled grimly.

Good bloody riddance.

For the last ten years of his life this drab and increasingly threadbare over-sized circus tent had been his millstone. Many was the night he'd wondered whether the smartest thing he could've done was let *everyone* in on the first night of the crash and let all of those poor bastards get on with it. If they wanted to end up like Wembley Stadium and tearing each other apart for tins of corned beef and bottles of water twelve weeks in, they could be his bloody guests. He could quite easily have delegated the nightmare to Brooks to handle, or one of the Cobra-appointed civilian safety-zone assistants and just walked out the front and gone back home to his South Bank apartment, emptied his drinks cabinet and then emptied his gun. But he'd decided to stay and do the dutiful thing, to be the one to make all the hard decisions these last ten years.

The quayside had sluggishly slipped far enough away for Jeff to spin the wheel and steer the tugboat out towards the middle of the Thames.

Good riddance to all of it.

Those poor bastards left behind probably weren't going to make it; weakened by months, years, of malnourishment, many of them already falling prey to ailments due to vitamin and protein deficiencies of one kind or another. Anybody with half a wit should have known that the acres of parking tarmac they'd managed to cultivate out at the front was little more than an exercise in window-dressing; smoke and mirrors. What they were growing was just about enough to keep half of them going a while longer — but nothing there that would keep them going through winter.

They were all going to die.

Or maybe they'd end up like those wild children; eating rats, dogs. Eating each other.

He watched the warm afternoon sunlight play across the dome and wondered what moronic government pencil-necks had thought it a bright idea to locate *any* of the zones in the middle of a city. For that matter, what moronic government pencil-necks had thought the global oil crash would be nothing more than a three-month-long economic crisis that could be more than catered for by setting up a couple of dozen over-sized soup kitchens.

So obvious now . . . Of course, armed with hindsight, he admitted that the old world had been heading towards something like that; an end-of-times event. Not just a twelve-week-fucking-crisis, but The End. He remembered an economist once calling it 'Petri dish economics' – where a bacteria feeds on a growth solution, expanding to fill its grow space and finally, upon consuming the last of the free food, it turns on itself.

Eats itself.

He looked back at the pale faces of the workers, gathering in ever larger numbers on the receding quayside, and realised all he'd achieved these last ten years was to duplicate the old world on a much smaller scale; a twenty-acre Petri dish.

The boat chugged heavily and slowly out into the middle of the Thames. Ahead, across the foredeck and the bobbing, excited heads of his boys, he could see the bend in the river, and in the distance the row of shell-like hoods of the Thames barrier.

Nathan watched London drift slowly past them. It reminded him of a riverboat tour of the Thames he and his cousins, mum and auntie had once been on. A warm day like today, ice-cream dripping onto his fist and pigeons pestering them.

From out here in the middle of the river, London really seemed to look no different to the way it had then. The buildings still stood. The tower blocks of Canary Wharf still glinted and shimmered proudly. This far away from the river's edge, all the small telltale details of dead London were lost; the weeds, the cracks, the broken windows, the overgrown lawns, the rusting cars, the cluttered streets. From where he stood on the stubby aft of the tugboat, Nathan imagined he was nine years old again as the vessel strained its way past Victoria Docks. London bustling in the distance.

He spotted the roof of the ExCel Centre beyond a row of giant freight cranes and dockside warehouses and shuddered at the memory of what had happened inside. He wondered if Leona actually did manage to escape, or whether – the thought turned his stomach – her bones had been added to that pile.

Coming to London had been a mistake. A huge mistake. But he knew they'd had to do it. Not knowing for sure, one way or the other, would have gnawed away at him and Jacob until they finally couldn't stand it any more and had to go see.

He shook his head sadly. Both he and Jake had thought the dome was nirvana. The beginning of the future; an epicentre of recovery and hope. But, despite all the lights, the arcade machines, the pounding music of party nights, he realised it wasn't a beginning, it was an end. It was denial, a last blast party with whatever could be scooped together out of the ruins.

He looked around at the other boys stretched out amongst the coils of diesel-stinking rope; all of them excited at their brand new adventure, smoking their cigarettes, stroking their guns with fingers heavy with gold.

It's like a game to them. Like a computer game. Like 'Grand Theft Auto'.

Here they were off to some place they knew absolutely nothing about other than Snoop had promised them it would have endless electricity and lots of women to play with. A new playground for them. A new party to go to. And as long as there was somebody coming along who was going to make sure there'd be booze and smokes they seemed content.

What the fuck have I done?

They were all heading to a place he'd called home. Where his mum lived. Where other people whom he'd considered extended family lived. And they were going to have a party there. Oh, yes, it was going to be a party. He could imagine any one of these boys, fired up with excitement, pissed or stoned, cornering his mum in some small cabin . . . his mum pleading.

Nathan felt something in his chest flip and turn with guilt, suddenly realised guilt.

The fuck have I done?

The cold sick feeling spread down into his stomach and started to churn there. He realised Snoop had talked him into believing this was a friendly visit; a pooling of resources, a combining of personnel. And he'd hinted, hadn't he? Hinted that the rigs would be a new kingdom, under their shared rule. Maxwell ousted and the praetorians in charge with Snoop and him as kings. These boys had been promised someplace even better than the dome . . . and they were going to have it.

'Oh, shit,' he whispered under his breath. 'Oh, shit.'

Chapter 71

10 years AC

'LeMan 49/25a' – ClarenCo Gas Rig Complex, North Sea

Valérie Latoc stood beside the railing and watched Howard and Dennis march Walter, hands bound behind his back by loops of gaffer tape, up the last flight of steps and across the helipad. They held him tightly between them – not that there was anywhere for Walter to run to if he broke free.

The wind gusted in an uneasy way this morning, rattling the protective plastic sheets so they snapped like canvas sails, stirring the field of tomato plants, sending white horses galloping across the restless sea far below.

Only about fifty members of the community were assembled up here to pay witness. The rest of them were lining the railings on the decks below.

Howard and Dennis finally came to a halt in front of Valérie. The old man between them looked surprisingly calm, given the fate awaiting him. Valérie had been hoping Walter would've started kicking and screaming on his way up here, pleading in an altogether undignified way for his mercy. Instead, he stood sullenly in front of him, eyes narrowed with bitter hatred and rage that was almost palpable.

'Walter Eddings, you understand why you are up here, yes?' asked Valérie loudly, his voice carrying across to the witnesses gathered on the helipad.

Walter's lips quivered slightly but he said nothing.

'It was decided collectively by these people – people who know you far better than me, people who trusted you – that you should be put to death for what you did to Natasha Bingham.'

'You know I did nothing,' Walter replied, struggling to keep his voice even. 'I didn't touch her.'

'She *was* on your boat, Walter. Do not try and lie about that. What things you did to her, how she died, I am afraid we will never know. Perhaps it is better that way—'

'I never fucking well touched her!'

'You are also being punished for what I suspect you may have done to the other girl, Hannah.'

Walter shook his head. 'I know it was you! I know that was you, you dirty bastard!'

'Walter . . .' Valérie said, reaching a hand out and placing it amicably on his shoulder. 'Why are you lying now? It is too late to change things, really. At least if you were to admit it now, and ask God for His forgiveness you could leave the world unburdened.' He smiled. 'You see, God really does love *everyone*. Even you. If you open your heart to him, this will not be the end for you. But the beginning of a period of redemption.'

Walter lurched forward and spat at Valérie, but the gusting wind carried his spittle away.

'You're a fucking lying pervert! You're a fucking sick bastard!' the old man screamed at him. 'I never touched either of them!' He twisted round to shout over his shoulder at the women gathered on the helipad behind him. 'Do you see what he's doing!! DO YOU SEE!!'

'Shut up!' shouted someone in the crowd.

'Why?' Walter's voice broke. 'Why me? Why don't you believe me? I'd never hurt Hannah. I'd never h-hurt anyone!'

'Shut up, shut up!!' screamed Mrs Bingham. 'JUST DIE!!' Her voice trailed away into a wash of burbling tears as Alice folded a protective arm around her. 'Why don't you just go, Walter.'

Walter's temper flared. 'You fucking bitch! After all I've

463

fucking done for you lot!! Why? Why??? Why are you doing this to me?'

That's better.

Valérie had hoped he'd crumble. Make a scene. Plead. Accuse. Snarl. Every word he spat at them only made him sound more guilty.

'Don't you see? Doesn't anyone see? It's him! HIM!! Latoc! I'd never hurt our girls! I didn't hurt Hannah!! I *loved* her for God's sake!!'

Yes, every single word damning him further.

'She was like my *own*. Like my own daughter!!'

Valérie gently squeezed his shoulder. 'Walter.'

The old man turned back to him. There was spittle on his cheeks, caught in his beard, his eyes wide and his face was mottled and crimson with fear. He couldn't have done a better job of looking like the right man to face the charge.

Thou protesteth much too much, sir.

'Walter,' said Valérie softly, just for his ears. 'I could spare you, you know? But these people feel betrayed by you. They are angry and hurt. Why not admit now what you did? Perhaps I could use that to help you. Show them that you understand what you have done is wrong. Perhaps then I could persuade them to settle for you just being evicted? Yes?'

Walter shook his head. He even managed to sneer. 'What? So you can be in the clear? Fuck you!'

Valérie let go of his shoulder. 'Then I am so sorry. I really cannot help you, if you will not help yourself.'

'Jenny knows,' he hissed breathlessly back at him. He turned to shout over his shoulder again. 'Jenny knows I never did anything!! That's all that fucking matters to me! That she knows!! Ask her!'

'Let us pray for this man's soul!' called out Valérie, dipping his head.

'Jenny knows I'm innocent!' Walter screamed, his voice ragged and breathless. 'SHE KNOWS!!'

'Lord, hear our prayer. This man has sinned against his family and his friends. He has taken the lives of two innocent young girls in moments of madness and selfishness. There can be no—'

'I DIDN'T DO IT!! IT'S *HIM*!!'

'—room aboard our ark for one who would take a young life for his own needs—'

'HE KILLED NATASHA! HE KILLED HANNAH! I'M NOT A PERVERT!!'

'—we hope, in this final moment, that he can understand the hurt he has caused to those beautiful children, to their mothers, to all of us. May God have mercy on his soul.'

Valérie dropped his hands and looked up. He nodded to the two men and they proceeded to wrestle Walter towards a narrow gap in the railing at the edge of the helipad.

'Dennis . . . Howard!!' gasped Walter turning to him. 'For fuck's sake! Please . . . don't do this!!'

'You brought this on yourself, mate,' grunted Dennis.

Walter writhed and twisted in their grip as they shunted him through the gap until he teetered on the very edge of the platform, nothing between his overhanging toes and the sea but one hundred and eighty feet of blustering air.

'PLEEEASSE!!'

Both men locked their free arms around the railing to brace themselves against Walter's weight, teetering and swaying over the edge. They both looked at Valérie, awaiting his nod for them to release their grip on Walter's upper arms.

'It's HIM . . . NOT ME . . . it's HIM!!'

Then, all of sudden, his desperate twisting and struggling was too much for Dennis to maintain a grip, the left arm pulled free and Walter swung around with Howard still struggling to keep a hold onto the right arm. Their eyes met over Walter's shoulder.

'Oh, God, no . . . !' he whimpered. 'Please . . . please . . .'

Howard grimly pressed his lips together. 'I'm really sorry, Walt,' he whispered. He let go and Walter pitched forward. He tumbled, spinning end over end, his hands bound behind his back, white-knuckled and clenched as if in prayer, his legs scissoring in a futile attempt to right himself. Nearly six seconds of descent, then he disappeared into the roiling suds that spilled between the platform's legs.

The Journey Home

Chapter 72

10 years AC

M11,
London

It was approaching twilight when they decided to stop. Leona hadn't worn a watch in years, but if she was going to hazard a guess at the time, then she would have said it was after eight in the evening.

Last night they'd hurried away from the Zone along the Blackwall Tunnel, expecting a hunting party of Maxwell's praetorians to be in hot pursuit. But no one had followed. Halfway along the tunnel, at its lowest dip, they'd had to wade through a puddle of stagnant water almost chest high. The result of ten years of rain and the accumulation of Thames water leaking through crumbling and neglected fissures in the structure.

An hour later they'd emerged into moonlight again on the far side, north of the Thames. They decided to hole up for the night on the first floor of an office block, sleeping fitfully between quiet cubicles and dust-covered desk tops.

Today's going had been slow. Leona had hoped they'd be out into the countryside by the end of the day, but instead they were still trudging along the M11 approaching the junction bisecting the M25. Beyond that was 'outside' London, according to Harry. But it was still very far from being outside the foreboding urban landscape looming down on either side of them.

'There they are again,' said Adam quietly.

Leona turned and looked over her shoulder.

A hundred yards down the motorway she could see them; about a dozen people, pale and ragged, old and young alike.

'There's a few more of them now,' she replied.

Adam nodded.

It had been about midday that she'd first spotted someone, as they picked their way along a high street. A curious face peering out of the dark gloom of a window above the empty shell of a shop.

Scavengers, Adam had said. No better than those wild children. He said they saw them here and there, but never in large numbers; pitiful, lonely figures managing somehow to continue to find scraps in the city.

'Never seen that many at once. They seem to be getting a little less nervous,' he said.

They were closer, and no longer darting to hide every time one of them turned round to check where they were.

'Why do you think they're following us?' asked Bushey.

'They see your uniforms.' She nodded at the faded and patched khakis Adam and the other men were wearing. 'Maybe they think you're, like, representatives of the government or something.'

They see hope.

'They want us to help them,' she said.

Walfield shrugged. 'We can't.'

'Not saying we should,' replied Leona. 'But that's *why* they're following us.'

It was an hour later that Leona and the others finally stopped. It was a beautiful moment that stopped them; in a way a reassuring thing, that life goes on quite happily without mankind's help. Just as the last pale stain of day was being chased by long shadows across the motorway, they watched in stunned silence as a small herd of deer ambled across the four lanes of the motorway passing within feet of them, their dark eyes expressing only a casual curiosity and not fear as they trotted by.

Here were several generations that had never known roads filled with *moving* vehicles, roads that could kill them. Or people that could shoot them.

Leona stretched a hand towards the nearest of the animals, a large doe bringing up the rear. She felt its hot breath coming in gentle puffs as it paused to sniff her outstretched fingers curiously.

'Hello,' she said softly.

It snorted wetly then broke into a trot to catch up with the others as they began to weave their way through a logjam of vehicles and down an off ramp leading into a cluster of low office blocks.

Adam shouldered his gun without a word of warning and fired a solitary round. An old stag, one of the largest animals in the group, dropped heavily to the ground with a clattering of its horns against the boot of a rusting Renault estate. The rest of the herd scattered, their pale rears bobbing like ghosts amidst the gathering gloom.

'Meat,' said Adam. 'Jesus, I haven't eaten fresh meat in . . .' he looked slowly round at them, a widening smile spreading beneath his beard. 'Shit, I can't even remember.'

'Come on, lads,' said Walfield to the other two men, 'let's get something for a fire.'

Leona nodded, glad at least that he'd not shot the doe that had sniffed at her hand.

'But they all seemed so young.' Leona chewed on the hot gristle in her greasy hands. 'I mean, those three smaller boys at the gate, they must have been eleven . . . twelve?'

Walfield shrugged and tossed another slat of fence wood onto the fire, sending a shower of sparks up into the sky. The deer's skinned and cleaned carcass hung from an improvised spit, dripping fat into the fire as it cooked; one hind leg already pared to the bone in places where cuts of meat had been removed.

'The younger the better,' he replied after a while.

Adam nodded, finishing a mouthful. 'Child warriors. They're often the most fearless. Certainly the most ruthless.' He swigged warm water from one of their plastic bottles. 'Maxwell was no fool. He set up his boys' army as "auxiliary staff", initially to help out the emergency workers. That's how it was for a couple of years until he staged that coup and had them turn our own guns on us and kick out the rest of the lads in our platoon.'

He picked meat from his teeth. 'There's a long history of dictators using child soldiers as a psychological weapon on their own people.'

'East Africa,' added Walfield. 'Somalia, Ethiopia, Eritrea . . . I remember reading about some warlord who ruled over something like a quarter of a million people with just a couple of hundred boys with guns. It was their totally *psychotic* reputation that did it. Kept all them people in line.'

'Boy soldiers,' added Adam, 'because they haven't lived long enough to understand right from wrong, to "grow" a morality. Older soldiers – men – have lived long enough to have wives, girlfriends, younger sisters, younger brothers, perhaps even sons or daughters of their own. It makes them pause for thought. At the moment of committing an act of atrocity, it gives them a reason to hesitate. And that moment . . . that second of hesitation can mean the difference between killing an innocent civilian or not.'

He sighed. 'If you want your people to be totally immobilised by absolute fear, you need a militia that can kill and r—' He was going to say 'rape', but casting a quick glance at Leona, he decided not to. There was no knowing what she'd been through in the arena. He could guess; beaten repeatedly for sure . . . and most probably worse. So far, she'd shown no sign of wanting to talk about it.

'You need a militia that can do the really *bad stuff*. Do it without batting an eyelid. Enjoy it, even. A powerful force of mind, that is.'

Bushey looked up at him. 'What is?'

'The arrogance of youth. You can do wonders with that kind of energy, that kind of self-belief. You can put the world to rights . . . or create dangerous little monsters.'

Leona shuffled uncomfortably on her rump. 'Not all kids are bad.'

'No,' Adam smiled at her. 'Not all bad.'

'Jacob wasn't bad,' said Leona. 'Didn't have a bad bone in his body.'

Adam said nothing. He didn't know anything at all about her brother. He'd only seen the lad from afar being given the red-carpet treatment by Maxwell; one blond-haired teenager, one black teenager, neither looking wild or malnourished.

'Nathan wasn't bad either,' she added. 'Do you think he's with those praetorians now?'

Adam shrugged. 'I suppose. Do you think he's actually going to lead Maxwell to your home?'

She wiped her hands on a tuft of dry grass stalks beside her. She stared into the flames for a long while, the still night filled with the crackling of fire and greasy fingers being sucked. She wasn't sure what a young man like Nathan would do in that situation. He'd always been a good friend to Jacob. He'd always been good with the younger children. But if he was with them, then he was with *very* different people at this moment in time. She really couldn't imagine what was going through his mind right now.

But there was one thing she was sure of. 'He loves his mum,' she replied eventually, as if that completely answered the question.

It was then they all heard the skittering of a small stone kicked carelessly across the motorway. It was somewhere out in the darkness beyond the flickering light cast by their fire. Adam snapped the torch on and panned it down the tarmac.

Caught in the glare, one hand held up beseechingly, a lean face crumpled as it winced at the intense beam. It was one of the people . . . the scavengers.

'P-please . . .'

A man of about forty or fifty. Dark grey tangled curls framed a creased and gaunt face.

'Fuckin' hungry,' his voice croaked.

He was wearing what looked like a threadbare police uniform; a fraying sleeve well on the way to dropping off its seam at the shoulder.

'Poor bastard,' she whispered.

Walfield racked his gun and shouldered it in one swift motion.

'NO!' shouted Leona. She raised her hand at him. 'No! Stop it! Can't you see? He's just hungry! That's all!'

The man was cowering on the road, his hands and arms cradling his head. She could hear his breathing, fluttering with fear. But he wasn't running.

'He just wants a little food,' she said. She turned back to face Walfield, Adam and the others. The smell of meat being barbecued had to be an almost unbearable smell for them.

'We could give them some,' she said.

The men stared at her. She could see they weren't sure it was such a good idea.

'We can carve off enough to do us for tonight, and let them . . .' she gestured out into the darkness to where she imagined the rest of those people were eagerly waiting to see what was going to happen, 'let them have the rest of it. After all, we've got guns and I'm sure there's no shortage of deer or rabbits between here and home.'

Harry nodded earnestly. 'She's got a point.'

'Let's show them a small kindness,' she said, annoyed at

the emotion in her voice. 'I don't suppose they've seen any of that in a long time.'

Adam turned to Walfield. 'All right. Danny, lower your gun, mate.'

He got up and produced a long kitchen knife that he'd liberated from a kitchen supplies store earlier. 'Hold this,' he said, passing the torch to Bushey. Then he started to hack at the large browning carcass on the spit. Fat dripped and spat on to the fire as he cut at one of the rear legs and eventually pulled it free. Then he worked on the other, tugging it loose a moment later with the sound of cartilage snapping.

Held by the hooves he carried a haunch of still sizzling meat in each hand and stepped out into the gloom towards the man.

The man's eyes remained on the food.

'There you go, mate. This is for you and the others out there,' he said, placing it on the road in front of him. Only when he'd backed up a few steps did the man come forward.

'Thanks,' he uttered quickly before reaching for each hoof and dragging the haunches off into the gloom, leaving a glistening trail of grease on the road.

They returned to their own meal and ate in sombre silence, listening to the faint sounds further down the motorway; murmuring and cries, the occasional sound of garbled half-words exchanged between them.

'We better try and get some sleep,' said Adam.

'You're kidding, right?' said Bushey. 'With them wild people out there?'

'I think they're harmless. All the same, we probably ought to take turns keeping an eye open.'

Adam sorted them into three watches. Leona and Walfield took the first watch, keeping the fire ticking over and listening to the noises the people were making. A couple of hours later, when Bushey and Harry relieved them, there was nothing to be heard but somebody moving far off down the slip road and amongst the dark streets of Chigwell. It could have been the children, it could have been dogs, it could have been that small herd of deer.

Chapter 73

10 years AC

Southend-On-Sea, Essex

Maxwell watched his boys messing around on the dodgems. They'd teamed up into groups of three; one in each car and two to push. Howls of delight and good-natured banter filled the deserted seaside fairground as they bounced heavily off each other.

Southend-on-Sea was the first obvious stop. They were more or less out of the Thames Estuary. Looking east along the coastline past Canvey Island was the North Sea. The tugboat had chugged and juddered slowly as it hugged the estuary shoreline. They'd travelled about forty miles today which was further than he thought they'd make. But it had made a significant dent in the boat's supply of diesel, according to Jeff.

Tomorrow, if they were lucky enough to have the sea as flat as they'd had today, the pilot assured him there was enough fuel to get them as far as Felixstowe where there was a large container port. With a bit of luck they'd be able to locate some more fuel, perhaps even stay a day or two and forage through all those containers and warehouses for anything that might be useful.

Felixstowe being a big container port was going to be a very useful stop. Southend, on the other hand, had nothing . . . except apparently endless unpowered fairground rides. The shops and cafés had been comprehensively picked clean over the years. A number of the once fine buildings along the seafront Marine Parade had caught fire; the blackened carcasses sandwiched between amusement arcades and banks of those 'claw' vending machines that still held hundreds of sun-bleached soft toys prisoner. And along the kerbside several brown husks that had once been recreational trucks sat rusting on stubs of melted tyre rubber and blackened wire. No doubt set aflame the same night as the buildings when the town's chavs came out onto the street to celebrate the lights going out and the promise of unpoliced fun and games.

'Sir? Mr Maxwell?'

He turned away from the boy-powered dodgems to see Nathan standing a couple of yards away.

'What is it?'

The lad looked uncomfortable.

'What's the matter, Nathan?'

'You . . . you said we was just going to *visit* them.'

'Your old home, yes, that's right. To pay them a visit.'

'But . . . but you've brought *everything* with you.'

Maxwell sighed and then smiled. There was no point bullshitting him. 'Yes, Nathan, you're right. It's not just a visit.'

The lad shook his head. 'Then what—?'

'We had to move, Nathan. This has been on the cards for months and months.' Maxwell waved the boy over to join him leaning against the rail. He did so and they both turned to watch the dodgems being pushed around by the guffawing boys.

'As Edward's second in command, I guess I should bring you into my confidence.' Maxwell lowered his voice ever so slightly. He was quiet for a moment, thinking how to proceed.

'Nathan, we couldn't have lasted another winter in the Zone. There just wasn't enough food being grown and we were supplementing every meal with a rapidly vanishing supply of tinned stuff. Just too many of us there. So that's

478

why we're on the move. I had to split us up. Those we left behind will have a better chance of surviving on what they can grow without having our mouths to feed as well.' Maxwell nudged his arm. 'But *you* were the deciding factor.'

'Me?'

'You and that poor lad, Jacob. When you told me there was someplace else that was like ours; organised, properly sorted and managing to get by. That was what finally decided me to get a move on.'

'So . . . so are you goin' to *join* them? Because, see, I don't think there's . . .' Nathan faltered and hesitated.

'Go on, Nathan,' said Maxwell. 'You can speak your mind.'

'Well, I don't think there'll be room on the rigs for us.'

He smiled. 'We're just going to talk, that's all, Nathan. Talk to the lady in charge.'

'Jenny Sutherland.'

'Yes. See if we can trade any supplies, any skills. See if she knows of any good locations nearby for us to set up a new home.' Maxwell turned to look back at the boys under the canopy. 'We need to be close together, do you see? If we really are all there is left of Great Britain; if I'm the last government representative left in authority and it's just our two communities that made it this far, then we've got to work together to make sure neither group fails. We have to co-operate.'

Nathan pursed his lips. 'But some of the boys are saying . . .'

'Saying what?'

'Well . . . that . . . they think we're going to live on a place that has lots of electricity and stuff. An' I . . . well I just wondered—'

'Whether they were referring to the rigs?'

Nathan nodded.

'Silly buggers. That's just their Chinese whispers. I'll be

honest with you, Nathan, because I think I can trust you. I'm inclined to let them carry on believing something like that for now. They have no idea where we're headed. Just you, Edward and me, we're the only ones that know. Truth is, when we resettle, hopefully someplace not too far from your old home, those lads will have to start getting used to a new lifestyle. Farming for themselves.'

'I don't think they'll be happy about that.'

'Well, you're right. But they'll have to get used to the idea anyway. But, for now, I'm happy to let them think whatever the hell they want. Once we've got together with your people . . . once the boys can see for themselves how well your lot are doing, they'll settle down.' Maxwell shrugged. 'I might even offer the services of myself and the boys to your Jenny Sutherland. Let her be in charge, eh?' He winked. 'I could do with a bloody rest.'

Maxwell could see that Nathan was encouraged by that. He'd obviously just wanted to be reassured this wasn't intended to be a raiding party. He'd needed to hear a few words from him that sounded genuine, sounded like *common sense*.

'Look, Nathan, these boys tell each other all sorts of silly stories. But then that's young boys for you.'

'I guess.'

'That's why I've got you and Edward to help me keep them in line. You're both older, more mature. The boys look up to both of you. To be honest, I think some of them hero-worship Edward. And I suspect, in time, they'll do the same to you, as well.'

Nathan shrugged, shuffling his feet. 'Oh, not sure 'bout that.'

'Sure they will. Edward says they gather round you like bees to honey. Says you make them laugh till they piss their pants.' He smiled. 'That's good. I need lieutenants like you, Nathan. Leaders the boys like.'

Nathan looked at his feet, uncomfortable with the praise. He wanted to pursue his concern a little further. 'So . . . we're . . . you're sure this isn't, like, some sort of invasion?'

'Christ!' Maxwell looked bemused. 'You really thought that? That I'm some sort of . . . of evil pirate? A Blackbeard. A Captain Hook?'

Sheepishly, Nathan nodded.

Maxwell dropped his head and laughed. 'Oh, to be so interesting!' He chuckled. 'All I am, all I've ever bloody been, is a mid-level administrator. A long time ago, long before the crash I was a history teacher. Not a particularly good one if I'm honest. Then I became a senior executive officer at the Department of Education. I'm a bloody civil servant. Nothing more, nothing less.'

He sighed. 'The only reason I ended up in charge of Safety Zone Four was because my name was on a Cobra emergency volunteer list. And you know the only reason I entered my details on that volunteer database? It would look good on my CV!'

He shook his head, grinning tiredly. 'I wasn't even meant to be in charge. The chap who was on the list to take charge was on holiday in the Dominican Republic when the crash happened. They couldn't get hold of him, I was next on the list.'

He looked at Nathan. 'So I'm not really the slash 'n' burn bandit leader type. Just a dull old pen pusher in charge of a hundred unruly boys.'

'Sorry, Chief, I just thought . . . I heard what the boys was saying and . . .'

'Think about it, Nathan, would I have brought you along if that's what I intended to do, hmm? You'd be a liability. I'd have to keep an eye on you. Wouldn't I?'

Nathan shrugged and nodded. 'S'pose so.'

'I can't believe that's what you were thinking, lad.' He offered him a warm smile. 'I'll let you off this time.'

His gaze fell back on the boys; all so gullible, so pliable. All of them had been so young when he'd 'recruited' them from amongst his zone intake. Just bewildered little boys ranging from eight to twelve years in age. Schooling – that's what he'd told everyone: they needed some sort of schooling if they weren't going to end up being illiterate scavengers like the feral children picking scraps out of the ruins.

Perhaps that might have been the original reason he'd started up those classes. But it was those armed RAF troops and Met police officers, particularly the Met officers, that he found himself worrying about. Too much talk from them about putting the Zone under police jurisdiction.

His lessons became subtle treatises on power and command, military geniuses, emperors and caesars – the sort of history all boys love. Soon the boys were given orange vests and assigned auxiliary civic tasks to teach them responsibility. No one objected to that, they were becoming a nuisance with nothing to do each and every day. A year after he started the schooling, Maxwell had suggested the boys be billeted in the central part of the dome where they'd be better placed for schooling and being given increasingly more important tasks.

It wasn't so long after that Maxwell learned that the Met officers were considering taking matters into their own hands. They had to go, and the RAF grunts they'd decided to involve along with them.

His boys, now his guards, his army, were infinitely more manageable than Brooks's men and the police officers – there was no need to explain things to them, to have to reason with his boys, they just did as they were told.

But, like performing seals, only so long as they're tossed a tasty fish.

The boys on the dodgems stopped their game and a shuffling of roles ensued, some of them fighting each other to get in behind the wheel. Maxwell watched them as the game finally resumed. So many of those boys, once so small and anxious away from their parents' sides, were now tall enough that they towered over his stocky frame.

Once upon a time they listened avidly in class, hanging onto every word as he described the battles of ancient Rome, the insane excesses of Emperor Caligula, the brutal wars and punishments of medieval times, the burning of witches, the impaling of heretics. Now, Maxwell suspected, they listened only because he provided them with the things they craved . . . and not, as he sometimes tried telling himself, out of some residual loyalty to a much-respected teacher.

It was getting dark now, getting hard to pick out the fun and games going on beneath the canopy of the dodgems' tent.

Maxwell gestured at the improvised game. 'Be a lot more fun, I imagine, if we could switch the bloody thing on, eh?'

Nathan grinned. 'Yeah.'

They watched in silence for a while.

'You know, one day we'll fix this country up again, just like it used to be. That's always been my goal, you know? Between your Jenny Sutherland and me, we'll get things sorted out.'

Nathan replied with a wary nod. 'That would be good.'

'Trust me, lad. The future, that's what I'm thinking about. Everyone's future. A better one. We're all going to work together on this.' Maxwell turned to look up at the evening sky. 'Anyway, I'd better get a move on and sort out arrangements for tonight.'

'We're sleeping-over here?'

'Overnight, yes. We'll be up early tomorrow if the sea's good. I want to make Felixstowe by the evening. Nathan?'

'Yes, Chief.'

'Will you organise the onshore guard roster for tonight? I know the place looks deserted, but you never know, do you?'

Nathan smiled. 'Sure, no problem.'

Maxwell could see he liked the idea of taking on the responsibility; being in charge.

Make him feel a part of things. Make him feel trusted.

'I'll leave the details to you. Just so long as the end of the pier is secure.'

'What about Snoop?'

'Oh, I think I'll let Edward have a well-deserved night off. I imagine he'll have a little fun with the girls.'

'Okay.'

'Good lad.' He slapped the boy's shoulder affectionately. Nathan nodded then turned away. Maxwell watched him weave his way through the funfair towards the pier. It stretched almost quarter of a mile out to sea; a long windswept and desolate ribbon of planking on rusting supports, lined with weather-worn arcades. At the far end, the tug-boat and barges were moored. The lad seemed reassured by their brief talk. He hoped so. He was relying on Nathan Williams to talk them onto the rigs; to have them drop their guard just long enough to get a few of his boys up there.

That's all it was going to take . . . a few of these psychotic little bastards.

Beneath the dodgems' low canopy the boys hooted with laughter as a couple of them upended one of the cars and turfed the driver inside out onto the rubber floor. He looked barely more than eleven or twelve. He railed angrily at them, pulling a knife out and flashing it around to the amusement of the others, who had been goading him on.

'Hey!' snapped Maxwell. 'Don't be bloody stupid!'

The young boy paused a moment, before nodding mutely. He tucked the blade back into his trousers as the other boys, still snickering, righted his car. They resumed their game, the incident already forgotten.

Chapter 74

10 years AC

MII,
London

By the steel grey of dawn's light they could see the number of people had grown.

'That looks like a hundred of 'em easy,' said Bushey.

'More,' said Walfield.

They remained fifty yards down the motorway watching them silently, warily. A wall of multicoloured faces, all lean, all smudged and dirty. All watching them with frozen expressions of hope and hunger.

'It's the smell,' said Adam. 'The smell of cooked meat that's drawing them.'

The first dozen, Leona suspected, had been following them all the way from east London, but the newcomers, however, must have been survivors scratching a living amongst the streets either side of this road. She wondered how far the smell had travelled, how far word had travelled.

My God. So many of them.

She wondered whether a far greater number of people had managed to keep going than anyone suspected. A hundred people or so from the immediate area. She wondered how many others like these, across Greater London, were still alive in their dark homes, living like rats.

'We should make a move,' said Harry. 'Sir?'

Adam didn't seem to hear that. 'So many of them,' he uttered. 'Jesus. Apart from the wild children, we thought the city was just dogs, rats and pigeons.'

'What's kept them alive?' asked Bushey.

'Dogs, rats and pigeons, at a guess.'

Leona studied the silent crowd; old and young, all of them far thinner than Adam and his men; by comparison they looked like they'd been gorging themselves.

'You from the guv'ment?' a voice from the crowd echoed up the roadway, breaking the silence.

The men looked at each other.

'We *can't* take them with us,' uttered Walfield. There were nods of agreement from the other men.

Leona finally decided to answer. 'Yes, we're from the government!'

Adam turned to look at her. 'What? Why the hell you tell them that?'

'If all that's left is your Chief, Maxwell, and my mum, then I reckon that makes *one* of them the closest thing we have to "the government", right?'

Adam and the others exchanged a glance.

'And I know I'd rather it was my mum,' she added.

'When is help comin'?' the same voice in the crowd asked.

Adam cocked an eyebrow. 'Well? It looks like you're the spokesperson now.'

Leona turned back to the crowd. Her first instinct was to tell them what they probably already knew. That there was no help coming from anywhere. But in that wall of malnourished bodies she saw the faintest glimmer of hope; more than just a feral existence. She saw braided hair on one or two, she saw mended and patched clothes, she saw a baby cradled in a woman's arms, she saw an improvised wheel cart. Not people who had given up, gone wild or gone mad, but people who were struggling on, hanging in there . . . just about.

It was all too easy, too convenient, to write them off with a simple label: *scavengers*. They looked threadbare and grimy. Painfully thin, yes, and some had that lost haunted expression that Mum would be looking out for. But there were people along that cracked and weed-tufted road who were still a part of the old world; older people who could remember how to fit a gas boiler, drive a truck, wire a house, fix an engine. People who Mum could use, people who could add rusty but invaluable skills to their community.

Was it possible that in other cities in the UK, perhaps the rest of the world, there were people like this subsisting? Somehow finding a way to keep going just on what they could grow, hunt and forage for? Could so many have survived?

My God.

She realised they'd spent long enough out at sea on those rusting platforms. The large raiding parties, the roving groups of hungry-eyed young men with guns were gone now. They were history; died out like the dinosaurs. Except for Maxwell and his boys. And if that's *all* they had to worry about, if they could beat those little bastards, then it seemed there was no one left that they needed to hide away from on the rigs.

If these pitiful beings could still be alive, then there really was hope. A better chance for them to be living on land; with soil, and easier access to fresh water, than on their artificial archipelago. She realised the time had finally come for them to live ashore once more.

'When is help comin?' asked the voice again. 'Are you guv'ment help?'

She stepped forward. 'No, I'm sorry, we're not help.' She looked back at the others before continuing. 'But there's a new start. A new government. It's in East Anglia. The northeast coast. We're doing fine there.'

'Can we come?'

Adam whistled softly to get Leona's attention. She turned back to him.

'Leona, we can't take them with us. Not now.'

'I know,' she whispered, then turned back to face the crowd.

'Listen to me! In one year's time,' she replied loudly so

that they'd all hear her clearly, 'in a year's time, we'll be ready for you. You'll be allowed in. It's a place called Bracton. Look for it on an A to Z. We're there.'

'Shit!' hissed Walfield. 'You're gonna be swamped!'

'A year!' she repeated, ignoring him. 'No sooner, you cannot come with us now. You have to stay here, and do what you've been doing to keep alive. But when you come, you'll find we have a doctor, we have an engineer, we have farmers, we have experts. We have rules, there's order and you'll be safe. We even know how to make electricity.'

She saw eyes widen amongst the crowd.

'But you have to give us time to get ready for all of you. One year! No sooner or you'll be sent away!'

She turned back to her companions and realised her legs were trembling. And yet her voice was steady and strong, steady enough that she felt she could even give these men something that sounded like a marching order. 'Right, let's get going.'

Adam's dark beard revealed the slender line of a smile as he nodded supportively. 'You heard her, lads. Let's go.'

They grabbed their guns and the webbing, and the remaining cuts of venison, and slowly backed away from the crowd, weaving through the logjam of vehicles and out onto clear road on the far side. As they made their way along the motorway she resisted the insistent urge to keep looking over her shoulder.

'Are they following?' she muttered to Adam walking beside her.

'Nope. Doing just as you ordered by the look of it.' He looked sideways at her. 'Ms Prime Minister.'

She laughed softly. The first time she'd felt capable of doing something as simple as that in quite some time. 'Oh no, not me. That's my mum. *She's* the really bossy one.'

Adam made a face. 'Really?'

*

They spent the rest of the day making their way north along the motorway, a journey she was familiar with in reverse. By the time the last of the hot and sticky day had deserted them they were just south of Cambridge. They found a campsite a mile off the motorway; rows of static caravans in a field, with a fishing lake at the bottom of it. There was nothing to eat, the camp shop had been picked clean of anything edible. They refilled their water bottles with green algae-tinted water, selected several caravans close together, and went to sleep.

The next day they found a storeroom behind the camp shop in which several dozen hire bicycles were chained up. They worked on the padlocks with a hacksaw. All of them needed their tyres pumping, and a couple needed an inner tube replacing. But by midday they were off the motorway, and coasting along the A-road heading north towards Thetford. On foot it would have taken them ten days or more. On bicycles, another two or three days at most.

Mid-afternoon she suddenly stopped pedalling and applied her squeaky brakes.

'What's up?' asked Adam.

She swung her leg over the bar and laid the bike down on the road. 'Yes! It's right there,' she said to no one in particular. 'I wasn't sure if I was going to spot it.'

'Spot what?'

'Raymond's enviro-dome!'

Walfield sat back in his saddle, wiping droplets of sweat from his forehead with the back of a hairy forearm. He looked at Adam. 'Raymond's dome?'

Adam shrugged. 'No idea what she's talking about.'

'Someone we came across on the way down,' she replied. 'He lives down that track. I'm going to go in and say hello. He might let us stay tonight. But I should ask first.'

Adam looked where she'd pointed. 'Track?'

She stepped across the road into tall grass and then rooted

489

around in some bushes until she found the hidden trellis. She pulled it aside. 'This track.'

He climbed off his bike and laid it down, joining her in the long grass and looking down at the twin muddy ruts leading into the dark forest. He slung the rifle off his shoulder.

'No,' she said. 'It's probably best if I go up there alone. He knows me. If he sees you and the gun he'll panic and shoot. I'll be all right, he knows my face. And it's just down there. Not far.'

He held out the SA80. 'At least take the gun.'

She shrugged and took it from him. 'A few minutes and I'll be back.'

She stepped into the opening and out of the sunlight, down the track which was almost as dark as a man-made tunnel. The branches above her were busy with the endless conversation of birds and the gentle hiss of shifting leaves.

She wondered how Helen was faring here. If this really was everything she'd wanted or whether she was now pining to come home. The girl could be so fickle.

Leona caught a glimpse of pale perspex reflecting bright sunlight in the glade ahead. A moment later she emerged into the clearing, the dome before her. To the right were several small turbines spinning excitedly in the breeze with a *whup, whup, whup*.

Raymond's truck was parked in front.

They're in.

She knocked heavily on one of the dome's perspex panels and called out their names. Neither answered. Gingerly she pushed her head through the plastic slats and immediately felt the warm, humid tropical air envelope her face. All seemed well; the palm trees either side of the walkway, the exotic chirruping of insects and birds, the seductive sound of pumped water trickling down through waxen leaves.

Still a going concern, then.

'Hello?' she called out again. Her voice was caught by the

dome and bounced around. 'Helen? Raymond? Anyone home?'

There was no reply.

Feeling like an unwelcome trespasser she made her way along the walkway until she reached the cluster of cabins. And she smiled. There were signs of Helen's feminine touch dotted around; flowers in pots, her clothes on a washing line alongside his, music CDs splayed untidily in a way that she imagined Raymond would find annoying. A thousand other little signs that all was well, and that if anyone needed rescuing, it was probably Raymond, from Helen.

'Raymond? Helen? Anyone home?'

No answer. They might be in the woods, foraging for chestnuts, mushrooms, berries. Raymond had said Thetford Forest was a larder of free food if you knew what to look for.

She studied the cabins, all with their doors open, apart from the one Raymond used to sleep in. She stepped lightly across the wooden decking and rapped her knuckles gently against the door.

'Guys? It's Leona.'

Still no answer.

She really didn't want to walk in on something she'd rather not see. So she knocked again, waited another few seconds, then slowly opened the door. It was dark inside the cabin. The diffused light that filtered down through the opaque plastic roof was blocked by a drape drawn across the cabin's window.

'Hello?' she said softly.

She could hear music playing and saw the pale square glow of Raymond's iPod in a docking station beside the cabin's double bed. And there they were, huddled together, like lifelong sweethearts, like two spoons in a cutlery drawer.

'Oh no,' she whispered.

Both quite clearly dead, mottled with purple blotches

491

where stilled blood had settled under the skin. Dead for a few days, a week maybe.

She stepped a little closer and saw that they'd gone peacefully; their eyes closed as if they were napping, Raymond's arm draped protectively over Helen's narrow shoulders.

'Oh why, guys?' she muttered. 'Why?'

On a chest beside the bed she saw half a dozen pill bottles, opened and emptied, and a folded sheet of paper pulled from a pad and scribbled on. She saw her name scrawled on the corner.

Leona
this is wot we both wanted. raymond and me. he's been very kind to me. i can't really explane why we decided to do it like this. but just in case u came back, i just wanted u to know we both wanted this. raymond told me you were planning to do the same. if u reading this, then i'm glad u didn't do it.
love helen xxxx
ps. i hope jacob and nathan found their lights in london.

Leona emerged into the sunlight five minutes later and carefully replaced the trellis barrier behind her so that the entrance was once more all but invisible.

'Well?' asked Adam. 'Did you find your friend?'

'No one's home,' she replied, handing the gun back to Adam. She picked up her bike and nodded down the long straight road, flanked on either side by the evergreens of Thetford Forest. 'Another couple of hours will get us to Norwich. Then tomorrow, I guess, if we start early we'll be in Bracton before it's too late.'

She led the way.

Chapter 75

10 years AC

'LeMan 49/25a' – ClarenCo Gas Rig Complex, North Sea

Martha gathered his dirty laundry. Valérie hadn't asked her to do that; she did it because it was a pleasure to do something for him. Because she felt closer to him than any of the others. She connected with him in a way she was sure no one else did; the others merely followed him but she actually cared for him — brought him meals and water. To do this as well . . . to take what few clothes he had to the ladies up on the top deck doing laundry duty and see that they were properly soaked and scrubbed, it was a small gesture really. After all, his time was stretched so thin now between the prayer meetings and giving instruction to the newcomers, explaining his message. He had precious little time for such banal things as seeing to his own comforts.

Just like Jenny used to be, she mused, always hurrying from one task to the next, worn down with the endless attrition of having to attend to a million different things.

She felt a soft stab of guilt for her friend.

Why didn't I see that coming? That nervous breakdown? That's what it was, wasn't it? A breakdown?

Jenny had just walked into their prayer meeting like that and fired a gun at him, point blank. Like some kind of automaton, no expression on her face at all. No anger. Just the empty, set, expression of someone who knows exactly what's coming next. It wasn't the scarring that made her look so unlike the Jenny she knew, it was those dead eyes. She thought she knew Jenny; never would have thought in a million years that she could do something like that out of spite because . . . what? Because they'd decided to vote someone else as the leader?

Crazy.

That wasn't like Jenny. Not like her at all.

How many times had she heard Jenny moan about being the boss? How many times had she half-seriously suggested walking away from the responsibility and letting someone else have a go at doing better? The carping from every quarter, the bitching, the complaining, trying to keep everyone happy? It wore her out. She never imagined Jenny would do what she did because . . . simply because she got *voted out*?

A breakdown, that's what it was, she decided. The accumulation of stress, the grief from losing Hannah, endless worry about her kids — and God knows, Martha knew what that felt like. There wasn't a morning she didn't wake up with a prayer on her lips for Nathan's safe homecoming or didn't send herself to sleep at night muttering the very same prayer.

Martha scooped up Latoc's shirt from the tangle of blankets, quilts and cushions on the floor of his quarters.

Jenny, though . . . Martha had always thought Jenny was stronger than that. Stronger than anyone else. Indestructible. Not the type to just *snap* like that.

I thought I knew her.

Four and a half years she and Nathan had been living here. Joined them, in fact, not long after they'd set up on the rigs. She and her boy, and about a dozen others, had been amongst the first to cross her path; making their way north along an abandoned road from London, clattering along on the back of a horse-drawn cart, and there she'd been standing in the middle of the road, almost as if she'd been waiting all the time for them. As if she'd known they were coming.

Why not join us? We've found somewhere completely safe.

She owed her so much.

494

Martha bent down again to scoop up more of Valérie's things. The dark blue khaki trousers he seemed to wear all of the time – all pockets. Some shorts he wore as underwear, thick woollen socks carelessly balled and inside-out on his bed. It was no different, she decided somewhat nostalgically, to going around Nathan's messy old bedroom, back in the good old days; untangling his scuzzy smalls from the game controller cables stretched across his unmade bed. Maybe that's why she enjoyed doing this. It felt like she was back then . . . back in another time.

Something fell out of the swaddle of clothes she was holding under her arm onto Valérie's bedding. She looked down at it.

A loop of hair; a thick tress of curly blonde hair, curled and tied up with a faded pink ribbon. She reached down and picked it up, spreading the soft loop of hair between her thumb and forefinger.

Oh . . . my . . .

She could have told anyone who that hair belonged to, even without looking at the ribbon. She'd run a brush through it often enough, trimmed it, plaited it, pulled it into cornrows, pulled it back into a ponytail Lord knows how many times.

Hannah's.

Seeing it there, nestling amongst Valérie Latoc's bedding, caught her by surprise; it stole a breath from her mouth. The lock of hair had dropped out of his blue trousers. Out of his one-of-many pockets.

A question arrived unannounced, unsolicited and very much unwelcomed.

Why was that in his pocket, Martha?

She looked at the bundle of clothes under her arm. And before she realised she was doing it, she had placed them down and was pulling his blue trousers from the pile.

That's the one. It came out of those. Now, why was it in his pocket?

For a moment she held them at arm's length; tatty blue army-style trousers, patched and mended several times. The kind of thing men do – pick a favourite item of clothing and hang onto it for dear life, nursing worn holes and unthreading seams, unable to toss them away. She held it at arm's length not because they smelled of stale body odour – they did, an accumulation of a week – but because . . .

Because, God help me . . . please no . . . because I might find something else.

Something that had no reason to be there.

Her hand drifted slowly towards a hip pocket lumpy with something inside.

What are you doing?

She answered that aloud, and dishonestly. 'I'm jus' emp-tyin' the pockets is all. Can't wash them with full pockets, right?' she muttered. How many times had she had to do that with Nathan's school trousers? Finding endless screwed-up balls of paper; 'pass-it-around' notes on exercise book paper, dog-eared Yu-Gi-Oh cards, shredding tissues stiff with dried snot.

Her fingers unbuttoned the pocket flap and curled inside. She realised her hand was trembling as she did so. A hand wanting to find nothing more than a sweaty old bandanna or a handkerchief.

She looked down at the lock of Hannah's hair on the bed and realised with an unsettling lurch in her chest that they'd condemned and killed a man on finding something less. They'd killed Walter because of a solitary gym shoe on his boat. Because they were so absolutely certain what finding that on his boat meant. Because there were those who'd been absolutely certain Walter was guilty even before they'd bothered to look for anything.

Then her fingers touched something soft inside. Material. Cotton. She felt her heart flutter and flip in her chest. She closed her eyes as she pulled it out, praying it was just a forgotten strip of bandage or a spare sock; praying it was only that one lock of blonde hair that she needed to find a way to explain away in her mind; to conjure up an acceptable reason for it being there.

She opened her eyes and stared at the small garment that dangled from her fingers.

'Oh, dear God, no,' she whispered.

A pair of sky-blue child's underpants with a constellation of five dark spots of dried blood on the white elasticated waistband.

Oh, God . . . no. Not him.

Chapter 76

10 years AC

Felixstowe,
Suffolk

Maxwell watched them dancing on the wharf; an impromptu party that had started only an hour or so after they'd tied up at Felixstowe and begun exploring the maze of stacked freight containers. Many of them had remained unopened all these years, their thick corrugated doors had obviously resisted earlier attempts by people to break in; scratches and gouges where levers and wedges had been banged into the gap between hatch and frame. A decade's worth of corrosion later, their hinges gave far more easily.

Each one they prised open proved to be an Aladdin's cave of treasures. Some of the boys had found a red Lamborghini in one and wheeled it out onto the wharf where they'd been pushing and shoving each other to take turns to sit in the front seat and pretend to drive the thing. The impromptu party, however, had begun shortly after some of them had stumbled upon a container filled with stacked pallets of alcopops and bottles of spirits.

A fire now shimmered in the afternoon light as the boys took turns in tossing on the bone-dry slats of broken pallets, throwing on bottles of brandy and vodka, delighting in the explosion of glass and rolling mini-mushroom clouds of blue alcohol-fuelled flames.

'S'getting out of 'and, Chief,' muttered Jeff.

Maxwell looked at his pilot, sitting beside him on the foredeck of the tugboat. Even from here they could feel the wavering heat of the boys' growing bonfire. 'Relax. They're just letting off some steam.'

Maxwell had smiled beneficently when a group of boys had emerged from the maze of containers to present Edward, Nathan and him with some of the bright orange and yellow coloured bottles of Froot-ka they'd discovered. The boys had already started opening and chugging away at them.

So he'd smiled and told them, since they'd all been such good boys, they bloody well deserved a party. The girlfriends had already been pulled out of their cots from the bowels of the second barge and plied with copious amounts of alcohol and were now, as he watched from afar, busy servicing clusters of boys. It had the look of a Roman orgy; a last-night bender before the end of the world. In fact, it very much had the look of the first few nights of the big crash. Maxwell wondered what would happen if he tried to flex his authority this second, right now – step ashore and announce that the party was over and it was time for them all to go to bed.

He felt the hair on his forearms stir and prickle.

They'd refuse, wouldn't they? One of the older boys certainly would.

It would be an open challenge to his authority; a dangerously open challenge. He realised the answer to that question was that he daren't step ashore. It wasn't a sudden realisation, more a gradual clarification, a truth he'd half suspected for a while that was now, finally, sliding into sharper focus for him. He didn't truly control these boys, not really. Sure, they were happy to follow orders, follow the schedules and routines that he'd assigned them over the years, happy to cheer his habitual party night opening speech, call him 'Chief' and knuckle a salute as he passed them by. But that was because he was the Chief, the guy at the top who made sure every one of them got their perks.

Another recurring, wake-up-sweating nightmare was that

one day he was going to publicly give an order to one of the boys and the boy would turn round and tell him to fuck off.

That's how slim your control is, Alan. You're just one 'fuck off' away from a mutiny; from being lynched by these little thugs.

What kept the boys knuckling their foreheads and nodding politely as he passed was a residual deference to him as their school teacher, as the official authority figure put in charge of Safety Zone 4. But more importantly, he was the man who made the lights happen, the arcade machines go on, who opened the sweetie-box and handed out grog and dope on party nights. He was the man promising them even more of that; promising them enough power that every night they could play on the games consoles they'd brought along, watch the library of action movie DVDs they had tucked away.

I'm in charge because I'm the chap who says 'yes you can'.

He shuddered at the thought of what would happen when he finally had to start telling the boys they couldn't have a party. If they'd stayed on at the dome, that day would have eventually come. And not too far off, that day, either.

With these rigs at least there was the leverage of limitless oil or gas, whatever their generator was tapping for fuel. DVDs, games and girlfriends would keep them busy, keep them happy for the foreseeable. And this container port looked like a useful place to come back to for more booze and fags later on, should he need to sweeten his leadership.

'You okay, Chief?' asked Jeff.

Maxwell forced a smile. It felt uncomfortable and ill-fitting and fled quickly. 'Fine.'

'We heading off again tomorrow?'

'I think we'll give it a day before we move on,' he replied, 'see what other supplies we can forage here first.'

Getting the boys to mobilise tomorrow morning, with their

heads pounding, was going to be difficult. At least back at the Zone the grog was under lock and key. He put some of it out for them once a week, and once it was gone, it was gone. Tomorrow morning, whilst the boys were all nursing their heads, he'd get what was left of that Froot-ka stored down below on the tugboat. After all, if they were going to have to fight their way on, the boys would be all the better fired up for a scrap with a little alcopop buzz inside them.

He picked Edward out of the milling crowd, his dark face shimmering on the far side of the vodka- and wood-fuelled fire; holding court, relaxed and reclining like a lord on a chaise longue of car tyres covered with fake-fur coats. Beside him, Jay-zee, now proudly wearing the 'second dog' jacket inherited from Dizz-ee; the jacket the other boy – Jacob – would have worn alongside Nathan.

He sensed, with a creeping disquiet, that the balance of power was one day going to swing Edward's way. The young man didn't need to bribe the boys with perks or parties. They followed his say-so because he was one of them, because he was like the big brother. He looked right, he sounded right. He acted right. The top dog.

That bastard's going to turn on me soon.

Snoop watched the boys queuing up to take their turns with the girls, shuffling forward with their trousers already undone and round their ankles. Most of the girls – mercifully for them – were so drunk they were barely conscious.

He watched the boys dancing around the fire like wraiths, playing with burning sticks and daring each other to leap over the flames as they waned. Snoop had tried a bottle of the sugary drink and curled his lip in disgust. In any case, he wasn't in the mood to get totally smashed. Not like these morons in front of him.

When they got this off their heads, this stupid and infantile, the boys truly embarrassed him. When they got too rough with the girls, he felt ashamed of them. Watching them now, he wondered what the real difference between them and those feral children was. They looked just as wild and out of control.

That's his trick, though, right? Keep 'em happy. Keep 'em bribed. Move from one stash of contraband to the next. Stay one step ahead of his boys. Above all, keep 'em grinning like idiots.

Snoop shook his head with irritation as two of them started to spray mouthfuls of whisky onto the fire and yipped with glee at the billowing clouds of flame.

'HEY!!' he shouted. The stupid fuckers were going to set themselves on fire. 'Stop that shit!'

They stopped and contented themselves with waving smouldering slats of wood in the gathering darkness and making smoke trails.

This was the Chief's plan, wasn't it? This is the long game. This. Just this. Keep them happy. He wondered if Maxwell had actually bothered to think any further ahead than taking possession of these rigs. Because *he* had.

How long does this shit last? Because at some point the hidden treasures that can still be foraged out of a stack of freight containers had to run out, right? It all runs out eventually; the bottles of alcopops, the cartons of cigarettes, the cans of corned beef and baked beans.

Just like the oil once ran out.

Then what?

He wondered if any of the other boys had bothered to think about that. He wondered if Jay-zee sitting beside him, whooping and clapping his hands as he watched the boys getting their ends away, had ever given that a moment's thought.

He wondered what Maxwell was going to do once they were on those rigs and running things. Was this going to be their home? A going concern? Or some place to simply strip clean and move on from?

That's the future then? Pick clean and move on? That's all we gonna be?

Just like locusts.

Chapter 77

10 years AC

Bracton,
Norfolk

Bracton looked unchanged to Leona yet seemed subtly different. As they cycled in silence through the old town, through the modern high street with its fading chain-store signs, towards the docks and gas terminal, she found herself appraising it anew. It contrasted with the choked urban space of London. Here there were overgrown front gardens, parks and greens gone wild, any and all of which could be cultivated far more easily than the cracked concrete spaces in the capital.

Oddly, it no longer seemed the forbidding and desolate shell she remembered; a place from which dangerous and desperate armed men might emerge at any moment. It was just an empty town, largely in fair condition, certainly repairable and habitable if they chose to settle ashore here.

Perhaps it was the sunny weather. Perhaps the warm breeze that stirred the birch trees along the high street and down Runcorn Way towards the docks. Perhaps the reassuring continuity of life: the rabbits, foxes and deer that impassively watched them pass instead of scattering at the sound of their bicycle tyres through drifts of dry leaves. It could've been any of those things that led her to believe there was a viable future here.

That was the *only* purpose left in her life now, she decided. To convince Mum once and for all that the days of hiding were over; that the time had come to move the community off the rigs and back onto the mainland. Just one single, bloody-minded goal that she was going to hang on to. To start over.

But that was okay with her. It kept the heartache in a box. It kept it manageable.

Their bikes rolled across the railway sidings between warehouses and parked forklift trucks onto the skittering gravel and crumbling concrete towards the quay. Finally, a dozen yards short of the water's edge, with a squeak of brakes, she came to a stop and the others followed suit.

'So there's the North Sea, then,' said Bushey, stating the obvious after a few reflective moments. 'Any idea how we get to your gas rigs?'

'Over there.' She pointed to a tugboat tied up on a canal lock alongside the large brick gable wall of an old brewery. Tied up there as it always was after Walter had returned it from a water run. 'We'll use that.'

'We'll need to scavenge some marine diesel,' said Adam. 'Is there any—'

'Walter normally leaves it topped up,' she said looking at the others. 'Always. He's very reliable. A creature of habit.'

Adam shielded his eyes from the sun as he stared out across the sea. 'And how far out is it?'

Leona shrugged. 'Take us a morning if we were sailing,' she said in answer. 'Over an hour in the tug though.'

Adam looked back at them. 'That would be about fifteen miles out?'

She nodded. 'About that.'

'On a clear day you can actually see the top of the rig's com tower from here,' she added. They all turned to look, squinting for a minute, but it was too hazy a day to pick out anything discernible on the flat horizon.

'You think we beat those others to it?' Harry asked.

Leona's gaze drifted along the perfectly flat sea line. It looked like Maxwell's boats had had the perfect weather to make it up here – an atypically glass-smooth North Sea. They could only hope something had gone wrong or delayed them.

'Yeah,' she said, 'I'm sure we've beaten them.'

'They may not even have left yet,' said Bushey.

Leona nodded thoughtfully. They could hope that. Who knows?

'You know which way to head, right?' asked Walfield.

'Of course,' she smiled. 'Straight out, north-eastish. On flat water like that we'll see something soon enough. I've done the trip enough times.'

Walfield laughed. 'Looks like you have.'

Adam looked at the tugboat. 'Do you know how to pilot one of those things? Because I sure as hell don't. Lads?'

Bushey and Harry shook their heads.

'Never been on one,' added Harry. 'I hate boats.'

'Can't be any harder to drive than a supply truck,' said Walfield. 'I'll have a go.'

Leona looked at the men. 'So, what are we waiting for?'

They made their way across the dockside towards the vessel, crossed over a small footbridge to the far side of the small lock in which the tugboat bobbed gently, and along the narrow walkway at the bottom of the brewery's red brick wall, finally hopping aboard the vessel.

Walfield let himself into the boat's cockpit and examined the small bank of toggle switches beside the helm.

Adam tapped Leona's arm as she looked on. 'You sure your mother is going to welcome us aboard? I mean . . . otherwise, we really are sort of left out on a limb.'

She studied him for a moment in silence as Walfield clacked switches and the others clambered aboard. Behind his dark beard, behind skin drawn economically tight against bone and muscle, she saw something of an intelligent young man. She saw eyes that didn't dart hungrily where they weren't invited, but instead met hers on the level. She thought she detected someone whose thoughts weren't on what could be *taken*, but what could be *made*.

She imagined Mum would see those things in him, too.

'You helped me. You've got me home safely.' Leona's

bittersweet smile ached as, for a moment, she'd give anything to be able to have Jacob standing here beside her. How she wished Mum was getting *both* her children back.

'She'll be grateful to you, Adam. Trust me. It'll all be hugs and kisses.'

He laughed. 'She sounds nice.'

She grimaced. 'Ugh, don't ever call her that. She hates that word. *Nice* is what you call ice cream, or a paper doily, or fluffy bunny rabbit print pattern. Mum's . . . well, she's a pretty tough case.'

For a moment, for the first time in ages, she spared a thought for how Mum was. She remembered, through the cloud of grief she'd been floating in, that Tami had assured her Mum would recover. She was healthy, fit. A tough case all right.

But how long ago had that been? She realised she'd completely lost track of the date, of what month they were in in fact. The trees were turning, the leaves falling. Autumn was just a spit away. Three months? Four, since they'd left?

Would she have recovered?

She'll pull through. Tough as nails. That's what Tami had said.

Tough as nails now. But not always so. Leona still remembered a different mum; more rounded with fewer angles. Comforting curves rather than sinews and muscle. A decade ago the hardest thing she'd had to do was argue the toss with the taxman once a year over the details of Dad's accounts. Or nag Jacob to get a wriggle on and do his bloody holiday homework. Since then, since the crash, she'd earned every single day of their lives; fighting for herself and her children. The first five years she was mother to her and Jacob. The last five years she'd been a mum to several hundred people. If that didn't make a person harder . . .

'She's . . . well,' Leona cocked her head, 'she's pretty *forthright*. But you'll see that soon enough.'

He laughed softly. 'If she's like you she sounds like someone I wouldn't want to get on the wrong side of.'

The tug's starter motor whined unhappily before the diesel engine caught, coughed and nearly choked before it settled into a rhythmic chug. Walfield grinned, pleased with himself as he held the helm tightly in both hands. 'Piece of piss.'

'So then, let's go home,' said Leona.

10 years AC

'LeMan 49/25a' – ClarenCo Gas Rig Complex, North Sea

Half an hour out from shore they picked out the platforms on the horizon; like a row of five fat ladies with thick shapeless legs, skirts held up and wading through ankle-deep water for cockles. Walfield opened the throttle and the engine rose a note. They carved across the flat sea, leaving a tail of tumbling suds behind them and Leona's spirits rose as she began to pick out more and more detail on their approach. Best news of all, she couldn't see any barges anchored nearby or tethered beneath any of the platforms.

We got here first.

'Jesus. Much larger than I imagined,' called out Adam.

Twenty-five minutes later the men were getting a much better idea of how large the platforms were, towering above them as Walfield eased back on the throttle and aimed the tugboat towards the base of the tallest platform amongst the cluster.

'It's like a bleedin' *jungle* up there,' said Walfield gazing up at the dangling terraces of foliage.

Leona detected movement along the decks; the ever-shifting green of endless leaves, lining every deck and walkway; the multicoloured fluttering of clothes strung out on laundry lines, and the movement of curious people emerging to gather along the safety rails.

She waved up at them, trying to see if she could recognise individual faces yet.

Walfield threw the tug into reverse to take the last of the

momentum off the vessel, and the deck beneath their feet shuddered. Leona shaded her eyes, looking up at the closest faces on the spider deck.

'It's us!!' she called out. 'It's me! Leona! Where's Mum?'

Several voices called back, over each other, lost against the idling chug of the engine.

'Mum?! You up there!!?'

A male voice called down. 'Who is that?'

Leona didn't recognise it at first. Then she remembered the newcomer, the foreign man. It seemed like a lifetime ago that she'd been teasing Mum about fancying him.

'It's Leona!' she replied. 'I also have some friends with me!'

She heard a chorus of voices stirring above her.

'Somebody go get her, will you!' she called out. No one was going to lower anything to them until Mum said it was okay to do so.

'How many friends?' It was that foreign guy again. She remembered his name now. Valérie.

She shrugged an answer. 'Four of them. Can you go get my mum, please?'

She saw him now, leaning over the cellar deck railing. 'Four men?'

Why is he *speaking for them?*

She wondered what was taking Mum so long. She wondered why Walter wasn't already manning the davits, being a nosy bugger and calling out twenty questions to them as he lowered the crane hooks.

Something's not right.

'Where's Mum? Where's Walter?'

Adam emerged from the cockpit and stood beside her on the foredeck.

'Everything okay here?'

Valérie Latoc's voice came down to them. 'Your mother is not in charge now! Things have changed!'

510

She looked along the crowd on the spider deck. She saw familiar faces. Deborah Hardy, her two toddlers, Ronnie, Moira and Audrey — white-haired old sisters — Saleena Chudasama, her children, Alice Harton, Denise Bingham. A deck up she recognised Tami Gupta, Howard, the Yun sisters, Keisha, Desirae and Kara and some of the other Bible-bashers. She saw Edward waving and grinning, David beside him. She saw Hamarra, Rebecca, the Barker sisters . . .

Familiar faces, but all somehow a little different. She'd expected smiles; teeth everywhere and waving hands. But instead the lined-up faces watched events impassively.

'What's going on? Why the hell isn't Mum in charge?'

Latoc's hesitation told her something. 'I have replaced her! The people here wanted this! It is for the best!'

'What?!'

'You should go!' called out Alice. 'It's not your mum's place any more!'

'Where's my mum? I want to speak to her!'

'Your crazy mum went and threw a bloody hissy-fit!' snapped Alice. 'She shot Valérie!'

Leona steadied herself on the foredeck as the tugboat bobbed gently. 'What? She wouldn't do that! Where is she?'

'She is in our prison!' replied Latoc. 'We have decided she cannot stay here any more! She is going to be evicted! She can leave with you!'

This is crazy. When she'd left Mum was in the infirmary dosed up to the gills on painkillers and antibiotics. Walter was ostensibly running things, maybe not a popular choice, but as her right-hand man, the obvious choice.

The newcomer, Valérie, is in charge? How the hell did that happen?

Leona turned to look at Adam. 'Something's gone wrong.'

She turned back to face the others along the railings. 'This is my mum's place, for fuck's sake! She took you all in! You can't just kick her off!!'

'This is now a place of God! A place of worship!' said Latoc. 'I asked her to join with us, to pray with us. Instead she took a gun and shot me,' he continued. He waved his bound hand over the side. 'Do you see? I cannot allow her to stay here any more.'

'This is *my* home, as well!' cried Leona. 'You can't stop me coming aboard!'

'Yes we can!' shouted Alice. 'You pissed off looking for something much better, didn't you? Well tough shit! It's the *faithful* only allowed on here. Do you understand!'

'Alice!' snapped Valérie, hushing her. 'I am sorry,' he continued. 'I cannot let you and your friends with their guns come onto our ark.'

Ark?

'This is a holy place now, Leona! These people have been waiting for me!'

Adam turned to look at Leona. 'That guy's a headcase,' he muttered.

She nodded.

Without warning, something landed with a heavy thud on the foredeck behind her. She spun round to see the bottom end of a rope ladder snarled in a pile of coiled rope and wooden slats. She looked up to see that it had flopped down from the main deck. At the top of it was Martha.

'NO!! This isn't no holy place!!' Her shrill voice cut across the space above them. She looked down at Leona. 'You come up, Leona, love!'

Valérie Latoc's eyes widened. 'Get that rope up now!' Several people, not too far along the main deck from where Martha stood, stepped towards her.

'Oh-my-God-grabbit!' hissed Leona.

Adam leapt across the deck and got a hand on the rope ladder before it could be yanked up beyond reach. Meanwhile, Martha had turned to fend off the people approaching her. 'You stay back!!' she screamed, slapping the face of the nearest woman with the palm of her hand. The others stepped forward and wrestled with her. The scuffle quickly became an undignified tangle of flaying hands; an almost comical bitch fight between her ample form and three others, hair-pulling and face slapping.

Adam turned to Walfield. 'Danny! A warning shot, please.'

The sergeant shouldered his SA80 and cracked a single shot into the air. The effect was instantaneous; everyone dropped back from the railings and out of sight. Except Martha and the others still slapping, scratching and screaming at each other.

Adam pulled himself up the first few slats of the rope ladder. It swung precariously over the side of the tugboat's foredeck with his weight, leaving him swinging above the water.

'Just cover me till I get my leg onto something!!'' he bellowed as he swung. Working quickly he pulled himself arm over arm, up the next dozen wooden slats until he was banging his hip against the side of the spider deck's safety railing. Several pairs of hands snatched at his khaki shirt trying to pull him off the rope ladder. Walfield fired another single shot that whistled close to them and zinged off the underbelly of the deck above. The hands disappeared back out of sight.

Adam swung against the railing again, this time letting go of the rope and grabbing at the rusty metal, hoping it wasn't so corroded that it was going to snap loose and bend out of shape and come tumbling down into the sea with him. He swung himself over the railing with the clumsiness of a man too exhausted to care how he landed. The spider deck rang with the impact. A moment later he appeared on his feet again, pulling the gun down from his shoulder.

'All right, everyone get the fuck back!' he screamed. '*Please!*' he added as an afterthought.

The nearest of them melted away from him, wide-eyed at

513

the sight of the levelled gun. A deck above them they could hear Valérie Latoc screaming an order for someone – *anyone* – to go and retrieve the community's weapons from Walter's trusty locker room.

Chapter 79

10 years AC

'LeMan 49/25a' – ClarenCo Gas Rig Complex, North Sea

'She's in here?' Leona asked incredulously. 'They shoved her in here?'

Martha nodded tearfully as they made their way down the dark, unlit and narrow passageway towards the battery storage rooms. They were on the same deck as the generator room and connected sludgery. Even though neither had been in use for several months, the stink was everywhere still; ingrained in the very walls of this place now. It was over-powering to Adam, a step or two behind Martha and Leona, and he fought an urge to gag.

'How could you?' she demanded, looking at Martha then turning round and glaring at Tami. 'Mum? Your friend, right?'

Martha sobbed as she led them to the door. She had no answer and instead she shook her head, ashamed, unable even to look Leona in the eye.

'He had a hold over them,' Dr Gupta uttered. 'He . . . we . . . there was nothing I could do . . .' Her voice broke and faded to nothing as she began to cry as well.

Martha slid the bolt and opened the door to reveal, in the gloom, Jenny perched on the cold hard floor, a bowl of cold uneaten broth at her feet. A toilet bucket in the corner. Leona's first reaction was a shudder of familiarity.

My God.

Leona pushed in past Martha. 'Mum? Mum, it's me.'

There was a faint spear of light coming in through a tiny

cracked window, clogged with bird feathers, at the top of the wall. Not much light, but enough that Leona could see her eyes remained locked on the scuffed and peeling wall opposite. Leona knelt down beside her.

'Mum?'

At her daughter's touch her trance broke and she turned to look at her, a momentary look of confusion on her scarred face.

'Mum? It's me!'

'Leona?'

'Yes!'

'I thought . . . it was. Like your father . . . just a dream . . .' Then the hazy look of bewilderment was gone, replaced as her eyebrows suddenly arched and her face crumbled. She wrapped her arms tightly around Leona and began to sob uncontrollably into her shoulder.

'It's okay, Mum, I'm back. I'm back.' She said *I* not *We*. Right now wasn't the time to tell her about Jacob. Not now. If Mum asked she decided some white lie would do for the moment. Jenny sobbed a stream of tear-soaked words into her neck, none of which Leona could untangle or make much sense of. She recognised Walter's name in there somewhere, however.

Adam stepped past Martha into the store room. 'Leona, we should make sure we find that fella. You know? Before he decides to rally his fan club and give us any more grief.'

He's right.

Leona loosened her mother's arms and pulled back slightly. 'Mum, we just need to go and straighten things out, all right? Then I'll be back and we'll talk.'

'Lee, don't go again . . . please . . .' she whispered.

'I'm not leaving you, Mum. I promise. I'm home now.'

She got up slowly, easing her mum's lean arms from her, and started to follow Brooks out of the room.

She stopped and turned to Tami. 'Dr Gupta?' Formal – she

didn't feel like indulging in first names with either of them right now. 'See to her, will you? Clean her up. Take her back to her quarters?'

'Of course, Leona. Of course.'

Outside in the passage, Adam turned to her. 'That was your mum?'

She knew what he was asking by the tone in his voice. *That's the tough woman you warned me about?*

'Yeah, that's my mum.' She wanted to add, *you're not exactly catching her at her best.* But she decided not to.

Adam seemed to understand. 'So, let's go find that fucking bastard, shall we?'

She nodded. 'Let's.'

Leona looked at the far end of the walkway: the primary compression platform, a crowd of people on the main deck just beyond the walkway's wire cage.

Not such a big crowd of fans now, though, is it?

Whilst she'd been looking up from the tugboat at the safety rails lined with once-familiar faces, Leona had assumed the *whole* community was in thrall to Mr Latoc. However, as soon as they'd managed to scale that rope ladder, as soon as his loyal followers had digested the sight of four soldiers bearing firearms . . . and Leona, looking like she was ready to cut herself a scalp or two, his support had quickly begun to fall away.

Funny, that.

And now they were staring down the walkway at his more loyal acolytes, those who had run back across onto 'Valérie's platform'. Her lips pressed out a hard smile. Little more than fifteen minutes ago that manipulative bastard had considered all five platforms to be his own personal fiefdom. It was now him and fifty or sixty of his followers over there and, having checked Walter's gun locker, there was a solitary gun somewhere amongst them.

517

She caught the glint of gun-metal, and saw it was Howard who was holding it shakily. Aiming it down the walkway at her. Right behind him, her head poking over his rounded shoulder, was Alice Harton.

'You fucking well stay back!' she screamed at them. 'Or he'll shoot you!'

Despite the warning, Leona stepped forward onto the walkway and into the wire cage. 'Where is that bastard?'

Alice angrily jabbed a finger over Howard's shoulder. 'You stay right there!'

Leona advanced calmly, unarmed, fortified not so much by any notion of courage as an unshakeable desire to wrap her hands around the bitch's throat. She'd never been a big fan of Alice Harton. Certainly much less so now.

'Where is he, Alice?'

The woman said nothing.

Leona felt the walkway grille under her feet vibrate and turned to see Martha joining her.

'Lee,' she said, her strong voice catching with emotion. 'I . . . I was as guilty as them. I listened to him. I believed in him. I . . . I'm so, so sorry, love. I was one of the *first* to turn against your mum. He told us God sent him to us. He told us we was *chosen*.'

'More fool you, then,' replied Leona coolly.

Martha nodded. 'Yes . . . yes, he did fool us.' She stepped closer until she was standing shoulder to shoulder with Leona, looking down the remaining fifty feet of walkway.

'He lied to us!' she shouted towards Alice and Howard and the others. 'Valérie lied to us!'

Alice was about to shout something back, but Leona saw Howard hush her.

'Valérie is a bad man. He did the . . . he was the one who killed Natasha! It *wasn't* Walter!'

There was a ripple of response amongst those at the end of the walkway, dark 'o's appearing on their faces.

'And . . .' Martha hesitated a moment, unsure whether to continue. She glanced at Leona's set face. 'And I think he was the one who killed Hannah!'

'It was an accident.' Leona turned to her. 'Wasn't it?'

Martha shook her head. 'We don't know for sure, love,' she replied quietly. 'But I found things in his pockets, things he kept.'

'What *things*?'

Alice Harton had heard enough. 'Martha! You bitch! You fucking traitor!'

Martha turned back towards the others. 'I found things, Alice! I found things amongst Valérie's clothes! Things that belonged to the girls!'

There was another ripple of consternation. Howard's gun dipped slightly.

'Yeah? Oh . . . just now? That's bloody convenient!' replied Alice.

'No.' Martha shook her head, ashamed. 'No, it was days ago!'

'You never said anything. You're a liar!'

'I was afraid!' replied Martha. Her voice wobbled. 'I was afraid! I didn't want to believe it was him . . . and not Walter! I didn't want—'

'What things did you find?' called out Howard.

Martha's voice quavered and broke. 'Hannah's hair!' she sobbed. 'Natasha's pants!'

Leona saw Howard's eyes widen, his bushy white eyebrows locked angrily. 'Her underwear?'

Martha nodded. 'He kept them . . . like a trophy.'

Howard stared at her in silence, the gun trembling, slowly lowering.

'And there was blood on them!' she continued, her words broken up by sobs and her breath hitching. 'He hurt her, he killed her! And then he blamed Walter!'

'You can't believe her!' snapped Alice. 'It's not true! She's making this up!'

'Fuck this!' shouted Howard. He turned round, pushed past Alice, and disappeared into the crowd.

Leona grasped one of Martha's heaving shoulders. 'You just said he had Hannah's hair *on him*?'

She nodded. 'A . . . a lock . . . and . . . and one of her ribbons.'

'Are you saying he killed my Hannah? He *killed* her?'

'I . . . I don't know, love. I . . . I just don't know.'

'What? Is he a . . . is he a child molester? Is that what he is?'

She looked at Leona through streaming eyes. 'I . . . I think we let a monster in.' Her lips quivered and she heaved in a shaky breath. 'An' . . . an' he made us think it was . . . it was p-poor Walter.'

The walkway was ringing with footsteps. Leona felt Adam's hand press the small of her back.

'Looks like they're folding over there. Let's take advantage of that and go get this fella.'

She nodded, leading the way across. As they approached the far side, Leona could see the uncertainty in Alice's eyes. She came to a halt in front of the woman. 'You've always been a vicious bitch, haven't you?' whispered Leona. 'Always the one moaning, bitching, causing trouble.'

Alice's mouth hung half open.

'What, not saying anything this time?'

Her mouth still hung open, her eyes seemed to be searching the far off horizon for inspiration.

'Let me guess, you were hoping you could spread your legs for Latoc? Become the queen to his king? Become the queen bee here? Was that it?'

Alice looked at Martha. 'I . . . I . . . just wanted . . . what was best for us all. That's all I ever—'

'Yeah, right.'

'It was for the children's sake, Leona. For Hannah's sake that I . . . that I thought Walt—'

Leona slapped her face hard. The crack of palm on cheek echoed between the platforms like a brittle gunshot.

'Don't you dare,' Leona whispered through clenched teeth. 'Don't you fucking dare say another word.' She pushed past her and finally stepped onto the firm footing of the compression platform's main deck. There was a commotion up ahead through the crowd. She saw Howard and William strong-arming Valérie Latoc towards them.

'That's the guy, is it?' asked Walfield.

Leona nodded. 'Yes.'

They wrestled him through the crowd on the deck, growing in numbers now as the curious and the less loyal made their way across the walkway in the wake of the soldiers to see what was going on. Howard and William stopped in front of Leona, Valérie held between them in an armlock.

'So, did you do it?' asked Howard.

'No, of course not,' said Valérie. 'I would never harm a child.'

'Why did you have those things in your pockets?' snapped Martha.

Valérie shrugged. 'I do not understand.' He pulled the pockets of his trousers inside out. 'I have nothing in my pockets. Martha, why are you saying these things?'

'Where is he bunked?' asked Leona.

'The plant monitoring suite on the top floor,' said Howard.

'Someone search it,' ordered Leona. Howard nodded, released his grasp on Latoc and pushed his way back through the crowd towards the external steps.

'I'm not telling a lie,' said Martha.

Leona's gaze remained on the man. 'I know, Martha. Even if Howard finds nothing . . . he's still going.'

She took a step towards him. 'So, *is* he going to find something?'

Latoc looked uneasy, his eyes darting from one armed solider to the next. Then to Leona. 'I never touched Hannah. I promise you.'

Leona suddenly buried her face in her hands. The thought of what might, or might not, have been the experience of Hannah's last few minutes was too much for her. She felt Martha's arm around her shoulders.

'I'm okay . . .' she said, rubbing away tears that she didn't want to share with everyone else. 'I'm okay.'

Adam took over. 'What about this other girl?'

Latoc hesitated. 'The other girl?'

'What are we going to find?' Adam turned to Martha. 'You found those things. What did you do with them?'

'I . . . I put them back where I found them. I was too s-scared to do anyth— I just didn't want to believe—'

Adam raised a hand to hush her and turned back to Latoc. 'So, chances are your little *trophies* are still up there some-where.'

Valérie's calm composure slipped for a moment. He dropped his head. 'I never touched Hannah. She was an angel. But . . .'

'But what?' asked Leona, her hands dropping away from her face. 'But WHAT?'

'The other one . . . I . . . she . . . I just wanted to be . . .'

'Wanted to be what?'

'Close.'

'"Wanted to be CLOSE". What the hell is that supposed to mean?'

From towards the rear of the gathered knot of people Denise Bingham sobbed noisily.

'To hold her . . . that is all. Just to hold her. The Lord told me to—'

'Don't do that!' snapped Leona. 'Don't you dare justify what you did with a *God-told-me-so*!'

'He is love. God is love. I am love . . . the physical form of love . . . that is love, too, yes?'

'Did you hurt her? Did you kill her?'

He shook his head. 'No . . . I . . . I just wanted to hold her. She was so beautiful. You know? That is all. Just to hold her and pray with her. But she tripped and hit her head—'

'Oh, that sounds like bollocks,' grumbled Walfield. 'Sounds like a load of shit, already.'

Leona grabbed a fistful of Latoc's shirt. 'Is that how it went with Hannah? You just wanted to *hold* her? And what? She tripped? Hit her head? Is that it?'

'Lee,' said Adam, placing a hand on her arm.

'What?' she replied over her shoulder, not taking her eyes off Latoc.

'We need some evidence, right? We can't just go on this. Why don't we see what's up in his rooms?'

Leona turned round. Between Brooks and Walfield she saw William was loosely holding the gun Howard had been aiming down the walkway at them moments ago. She quickly pushed through and snatched the gun out of his hands.

Adam stood in her way. 'Leona? What're you doing?'

'Out of my way!' she barked, pushing him aside and jamming the barrel of the gun into Latoc's ribs. 'MOVE!'

He stepped uncertainly backwards.

She prodded him across the deck, the crowd parting either side of them.

'You want me to leave?' asked Latoc. 'If that is what you wish, then I—'

She prodded him hard again, Latoc taking faltering steps backwards until his backside bumped up against a safety rail.

'Now fucking climb it.'

He turned round to look at the railing, the smooth grey sea eighty feet below. He shook his head defiantly. 'Leona, anger is the devil's way in to your soul. Do you not see that? You are letting him in. I know you are better than—'

523

'CLIMB OVER IT!'

He remained rooted to the spot. Leona aimed the barrel of the gun at his face and let her finger slide onto the trigger.

'D-don't,' he whispered. She saw another crack in his calm demeanour, his eyes narrowing into a wince.

She aimed the gun a couple of inches to the left and pulled the trigger. The shot passed his head and echoed out across the stillness on the deck. He cowered at the deafening sound next to his ear.

'CLIMB!'

Latoc hesitantly swung a leg over the safety barrier, then the other, eased himself over the rail and stood on the narrow lip of rusty metal beyond, one hand tightly holding the upper bar, his other arm, with its bandaged hand, wrapped around the stanchion.

Adam pushed his way through the crowd towards them. 'Leona, we can't do this just on someone's say-so!'

She ignored him. 'You . . .' she started, her voice faltering to nothing but a croak. She hawked up and spat on the deck by Latoc's feet. 'People like you,' she continued. 'Takers. You take what you want, and fuck anyone else.'

She swung her aim back onto his face. 'People like you, shit like you, took my father, took my daughter, took my brother, took . . . *me*.' She found herself trembling, her voice robbed of the brittle force of righteous vengeance. Now it was little more than a fluttering whisper. 'Takers . . . takers . . . takers. Fucking parasites. People like you,' she said, leaning forward and prodding the muzzle against his cheek, 'people like you fucked the whole world up; sucked it dry until everything collapsed.'

Brooks put a hand on her arm. 'Leona.'

She shook it off, her eyes still on Valérie Latoc. 'You. I hate men like you. Pricks . . . fucking selfish pricks.'

Valérie shook his head and smiled. Some sense of his calm

composure rebuilt one more time. 'You have me all wrong, Leona. I am not like other—'

'NOW LET GO OF THE RAIL!' she screamed. She hated the sound of her voice. It sounded like someone else. High-pitched and shrill and desperate.

Latoc's eyes dipped and the smile slipped away. 'I . . . I am human. I have human weaknesses. That is why the Lord came to me. Because, yes . . . I am . . . I *was* the lowest form of life, once. I was hated. I . . .' He looked down in shame. 'I was in prison for this kind of thing. I was spat at before the crash. I know what it is to be despised, Leona.' He looked up at her again. 'But He came to someone like *me* to show us all that anyone can be forgiven. *Anyone!*'

She laughed. 'Oh, you want me to forgive you? Is that it?'

'You . . . I see in you the strength to . . . to forgive.'

'Just SHUT UP!' she snapped at him. 'Shut up!'

Adam tried again. 'Leona,' he said in a soft voice. 'C'mon, Lee, this isn't you. You can't execute this man just on someone's say-so. Give me the bloody gun.'

'Leona,' said Latoc, 'this place, these rigs . . . this is a *sacred* place. It is the beginning.'

'What?'

'I was sent here. Do you see? Sent here. This place is the *ark*. I was sent here for a purpose. I—'

'Is that the kind of crap you've been telling them?' She laughed bitterly. 'This is a . . . what? A *Noah's ark?!*'

'Yes,' a woman called out from behind him. Leona turned round to see her mother pushing her way to the front. 'That's exactly the crap he's been peddling. That we're special because we're going to be the last humans in the world.'

She joined Leona beside the railing. 'But I think all he was really after was his own little brothel.'

'No, that is not it, Jennifer,' said Latoc quickly. 'You have made a very special place here. God sees that. A very special place. God is grateful for all that you did.'

'God's grateful is He? Oh, yeah, God's been a really nice guy. Was it God's call that Walter be killed?' She turned round to look at the others. 'Or did you all have a hand in it?'

The crowd shuffled uneasily under her gaze.

Adam slowly extended a hand towards Leona. 'This isn't the right way to deal with this. Trust me, it'll haunt you. Give me the gun.'

She turned to look at him and saw in his eyes that he was talking from experience.

'Seriously.' He rested a hand on the gun's still-warm barrel. 'Don't do this.'

They heard the sound of a door swinging shut and the clang of feet on the metal rungs of the stairs. All eyes drifted up and watched Howard hasten his way down, wheezing and puffing at the bottom of each flight. He was holding something in his hands.

'Leona, wait, I've got—' he called out from the top of the last flight of steps, the words were pulled away by the wind. Finally, he made his way across the deck, pushing through the crowd towards her, finally spotting Jenny and Leona by the railing. For a moment he gasped, trying to catch his breath.

He'd told her to wait. That meant he must have found something that mitigated the circumstances. She felt the resolve to kill without mercy begin to ebb away. Her hands loosened their grip on the shotgun and she let Adam silently relieve her of it. She turned towards the sweating, gasping old man beside her. 'Howard, what did you find?'

He opened his left hand. 'Martha was right.'

She saw a single loop of blonde hair in his fleshy palm. She reached out and touched it with the tip of her finger. The right texture. She picked it up and held the lock of hair to her nose. Her smell.

Hannah.

Unmistakably Hannah.

'NO! I . . . I did not t-touch her!' said Latoc. She turned to him and saw his eyes were wide with fear, the last vestige of composure torn from his face like a cheap plastic Halloween mask. 'Understand . . . God told me I could *have* the other one . . . Natasha. But not Hannah! He s-said I could have—'

'Oh, fuck off!' said Leona, lifting a booted foot off the deck and kicking his groin through the gap between the railings. Both his feet lost purchase on the narrow lip of metal and he flapped desperately with his hands to keep hold of the railing. His unbandaged hand found the vertical stanchion, sliding down the pitted metal, cheese-grating the skin of his hand on the way down. The other arm lost its hold completely; the hand swathed in layers of bandaging gave him little more than a mittened hook to grasp with. He hung there for a moment, bloodied and scraped, wrapped tightly around the base of the stanchion, the rusting post creaking perilously with his weight. He swung, knuckles and sinews in his hand bulging as he clung on desperately. The bandaged hand flapped around the pole, trying ineffectually to get a purchase on it, too.

'PLEEEAASSE!!' he screamed, his long Jesus-like locks flickering and dancing in the updraught.

'My daughter told you to fuck off,' hissed Jenny, delivering a swift kick at his fingers.

Valérie Latoc's wide-eyed face and his bloody hand disappeared from sight.

Chapter 80

10 years AC

'LeMan 49/25a' – ClarenCo Gas Rig Complex,
North Sea

I look at this place and I see something very different to the dome. I don't see floodlights piercing the night sky. Instead I see candles made from animal fat. I don't see London's lifeless horizon of glass tower blocks. Instead I see the North Sea. I don't hear the thudding beat of a boom-box, I hear the soft murmur of the tide. In the evenings I hear the strumming of a guitar, snatches of conversation from open portholes, the giggle of children's voices.

And chickens, lots of the stupid little things.

What I see when I look around is a time before the oil age, before the steam age, even. This is what they've built out here, a life that I guess wouldn't look out of place in the middle ages. Minus the ignorance, minus the superstitions, minus the witch burnings.

Who would have thought you could actually turn five rusting gas platforms into a self-sustaining village? They managed it – Jennifer Sutherland and her family and followers.

I used to miss the pre-crash world with its conveniences and distractions. I used to miss a million and one little things during those years we were at the dome. But now I've seen this place, I don't miss that dead world any more. I think this is what the future should look like. Not these ugly rigs, but the plants, the chickens, the animal-fat candles. Life without taking endlessly.

There were a few painful days after we arrived – bridges

needed to be rebuilt. These people were so utterly divided by that mad bastard. About a third of them had completely bought into his preaching and another third had joined him, not wanting to be left in the minority. I wonder, if we'd not arrived when we did, whether the first two thirds might eventually have turned on the last — the non-believers.

Mankind has plenty of form with that sort of thing.

There are wounds that are going to take years to heal. A lot of work for Jenny Sutherland. There was also the news that her lad was gone. Truth be told, I think it hasn't sunk in yet, or maybe she'd come to terms with never seeing either of them again and to have at least one of her children back was a blessing.

There was also news for the big woman, what's her name? Martha. News that her son is with Maxwell's little army. That has certainly focused minds to pull together again: the knowledge that something worse than the mad priest is out there and will turn up one day soon.

I look at both the Sutherland women and I'm amazed at their bloody fortitude. Mother and daughter, natural survivors . . . tough buggers, the pair of them. It does make me wonder whether true 'toughness', 'true grit' isn't the size of the muscles you can bench-press out of your body, or how many miles you can jog with eighty pounds of field kit strapped to your back, or how big a gun you can hold in your hands.

I think it's in how much crap you can endure, how much brutality you're on the receiving end of and yet still keep your humanity.

In a world like this with no laws, no charter of human rights, it's the women who suffer. It's the women who learn what it is to be tough, not the men.

Adam Brooks

*

'. . . because you never *listened* to anyone,' said Tami Gupta. 'That is the truth, my dear. I am sorry to say that.'

The mess erupted with a chorus of voices. Most of them agreeing with the woman. The chairs and tables had been cleared away to allow as many people in as possible. Pretty much everyone was here. Those unable to fit in the mess stood amongst the rows of preparation surfaces in the galley, sat on the serving counter, the large roller-shutter fully retracted to make it more like one large meeting room. There were even people crowded on the gantry outside, and sitting on the steps all the way down to the accommodation module's first floor; mostly children, more likely to find the 'town hall meeting' somewhat boring.

'You know I'm very fond of you, Jenny. I say this because it needs to be said. In the early days, when there was just the few of us, it was right that we had someone take charge. And I think we would never have managed without you making the decisions. Perhaps we would never have settled here. We needed you.'

Tami, seated in the chair next to Jenny, behind the one table they'd not stacked out of the way, reached a hand out to her friend. 'I love you like a sister, Jenny, but we now need to have some sort of a democracy. There are too many people with different opinions. Too many people whispering because their voice is not heard.' Tami glanced pointedly at Alice Harton. 'That is how that man came between us. Like an infection from a simple cut, he exploited the discontent . . . the whispering.'

Jenny sat still and looked down at her hands. 'Maybe . . .' she began, then paused. Her words quietened the hubbub in the mess. They awaited more from her. 'Maybe it's time, then.' She looked up. 'I *am* so bloody tired of it.'

Leona, sitting on her other side, nodded. 'We know, Mum.'

'I suppose I just never trusted anyone else,' she continued. 'I promised Andy to take care of you both and I just couldn't put us in a situation where someone else was deciding your fate.' She sucked in a breath, looking up from her twisting hands at the women and men crammed into the room. 'But things are different now, aren't they?'

There were murmurs of assent, nodding heads.

'I'll stand down then and we'll vote on someone new.'

A spattering of applause rippled through them. But Adam, sitting at the end of the table, raised his hand. The applause quickly faded away.

'But maybe not right *now*, Mrs Sutherland?'

There were a few muted giggles at the man's formality.

Jenny offered him a smile. 'Jenny . . . that's what everyone calls me, Jenny. All right, Flight Lieutenant Brooks?'

'All right, Jenny.' Adam tipped his head in acknowledgment. 'But this election can't be now. Not until we're done with Maxwell.'

'He's right,' said Leona. 'They'll be on their way. In fact, I'm surprised we beat them back here.'

'How big is this army?' someone called through from the galley.

Adam shook his head. 'Army's the wrong word for them. They're not proper soldiers. They're boys with guns. About a hundred of them.'

A ripple of gasps.

'You said a *hundred*?'

'They *all* have guns?'

Adam nodded.

The room filled with voices. It was Leona who raised her hands to quieten them this time. 'But they're *boys*,' she said. 'No more than that. They've never fought in a battle, they've never had guns fire back at them. They're *children*.' She looked at Adam. 'At the first sight of their own blood they'll run, right?'

He nodded. 'They're green, untested. The only warfare they've experienced is on their games machines.'

'What about you?' asked Bill Laithwaite. 'Are you green?'

Adam glanced at Walfield and the other two, leaning against the back wall. 'Danny?'

Walfield grinned. 'Three fuckin' tours back-to-back providing perimeter security in and around Camp Bastion in Afghanistan. Mostly on the receiving end of mortar and rocket fire.' He shrugged. 'We had a few toe-to-toe stand-offs. The local Pashtuns fired smarter than the Taliban-imports ever did. An' I'm pretty fuckin' sure both will fire much better than those boys will.'

'We also have the advantage of the defensive position,' added Adam, looking through the faces for one in particular. He found Martha. 'If *you* hadn't thrown us the rope ladder, miss, we'd have been unable to get on your rig. They may come with ropes and hooks and have to scramble up to those lowest decks . . . what do you call them?'

'Spider decks,' said Jenny.

'If they've brought ropes and hooks, then they'll have to toss and secure 'em under fire. That's not going to be easy. Not even for experienced soldiers.'

'But we've only got nine guns, sir,' said Bushey.

Leona cut in. 'So? We can make other weapons, can't we? On the chicken deck there are rooms full of iron rivets and bolts, some of them as big as my hand. We can throw those down at them. There are lengths of bungee cable we could make slingshots or catapults from.'

Adam grinned back at Bushey. 'Hear that? What she said.'

'Or we could leave now, whilst there's still time,' said William. Heads turned towards him. 'I'm serious,' he added. 'I'm . . . I've never fired a gun. I'm not really soldier material.'

Leona shrugged. 'Yes, or we could leave now. But if we did? If we all left now? I don't think there's enough food left ashore to forage – not for four hundred and fifty mouths. We'll go hungry.'

'And the fact is Maxwell's boys might attack us ashore anyway,' said Adam. 'Maxwell's made them dangerous, *predatory* . . . do you understand what I mean by that?' Not many of them seemed to. 'You're mostly women. Those boys have come for that as much as anything else.'

A ripple of whispers across the room.

'We can't let them on,' said Leona.

'We'll have much better odds fighting them here,' said Adam.

'Perhaps this Maxwell is coming in peace?' said Rebecca. 'Is that possible? Could he be coming in peace? Maybe planning to co-operate with us?'

Adam and Leona looked at each other.

Adam shrugged. 'Maxwell's a power junky. If he comes he'll want one thing only; to be in charge. That's why he created his boys' army and called them his praetorians. It was all about prolonging his authority at the dome . . . at any cost.'

'If he did take charge here,' added Leona, 'his boys would be in charge. And the women would have to . . . *submit*.' The word spelled out more than enough without her having to qualify what she'd meant by it.

'Abandoning the rigs and running ashore,' said Tami, 'does sound like a very bad idea. But after this is done, going ashore is what we will eventually do?'

'Eventually,' said Jenny guardedly.

'We could move now if it wasn't for Maxwell,' said Adam.

'Is it really safe to do this yet?' asked Sophie Yun. Her sisters nodded at the question being asked.

Leona nodded. 'Yes, Sophie.' She turned to her left. 'It's finally safe, Mum. It's not the same place we ran from. Maxwell's praetorians are the last of the *men* with guns.'

'Did you see others ashore?'

'A few. There're a few people out there,' replied Leona. She recalled those people on the motorway; a mute crowd of the hungry. Not menace in their eyes, just lingering hope that someone, somewhere, had an idea how to reboot this world.

'If we start something ashore, we need to take our time about it, a phased migration. We prepare, plant, grow . . . those people still out there will come. They won't take it from us, they'll join us.'

The room was silent.

'I think − no, I'm certain − we're probably the largest group left in Britain still managing to make a go of it. Do you see? The community we build ashore, the way we set it up, the rules and values we agree on now, well, those things will set the tone for our future.' She smiled. It was a hopeful smile, the ghost of which seemed to spread across the mess table to those standing in the room.

'We'll be deciding how the future is going to look . . . in a way.'

A soft breeze tickled through the portholes and filled the moment with a portentous whisper.

Jenny nodded. 'The future.' She pulled herself wearily out of her chair and met the eyes of those that had deserted her for Latoc as well as the few who had remained loyal. 'So maybe then, heading ashore . . . this should be the first thing we vote on. What does everyone think?'

Heads nodded silently.

'All right. This is how it is. We stay here and fight . . . let me see your hands for that.'

One or two at first, then others, encouraged by that, joined. Soon the room's low ceiling was almost held aloft by a sea of hands. It appeared to be almost unanimous.

'Afterwards, we make our plans to move back ashore. Hands for that?'

The last few unraised hands appeared.

Leona looked at her mother and thought she saw the clearly defined angle of her shoulders droop ever so slightly beneath her thin cardigan. She knew that gesture so well, she'd seen it so many times before back in the old days; after a long grocery shop when the plastic bags were off-loaded on the kitchen counter and she'd let out a sigh. It wasn't the sagging shoulders of someone defeated, it was relief.

If that gesture of hers had words it would be this: *Job's done.*

Chapter 81

10 years AC

'LeMan 49/25a' – ClarenCo Gas Rig Complex, North Sea

'I missed up here,' said Leona. They both listened to the rustle of leaves, soothing in the darkness. The moon peeped out at them, painting the helipad a perfect blue momentarily before hiding away again behind a relay race of scudding clouds, all racing each other to reach the distant shore first.

'How did our old house look?' asked Jenny.

'Just as we left it, I suppose. We got weeds growing in the lounge. Oh, and the lawn needs mowing.'

Jenny laughed softly.

'It's not our home any more, Mum. It doesn't feel like that any more. It's just a place we used to live.' She plucked at her lips thoughtfully. 'I thought going back there, I was going home. I thought that's where I wanted to be. With Hannah gone it seemed pointless struggling on. I just wanted to curl up in my bedroom and, you know . . . ?'

'I know,' she replied squeezing her daughter's hand.

'But it's not our home any more.' *Just an empty house with broken windows and damp curls of wallpaper and leaves in the hallway.*

'Is . . . ?'

'Is Dad still there?'

Jenny nodded.

'Yes, he is.'

The night was warm, even with the breeze. The sea hissed and splashed nearly one hundred and eighty feet below, bumping gently against the platform legs like some giant turning over in its sleep.

'Tell me, Lee, how did Jacob die?'

'Defending me, Mum.' She could have described her small stifling cell, the smell of shit, the sounds coming through the walls, the night after night of fighting off that scrawny bastard who wanted to tame her, to make her his plaything. All unnecessary details.

'He was protecting me from another boy.' She swallowed, pinching at her lips again. 'He died just like Dad died.'

She felt her mother's shoulders gently shaking. It might have been easier to change the subject, move on, but Mum needed to hear what she had to say.

'I think, in some way . . . I think Jake was *proud*? I dunno, like he figured Dad was watching over us and giving him the thumbs up. I think he died sort of knowing Dad was pleased with him.' Leona wiped her damp cheek on the back her hand. 'I don't know . . . that sounds silly doesn't it?'

Jenny shook her head. 'No it doesn't, Lee. I sometimes think he is there, watching us, somehow.'

'So maybe they both are now?'

'Maybe,' Jenny smiled, 'maybe . . . all three of them.'

Leona suddenly felt her own façade slipping. *Oh, screw it . . . cry if you want, girl.*

She did. They both did, for Jacob, for Hannah, for Dad. For quite a while.

Presently, Jenny wiped her nose on her cardigan. 'Oh, hark at us defenceless wimpy, weepy women.'

'Mum?'

'Yes.'

'I'm so proud of you. You're not some wimpy, weepy woman. You've been a wall, protecting me and Jake, and Hannah. A solid wall. For all the others here, too. Even those ungrateful bitches who turned against you. You made this place happen. You kept us safe.'

537

Jenny said nothing. Not for a while. Finally she sighed. 'I am so tired, though.'

'I know. So am I.' Leona reached out and hugged her mother. 'You and me, like two peas in a pod.' *Both grieving mothers.* She left that unsaid. Didn't need to be said. Mum knew what she meant.

Jenny cleared her throat, blew her nose. 'Those men you brought with you seem like decent types.'

Leona watched as the moon cleared a thin skein of a combed-out cloud. 'Yeah, I think they are.'

'Particularly Adam?'

Leona snorted. 'Oh, come on.'

'What? He seems quite nice now he's shaved that awful beard off.'

'And more *your* age than mine, Mum.'

'How old is he?'

She thought about it. 'I think he said he was twenty-nine when the crash happened.'

'Thirty-nine, then.' Jenny grinned. 'Now, if I was ten years younger . . .'

Leona shrugged. 'Or if I was ten years older . . .'

They both laughed. It felt good; like gulping fridge-cold lemonade on a hot summer's day. Wasn't even that funny, but still, it didn't stop them.

'It's much quieter, ain't it?'

Adam nodded. Even when it *wasn't* a party night back at the dome, those boys made a racket arsing about; shrieking, singing tunelessly, cackling like hyenas. He certainly didn't miss any of that.

'Nice an' fuckin' peaceful,' added Walfield.

They gazed out at the moonlit sea; dark swells that bobbed and dropped gently; like a micro mountain range fast-forwarding through geological eras.

The darkness on the rigs was total. It had been Adam's

538

suggestion; tonight, and every night for the foreseeable future, no oil lamps, no candles, nothing after dark. Nothing that could give them away. No point of light guiding Maxwell and his boys in if they chose to make their approach after dark.

Murmurs of conversation drifted across the restless fidgeting sea from the other platforms. There were people on lookout duty on each platform, looking north, east, south and west. But it was this one at the end – the drilling platform – that was the most vulnerable. Its spider deck was the closest to the water, more often than not catching the tips of larger swells when the sea was in a spirited mood.

Adam silently scanned the sea, looking for the telltale sign of a faint grey skirt of suds amidst the shifting black hillocks. The last twenty-four hours had been busy. There were now little ammunition piles of rusting bolts and nuts and rivets set along the perimeter of the main deck of each platform at regular intervals. A number of women had been busy with needles, threads and scissors making hand-held catapults and slings from lengths of bungee rope, and – believe it or not – the cups of bras. Others had made an array of clubs and spears and cloth-wrapped handles on a number of cutting weapons fashioned from jagged strips of aluminium sheeting. Then there were their eight firearms; the five SA80s they'd taken from the boys and the three remaining assorted guns this community had been relying on for the last five years.

There was a plan of sorts. Adam could only guess that Maxwell would try for the lowest platform first and, with that bridgehead taken, move down the row attempting to take the production platform next, then the secondary compression platform, the accommodation platform, and then off to the left of that, the primary compression platform. Hopefully, if they threw everything they had at them before they could get a toehold on the drilling platform's spider deck, the boys would think better of the idea, turn tail and sail away. That's what Adam was hoping; the first sight of one of their own lying dead, they were going to bolt like rabbits. Failing that, though, if they got on, then with each of those hundred-foot-long walkways, there was another chokepoint on which they could hold them back. He doubted whether a single nut or bolt propelled from the cup of one of their bras was actually going to find a target, but with the air around them whistling with projectiles, perhaps Maxwell's boys might decide these rigs weren't such a soft target.

There was a football horn used to summon people for their meal sittings. That was going to be their battle horn. One honk meant everyone on the first platform was to retire across the walkway to the second. Two honks was the sign to retreat to the next. Three honks, the next . . . and so on. A simple plan. But simple was always best.

'Danny?'

'Yeah?' replied Walfield.

Adam looked at him, caught the glint of his eyes in the moonlight. 'Reckon we're going to be able to hold them off?'

Walfield sucked his teeth like a builder giving an estimate. 'Dunno, maybe. It's a bit of a bastard of a place to try an' take under fire, to be fair. I guess it depends how much those little bastards really want it.'

'Maxwell won't go back to the Zone. He knows the Zone hasn't got a future. He knows he's got to take this place. That or face a mutiny.'

Walfield shrugged. 'His boys might not know that. They're a pretty stupid bunch, the lot of them. Maybe they're thinking this is just some bloody raiding trip.'

'If I was in his shoes I'd tell them. Tell them this isn't just a raid for booty. This is their survival. Take this place or face starving.'

Walfield whistled softly. 'Them boys're too fuckin' stupid to explain things to. I reckon he won't have told 'em any-thing. They'll just be thinkin' it's a lark. A day out.'

They leaned against the railings in silence for a while, savouring the fresh salty breeze. They heard Bushey fart on the other side of the platform and Harry's dirty Sid James cackle. Pair of bloody idiots.

'And that's how you charm the ladies,' said Adam. 'They do love a man who can hold a tune.'

They listened to the soft rustle of leaves above and below them, and the thump and wallow of the sea. Adam scanned the dark horizon, a mottled quilt of drifting moonlight and shifting shadows.

'They're something, though, aren't they?' said Walfield after a while.

'What?'

'Mrs and Miss Sutherland. Tough ladies.'

Adam nodded. Jennifer Sutherland with that tomboyish short brown hair, there was something of a GI Jane look to her, what with the khaki pants and the scarring down her cheek and neck. Tough. Very tough. She'd had to be.

Leona, on the other hand, was a puzzle. She seemed both vulnerable and strong. She was fragile like a vase with a handle broken off and glued back on again; never quite as fixed as it once was. But there was something about her, an inner strength she seemed to be finding. He realised both of them, mother and daughter, were women he might find himself putting on a pedestal, idolising even, if he wasn't mindful of that.

He shook his head. Now really wasn't the time to start thinking that sort of thing. In the old world, he suspected neither of them would have looked twice at him anyway.

Harry's voice broke the silence, echoing across the flat deck.

'Hey!! Shit!! There's something out there!!!'

Chapter 82

10 years AC

'LeMan 49/25a' – ClarenCo Gas Rig Complex, North Sea

Maxwell watched the dark looming silhouette of the nearest platform as it drew closer. The tugboat was approaching slowly and noisily, sputtering fitfully like an old man choking on a mouthful of unchewed meat.

That's exactly what he wanted; no discretion, no quietly sneaking up. Just a very noisy arrival; enough to rouse everyone.

A floodlight mounted on the roof of the pilot's cabin snapped on, bathing the gently lolling sea in front of the boat's prow with a brilliant cone of light. The beam swung across several hundred yards of water onto the nearest platform, slowly panning over its dark corroded legs, across the lattice of the spider deck and the drilling core's support jacket. It swung up across the cellar deck, cluttered with flaking yellow Portakabins, onto the main deck where, finally, Maxwell thought he saw several faces watching them intently.

So they know we're here.

The floodlight arced down the side of the nearest platform, dimly picking out the next one along, a hundred feet further away. They were doing a good job of clearly announcing their arrival. There were more faces now lining the railings. More and more.

As the tug chugged closer, Maxwell tried to pick out individuals; how many of these people were adult, young, old? How many men were there? But the floodlight was dancing around too quickly, not lingering long enough to pull a single face out of the growing crowd.

'Just put her over there, near that support-leg, Jeff,' he said, picking up the loudhailer and stepping outside the cockpit, along the runner and onto the foredeck.

'Hello?!' His voice echoed over the thrum of the diesel engine and the churn of water past the bow. It sounded tinny, almost comical, over the loudhailer.

'Hello there! My name's Alan Maxwell! Who are you?'

There was movement amongst those gathered on the main deck but no answer.

'I heard about this place from some people who came from here! Would it be possible for me to talk to someone?'

Maxwell was getting the response he wanted with this noisy well-illuminated arrival; everyone's full attention. He'd made sure the tugboat appeared as harmless as possible; only Nathan and another lad were on the foredeck, Jeff in the pilot's cockpit, the other boys – a dozen of them – were down below, armed to the gills and out of sight.

He glanced down at the bobbing troughs and hillocks of seawater and tried to locate Snoop and all the other boys in their rowing boats. He was pretty certain they'd be in position by now, waiting in the moonless gloom beneath the drilling platform, tied up to one of the legs and awaiting the signal to come out.

The tugboat's engine finally dropped in pitch as it approached the base of the platform and bobbed slowly forward under its own momentum.

Maxwell craned his neck to look up again at the distant faces lining the main deck. He thought he could see one or two men standing up there.

'Hello?!' he called out again. 'Is there someone I can speak to? We've come in peace!' He smiled to himself at how corny that last bit had sounded.

The diesel engine had settled down to a quiet throaty

543

mutter, accompanied by the slap of water against the boat's hull.

'We heard about this place!' Maxwell said again. 'Can we talk?! We've got a boat full of supplies. We'd like to join you, if . . . if that's okay?'

'Wait a moment!' shouted a female voice back down to them.

He glanced across the foredeck at Nathan and the other boy standing right next to him; Notori-us. The nickname suited the young lad; a completely bloody psychotic little pit bull. He was packing a handgun and a knife under his orange jacket, and had orders to jump Nathan and slit his throat if he showed any sign of blowing the whistle on them. Even though Notori-us liked Nathan, he was happy to do it – there was the promise of double dope rations for a month if he did his bit well.

Maxwell was banking on the simplest approach. To talk these people into lowering a ladder and to allow him – just him, he'd assure them of that – to come up and talk. That's where Nathan's assurance of their good intentions came in. Lulling them into lowering a ladder. Of course, once the ladder was down, Notori-us was going to grab hold of it, whilst the boys hidden down below in the tugboat would spring out of hiding and storm up the thing as quickly as possible.

And with that going on as a distraction, Snoop and the rest waiting quietly in their rowing boats had knotted ropes and hooks which they'd sling onto the spider decking and pull themselves up.

Nothing particularly clever there in that plan. All nice and simple. Maxwell had been into the Bracton gas terminal, found an office block shared by Shell, ClarenCo, ATP and several other North Sea players. He spent most of yesterday rifling through their filing cabinets and found what he wanted; a proposal brochure on the platforms and modules manufactured for those oil companies. It wasn't specific information about these particular gas platforms, but it was good enough ball-park information about this *class* of rig for him to work from. He now had a pretty good idea of the layout of the underbelly of these rigs, and that this one, the drilling rig, was going to be the easiest for them to scramble up onto.

Of course, the boys were all pumped up for this; giddy with excitement and slightly stoked on the last crate of that sugary alcopop. A bottle for each of them before they went in; a celebration drink to toast the victory. Just enough of a buzz to take the edge off any last-minute nerves, just enough to make each of them feel like invincible Super Army Soldiers.

Maxwell shot a glance at Notori-us. He was grinning with excitement, ready for the fun and games to begin; probably sporting a raging hard-on in his tracksuit bottoms. Maxwell looked at Nathan. *You going to be a good lad and play along for me?*

Nathan smiled back at him, hoping his cavalier grin gave away none of the twisting, churning emotions going on inside him.

Oh, crap. Oh, crap. I've got to do something.

Nathan wished he'd chugged another bottle of Froot-ka. He realised he was trembling from head to foot. He was hoping, desperately hoping, that they weren't going to fall for this. That Maxwell's plan to sweet-talk his way on was going to fall on deaf ears. And if he got Nathan to say hello there'd be a way to let them know, a tone of voice, a choice of words that would subtly warn them this was a trap waiting to be sprung.

He glanced at Notori-us, grinning like an over-sugared toddler. He knew exactly why the boy was on the foredeck standing right next to him.

Fuck.

A voice he recognised instantly echoed down from the

main deck. 'Hello?' It was Mrs Sutherland. 'I'm in charge here. What do you want?'

'To talk. That's all. We heard about this place. That it's a safe place!'

A pause.

'No! You should leave now! We have guns aimed on you!'

'What?! I'm not armed!' shouted Maxwell. 'I . . . I was just hoping we could talk!'

Jenny Sutherland said nothing.

'Look, I've got someone you might know down here with me!'

Nathan felt his bowels unknot and loosen.

Oh, shit . . . Nate . . . you have to say something.

A torch snapped on from above, lanced down eighty feet and dappled its way across their upturned faces.

'Nathan?' A syrup-thick voice that he recognised instantly echoed down to him. 'Oh, God! Is it *you*, Nathan?!'

'Hey, Mum!' he called out limply. He couldn't see where she was.

Maxwell touched his arm lightly. 'There's a good lad,' he muttered quietly. 'Talk to Mum. Let's go up and see her, eh? I promise she won't be hurt, lad.'

'Oh, my!' Martha cried. 'Oh, Nathan, love! You all right?'

'Nathan led us here!' called out Maxwell. 'Said you were decent people. He wanted to come home. So I brought him back!'

The torch beam flickered across their faces, across the deck onto the cockpit. Probing the boat for any secrets.

'So, how many of you down there?'

Shit, no . . . they're going to fall for it.

Maxwell smiled. 'Just us three . . . and there's Jeff in the cockpit.'

Jenny said nothing in response, and they bobbed in silence for a few moments.

Don't do it. Don't do it.

'You can send Nathan up alone,' called down Jenny. 'Just him.'

Fuck. No. Don't lower anything!

Maxwell shrugged. 'Sure, okay.' He made a show of smiling at Nathan like they were inseparable buddies; favourite uncle and favourite nephew. 'That okay with you, fella?'

Nathan stared out into the dark, unwilling to say anything, even nod silently. Then he heard the cranking of a windlass above.

Shit-shit-shit. You gotta do something, say something . . . now.

'MUM!' he blurted. 'THEY'RE DOWN HERE! THEY'RE EVERYWHERE! THEY'RE GOING TO ATTACK YOU!!!'

Maxwell's face split into a snarl. 'Ah, for fuck's sake, you little fucking shit!!!'

Nathan saw Notori-us reach quickly under his jacket and he heard his mum's distant voice screaming down at them not to touch her baby.

God, she could be embarrassing like that.

He turned to face the boy next to him, hands held out in front of him to protect himself, but Notori-us was already on him. Nathan felt several rapid punches in his stomach – like a boxer furiously working over a punchbag, except he knew each blow was more than that.

He could still hear his mum's voice, stretched thin and reedy, screaming down as his knees started to buckle beneath him.

Adam realised the conceit was over and all the talking was done.

He shouldered the gun, aiming through the SA80's night-vision scope down onto the tugboat's deck. If he could get Maxwell, maybe that would be enough to nip this whole thing in the bud.

Before he could get a bead on his target, dropping and

547

rising on the gentle swell, Maxwell shouted something and a dozen of his boys emerged from the pilot's cabin, their orange jackets glowing like beacons in the torchlight.

He glanced at Walfield, clearly thinking the same thing: *why the fuck are those morons wearing those glow-in-the dark jackets for a night assault?*

The tugboat's floodlight blinked out and then all of a sudden its foredeck was illuminated by the strobing light of a dozen muzzle flashes. Sparks danced along the rim of the deck and the railing and the torch that someone further along the deck had been holding tumbled down spinning end over end into the water where it glowed greenly for a moment beneath the froth before disappearing.

'Shit, shit!' hissed Adam, ducking back as he felt the warm puff of a shot whistle past his ear, too close for comfort.

Walfield popped his head over the side of the main deck to look down. 'Bollocks!' he shouted. 'They're all over that bottom deck already!'

Adam snapped his teeth angrily. The bastards must have sneaked in some boys underneath. They were swarming the spider deck now and there were too many stairwells and rung ladders from there up to the cellar deck, then the main deck, for them to risk making a stand here. He realised he should have had everyone on watch up *this* end of the string of platforms instead of spread out amongst them all.

For fuck's sake. Great start.

The spider deck was the big hurdle he'd been hoping would stop them. Clearly Maxwell's parley had been intended to be nothing more than a distraction whilst the rest of them found a way to scramble up. Never mind, they still had the choke point of each connecting walkway.

'All right, screw this, Danny, they're on. We've already lost this platform.' He looked around. 'Where's Bushey? BUSHEY!'

'Over here, sir!'

'First horn! Everyone back across the walkway.'

'Right.'

A moment later the horn belched a loud football terrace honk above the clatter of gunfire and the heavy metallic ringing of boots on the stairwells below them.

'Go, go, go!' he said, slapping Walfield's arm.

He waited until the last of those who'd been stationed on this platform scrambled past him, then set off after them, stumbling a moment later over the prone form of somebody. He didn't know her by name, but recognised her: a mature woman with long grey hair in plaits. He'd listened to her strumming a guitar a couple of nights ago. Presumably she'd been the one holding the torch aimed down on the tugboat.

From below he could hear the boys whooping with delight as they charged up stairwells on the decks beneath them, a multitude of heavy feet clanging on metal rungs.

He looked around and saw Harry still firing over the rail in controlled three-shot bursts. 'Harry! We're pulling back! Move your bloody arse!'

'Right!' he called back over his shoulder. 'I'll cover you, sir!'

Adam nodded. He sprinted back across the deck picking out, by the flitting moonlight, the obstacle course of redundant junction boxes and cable conduits ready to trip him up, listening for Harry's pounding footsteps behind him. He heard chattering gunfire. Short double taps — Harry's . . . and long undisciplined pray-n-spray bursts — the boys.

Come on, you idiot, just run!

A moment later his feet clattered onto the mesh floor of the walkway, it rattled and rang beneath his boots. He turned back, looking for the lance corporal, listening for his following footsteps.

'Come on, Harry!' he shouted.

The silly bugger must have got himself lost. Even on this small deck, a third of an acre of it, it was all too easy to get lost amidst the maze of rusting metal pipes and Portakabins. Especially in the dark.

He heard another couple of double taps, then a volley of return fire from several guns that seemed to go on for ages.

Jesus.

Then it was quiet.

Chapter 83

10 years AC

'LeMan 49/25a' – ClarenCo Gas Rig Complex, North Sea

Leona tripped, stumbled and spat a curse as she rubbed her barked shin. She could hear the distant rattle of firing and voices screaming. Where she was, at the opposite end of the row of rigs, standing on the main deck of the primary compression platform with Rebecca and Claire, they'd spotted the flicker of a floodlight lancing up from the sea. Leona had decided they should stay where they were, keeping a vigil at this end of their archipelago. Just in case. But then things had suddenly kicked off all the way over there and she cursed the fact they were too far away to be able to help out.

Her feet slammed down the walkway, Rebecca behind her clutching her bra-and-bungee cord catapult – for what it was worth – in both hands. They emerged onto the main deck of the accommodation platform, turned right, skirting the edge of the deck to avoid tangling with any obstacles.

People were spilling out of their cabins, brandishing their home-made weapons, and heading towards the noise. Leona converged with them, pushing and stumbling along the walkway cage towards the second compression platform, towards the sound of gunfire.

She emerged from the cage moments later, and then weaved her way across the platform's main deck until she could see the far side, and the next walkway. Across the dark empty space between platforms, she watched for a moment. Trying to make out the situation. She saw some flickers of light, and the occasional flash of gunfire, but nothing that clearly explained how things were. She suspected the shots were coming from the furthest platform.

Rebecca hunkered down next to her, wheezing from the sprint thus far.

'Can you see anything?'

'I think they're on drilling. Come on,' she said, stepping onto the walkway taking them across with the sound of her heavy steps ringing in her ears.

They emerged twenty seconds later onto the firm deck of the production platform into a confusion of panicking people, some scrambling past her to head back along the cage away from the fighting. She pushed her way through the mingling confused bodies and crossed the deck, catching sight of the skirmish going on ahead of her.

Along the edge of the deck she could see Adam and his men, and one or two of the old men – Howard, Bill, Dennis – firing potshots across the void between platforms at the boys on the far side. They, too, were firing back, sparks erupting from the deck, from the vent stacks and deck lockers the men were huddled behind.

She felt a puff of air on her cheek, heard a metallic clang against the metal wall beside her head and a hot spark jumped onto her bare arm.

'Ouch!' she yelped before instinctively dropping to her hands and knees. She crawled across the deck until she was huddled beside one of Adam's men.

She recognised his outline. 'Bushey! It's Leona.'

He turned and grinned manically at her before turning back to aim down the barrel of his assault rifle. 'The little shites surprised us!' He fired two aimed shots one after the other, the hot bullet casings almost landing in her lap.

'Where's my mum?'

'Dunno, she's somewhere along here,' he said, firing again.

Leona craned her neck, looking down along the row of

people cowering behind assorted cover, in two groups either side of the walkway cage. She picked out the huddled forms of Walfield, Howard, Sophie and one of her sisters and Dennis. She saw Alice and her friend Rowan both blindly flinging walnut-sized rivets across the void with their catapults. She picked out Adam in the group to the right of the walkway entrance, aiming and firing methodically, Martha loading up a dainty lace bra cup with another projectile.

She looked down the length of the walkway and thought she could pick out the detestable orange flash of those jackets, several of them, lying prone along the first thirty feet of it.

Bodies. They'd already made a first attempt to force their way across it and failed.

On the far side of the walkway, amongst the clutter of the drilling platform's deck, she saw the strobe-flicker of muzzle flashes from their guns and heads bobbing in and out of sight.

They're stuck. She found herself grinning. Adam was right. The caged walkways were turning out to be perfect chokepoints.

The firing on both sides began to ease off.

She looked around for Rebecca, assuming she was still with her, but she must have gone to ground somewhere else. Leona decided to press on. See if she could find Mum. Taking advantage of the lull in firing, she crawled on hands and knees, from one huddled person to the next, then, waiting for a moment of calm, she leapt across the open space beside the walkway's entrance and a second later joined the others, hunkering down behind a long and low mechanical store locker, gasping for breath.

Jenny looked down at her, panting on the floor beside her. 'Lee! Christ! I thought I told you to stay back! Are you all right? You okay?'

'I'm fine,' Leona huffed, trying to catch her breath. She swallowed, sucked in more air. 'What's happened?'

'They pulled up in a boat,' replied Adam. 'Maxwell tried distracting us. The rest of his boys were already waiting underneath. Then it all kicked off.' He shook his head angrily. 'We should have had *everyone* on that far platform instead of spread out. We might have spotted the rest of them sneaking under.'

Leona pulled herself onto her hands and knees and stole a look round the edge of the storage locker. 'But they're stuck there now, right?'

Adam nodded. 'For now.' Adam turned to Jenny. 'There's no way up onto the other platforms, right?'

She shook her head. 'The other platforms are much, much higher. They'd need us to lower them *something* to get aboard.'

'Then sod it, this is fine,' he said, trying a reassuring smile on them. 'We've got them plugged right here.'

Maxwell glared at Jay-zee. 'Are you calling me a *liar*? Is that it?'

Jay-zee met his challenging stare. 'Shit, man, you said this place was all powered up. That's what you fuckin' told us!'

A dozen of the praetorians crouching nearby glanced at them, eyes switching from Jay-Zee to Maxwell as they spoke.

'Man, you tol' us this place was lit up like some fuckin' light show. All I see is the whole thing is dark as shit. There's no fuckin' power here!'

Christ. This is it, thought Maxwell. *The bloody challenge.* He suspected it was going to come from one of the older boys, if not Edward himself, but not right in the middle of a bloody battle. The alcohol from that sugary fruit crap mixed with what must be a tidal flood of adrenalin surging through his veins had made Jay-zee wired.

Maxwell looked at the others nearby. They were, all of them, wide-eyed, talking ten to the dozen, chomping chewing gum in a dry mouth, stoned on adrenalin and buzzing like violin strings; hungry little tiger cubs looking for a gazelle to pull down and tear apart.

'You *ever* talk to me like that again, Jay-zee, I'll kill you myself!'

The boys recoiled uncertainly.

'The lights are all out, you idiot, because these people were warned we were coming. They didn't want to stand out like some fucking beacon. That's why everything is off!'

Uncertainty made Jay-zee waver; robbed his defiant posture of some of its challenge.

Something heavy pinged and rattled off a wall near to him. He flinched and ducked. His tall frame made him easier to see than anyone else. He crouched down to make sure his head wasn't a target that could be picked out from the platform across the gap.

Another clatter nearby. Maxwell ducked this time. A nugget of pitted metal bounced and rolled across the deck and ended up rocking to and fro in front of his foot. Those silly bitches were throwing nuts and bolts at them like frigging peanuts. That would have been laughable if he hadn't already witnessed one of his boys knocked senseless – left with a gushing cut across his scalp by one of those projectiles.

Jay-zee was still defiant. 'This place ain't worth this shit!'

Maxwell pointed up to a bulb dangling above the walkway entrance, and loops of sagging power flex dangling from ties all the way down the wire cage to the far side. 'See the cables?'

Jay-zee looked up, frowned and nodded.

'All of you boys?' Maxwell raised his voice for the benefit of those crouching nearby. 'Do you see these cables?'

They nodded.

'It means they've got power. All right? Plenty of it. Why else would they be living out here on a bloody rig? They're tapping oil or gas or whatever's down there. And I'm telling you now they'll have more fuel down there than we can ever use! All right?'

Some of the boys began to nod, reassured the Chief knew what he was doing and hadn't led them down a dead end.

'In an hour's time we'll have this place LIT UP LIKE A FUCKING CHRISTMAS TREE! ALL RIGHT?!!'

Some of their uncertain faces split with grins, the buzz of excitement flooding back.

Maxwell looked for Edward's face and found him, listening in, and so far staying quiet.

'Isn't that right, Edward . . . Snoop?'

The boys all turned as one to look at him, studying his face, his reaction, wanting to know what to think.

'Am I right?' said Maxwell.

Snoop finally pursed his lips and shrugged. 'Yeah, reckon they got power.'

'Right then.' Maxwell nodded towards the walkway. The bodies of three of his boys lay there, one behind the other. That little pit bull Notori-us was one of them, charging across like a rabid dog let off a leash, drawing fire and spinning like a cartwheel as he went down. If a few more of his boys had been equally fired-up and been following in his wake they probably would have made it across and already overrun those bitches on the far side by now.

'So, boys. We need to figure out a way across that. They've got it covered.'

Snoop looked around the cluttered deck. Most of the boys were up here now, clustered in groups amongst the Porta-kabins and looking anxiously at him and Maxwell to figure out something for them. Snoop's eye rested on a supermarket shopping trolley knocked over on its side, spilling its load of plastic seed trays filled with compost and little green shoots of something-or-other across the deck.

'Got an idea, Chief.'

556

10 years AC

'LeMan 49/25a' – ClarenCo Gas Rig Complex, North Sea

With no one firing right now, the only light was coming from the moon. Adam squinted to see what was going on on the far end of the walkway.

'See anything?' asked Leona, crouched beside him.

'Those buggers are up to something, no doubt.'

His gaze swept either side of the far end of the walkway. He could see the occasional head popping up from behind cover and ducking down again.

He dropped back, resting against an exhaust bell. 'I'm sorry,' he sighed. 'Sorry, we screwed up.'

Jenny hunkered down beside him. She pressed her lips together and smiled. 'Don't be, you've done all you could.'

Leona was still studying the far side. She couldn't see anything now that the firing had ceased, just flitting silver moonlight across the deck, cabins and pipes. 'They seem totally fearless,' she uttered. 'Afraid of nothing.'

'They're boys, it's all just a big game to them,' replied Adam.

'They remind me of the gangs that were partying in London. Were you in London during the week of the crash?'

'I was. We were manning the dome's perimeter.'

'You must have seen your share of the riots?'

'Oh yeah . . . we saw a lot of that.'

'I still have nightmares,' said Leona. 'Teenage boys stabbing, shooting, raping.' She nodded. 'You're right, it was some sort of a game to them . . . like some bloody computer game.'

'Young men never change. Two powerful ingredients at work inside them: the arrogance of youth and testosterone. Mix those two with a dose of anarchy, and yeah, they'll want to party.'

'Party . . . *part-eee*,' Leona whispered and shuddered.

'Truth is, they're still just boys,' he continued. 'Just boys. If you can get them to shut up and sit still for five minutes and actually listen to you, they quickly become children again.'

Leona made a face. 'Yeah, right.'

'Seriously, Leona. They're just kids. You forget, I know them. I've lived with them for years. They're children. It's just that that crazy twat Maxwell has indoctrinated them into thinking they're super-soldiers.'

'Right,' said Jenny. 'Just kids. They just need someone to pull their trousers down and smack their legs.'

Adam laughed. 'Maybe.'

'Maybe we should—'

'SIR!' it was Bushey. 'There's something on the walkway!'

Adam grabbed his gun and poked his head above the locker. He could see movement, something wobbling towards them. He could hear a tinny rattling now, getting louder.

'Torch! Someone get a torch on it!'

Walfield snapped one on and aimed it down inside the wire cage of the walkway.

'Fuck!! That's . . . that's Harry!!'

Adam squinted. It was. It was Harry, straddling what looked like a shopping trolley. 'HARRY?' shouted Bushey. 'Mate? You all right?'

Rattling closer to them, Adam could see that he wasn't *riding* it; he was stuffed onto the shopping trolley like some home-made Guy Fawkes, tied on. Clearly dead. He was perched on top of another body. And another.

'He's already dead!' said Adam.

The trolley was halfway across now, and craning his neck to look down the length of the walkway's cage he could just about see around the side of the shopping trolley; dozens of legs and bobbing orange jackets crouched stealthily behind it, trailing all the way back to the far side of the walkway.

Oh shit-shit-shit.

'It's a shield. They're right behind it. FIRE!!'

Bushey turned to him. 'It's Harry! We can't—'

'He's dead already! FIRE!!'

Walfield opened up on the trolley, his bullets thudding into the stacked corpses. Harry's body rocked lifelessly as puffs of crimson and shreds of shirt erupted from his chest. From either side of the walkway, those armed with catapults launched their projectiles at the wire caging. Most of their nuts and bolts rattled off the side and disappeared down into the void, but some whizzed through the grilles, some even finding targets.

Adam aimed down the gap between the loaded trolley and the sides of the walkway cage, and fired off three or four single shots. His bullets found a shin, shattering it, causing a boy to shriek and drop down onto all fours.

But the trolley was still coming and they were nearly all the way across.

'Bushey!'

'Sir?'

'Sound the horn!'

Bushey picked up the horn and pressed the trigger. Compressed air made it bark deafeningly, right next to Adam's ear. Two long blasts.

'EVERYONE BACK!' screamed Jenny. 'BACK TO THE NEXT PLATFORM!! HURRY!!'

They scrambled to their feet, a panicking flood-tide of women and a few old men, streaming back between the Portakabins and obstacles, legs tangling with pipes and each other as they raced towards the next walkway and the temporary safety of the far side.

The night lit up with muzzle flashes once more as the boys yet to file onto the walkway behind the rattling supermarket trolley fired across from the drilling platform.

Adam could see the trolley was nearly at the exit and the boys were going to spill out of the wire cage onto the deck. If they stayed put a moment longer, they were in danger of being overrun.

'Danny! Bushey!'

Both men turned to look at him.

'Fallback positions on the far side of the deck, now! We'll buy Jenny's people time to clear the walkway then follow them. Got it?'

They nodded.

'Let's go!'

They scrambled to their feet, abandoning their positions on the edge of the deck either side of the walkway cage and retreating several dozen yards back until they found new covered positions.

'Fuck it! Stop here!' shouted Adam. He dropped down onto one knee behind the fat curve of an exhaust pipe. 'We can take them as they emerge.'

The other two nodded and dropped to their knees behind cover.

A moment later the shopping trolley, with Harry's corpse lolling lifelessly on top of it, rattled out of the cage and onto the deck, orange-jacketed praetorians spilling out after it.

Adam, Walfield and Bushey fired targeted double taps that picked off the first four of them emerging from the cage. The rest of them spilled out in their wake, diving for cover and firing back at them; full-clip volleys unaimed, yet in their general direction, which had them ducking down out of sight as showers of sparks cascaded off the metalwork and deck clutter around them.

And even more of them were streaming out of the walkway cage as they cowered.

Shit.

Adam popped up and fired three more shots to slow them down. Returning fire zeroed in on his muzzle flash. Flakes of rusting metal and paint stung his cheeks. He poked his gun over the top and fired the last four rounds in his clip blind. Then the gun was clacking on empty.

One more clip, then I'm down to firing bolts from a bloody bra-cup catapult.

He pulled the last ammo clip out of the thigh pocket of his khakis and rammed it home.

'Danny, Bushey . . . new position. Far side of the deck where the walkway—'

Walfield was gone; splayed out on the deck several yards from him with a sizeable chunk of his head missing; one foot lazily twitching from side to side as if he was enjoying some tune over an iPod.

Bushey was staring down at him.

'Come on, we're going!'

He grabbed the lance corporal's arm and tugged him to follow. They rounded the main process control cabin, weaving their way through a row of water butts, and stumbling through several rows of bamboo tepees up which a wall of beans had done a good job of climbing. Adam's legs tangled with something and he went head over heels amongst them.

Bushey pulled him up roughly. On his feet again, they left the clatter of bamboo poles behind them and vaulted over a waist-high junction box, finally reaching open deck. Ahead of them was the walkway; the last few people pushing each other to get into the wire tunnel. He tried to see whether either of the Sutherland women were amongst them, but the moon showed him little more than a press of dark bodies stretched out along the walkway.

'Here!' said Adam. 'Here. We'll have to slow 'em down again here.'

Bushey nodded, found himself a niche of cover to squeeze into and readied his aim on the way they'd just come, around the right side of the platform's central building module.

Adam did likewise and set his aim up on the left hand of the module. Already, he could hear the boys coming. He could hear jeering voices, hoots of delight. Getting closer . . . And the flickering glow of several flashlights arcing like light sabres amongst the pipes, gantries, junctions boxes, exhaust stacks.

'You ready?'

Bushey nodded.

'Just fire enough to make 'em duck for cover. Then we'll scarper, too, okay?'

Bushey licked dry lips and pressed out a grim smile. 'Right-o, sir.'

Adam aimed down the trembling sights of his assault rifle, waiting for the flash of enough orange jackets to appear to make his shots count.

Bollocks, I fucked this up.

He'd been banking on the boys turning tail and rabbiting at the first exchange of gunfire. Maxwell must have got them totally stoked up somehow, or got them all stoned on coke or something. Or maybe he was right. Maybe the boys really were convinced this was just one big computer game; that a shot landing home wasn't actually going to hurt them.

'Sir!'

'I see 'em. I see 'em!' replied Adam.

He caught the pale flicker of a baseball cap, a head poking around the corner of the module to check the lie of the land ahead, then ducking back. He saw more heads now, emerging from the maze of buildings, pipes and exhaust bells. Cautious steps forward towards the open area of deck and the walkway.

Bushey fired first. Half a dozen quick shots that appeared to find one of the boys. Adam joined in and all the heads and shoulders dived quickly out of sight.

A moment later return fire sputtered out from a dozen places, several shots whistling up the walkway between them. Adam hoped the others were all out of there now, although he thought he could still hear the distant rattle of feet on the mesh.

'That's it, I'm out!' hissed Bushey.

Adam was on his last clip. 'All right, fuck it, we're done here. Go, Bush. I'll cover!'

Bushey nodded, scuttling low out of his niche and across the open deck towards the walkway. Adam waited until he saw heads had begun popping up again, and fired another half a dozen shots to keep them down a while longer. Then he, too, was on his feet, a low loping sprint across a few yards of open deck, then his boots clanged all too heavily onto the walkway. He could see Bushey up ahead, jogging to catch up with the last of the civilians.

Adam ran sideways, like a crab, keeping his assault rifle hip-aimed backwards down the wire cage, waiting for one of the boys to be stupid enough to press the pursuit too closely.

Twenty yards along and starting to feel sure he was going to make it over without incident, his foot found something soft and he stumbled.

'Shit!' he gasped.

He looked down. It was that relentlessly cheerful black woman who was Jenny's friend. She seemed to be alive, but whimpering pitifully.

'You're wounded? Can you walk?'

The woman moaned. 'Can't feel my legs.'

He reached down with his spare hand and grabbed a fistful of damp clothing. He tried dragging her along the walkway, but she shrieked with pain. 'No! Please! Stop!'

'Come on, love. You've to got help yourself!'

'I can't!' she cried. 'I can't!'

He knelt down closer to her. He remembered her name now. 'You're Martha?'

She nodded. He looked down at what she was cradling in her hands; a mess of tattered skin around an exit wound and dark coils of soft tissue from inside. 'Dr Tami can't fix this sort of mess,' she whispered. 'You go.'

'I can drag you,' he said, shouldering his weapon and getting his other hand under her armpits.

'No!' she spat. 'Please, no! Hurts!'

'Just shut up and let me—'

'I want to die,' she sobbed. 'My boy, I know he's gone . . . I just wanna go an' see him now.'

He could see her face; damned if there wasn't something that looked like a smile on there. 'He's such a good boy,' she whispered. 'Did you hear him? He warned us.'

Adam nodded. He had heard the shout from the tugboat's foredeck just before everything kicked off. 'Your boy? That was brave.'

She grinned, grateful it seemed, that someone had noticed.

A shot rattled off the wire cage a dozen yards down, sending sparks onto the walkway.

'Go!' hissed Martha. 'Go now . . . an' you tell Jenny . . . say "sorry" from me?'

'Sorry? Yes, okay.'

'I let her down . . . so badly.'

Another shot rattled against the wire and he could see down the far end the boys were beginning to cluster around the entrance.

'Martha . . . I better . . .'

She nodded, let go of his hand and shoved his shoulder. 'Go! Go, go, stupid!'

He stepped away from her as torchlight from the boys' end flickered down the walkway and onto them both. Adam dropped down quickly on to one knee and aimed a shot at the torch. He heard a cry and the torch spun and dropped, lancing light in all directions. There was a clattering sound as the boys ducked backed behind cover.

'Yeah!' Martha cheered weakly. 'Now go, go,' she said again, shooing him away with a flapping hand.

'Sir?' It was Bushey's voice calling down from the far end. 'Better move it!'

'Take good care of her . . . she *needs* you,' whispered Martha still smiling. 'She likes you . . . now go!'

He turned to abandon her, feeling like the lowest form of life for doing so. Then he stopped. 'Martha, do you want to . . . to *leave* now? Right now?'

She looked at him. 'You mean . . . die?'

He looked up at the far end of the walkway. 'You don't want those boys to get hold of you alive.'

She gave it only a heartbeat's thought, then nodded. 'Oh, yes, please.'

Don't fuck around, Adam. Make it quick for her.

'Close your eyes, then,' he said, reaching for her shoulder and squeezing it affectionately. She did as she was told and then clasped her hands together under her chin. 'Mum's coming, Nathan,' she uttered softly. 'Just hang on for me, baby.'

Adam shouldered the gun, aimed at her forehead and closed his eyes as he fired.

Then he was running; running with the sound of his boots making the walkway ring and rattle in his ears. Sparks chased him and he felt the air on one side of his hunched-over head and shoulders hum as a solitary shot narrowly missed its mark.

He was out of the other end and lying on his back next to Bushey less than ten seconds later, gasping ragged lungfuls of air and looking up at shifting clouds above haloed by the moon. The silhouette of Bushey's head leaned over him and he was saying something. Adam felt like he was a thousand miles away, watching the moon above, the skimming silver-haloed clouds, the dark outline of head and shoulders and the muffled bellow of a faraway voice. Watching it on a telly; a storefront telly through the plate glass of a window.

'Sir!' Bushey's voice was getting louder, cutting through, pulling him back, reluctantly, from this odd sensation of calm detachment.

'Sir! Adam!! You okay? You hit?'

Bushey was shaking his shoulder. Adam took in another breath of cool night air and finally managed to sit up. 'I'm fine,' he grunted. 'I'm fine.'

'I thought the bastards'd got you.'

He turned over, propped himself up on his elbows to look back down the walkway. There was plenty of movement on the far platform. The boys gathering their numbers again. Probably stacking up bodies on yet another supermarket trolley, getting ready to run the same tactic again.

Bushey leaned closer to him so he wasn't overhead. 'We're fucked now. We're out of ammo.'

Adam said nothing. If they tried the trolley trick again that was going to be it for them. In fact, even if they just ambled over without any cover at all, that was pretty much it for them. He was down to half a dozen rounds left in his clip.

'Maxwell will make an example of us,' said Bushey. 'I know he will. The bastard's going to let the boys rip us to pieces.'

'So let's make sure we hold back a couple of rounds, all right?'

Bushey pressed out a scaffold-smile. 'Yuh. Just don't fuckin' fire 'em by accident.'

Adam felt an arm on his shoulder. He turned to see Jenny settling to a crouch beside him. 'I thought we'd lost you,' she said.

'I'm all right.' He mentioned nothing about Martha. If

there was time later, if there was a later, he could pass the message on then.

She bit her lip. 'My lot want to surrender. They're all talking about surrendering.'

'And you?'

'I . . . I don't know. Maybe that Maxwell won't be quite so bad? Maybe—'

'He'll do whatever he needs to do,' said Adam. 'That means keeping his boys happy.'

She stared at him. 'You mean—'

'Whatever those boys want, they'll have.' He gestured at those around them, cowering, crying, waiting for the boys to make their way across. 'All these women? Do you understand?'

She looked back over her shoulder at them; women young and old and children . . . all of them so vulnerable. She couldn't bring herself to visualise what this place, their home, would become once those boys came across; a charnel house of raped and broken female bodies, and those thugs dancing like wild savages around them. And, yes, there'd be an element of revenge to whatever those boys did to them; revenge for their fallen comrades – in their minds it would justify doing just about *anything* they wanted to them, wouldn't it?

She shuddered at the thought. Five, nearly six years of endless grinding effort to build this safe haven, only to have it picked apart by a feral gang of boys . . . just for the fun of it.

No. I'm not having it.

She gritted her teeth and turned to face the people nearby, faces full of hope that she had an answer, a plan. Something up her sleeve.

'I'm not surrendering,' she said. Whispers rippled and spread amongst them. She saw them stir, shoulders slump with despair. She decided if her tenure as their community leader was finally at an end, then her last leadership decision wasn't going to be to surrender her people to whatever entertainment those little bastards had in mind. 'We can't let them over here,' she announced to them. 'There'll be raping . . . and worse. We can't let them over. We have to fight.'

She turned back to Adam. 'Let's give them all we've got left when they cross.'

Adam nodded. 'That's the plan.'

Maxwell could see the boys had had enough. This wasn't the pushover they'd been promised. To be honest, this wasn't the pushover he'd hoped for either. He'd expected nothing more than several hundred wobbly-kneed women fool enough to welcome them aboard and offer their complete submission at the first sight of a gun.

He looked at the boys, many of them spattered with blood, some of it their own. A headcount showed about twenty of the praetorians were down; most of them dead, a couple of the wounded probably weren't going to last the night, their pitiful cries weren't helping morale at all.

He'd sent Jeff to pilot the tug back to where the barges were moored at Bracton and then to tow them back over to the rigs. There were supplies aboard for the boys. Food and water and a few more crates of that cheap booze to get them back into the mood for the final push.

A top up of vodka and adrenalin . . . that's what they needed now.

Several hours ago ashore at Bracton he'd had them roaring with excitement, jumping up and down like over-sugared birthday boys on their way to a Laser Quest party; convinced they were invincible and everyone was going to get as much sex as they wanted tonight.

In truth, a break for several hours was no bad idea. Those people across the way weren't going anywhere, and given enough time to mull over their predicament, they might just decide they'd had enough and wave a white flag.

He gave Snoop orders to set a dozen lads on watch over the walkway, the others could get whatever rest they could. He handed out cigarettes to them all, with a word of encouragement to the youngest lads, and for the older boys, whose eyes betrayed the beginnings of distrust, he reassured them that tomorrow, after they'd tidied up the mess, fixed whatever damage had been done, and the barge with their girlfriends and games consoles had been unloaded, they were going to have one hell of a party; lights, music, games . . . and plenty more ladies to choose from.

Finally, he sat down with his back against one of the deck lockers, suddenly feeling like he'd run a marathon over the last twenty minutes.

Tomorrow morning, dawn . . . as soon as it was light enough, Maxwell decided. If they'd not waved a white flag, he'd better get out there and sort this out himself.

I'll parley. Talk those bitches into surrendering.

At the very least it was another chance to show his little soldier boys just who was in charge. Not Edward *Snoop* Tindall, but him, *The Chief* . . . the fella responsible for feeding them all this time, handing out the booze, the fags, finding the means and ways so they could enjoy their privileges; the fella who kept Safety Zone 4 going ten years after every other one had gone belly-up.

I'll show them. I'll sort it.

Chapter 85

10 years AC

'LeMan 49/25a' – ClarenCo Gas Rig Complex, North Sea

'Hello?'

The voice echoed across the silent blue-grey light of pre-dawn.

'Hello?'

Leona's leg jerked. She couldn't believe she'd actually fallen asleep. She turned on her side, propped herself up and looked over the top of the rusting hulk of the storage drum she'd been sheltering behind. There was a man on the walkway, about a third of the way across. He held a rag of white cloth in one hand.

'Hello? Can I speak to your leader, Jennifer Sutherland?' he called out.

The praetorians were all awake and crowded along the edge of the platform opposite – she could see flashes of their orange vests, the glint of gold chains here and there.

Next to her, Mum stood up.

'Mum!' hissed Leona. 'Get down. It's a trick!'

She ignored Leona, stepping out from behind cover. 'I'm Jennifer,' she replied.

Leona looked at Adam. Her face said *can't you stop her?*

He gave her a shrug. Too late.

'I'm Alan Maxwell, by the way!' shouted the man. 'Can you and I meet in the middle?'

Jenny stepped onto the walkway and slowly made her way a dozen yards along and finally stopped. 'Just here is fine for me. I can hear you well enough.'

'So.' He shrugged and smiled. 'This is a bit of a bloody mess, isn't it?'

Jenny said nothing.

'Thing is, it's not exactly a stalemate. We've got a whole load of guns over here, and, well . . . you've got these,' he said, holding up one of their improvised bra-slingshots. Some of the boys laughed at that. He scratched his salt and pepper beard. 'So, if we have to come over there and get you it's just that you're going to annoy my lads even more if your lot decide to carry on throwing things at them on the way over.'

'That's exactly what you're going to get if you do.'

Maxwell laughed. 'I figured that. In fact, during the night I've had time to do some thinking. And you know what?' He shook his head. 'This is really very bloody stupid! That's what it is. Stupid. Fighting like this, when, let's face it, we're probably the two largest organised groups left in Britain!'

He laughed and took another step forward. 'I mean, we've got to rebuild, haven't we? Make Britain Great again.'

'We were doing just fine before *you* attacked us.'

'And we were doing okay in London,' replied Maxwell. 'But, you know what? Your group and my group are what's left. There's no bloody government. In fact, you and me . . . I suppose *we're* the government, aren't we? It's down to us to do something about the country. Get it on its feet again!'

'And this is how you go about doing that?' she replied, her voice echoing across the stillness. It was surprisingly quiet. The sea was chastened like a child scolded, lapping softly at the legs a hundred feet beneath them. The endless North Sea breeze just a soft flutter.

He shrugged apologetically. 'No, maybe you're right, Jennifer. Which is why I'm standing out here like a right lemon.'

'So?'

'So . . . why don't we call an end to the fighting? Pool our resources. I've got about eighty lads here with me, and another one hundred men and women who'll be arriving soon. And we've got barges stuffed full of supplies. Together, your lot and mine, that's, what? Nearly a thousand people?' He spread his hands. 'You know what I call that?'

'What?'

'A bloody good start.'

'And of course *you'll* be in charge,' said Jenny.

'No,' he shrugged. 'Shit, you can be if you want! I'm just trying to make a deal here. There's been enough bloodshed, for fuck's sake.'

Jenny looked past him at the boys gathered around the entrance to the walkway. 'And those boys?'

He turned to look at them. 'They'll do what they're told. Alan knows best.' A fresh breeze tugged at his anorak, flipping the hood up. He smoothed it back down. 'Look, we've got loads of goodies to share and you've got oil or gas, you know? We're both bringing something to the party—'

'Oh, we don't have oil or gas. That's for sure.'

Maxwell's eyebrows arched. He looked perplexed.

Jenny laughed drily. 'Oh, I get it . . . I see,' she shook her head. '*That's* what you came for, is it?' She nodded towards the drilling platform. 'You thought we were pumping stuff out of the sea?'

Maxwell said nothing.

'Take a look,' she said. 'The drilling platform . . . see?'

Maxwell turned to look, craning his neck one way then the other to get a look past the low structures on the production platform to see the empty support jacket on the far rig. After a few moments squinting at the structure, he turned back to her, a look of confusion on his face.

'There's no drill apparatus, do you see? It's just an empty jacket. This field was dry even before the crash.'

He smiled and wagged a finger. 'You've been running a generator,' he replied. He looked up at a loop of power flex dangling from the roof of the cage and flicked it with a finger.

The heavy flex swung and creaked. 'Oh, you've got power all right.'

'We did. But we've never been pulling up oil or gas. Like I said, this place was dead. Being mothballed.'

Maxwell laughed. 'Don't be modest now. You expect me to believe that?'

'We had a generator running on methane. Running on human and chicken shit. That's all.'

Maxwell looked stumped. 'But . . . but it's a gas rig,' he said again. 'It's a fucking gas rig! Why the fuck would you be living here in the middle of fucking nowhere, Mrs Sutherland, if it wasn't producing something? Hmm?'

'To keep away from bastards like you.'

Maxwell laughed a little too shrilly.

'We managed to produce enough methane to get a couple of hours of light a day. That's all,' said Jenny. 'You could quite easily have done the same yourselves.'

Maxwell looked sceptical. 'All this cabling . . . you're telling me all this . . . for just a couple of hours of light?'

'A couple of hours of light, sometimes less. But not any more. We had an accident. There was an explosion several months ago. I'm not even sure we'll ever get it working again.'

She noticed, over Maxwell's shoulder, the boys keenly listening to the shouted exchange. She could see them looking at each other, whispering.

'Maxwell,' she said, raising her hoarse voice a little more to be certain all the boys were hearing her loud and clear. 'Is that what you've been promising those kids? Unlimited electricity?'

The man seemed momentarily stumped for a reply.

'Because you're a terrible fool if you did. All we've got here is what little we manage to grow. You'd have been far better staying wherever you came from.'

573

Maxwell put out his hands, as if trying to hush her voice. 'No, course not. This is—'

She laughed. 'You did, didn't you? You stupid fucking idiot!' She leaned to one side to address the boys directly. 'There's no gas or oil here! There's no power! He led you here for nothing!!'

'Shit!' snapped Maxwell, lowering his voice. '*Shut up!*'

'You wasted your time, lads!' she called out again. 'You stupid idiots! There's no power here! No lights! There's nothing!! This man is a fool!'

Maxwell turned away from Jenny to face his praetorians. He sighed. 'All right, boys, maybe she's right. We'll find out for sure soon enough. But we're here now, aren't we? And we're nearly done. Over there are several hundred new women for you to enjoy. So let's get on with it, boys. You can have a couple of days' fun, then we'll grab everything worth taking. And I suggest we head back to Felixstowe. What do you say to that? Hmm? Who knows how many more containers of grog we'll find there?'

Snoop emerged from amongst the crowd of praetorians and stepped onto the walkway. Maxwell glanced at him and smiled. 'What do you reckon, Edward? That sound like a plan?'

'Sounds like a really shit plan, Chief,' he replied.

Maxwell's eyes narrowed and then he nodded. 'Oh, I see, and this is the point where you've finally decided to take charge of the praetorians, is it?'

Snoop said nothing.

'You know absolutely nothing, Edward. You're still just a child. A big boy who knows nothing more than the dome. What? So you're going to take charge now? Find food for these boys? Care for them? Plan for them? Educate them? Are you *that* organised, Edward?'

Snoop shrugged. 'I know enough that we can't just live on the shit we find in containers for ever. Or did you think I was too stupid to figure that out for myself?' Snoop turned round to face the boys. 'The shit out there ain't going to last for ever. You boys know that, right?'

'Edward! Give it a fucking rest, will you?' snapped Maxwell.

'Our shit can't jus' be one party night after another. You gettin' that, right? You all figured out the party's gotta end one day?'

Some of the boys glanced at each other.

'Edward!'

'Well,' continued Snoop. 'The shit needs to change, or one day we end up like them fuckin' London wild kids an—'

'Edward! SHUT UP!'

'Or what?' He spun round. 'You gonna' do what, fool?'

'You'll be kicked out, that's what! Kicked out of the praetorians. I'll make . . . I'll make Jay-zee my new top dog!' He leaned round Snoop and addressed the cluster of faces watching events from the far end of the walkway. 'You hear that? How's that sound, Jay-zee? You want to be my new top dog?!'

He looked back at Snoop. 'Now why don't you shut up and let me finish what I'm—'

'This place,' Snoop cut in, '*this* place has figured it out. You see all this green shit everywhere?' He pointed at the rustling leaves dangling from every level, on the platforms either end of the walkway. 'That's all food. That's all grow-again, come-again food. That's like making a real future.' He jabbed a finger at Maxwell and turned to address the boys. 'And you know what he is, what the Chief is? He's like a piece of the past. The use-it-up past. And when whatever shit lying around is all used up we'll be fucked, too.'

'He's right!' called out Jenny. 'There's no future in this.'

'Oh, don't you start,' snapped Maxwell. He pulled a hand-gun out of the pocket of his anorak and levelled it at Jenny. 'You really need to shut up now.'

575

Snoop pulled the assault rifle from his shoulder and aimed at Maxwell.

'Chief!'

Maxwell turned to look at him. 'EDWARD? WHAT THE FUCK DO YOU THINK YOU ARE DOING?'

'You should lower the gun,' replied Snoop hesitantly. 'Lower the fucking gun!'

'Or what, Edward?'

'My name's *SNOOP*, not *EDWARD!*' he replied.

Maxwell laughed. 'No, you're just a stupid twat called Edward, who thinks he's some sort of hip-hop gangster!'

'Fuck you!' A dozen rounds ricocheted up the walkway, spinning Maxwell and knocking him heavily onto his back.

Leona was on her feet. 'MUM!!!' she screamed. She grabbed the gun lying beside Brooks, leaped over the storage drum and into the walkway cage.

'NO!!! NO-NO-NO!' The scream filled her ears as she watched her mum's knees slowly begin to buckle. She collapsed on her haunches, sitting uncomfortably on her bottom, swaying unsteadily, both of her hands clasped over her left breast.

Leona clattered down the walkway as Snoop looked on in confounded silence. She slewed to a halt beside her mother. 'Oh, God, Mum, no!'

Jenny looked up at her, with an expression of puzzlement. 'I think I got hit,' she said matter-of-factly. She looked down at her hands, both clamped over a small hole, several inches below her collar bone, that was vigorously pushing blood out between her spread fingers.

Leona dropped to her knees and pressed her hand against the wound, three hands, hers and Mum's, all trying to do the same futile thing; stem the flow.

'Mum . . . Mum . . . Mum,' she whimpered. Jenny wobbled sideways like a drunkard and Leona caught her in her

576

arms. 'Mum . . . please!!!' She looked up. 'WHERE'S Tami? WHERE'S TAMI?!'

She looked down at her. 'Mum . . . please . . . don't . . .'

Jenny looked crossly at her. 'Oh for God's sake, Leona, you've got my mess all over your hands.'

Leona shook her head and cradled her mother's. 'Mum, don't do this.' Her voice broke into a pitiful whine. 'Mummy . . . please . . .'

'I'm all right, honey . . . just a bit tired . . .'

Jenny's head began to loll heavily against her daughter's arms. 'Just like your father . . . so messy . . .'

'Like *you,* Mum,' she whispered, 'I'm like *you*, Mum.'

'. . . You're . . . you . . . like . . . ?' She wasn't making sense, her eyes were losing focus, starting to roll to one side as a single line of dark blood emerged from one nostril and streamed down across the bumps of her scarred cheek.

'You're so strong, Mummy.'

'. . . Hannah? Now be a good girl . . . just . . .'

Her head kinked over slowly to one side and her eyes seemed to be regarding the sea below, visible through the walkway grating, softly swirling eddies between the rig legs. One last breath came out as a protracted sigh of relief.

Then she was gone.

It was quiet and still there, a hundred feet above the grey void. A breeze rustled through the wire and whipped playfully with the corner of Jenny's tan cardigan. Leona heard the clang of feet slowly approaching and looked up to see the tall black kid in a tracksuit approaching her. He wore an orange vest with the fading word 'staff' stencilled across it and wore several heavy gold chains round his neck. He was holding a gun in both hands. It wasn't pointed at her, it was pointed down. No threat. Instead, he looked almost chastened; like a schoolboy asking for his ball back having broken a pane of glass in a greenhouse.

She vaguely recognised him through a foggy recall of the aftermath in that small room that stank of her own faeces.

'That your mum?' he said quietly, not seeming to recognise her. 'I'm sorry. Real . . . real sorry what just happened. Don't know if it was me hit her . . . or . . .' He glanced at Maxwell's body, skewed awkwardly across the walkway, the gun still held in his hand. He might have fired it, might not have.

Leona could see the boys gathered beyond him at the mouth of the walkway, looking much the same way as he did. Lost. Not sure what should happen next.

More fighting? Or something else?

No longer Super Army Soldiers . . . just lost boys.

'Yeah.' Leona nodded slowly, stroking her mother's scarred cheek. 'Yeah, that was my mum.'

The boy squatted down beside her and reached for one of Jenny's wrists, feeling for a pulse. Leona already knew she was gone. Perhaps to somewhere she'd be happy. Perhaps not.

She pulled herself to her feet. 'All of you,' she croaked. She cleared her throat, dry as parchment, hawked, spat and tried again. 'All of you boys,' she said, her voice louder, stronger.

'Why don't you put down those guns?'

Epilogue

I look back now and realise how different things might be today if we'd been overrun by that mad bastard's boy army. We just wouldn't have survived under Maxwell. Him and his army would probably have taken what they wanted and moved on like a horde of locusts.

But something happened on those rigs that morning. Something quite remarkable. Leona Sutherland shamed those boys into putting down their guns. She shamed them into taking off their orange jacket uniform. That morning, she stood up and stared them all in the eyes and somehow made them see the truth . . . that their guns and swagger, their gold chains, their rap-star nicknames were all just a pitiful, needy, grasping for the past.

She made them see that. That there was no future in it. Fighting over the scraps of what remained, the last tins, the last bottles, the last drops of oil.

I saw her transform there and then. Become every bit as strong as her mother. Perhaps even stronger. I saw her stare at those boys until they could only look at their own feet in shame.

A year and a half after that battle on the gas platforms, the last of the moving ashore was completed and the area around Bracton became our home; the soldier boys, the women, the workers and the steady trickle of newcomers — those that had heard the country was rebuilding itself here in East Anglia — all of us working together.

She led that unlikely collaboration for nearly thirty years.
She's dead now, Leona.

Died ten years ago from cancer. Still, we had a wonderful
life together. I wake up every morning missing her. Then I
open my eyes and realise I'm living out my days in a world
that is a reflection of her. So in a way, she's not gone. She's
all around me.

I was looking the other day through my old diaries. And I
found an entry written not long after we'd started the move
ashore. She'd just discovered she was pregnant. I remember
asking her what she'd want to call our baby and she said she
already knew what names she was going to call it, boy or girl.
She was like that . . . bossy sometimes. So certain and so
clear in mind.

But I think it was knowing she was pregnant – that was the
source of her determination and strength in those tough early
days after we moved from the rigs; when there was so much
to do and so many things that could still have gone wrong for
us. It was that determination to be damned sure our children
inherited something better that fuelled her, drove her on,
gave her such seemingly endless energy.

And I think our son has inherited a much better world . . .
and, of course, so have his children: Jacob and Hannah.
Here I am at the tail end of my life, and I can see that now;
looking around at windmills, and roads filled with bicycles
and people having so much less, yet living more. People no
longer tucked away in isolation surrounded by an Aladdin's
cave of mail-ordered possessions; no longer tapping anonym-
ously on keyboards to an internet world of other lonely
people. Instead, I see people tending allotments together,
repairing things together, reaching out and connecting with
each other in a way that never happened before the oil age
crashed and burned.

I'm living in the world Leona and her mother made. I can
honestly say that I see a little bit of her in everything around

me . . . and not just in the occasionally stubborn expression on our granddaughter's face. She's here in spirit, I suppose, in the way we all live now.

When young people ask me how hard it was just after the crash, how did we manage to get through those tough, dark times and build things anew, I find myself thinking that it was 'power' that got us here. Not the sort of power that comes from burning oil or gas, or spinning turbines, but the kind that comes from a mother who wants something better for her children.

There truly is nothing more powerful, more world-changing, more complete than a mother's love.

Adam Brooks
21 December, 51 AC

Author Notes

Afterlight was something I wanted to write directly after I finished writing *Last Light*. The temptation I suppose was to follow straight on with the tale, following the Sutherland family out of London and into whatever post-oil survival nightmare awaited them. But, I decided to let another book intercede (*October Skies*) which took me somewhere else for a while and allowed me the time and distance to think about how I was going to conclude the Sutherlands' tale.

The main result of giving myself that time was the decision to follow on *ten years* after the events of *Last Light*. And I'm so glad I did that because I think, certainly from my point of view, it's been a far more interesting exercise looking at the world long after the dust has settled, than just to write a continuation of the unravelling chaos of a collapsing world. Anyway, we've seen all that before in countless zombie movies; all those chaotic scenes set in shopping malls and petrol stations.

This was a chance to see what a world without oil looked like. And quite a sobering experience it's been. I never really imagined it being the commune-living-in-the-Welsh-valleys post-apocalyptic idyll that some survivalist types seem impatient to experience. Instead in this book I've imagined it as being a relentlessly hard life of grim endurance, where every day is a constant reminder of all the little luxuries we once had, and lost. Hot water at the twist of a tap, light and heat at the flick of a switch . . . a hot meal at the push of a micro-wave button.

So this book has ended up being less about railing against our evil, greedy, consumer ways and more a swansong to those times. See, I know despite all the moaning I do about waste and greed, and consumerism and selfishness and this dumbed down me-me-me culture . . . that given a week in a wet forest with nothing but damp firewood and a diet of scrawny trapped rabbits, I'd be pining for these times.

And that's exactly what the characters do. They ache for that old world. They pine for it.

Afterlight has certainly turned out to *not* to be a manifesto for the hardcore survivalists out there. It's not a celebration of anti-consumerism nor a yearning for a simple smallholder lifestyle. Sorry, that's just not me. But, what it is — just like *Last Light* was — is a warning that we can't go on consuming the way we're doing now. Simple maths dictates that this world won't support eight billion people all wanting their TVs and cell phones and cars. In fact, if I'm being brutally honest, it won't support eight billion people wanting something as simple as . . . *meat*. (Yes, in our time, I'm convinced we'll all have to become vegetarians if everyone's going to have enough to eat. And believe me, as a bacon-lover that's a bitter pill to swallow.)

Tough times ahead. Tough decisions ahead . . . and it's unavoidable. Perhaps the only positive note I can tack on the end here is that the sooner we wake up and start making the really hard decisions about the future; decisions about how much we in the first world should really *own*; decisions about how best the third world can control its population growth . . . then, the less likely we are to face a scenario like the one portrayed in these two peak oil books.

But, do I have faith that everyone will wake up *sooner* rather than *later* and make all those really hard decisions? Pfft. Nope, can't say I do. In the end, we've all become children . . . unable to delay gratification, unwilling to wait for our goodies, unwilling to do without all our shiny things . . . and content to sit back and watch the world walk towards a big crunch point.

The sad thing is . . . even though I've had my head in Peak Oil for years and written these two books, I'm just as childish and selfish and short-sighted as anyone else.